L.A. HEAT

L.A. HEAT

P. A. Brown

Manufactured in the United States of America.

This trade paperback original is published by Alyson Books,
P.O. Box 1253, Old Chelsea Station, New York, New York 10113-1251.
Distribution in the United Kingdom by Turnaround Publisher Services Ltd.,
Unit 3, Olympia Trading Estate, Coburg Road, Wood Green,
London N22 6TZ England.

First edition: July 2006

0607080910 a 10987 6543 21

ISBN 1-55583-948-7
ISBN-13 978-1-55583-948-2

A Library of Congress Cataloging-in-Publication Data application is on file.

Cover design by Taylor Johnson.

To my mother, Faith Evelyn Brown,
I wish you could have held this in your hands

CHAPTER 1

Saturday, 12:25 A.M., North San Miguel Road, Eagle Rock, Los Angeles

THE JOHN DOE had been dead for days.

Flies buzzed around the corpse, crawling over sunken eyes and up collapsing nostrils. From the doorway LAPD Homicide Detective David Eric Laine could see the skin sloughing off dehydrated muscles. He held his breath against the stench. After fourteen years on the force he figured he had seen it all. But sometimes the perps still managed to surprise him with their brutality.

The body had been posed on its back, legs splayed on the blood-soaked rug, hands already bagged to preserve evidence. He knew that death had occurred somewhere else. The lack of blood anywhere but on the carpet, and the body itself, confirmed that. Abruptly he turned away. John Doe wasn't going anywhere; he could concentrate on evidence the killer might have left behind.

This was no drug buy gone sour, or a bad domestic. The way the body lay in the hot, breathless room, empty eyes staring at a filthy window, told him this was worse. He knew the rug had been used to carry the body to this dumpsite. Just like the others. David felt a familiar tightening in his gut. He had hoped they'd been wrong about the last body, found less than a month ago in a similar state. He had hoped then that there would be no more.

Now he knew how naïve that hope had been.

Physical damage to the John Doe was extensive. Vivid purple abrasions marred the pale skin above the Adam's apple and dozens of shallow cuts covered the victim's chest and arms.

If he was anything like the others, he had been a good-looking youth. So how did he end up in a slumlord's firetrap, dying to satisfy some twisted freak's perversions?

David smeared wintergreen under his nose and the smell of decay faded, though he knew it would cling to him for hours, haunting his restless sleep. Assuming he got any in the next forty-eight hours.

He pulled on a Tyvek sterile suit, complete with plastic booties, and ducked past the crime-scene tape. Teresa Lopez, the deputy coroner from the Los Angeles Coroner's Office, nodded at him. A few strands of white hair spilled from under her sterile cap and framed her lined fifty-year-old face.

She smiled at him, but as usual he pretended not to see the question in her eyes. He knew her interest in him was based more on the fact that he was one of the few unattached men she met on a regular basis rather than any kind of physical attraction. He knew only too well how he looked. Either way, that was a road he wasn't going to travel, no matter how safe it might make him.

Darkness engulfed the apartment when Larry Vance, senior technician for the Scientific Identification Division—S.I.D.—ordered the lights cut. He scanned the floor with his handheld ultraviolet light. Vance was little more than a trace himself. Thin and sinewy like catgut, he always seemed to be able to insinuate himself into small places and find what others couldn't.

The hiss of traffic on the nearby 134 came through the dirt-spattered window. The only furniture in the room was the threadbare rug under the body and a single ladder-backed chair near the bathroom door.

Officer Kurt Henderson, who had been the first officer on the scene, appeared in the doorway. David nodded at the muscular black cop. They had crossed paths before. David tried not to stare at the striking dark-skinned black man. He kept his face neutral when Henderson nodded at him.

"Where's the building manager?" David asked.

"Partner's baby-sitting him downstairs."

"Name?"

"Collins. Harvey Collins."

"Get him."

Henderson left. Waiting in the hallway for him to return, David reviewed his notes. At ten minutes past midnight, the switchboard at the Northeast Community Police Station, on San Fernando Road, had received a frantic call. Responding to it, Henderson and his partner had found Collins in the hall and the body in room 317.

Henderson returned, leading a heavy-jowled Anglo.

"Mr. Collins? Detective David Eric Laine." David suppressed his sympathy for the traumatized man. Better for both of them if he did this as dispassionately as possible. "I need to clarify a couple of things. How did you come to find the body?"

"I got a phone call," Collins said. "I checked it out . . . " He swallowed and rubbed his bulbous nose. His gaze tracked around the hallway, settling everywhere but on the open door to the apartment.

"What phone call?"

"He said the police were too slow, that I gotta call them."

"What time was this, Mr. Collins?"

"I always watch the news at ten . . . KTLA. It was right after that was over. He told me the police had to find this body."

"So that would have been around eleven, eleven-ten?"

"Yeah, I guess so."

"And you waited over an hour to call 911?"

Collins's jaws worked around something bad-tasting. "Hey, I thought it was a crank."

This got better by the minute. "Did you recognize the voice? A former tenant, maybe?"

"I don't think so."

"When was the last time the unit was rented?"

"Two months." Collins scrubbed his hand through his thinning hair. "The last guy did a midnight run on me end of June."

"Anyone look at the place since then?"

"Nobody who'd do this."

David didn't pursue the non-answer. He'd get to Mr. Collins's evasions later. Maybe they were just the usual lies and half-truths everyone tried when faced with suspicious cops. Sometimes he saw the lies before they formed. Sometimes he saw lies that weren't there at all.

"Place is unfurnished. That the way you rent it?"

"Sure, tenants gotta bring their own stuff."

"What about the chair?"

"Musta been left by the last tenant."

"The fly-by-night one?"

Collins scowled. "Yeah. Him."

Lopez, the coroner, emerged from the apartment. Her stained Tyvek suit ballooned off her undersized frame. "We're ready to bag it."

David motioned to Henderson. "Take Mr. Collins back to his apartment. I'll be along later to get a written statement. We'll get a list of incoming calls, see where our helpful friend called from. See if you can get a list of tenants, too. Past and present."

His cell phone rang. He held up one finger to stall Lopez.

"Laine here."

"Davey," the voice on the other end said. It was his partner, Detective Martinez Diego. No one else had the temerity to call him Davey. "I'm stuck in traffic. Looks like a semi was dancing with a pickup out here." Martinez grunted. "Pickup lost."

"Lopez just called me back in to the apartment."

"How's it looking?"

"Like our guy." David glanced at Lopez, then looked away from the friendliness in her dark eyes. "Same injuries. Body wrapped in a rug."

Martinez swore, then said, "I'm clear here. I'll be there in two."

David hung up and clipped the cell back onto his belt.

Lopez raised one silver eyebrow. "Martinez?"

"On his way."

"So how'd you luck into this?" Teresa glanced over her shoulder at the room behind them. "Spending too much time loafing at your desk?"

"Just finished a drive-by on College when the call-out came." David gave her a thin smile. "I think the watch commander's words were 'Sleep can wait. Get your ass over there now, Laine.'"

"They're working both of you too hard. When was the last time you went home?"

"What year is this?"

"Seriously."

He shrugged. "Goes with the territory, right?"

David reentered the apartment.

Silver powder coated doorjambs and window ledges, revealing the smudges and swirls of the usual collection of latent prints a place like this collected. Scientific Investigation Division had set up spotlights. Larry had replaced the UV scan with a hand-held vacuum, which he ran over the carpet and floor, collecting and labeling bags of debris.

David scanned the room, along the walls, up toward the unlit ceiling light, then back to the corpse, where the fly feast continued. Then his gaze flew back to the light fixture, a simple white shield over a single lightbulb. A shadow on one side drew his eye.

David heard Martinez and one of the EMTs joking and laughing about their respective families before he ducked past the crime-scene tape. His Tyvek suit clung to his beefy form.

"You starting this party without me?" Martinez asked.

"Just warming things up."

Martinez, David's partner for the last five years, peered down at the body. "Looks like somebody let their party get out of hand."

Teresa approached, stripping off one pair of stained gloves and replacing them with clean ones. "You're late, Martinez."

"We got reporters outside. They wanna know if this is their Carpet Killer."

Teresa winced. "'The Carpet Killer.'" She shook her head in disgust. "Whatever you call him, he's got four vics now in six months, raped and butchered. The first one we know about was back in March. Prolific guy."

Martinez paced the narrow confines of the apartment. He elbowed the bathroom open to look inside.

"He likes what he's doing." David looked back at the light fixture. "Can we get a ladder in here?"

A technician entered carrying a folded stepladder under his arm. David pulled on his first pair of thin, latex gloves and clambered up the rickety steps. He withdrew a thin leather billfold from the fixture.

"I think our perp likes being recognized for his talents." He held up the billfold. "How can we give him proper credit if we don't know the identity of his vic?"

Back on level ground, he flipped it open under Martinez's speculative eyes. The face that stared back at them from the California driver's license was significantly better-looking than that of the damaged corpse at their feet, but the match was obvious.

"Jason Blake," David said. "Anaheim."

They both looked at the chair. It had already been printed.

"Check the seat for footprints," David said.

A technician hurried to comply.

Martinez reached past David and flipped up a second row of various cards. He tapped a plain white card with a rainbow on the upper left corner. "What's PFLAG?"

"Parents, Families and Friends of Lesbians and Gays—actually it is PFFLAG," David murmured, feeling the heat on the back of his neck when both Martinez and Teresa looked at him.

"*Dios,* there's an organization for everything," Martinez said. "How the hell do you even know that?"

David was saved from answering by Lopez.

"You better see this before we bag him," she said.

While Martinez took his initial impression of the corpse, David changed gloves. The powdery residue inside them felt cool against his damp skin. At only 2 A.M., heat already filled the room. The day to come promised to be another L.A. August scorcher. If the body hadn't been phoned in last night, it would have been found soon anyway. By tomorrow the whole building would have known about it.

He knelt, knees popping in protest. At thirty-seven old age was creeping up on him.

The rich stench ripened in the expanding heat. David loosened his tie and tugged the stiff collar away from his neck. Already sweat saturated his armpits; the hurried shower he'd had earlier that evening seemed a dimly remembered luxury.

"Someone brought him here several hours after death," Lopez said. "This guy's careful—and he plans."

"Scary thought."

"He's a scary guy."

On the other side of the body, Martinez squatted, arms resting on his knees while he studied the corpse. He tilted his head sideways.

"Ever notice how much more violent faggots are when they kill each other?" Martinez said.

"We don't even have any proof our perp's gay."

Martinez gave him the look. "Yeah, like some straight mofo's going to get his kicks this way."

"Wouldn't be the first time."

"Hey, Lopez. What can you tell us?"

"Rigor has settled out." Teresa demonstrated by bending the corpse's right knee. "Livor is almost entirely on the buttocks and feet." She lifted one foot and indicated the purplish marks on the bottom of the vic's foot where the blood had settled after his heart stopped pumping, technically known as livor mortis.

"Meaning?" David asked.

"He was in a crouched or sitting position for at least two hours following death." She ran a gloved hand up the right arm, touching a ring of bruised flesh around the slender wrist. "Bound."

David met Teresa's eyes. "Like the others."

"'Fraid so."

"Full rape-kit run?"

"Already collected some swabs and I'll do a pubic comb-out at post. Tox screen, too."

With a technician's help Teresa rolled the body over.

"*Calliphora* activity is only starting," she said, referring to the fly family most commonly found on corpses. "The first instar is approximately seven millimeters in length. That puts death about three to four days ago. We'll hatch some of these instar out to verify species."

David caught his breath when she finished rolling the body onto its stomach. A seething mass of tiny maggots spilled out onto her gloved hand. Almost gently she brushed them aside, revealing a yawning wound between the dead man's buttocks.

"Just like the others. Your killer's penetrating them anally with a knife. And this poor guy was very much alive when he was doing it."

CHAPTER 2

Saturday, 12:40 A.M., The Nosh Pit, Hyperion Boulevard, Silver Lake, Los Angeles

CHRISTOPHER BELLAMERE STARED down at the dark head of the most beautiful man in the world and knew he was in love.

"What did you say your name was?"

Mr. Beautiful grinned as he climbed to his feet wiping his mouth. "Bobby."

As Chris's breathing steadied, the BlackBerry on his belt vibrated. He fumbled for the palm-sized device, squinted through the fog of fading lust, and groaned. It was his boss, Peter C. McGill, chief information officer of DataTEK Systems. Petey had hired him six years ago. He had been trying to figure out a way to fire him for four. Chris hadn't been laid in over ten days. He wasn't about to let Petey spoil this evening. He forwarded the call to voice mail.

"Who was that?"

"Nobody important," Chris said and shoved his still semi-hard dick back into his Diesel jeans.

Bobby took his hand and pulled him out of the stall just as a pair of overweight queens teetering on four-inch Manolo Blahniks crowded into the bathroom.

One of them licked her scarlet lips while her hand groped under her hot pink thigh-length skirt to adjust herself. They stared at Bobby's crotch.

Chris grabbed his hand. "Sorry, ladies, I saw him first."

"He looks like he's got enough to share."

He steered Bobby back out into the pulsing music of the crowded

Saturday night bar they had abandoned less than ten minutes ago. Pushing through to the bar, he kept one hand on Bobby's hip. He wasn't letting this one get away.

He nibbled Bobby's perfect ear. "I've got a bottle of Elsa Malbec chilling at home."

"What's that?"

Okay, so he wasn't so perfect. But with those blue eyes and that gorgeous bubble-butt, who needed good taste? He only had to taste good.

"It's wine," he said.

Bobby shrugged and braced his elbows on the bar. "I'm more of a Bud man, myself."

Chris caught the eye of Ramsey, the bartender, and nodded. Ramsey grabbed the Cîroc off the top shelf and assembled Chris's usual Cîroc martini.

Bobby pressed his well-packed groin against Chris's hip. He plucked at Chris's waistband, and Chris couldn't help but wonder what made Mr. Perfect so desperate.

Ramsey dropped a Bud beside Chris's martini and scooped up his twenty. The press of bodies at the bar made movement nearly impossible. Thundering techno music kept conversation sparse. That suited Chris. He had the feeling if Bobby opened his mouth for talking, anything that emerged would only lessen the illusion of perfection.

Bobby worked one hand down the front of Chris's jeans. "You like to live dangerously?" He nipped Chris's ear, tugging his single diamond stud. "Let's take this someplace more private. I got beer at home."

Chris thought of renewing the invitation to his place, then realized that taking Bobby home might sully the illusion further. He grinned easily. "Who's driving?"

"You are." Bobby grabbed his balls. "At least until we get to my place."

Saturday, 1:50 A.M., Bluebird Motel, Santa Monica Boulevard, West Hollywood

The hot spray washed the last of Bobby's fluids down the motel drain. The heat helped wake him, but all Chris wanted to do was go home and crawl into his own bed. As happened all too often lately, the production never lived up to its advanced billing. Bobby was a major disappointment in the sack despite his brag about the porn he shot on a regular basis. Rather than argue, he had let Bobby press a couple of cheaply produced DVDs into his hand.

"Watch them later and think of me," Bobby murmured before diving down to work through another frenzy of feigned lust.

Chris stepped out of the shower onto the worn-out bath mat amid a cloud of steam just as his BlackBerry trilled. He dragged it out of the pocket of his jeans and flipped it on. Without checking caller I.D. he knew who it was.

"Tell me you're not busy," his boss said.

"Petey?" As always, using the hated name gave Chris a few seconds of silence to gather his thoughts. "Did I miss it?"

"Bellamere—" Petey stalled again. "Miss what?"

"Hell freezing over. That's the only time you ever call, isn't it?"

Given Petey's attitude, Chris always made sure his work was unimpeachable, and Petey was never able to forgive him for that.

"We've got major trouble at Pharmaden." Petey's voice rose, losing his normal MBA-trained cool. "That new server you put in has been down half the night. Their techs can't do anything with it."

"The server *I* put in?" Chris did some quick calculation—the first phone call couldn't have been more than three hours ago. *Half the night indeed.* He dragged a towel around his narrow hips, struggling to escape the lingering affects of one too many martinis, too much Bobby, and too little sleep. He scrubbed his face with a second towel, then used his fingers to work his short blond hair into damp spikes. "Which server would that be?"

"The one you signed off on," Petey said. "Pharmaden is holding us responsible—"

"I signed off on your orders." Chris couldn't resist digging at the man. "I told you not to roll those servers out without more load testing. But you had to let Golden Boy call the shots, didn't you? The guy wants my job and you're all set to give it to him—"

"Now hold on just a minute, Tom's a good worker—"

Yeah, right. "Then call him in to fix things."

"Are you refusing to go?"

"Are you threatening me?"

Petey coughed and cleared his throat. "Tom's only been with us eight months. Cut him some slack."

"Why? Wasn't he the genius you got from Berkeley? The ink on his degree was still wet when you put him in charge of Pharmaden. Now you're claiming he's inexperienced?"

"If you two had worked as a team from the start—"

"He'd still have screwed up." Chris furiously rubbed the towel over his already dry chest. Petey had a lot of gall denigrating his skill after all these years. "I'm not even on call this week. In fact I'm supposed to meet with Ortez later today. You remember that studio rep who wants us to handle their payroll servers?"

"And I want you at Pharmaden. You'll be done in plenty of time to meet with Ortez."

A dull headache pulsed behind Chris's eyes. "Then I'll be there." He hung up. "Asshole."

It was already after five-thirty by the time he climbed the single stone step to the two-story Art Deco Silver Lake house his grandmother had left him at her death five years ago. Hurried or not, he dressed with care, knowing it could be hours before he got home again.

On the Hollywood Freeway, early-morning heat spilled into his Lexus SUV. He dodged a slow-moving produce truck and picked up speed as the lanes ahead of him cleared. On his right, downtown L.A. was dominated by the phallic seventy-three-story First Interstate World Center, which glowed pink in the advancing daylight.

He pulled into Pharmaden's parking lot just as the sun cleared the row of ragged palms that lined the cracked asphalt lot.

Pharmaden's front door opened and a figure stepped out. Chris trotted up the shallow steps to greet him. His steps faltered as the man stepped into the light.

Tom Clarke, a.k.a. Golden Boy, folded his arms over his chest. His hair looked damp, like he had just stepped out of a shower.

CHAPTER 3

Saturday, 6:55 A.M., Lansdowne Street, Los Angeles

TOM BLOCKED THE steps. His full lips curled in a half-smile that would have been sexy as hell if Chris had felt an ounce of attraction to the guy. He didn't.

"Petey sent you?" Chris asked.

"He says we lose this account, we're screwed." Tom swung the heavy glass door open. A thatch of heavy blond hair fell over his face, momentarily covering his eyes. "We can't let this go down the toilet."

Fine words from the man who had put them there in the first place.

Chris pulled the door shut behind them. Their footsteps echoed through the empty building. They headed for the stairs that led to the basement. All six of Pharmaden's sixty-four-bit UNIX servers resided down there in the temperature-controlled server closet.

"You get a chance to talk to anybody?" Chris asked.

"The head tech, DePalma. They've rebooted the server a half dozen times. It won't come up."

From the other end of the hallway a thin black man appeared. He sported a lush growth of salt-and-pepper hair covering both his head and most of his face. Phil DePalma, Pharmaden's senior technical analyst, glanced at Tom before holding his hand out to Chris, who shook it vigorously.

"Glad you could stop by." DePalma grinned. "What kept you?"

"Life." Chris smiled in return. "You met Tom Clarke?" he asked, knowing the two had to be well acquainted. He wasn't surprised when DePalma blinked three times in rapid succession. Tom had that effect on people.

DePalma opened the door with an electronic I.D. card. They entered the cool, well-lit data center and crossed toward the wall of rack-mounted servers.

"Quickest solution is restore from backup," Chris said.

DePalma nodded. "But we'd lose today's transactions, wouldn't we?"

Chris nodded. "They'd roll back. You'd have to input them again." Chris pointed at two yellow blinking lights. "When did this start?"

"Last night around ten," DePalma said.

Chris restarted the server, this time with a diagnostic disk in place. Keeping his eyes fixed on the screen he watched it go through its boot-up process. Yellow lights flashed green briefly before flaring yellow again.

"Diagnostics say there's nothing wrong with the hardware," Chris said. He pointed at the yellow lights. "That says otherwise."

"So which is it?"

Chris glanced at Tom and decided to see if the guy had a clue. "What do you think?"

"If it's not hardware then what is it?" Tom asked.

"Bad parity."

"Parity?"

"The server will have to be rebuilt." Chris pulled a disk out of his CD case. "There's no way to recover the most recent data, I'm afraid."

DePalma sighed. "How long are we looking at?"

"Couple of hours at least."

DePalma swore, then nodded.

It took just over three hours to rebuild the server and restore the available data from backup. Another hour was spent verifying the restored data. Back outside, the empty parking lot sizzled like the African savanna. In the distance a siren wailed. His gold-tinted SUV threw the sun back at him. His head ached, his legs felt weak, and he desperately needed a shower. Why hadn't he parked in the shade?

He cranked the air conditioner on and was about to throw the SUV into gear when Tom appeared beside the driver's door.

Reluctantly Chris powered his window down. Hot air rolled into the cab. "Yeah?"

"Can I catch a lift?"

"Sure." Chris stared at the man as he crossed around to the passenger side and slid in. "How'd you get here if you didn't drive?"

"Cab."

"Car in the shop?"

Tom looked away. "Don't have one."

Chris had heard about people like that. He'd never actually met one. He threw the SUV into gear and wheeled out of the parking lot.

"Where you going?"

"Drop me at L'Orangerie. I'm meeting my uncle for lunch."

"You can eat at L'Orangerie but you can't afford a car?" Before he could answer, Chris shot a glance at his watch and swore.

He was late. Des was going to kill him.

Chris braked hard at the next set of lights. Plastic rustled and snapped and he glanced over in time to see Tom staring down at the cheaply produced cover of one of the DVDs Bobby had given him. It had slipped out of its bag. Even from where he sat, Chris could see the enormous erection halfway down Bobby's perfect throat.

Tom's face was stoplight red.

Chris almost felt sorry for him.

He left Tom in front of the stone door of the venerable eatery on La Cienega Boulevard, and sped east to his place in Silver Lake. Thirty minutes later he pulled into his driveway. He groaned as three figures stepped out of the shaded courtyard.

"Don't tell me you forgot lunch?" His best friend, Desmond Hayward, pulled the driver's-side door open.

He smiled weakly before focusing on the tallest man in the group, Trevor Watson. "Hey, Trev," he said, wondering if he'd blown things big-time. Wondering how much he cared. Trevor wasn't normally his type. Chris wasn't big on blond, blue-eyed pretty boys; he preferred his men dark and lithe. But Des had been persistent in setting the two of them up. "Sorry I'm late. How long were you waiting?"

"Longer than you deserve," Kyle Paige said. He sniffed at Des. "I told you we should have left an hour ago."

Des put a hand on his lover's arm. "Now, hon, don't be such a stress puppy. We haven't been here anywhere near that long. Barely forty-five minutes. I'm sure Chris has a good reason." Des glared at Chris. "And please tell me it wasn't work."

"Okay, I won't." Chris slammed the SUV's door. "But it's going to make my explanation a tad on the short side."

He caught Trevor studying his SUV, but before he could say anything Des cut in. "Oh, don't let the wheels fool you, sugar. It's the butchest thing about him."

Chris threw him a look, but Des only smiled before he said, "We had reservations at the Blue Cactus."

"I know, and it took you weeks to get them." Chris led the way into his blessedly cool house, the others followed. "What can I say? I'm sorry."

"Say you'll take a shower. You are ripe, boyfriend."

"Give me five minutes. I'm sure we can find someone who will take our money." Chris paused at the foot of the stairs. "Maybe even someone with decent food. Hey, how about Crazy Fish?"

"*South* of Wilshire? Please," Des said. "No one who's anyone eats south of Wilshire."

"Right, just what was I thinking." Chris rolled his eyes and caught Trevor's grin. Damn, he was a hot-looking guy, all coiled muscle and lazy, dangerous eyes. Maybe this could turn into something after all. Chris felt a lot better all of a sudden. He bounded up the stairs, calling over his shoulder. "Be back in five."

They ended up at Spago, one of Kyle's favorites. At least they deferred to Chris in their choice of wine, though he had a spirited argument with Trevor over the Australian zinfandel he ordered. Chris was surprised. Most of Des's acquaintances didn't know Chardonnay from zinfandel.

Trevor played kneesies with him under the table and regaled them all with stories about the up-and-coming actors who plied their trade for the low-rent production company he worked for. Chris was sorry when lunch ended. Especially when he wound up with the bill.

"Paybacks are a bitch," Des said and patted Chris's smooth cheek. Then he leaned forward to brush his lips across Chris's mouth. "Why don't you invite Trevor home," he murmured. "He'd be good for you."

Des the matchmaker. Chris smiled his regret, wishing he hadn't agreed with Petey's request to meet with the studio exec. For one brief instance he considered canceling the meeting, then common sense overrode his lust. "Can't, I've got to work."

"All work and no play makes Chrissy a dull boy. You need to get out more."

Chris thought of Bobby from the night before. But he knew what Des would say about that. He hated it when Chris picked up strangers in bars. "You deserve better," he always said. Chris never bothered telling him he didn't agree.

Chris looked regretfully at Trevor. "Maybe we can do it again sometime."

Trevor frowned. "Sure, I guess."

After meeting with Ortez and making what he thought was a persuasive argument for having DataTEK take care of the studio's data, Chris found himself really regretting the brush-off he'd given Trevor. Maybe he should have gotten the guy's number. He wondered if Des knew it, then decided he didn't feel like hearing his friend's I-told-you-so's.

Maybe a drink would tame his regrets.

The Nosh Pit on a Saturday night was busy. He got his regular Cîroc martini from Ramsey, then grabbed a place at the end of the bar where he could watch the action.

There was lots of the usual trashy eye-candy spilling off the tiny dance floor and crowding the tables. The music was bone-jarring techno glitz, making even the simplest conversation difficult. Chris got his share of attention and before long was sharing some close space on the dance floor with a twenty-something music producer slumming it from West L.A. He had almost let the producer talk him into taking it to the backroom when someone bumped into them hard enough to break their embrace.

"Hey—" Chris protested, then froze when he found himself face to face with Trevor. "Oh, hey, man . . . "

"Work, huh?"

Chris flushed. "Well I was working, but . . . I meant to get your number earlier . . . "

Trevor eyed Chris's glassy-eyed companion, who was still swaying to the music. "I can see that."

"Listen," Chris said. "I was just heading out, why don't you come back to my place for a drink—"

"Can't." Trevor showed his teeth. "You're not the only one has to work."

Before Chris could react, Trevor slipped through the crowd and was gone.

Chris swore, then tried to walk past the producer. The younger man grabbed him.

"Com'n man, I wanna fuck."

Chris stared toward the exit, hoping to catch sight of Trevor. No luck. He looked at the dark-haired, sloe-eyed bombshell trying to hump his leg.

"Not tonight." He disentangled himself and made his way back to the bar.

"Ah, Silver Lake's own Lothario." Ramsey grinned at him. "You're blowing hot and cold tonight."

"Just give me another drink and keep it to yourself."

"Well don't I know who's sleeping alone tonight." Still grinning, Ramsey pulled the Cîroc off the top shelf and mixed Chris's drink. "What happened to the cutie you were with last night?"

"That was last night," Chris muttered and buried his nose in the glass Ramsey handed him. The sharp odor of top-shelf vodka tickled his sinuses.

He finished the drink and decided against another one. Tossing a ten on the bar, he wove through the press of warm bodies and made his way back out to Hyperion Avenue. His SUV was parked less than a block away, in an alley off De Longpre Street. He approached a crowd gathered at the mouth of the alley and hoped he wasn't interrupting anything violent. He watched the all-male crowd warily, until he recognized a guy who went to the Pit occasionally. When he tried to catch his eye the guy turned away, shuffling through the tension-filled crowd away from Chris.

A low mutter of excited voices rose and drifted over the whisper of traffic on Hyperion. A high-pitched voice giggled and cried, "My God, do you think it's true?"

"Get a grip, Michael. Would the guy advertise?"

"That's sick," Michael—at least Chris assumed it was Michael—said.

He rounded the corner, and it took him a full thirty seconds to realize that the source of the attention was his Lexus. It was another five seconds before he saw what the words spray-painted in red on his vehicle actually said.

CHAPTER 4

Saturday, 10:30 P.M., Piedmont Avenue, Glendale

DAVID CARESSED THE tone arm of the Victrola windup phonograph. It felt like warm silk. He carefully lowered it on Gene Greene's "Alexander's Got a Jazz Band Now" and listened to the opening whisper of scratchy words. The old jazz tune filled his small living room.

David lived on the flats in Glendale, off Lexington, near enough to the 134 for him to hear the steady hiss of freeway traffic day and night. The house was a small brick and wood-sided bungalow, one of the thousands that had been thrown up after the Second World War.

On the muted TV screen atop the bar between the kitchen and living room the Angels blew a pop fly and the Boston Red Sox took the lead in the bottom of the ninth. David shook his shaggy head and shut the thing off, not needing to see the final humiliation.

The Victrola wound down and traffic sounds flowed back into his tidy space. He slid the 78 off the spindle and back into its protective sleeve.

This time he pulled out his newest acquisition from the oak cabinet: Chuck Berry's "Oh, Baby Doll." He laid the platter on the turntable and finished his beer while the song played. Once it ended, he ran the tips of his fingers across the wood cabinet one more time. Satisfied the refinishing job wasn't going to get any better with more work, he put the music away and closed the Victrola. Glancing at the wall clock, he debated turning the late news on, finally deciding he didn't need any more bad news.

A pale shadow slipped out of the kitchen and followed him into the bedroom. David rubbed the small Siamese's head. The cat purred, a warm sound that took away his stress.

"Rough day, Sweeney?" The cat butted against his hand when his fingers slowed down.

The phone rang. He stared at it while it rang twice more before he gently pushed the cat aside and answered it.

It was Martinez.

Saturday, 11:30 P.M., Northeast Community Police Station, San Fernando Road, Los Angeles

Flanked by the two uniformed cops, Chris reluctantly entered the police station. His Dockers scuffed the faded linoleum floor; overhead fluorescent lights washed the color out of his Diesels and left his skin looking wan and sickly. A little like he was feeling.

When the cops had first shown up at the Nosh Pit to take the report on his vandalized SUV, he had expected them to write up the incident and leave him with shallow promises to look into it. Instead, after nearly twenty minutes of standing around talking on their cells, he had been invited to the police station.

The building smelled of sweat, stale food, and despair. A low hum of suppressed rage buzzed around him. Puke-green walls were plastered with yellowing posters and community bulletins. He glanced left at Officer Dale McEwen, the bull-necked cop who had been the first to arrive at the scene. The man's creased face desperately needed a shave. His rubbery lips were in constant motion, as though he kept a conversation going under his breath.

On his right, McEwen's partner, Orren Bulkowski, kept glancing at Chris with open contempt.

They passed through an open area, then into a second, this one labeled DETECTIVES. Several of the ancient desks were occupied, and Chris felt eyes on him as he threaded his way through the room. McEwen led him through to the back, where a bear of a man, six-four at least, climbed to his feet. He looked like a taller, heavier version of Tommy Lee Jones. His hair was a mass of tight dark curls touched with gray. A light smattering of old acne scars gave his face the rugged look of a TV cowboy. A thick mustache framed his full mouth. His brown eyes had just enough green to make them interesting. Chris figured him for around forty.

"Detectives Laine and Martinez will take care of you now, sir," McEwen said. His partner snorted and the two turned away. Chris watched them strut out of the room; glad to see them go, wishing he could follow.

Saturday, 11:40 P.M., Northeast Community Police Station, San Fernando Road, Los Angeles

"Christopher Bellamere?"

When David called Bellamere's name the vic's head snapped around, his face a mask of growing confusion and fear. David caught his breath; the light filtering through the vertical blinds fell on the face of the most beautiful man he had ever seen.

"Yeah?" the victim asked. His eyes darted from David to Martinez, then back to David. "What's this about?"

David introduced himself and Martinez. Bellamere nodded, his eyes glazed.

"Could I get your full name, please?" David's pencil was poised over the notepad. "And contact information."

"Christopher Robin Bellamere." He rattled off his address in Silver Lake and work and home numbers.

David wrote everything down. "Where do you work, sir?"

"DataTEK, in Studio City, in the Valley. Why am I here?"

"Your sport utility vehicle was vandalized," David said. "Is that correct?"

"Yes, but—"

"What sort of work do you do, Mr. Bellamere?"

"I.T.—computer support."

David slid a stack of photos of the vandalized vehicle across the desk. In most of them the words were all too clear: COCKSUCKER'S KILL. CARPET KILLER. FAGGOTS!! and finally, FAGS DIE. All in scarlet paint the composition of which was even now undergoing analysis. David doubted that this point would erase the look of outrage on the man's smooth-skinned face.

"Can you tell me what happened?" David asked.

Bellamere's face twisted into a grimace of rage. "Some asshole trashed my truck. Why aren't you out looking for skinheads or some religious nut with a god complex?"

"Any reason that type would single you out?" Martinez asked. "You piss someone off?"

The idea seemed to puzzle him. "Not that anybody ever said to my face."

"Maybe they didn't feel like talking about it," Martinez said.

"What time did you park your vehicle this evening?" David asked.

"Seven, seven-thirty, I guess. I wasn't paying attention."

"At that time you went to . . . the Nosh Pit, is it? That a regular hangout?"

"What's that got to do with what happened to my truck?"

"That's what we're trying to determine, sir," David said. "Do you usually park in that area?"

"I park wherever I can find space. This is because I'm gay, right?"

Martinez snorted and looked away. David stared at a spot on the nearest wall.

"You see anyone hanging around? Maybe somebody going into the alley? Or walking down the street toward it? Someone who looked out of place?"

"You mean straight? No. Listen, where's my SUV? Those other

cops said it was being towed—"

"It was. Our forensics people need to look it over. Once they're done we'll see you get your vehicle back."

"When's that going to happen?"

David shrugged. "Can't say, sir." He scooped up an eight-by-ten from the desk and studied it. Of the half dozen words the pricey SUV had been spray-painted with, the most prominent, and the one that had attracted their attention, were the words "The Carpet Killer," the term the local media had pinned on the killer in the recent murders.

Before Bellamere could say anything else, Martinez propped his hip against David's desk and leaned over Bellamere. "Ever hear the name Jason Blake?"

He turned at the sound of Martinez's voice. David took advantage of the distraction to study the younger man more closely. Bellamere's eyes were the same shade of blue as the ocean he had seen during a trip down the Baja. The color of his blond hair looked natural and it was cut short and spiked. He wore what David recognized as expensive designer clothes. The overall effect was stunning.

Bellamere shook his head. "I'm sorry. I don't—"

"Are you familiar with Eagle Rock, sir?" David asked.

"I've been there once or twice—"

"What about San Miguel Road?"

"No—"

"Mission Road?"

"Sounds like something downtown. Like Skid Row."

"Ever been there?"

"Skid Row? I hardly think so—"

"Let's get back to Jason Blake," Martinez cut in again.

"I think he called himself Jay," David said. "The name familiar to you?"

Bellamere screwed up his face and stared over David's shoulder.

"Jay? I met a Jay once. You don't think he had anything to do with this, do you?"

David kept his voice carefully neutral. "You remember what this guy looked like?"

Martinez stepped around to his own desk and pulled out a thick blue binder—Jason Blake's murder book. While he flipped through it, David worked at keeping the other man distracted.

"Any reason to think this guy might have had something to do with vandalizing your truck?"

"No."

"What can you tell me about him?"

"Not much." Bellamere picked at the skin around his thumb. "I didn't really know him very well."

"Well enough to recognize him if you saw him again?" This time when Martinez stepped back around the desk he edged right into Bellamere's space. He ignored Bellamere's alarm and shoved the picture of Jason Blake under his startled eyes. "Is this Jay?"

Bellamere stared down at the head shot, a high school graduation picture that David had acquired from Jason Blake's older brother. It showed a skinny youth in a blue and gold gown, a slightly dazed look on his pimply face. He had died three years after the date of the picture, just two months past his twenty-first birthday.

"Well, Mr. Bellamere?"

"I'm not sure . . . " David saw a flash of recognition in Bellamere's eyes. "I might have met him. But he was older."

"No need to get defensive, Mr. Bellamere."

Bellamere bristled. "I know the way you guys think. We're all a bunch of pedophiles." He poked his finger at the picture on the desk. "If I knew him he was old enough to be in the bar where I met him in."

"You mean where you hustled him?" Martinez asked. "Would that be the Nosh Pit? That your usual pickup spot?"

"It's a bar," Bellamere said. "I go there to drink."

"You just get lucky sometimes, that it?" Martinez said.

Bellamere stood, hands curled into fists at his side. "You really think I had something to do with what happened to my SUV? You think I pissed someone off? That I slept with the wrong person? Maybe I got some religious fanatic mad at me. Is that it?"

"I don't know, Mr. Bellamere," David said softly. "But if you know anything, now would be the time to tell us—"

"What happened to this guy? What the hell is going on here? This isn't about my SUV is it? It was never about that."

"He's dead, Mr. Bellamere," Martinez said. "Jason Blake was murdered."

CHAPTER 5

Saturday, 11:50 P.M., Northeast Community Police Station, San Fernando Road, Los Angeles

CHRIS STARED AT the Latino cop. The skin of his face felt hot and tight. "Murdered?"

"Yes, murdered."

Chris didn't know what to say. "Murdered."

"Yes," Martinez said.

"The message on your vehicle refers to a very specific crime," Laine said. "And if you have any information on that crime I need to hear it."

"You mean that serial killer?" Chris looked sideways at Martinez. "Tell me he's joking."

"I don't do standup, Mr. Bellamere," Laine said. "Do the words on your vehicle mean anything to you? Anything at all?"

The air Chris was trying to breathe suddenly seemed too thick to draw into his lungs. He'd known plenty of people who had died over the years—it was hard to be gay in Los Angeles and not know firsthand the swath AIDS had cut through the gay community—but he'd never known anyone who had been murdered.

"If I can help, just tell me how. What do you want to know?"

"Can you think when you last saw Jay?" Laine asked. "Was it at the Nosh Pit?"

The detective had surprisingly soft eyes. Chris always thought of cops as being tough—hardened by the world they lived in. Cynical tyrants who ruled the streets with their rules and their guns and their hard-assed attitudes.

"Or did you and Jay go to your place that night?"

Chris felt like he was drowning. What were they trying to suggest? He closed his eyes and opened them to stare down at the desk in front of him. "Yeah, we went back to my place."

"You live alone, Mr. Bellamere?"

Chris nodded. It was no secret. He always had—well, except for that disastrous year he'd spent with Geoff before the man had moved on to greener—and younger—pastures.

"I don't understand any of this, detective. What have Jay and this"—he indicated the pictures of his SUV—"got to do with each other?"

"How many times did you see Jay?"

"Only the once." Chris shrugged, trying to loosen the knots in his shoulders. What was it with these guys? They never answered a question? "I saw him around a few times, but we never said more than hi."

"He do something to tick you off?" Martinez said. "Or maybe he just wasn't very good in bed."

"We didn't click. It happens."

"How often it happen to you?"

"Not often—"

"How many men you fuck over the last six months?"

This guy was really beginning to get on his nerves. He decided it was time for some shock treatment. *He liked dishing it out. Let's see how much candor the asshole could take.* "Actually I don't fuck very many of them. I'm more of a bottom, myself."

"You're what?" Then Martinez flushed a deep red and his head turtled into his shoulders.

"Too much information, detective?" Chris smiled. "Don't like the pictures it conjures up?"

He glanced at Laine and was surprised to find the other man looking back at him. If he was disturbed by Chris's frank admission, it didn't show.

"I'd like to go now," Chris said.

"Sure," Laine said. "Just a couple more questions—do you remember seeing Jay with anyone else? Maybe someone who came into the bar some night?"

"I'm sorry. No, I didn't." Chris fumbled for his BlackBerry. "I'd like to help you. Really. I just don't know anything."

Laine removed the pictures of his vehicle from the desk and held out a business card.

"Thank you, Mr. Bellamere," he said. "If you think of anything—anything at all—give me a call, okay?"

"I don't know what it is you want from me, detective. I've told you all I remember." A lie, but he didn't think even this guy could remain cool-headed if Chris got into the details of the night he had spent with the young and very energetic Jay, so it was a nice lie. "But if I remember anything, I'll let you know. Promise."

He gave Laine his most beguiling smile and was startled when the man blushed.

He speed-dialed Des and was relieved when his friend's soft voice answered almost immediately.

"Hey, babe." He turned away from Laine's overly inquisitive gaze. He gave Des the truncated version of the night's events and was gratified when his friend said he'd be right there to pick him up. He was damned if he'd ask those buffoons for a ride.

Then Laine's graceless partner was back in his face, fully recovered from his embarrassment.

"We'll be watching you, Bellamere. Bank that."

Sunday, 12:10 P.M., Northeast Community Police Station, San Fernando Road, Los Angeles

They watched Bellamere as he was led away by a junior female D who was clearly interested in the good-looking young man. In disgust Martinez took the vehicle pictures and shoved them into a folder labeled with the date and incident number. "File that one under another accommodating citizen."

"It might not have been so useless. We know where he works and where he parties. We can ask around, maybe something will stand out." David swiveled around and began tapping away at his computer, laboriously entering the notes he had made from his interview with Bellamere. "Check with D.M.V., see if we can find any paper on him. See if there are any parking tickets or traffic stops."

Martinez nodded. Manson and Son of Sam had both been nailed thanks to traffic citations stored with the Department of Motor Vehicles that put holes in their alibis. Maybe they'd get as lucky with Bellamere. Even a paid-up traffic ticket could still be used to put him at a specific location at a specific time.

"I like the way your mind works, partner," he said. "You really think that *joto* has anything to do with this?"

"Someone sure wants us to think so. Besides," David said shrugging, "we don't have anyone better on the table right now."

"Well I ain't buying it. Look at the guy. I doubt he could pop a fruit fly." Martinez laughed at his own joke.

"Jeffrey Dahmer didn't look like he could, either."

"*Cabrón,*" Martinez muttered. "I still don't buy it."

David shook his head. He didn't want to buy it either, but his reasons were different. He didn't want to believe that a man who looked like that could be capable of the things he knew the Carpet Killer had done. And how stupid was that?

"There's no proof he's involved."

"Oh *dios,* here comes another one."

David looked over in time to see an impeccably dressed black man rush over to Chris, who was standing in the corridor. The two embraced and David felt heat rush to his face as in a heartbeat he found himself wondering what it would be like to do the same. Fool. As though anyone who looked like that would give the time of day to someone like him.

"Forget them." David refused to let his thoughts linger on hopeless fantasies. "I want to talk to Jason's brother again."

"Why?" Martinez asked. "He wasn't very helpful the first time we interviewed him."

As senior detective, David had taken on the unpleasant task of informing Jason Blake's family of his death. The brother, Richard, had been too distraught to offer anything useful. But more than one witness had their memories improved by a second interview.

"You don't think Jay mentioned this Chris guy, do you? Would he tell his own brother about his latest *puto*?"

David frowned. "We won't know until we ask."

CHAPTER 6

Sunday, 12:40 A.M., Cove Avenue, Silver Lake, Los Angeles

AFTER DROPPING CHRIS off at his house and declining his offer of coffee—"Really, hon, it's after midnight!"—Des pressed two small white pills into Chris's palm.

"It's nothing, just Percs. It'll help you sleep," Des said before climbing back into his silver Mercedes and leaving Chris alone.

Chris retreated to his media room, where he curled up on the love seat with a glass of wine and watched an hour of inane talk shows before drifting off to sleep. The wine on top of the Percodan might have been a mistake.

His dreams were turbulent and disjointed. He was cruising Boystown. The rainbow-hued streets were wall-to-wall men, each more gorgeous than the last. Except for one familiar face. The acne scars made David Laine's skin look pitted and diseased in the gaudy lights of West Hollywood. The cheap cut of his clothes looked even more frumpish as he kept appearing and disappearing in the wandering crowd.

Abruptly the crowds vanished. The dark streets were empty. Chris looked around for his SUV, but every time he found it, his keys wouldn't work, or they slipped from his fingers and disappeared into the shadows pooled around his bare feet.

Someone else was there.

"David?"

Only he knew it wasn't David.

He spotted the SUV, parked by itself down an empty street,

covered in graffiti. Hurrying toward it was like plowing through deep water. When he reached it he pounded on the golden door panel, smearing red paint all over his hands until it looked like they had been dipped in blood.

The door popped open.

"About time," he muttered and jumped inside. The door slammed shut with a solid *hunk*.

Someone ran down the street toward him. In the kaleidoscopic streetlights he recognized David. Chris jammed the key into the ignition and the Lexus rumbled to life.

David shouted something, shaking his shaggy head and waving for Chris to pull over. Instead Chris goosed the gas pedal and shot out into the midnight black street. Odd, his headlights didn't come on.

"Chris."

The fingers that closed over the bare skin of his shoulder were boneyard cold. In contrast the breath on his cheek was a furnace.

He turned and found himself staring into a smiley-face mask. The lipless chasm of its mouth was open in a humorless grin.

The oily barrel of the gun pressed against his left eye. Chris heard an odd buzz as the trigger was depressed.

He woke with a scream buried in his throat. The buzz came again.

He jerked upright; the issue of *Linux* he'd been leafing through was slithering off his lap. Belatedly he realized the sound was his doorbell.

Head woozy, heart trip-hammering in his chest, he nearly tumbled to the floor, only catching himself at the last minute with a painful bump to his shin on the granite coffee table.

He staggered to the front door, leaning forward to peer through the mullioned window.

At first he confused the figure standing under his porch light with the faceless killer in his dream. Then the figure turned into the light.

He flung the door open. "Trevor?"

"I was cruising the area and saw your lights on." Trevor glanced back over his shoulder. "Did I wake you?"

"No—yes." Chris rubbed his sore ankle on the back on his leg and tried not to let his eyes dart around while he scanned the shadows beyond his door. "Sort of, I guess. I think I was dreaming."

"Nothing fun, from the looks of it."

"No," Chris said, remembering the sound the gun had made as the masked man pulled the trigger. "Not fun."

"Want some company? I picked up a bottle of Silver Oak Cabernet the other day. You can tell me if it's any good."

"Silver Oak?" Chris glanced at the plastic bag in Trevor's hand. "What year? Ninety-eight?"

"Is there any other?"

"Come on in." Chris closed and locked the door behind him. When Trevor walked by he breathed in the scent of Yves Saint Laurent and soap. He inhaled and began to think this evening might not turn out so bad after all.

Chris briefly told him about his SUV while he led him back into the media room, where a pair of talking heads filled the sixty-inch screen. Chris grimaced as he overheard the last of the newscast.

" . . . another apparent victim of the so-called Carpet Killer, who has been terrorizing the gay community of Los Angeles and environs for weeks now."

The image on the screen shifted. It was night, but there was more than enough light to see the blue-garbed EMTs emerge from behind a crumbling building with a sheet-draped gurney. Other people clustered around, several of them cops.

Chris leaned forward when he recognized Detective Laine standing apart from the uniformed cops, taking notes in his notebook.

"A call from an unknown source tipped off police to the body."

Laine looked straight into the camera. He was too far away for

Chris to read his expression.

"No identity has been released at this time," the announcer stated. "Up next: Terror in a peaceful community."

"Nasty stuff, isn't it?" Trevor dropped into the depression where Chris had been sleeping earlier. He held up the bag. "Why don't you round up some glasses and a corkscrew? I'll find something more interesting to watch."

After pouring the Cabernet, Trevor flipped through Chris's DVD collection, pulling out one of the movies Bobby had given Chris. Chris had almost forgotten them. Curious, he let Trevor put it on. The startling blue of a clichéd kidney-shaped pool appeared on the screen as the camera panned around.

Chris wasn't a big porno fan but he watched without protest as a trio of guys—two hot blonds and dark, sexy Bobby—moved away from the pool and climbed a set of marble steps to a pool house, where they got down to what was apparently the heart of the movie. The production quality was poor, but there was some amateurish spark between the three actors that made up for the bad lighting and rough sound.

"So that's where he learned that," Chris murmured.

"What?" Trevor's pale blue eyes were already hooded in passion. "Something wrong?"

"No, it's just . . . I know that guy."

"Who?"

"The dark-haired one."

"Yeah?" Trevor leaned forward. "Didn't know you were a porn groupie. He an item?"

"No."

"You mean not now?"

"I mean not ever."

"Too bad." Trevor sipped his wine and flicked his tongue out over his full lips. So, tell me all about your deliciously kinky sex life . . . "

"Hey!"

Trevor grinned and turned back to the video. Still woozy from the wine and drugs, Chris dozed off with his head on Trevor's shoulder.

He awoke to find himself alone in his bed. Naked. Blearily he saw the slip of paper taped to his dresser.

"Too bad it didn't work out. Guess next time we'll stay away from the wine. Sorry about your truck." It was signed with a loopy T and a cell-phone number.

Chris wondered how far things had gone last night after he passed out. He didn't feel sore; they hadn't fucked. He glanced at his watch. It was barcly six. Too early to call. Later. And he would stay away from the booze and the pills. He had the feeling Trevor would be fun in bed. If they ever managed to get there.

In the bathroom he grabbed his shaving gear and turned the shower on. His bedside phone rang.

He ran out of the bathroom and scooped it up. Maybe Trevor was calling for a rematch. Only silence met his initial greeting.

"Hello?"

Nothing.

Christ, he hated wrong numbers who wouldn't admit their mistake.

"Who is this—"

The phone went dead.

He clicked recall but all he got was unknown name, unknown number.

"Asshole."

He dumped the phone back on his bedside table and went in to take his shower.

CHAPTER 7

Sunday, 3:15 A.M., North Mission Road, Los Angeles

"PACK OF FUCKING jackals," Martinez snapped.

The uniformed officer who had been called in to help with crowd control threw him a wary look. "Sir?"

"Just watch everybody, Schmidt," David said to the confused man. Personally he could never figure out where the crowds came from, but no matter what time of day or what location, they always seemed to show up. And they always managed to get in the way if you let them. "Keep them all clear of the crime scene."

"Sneaky bastard is what your average reporter is," Martinez added, as though someone might have missed his point. "Don't ever trust 'em, Schmidt. Them or lawyers. If any of those assholes so much as pokes a nose hair over that line, bust them."

Schmidt smiled weakly. "Yes, sir."

"What do they teach 'em these days?" Martinez muttered after Schmidt left.

David crouched to examine an impression in the stained and cracked pavement in the alley behind North Mission Road, where the latest body had been found. "Same thing they taught us. Why?"

"So how come we're so much smarter than them?"

He couldn't help it. He laughed.

"What? You're saying we're not smarter?"

"Come on, Einstein." David clapped Martinez on the back. "Let's have another go at your wit. See if we can wrap this up before morning. I really don't want to see what this place looks like in broad daylight."

Two men loaded the body into the coroner's wagon. The flashing lights of the emergency vehicles strobed over the alley.

After making sure the vehicle got through the growing mob, David slipped back between the two buildings. He watched where he put his feet. Gelatinous puddles littered the alley; the odor of urine underlay the stench of rotting garbage. S.I.D. had already been over the whole length, photographing and sampling everything. Photos were taken of the crumbling walls and cardboard boxes and even a discarded bicycle found behind one pile of garbage.

He followed Martinez back to the dumpster where the body had been found. A luckless scavenger had made the discovery while looking for tin cans to exchange for a bottle of Thunderbird. The shivering man now huddled under a broken lean-to that some inventive soul had erected using discarded tin and rotting pallets.

Martinez had sent one of the uniforms to get coffee for their witness. Now he hovered around while the man greedily sucked back coffee and mumbled answers to Martinez's questions. The witness, in a cast-off overcoat two size too big, and Martinez, in a green jacket over a paisley shirt and dark brown pants, made quite a pair. Fashion was not Martinez's strong suit.

"Any luck?" David asked.

Martinez shook his head. "Guy's having trouble giving me his name, at least one he can remember more than five minutes. He does claim he found the body before it got completely dark. I checked with LAX, sunset was at 19:25 tonight. Full dark would have come twenty, thirty minutes later."

The call hadn't come into the switchboard until nearly nine o'clock. Long after sunset. "Is he saying he hung around for nearly an *hour* after he found the thing?"

"He won't say. I think he took advantage of the light that was left to collect more cans."

"He hung around a body that Lopez thinks has been dead at least three weeks looking for scrap?"

"Hey, S.I.D. got the cans away from him. A couple even contained fluid from the body. At least one housed some wandering maggots."

David grimaced. "How'd he call it in?"

"Pay phone at the end of the alley. Good Samaritan, huh?"

"Any chance your guy knew the vic?"

"He didn't seem to think so. But then I'm not sure at what level he's actually thinking. Lopez seems to figure this vic's another young guy. Can't see them running in the same circles, can you?"

"So, this is just another dumping ground."

"Techs are still running luminol tests, but so far there's precious little blood." The luminol spray reacted chemically to blood and this released light. "One thing I'll give him, our perp's tidy."

"He's not geographically impaired, either," Martinez said. "He likes to move around."

"A mobile serial killer. Not exactly unique."

David had seen the body after Lopez was done with it. Maggot activity had been so far advanced there was no telling what condition that body had been in when dumped. Still, he had to ask, "Raped?"

"You think Lopez would say? You know she keeps things close to her chest. I figure we're lucky to get her to speculate on his age."

"Your guy see anyone else hanging around?"

"I was working on that when the coffee got here. I'm kinda hoping the stuff will wake up a few brain cells. Who knows, if he hangs around here all the time, maybe he did see our perp. Wouldn't that be a nice break."

Their witness watched them approach, clutching his empty Styrofoam cup in one dirt-encrusted hand.

David flashed his tin. "Detective Laine. We'd like to ask you a few questions, if that's okay, Mr.—?"

"Dante!" The man shouted. "Circles of hell!"

"Your name, sir?" David asked.

"The elves did it."

"The who did it?"

"The elves. The elves!"

The babbling man sprayed spittle, which David wiped off his cheek. "Yes, sir."

"The elf was golden."

"Can you describe this . . . elf?" He glanced at Martinez, who shrugged.

The elf man drew himself upright, wrapped in the dignity of delusion. "The elves are golden, but cold."

"Okay, we've got one golden elf," David said. "Was he alone?"

Martinez cut in. "Did you see this elf, or anyone, put something in that dumpster?"

"A golden chariot," he shouted.

"Great, did Charlton Heston bring a body to the dumpster?" David muttered. "What did this guy look like, anyway?"

"I'm dry." The elf man licked his lips, tugging at the filth-encrusted beard covering his face. "Got a buck you can spare?"

"Tell me about the elf."

"Will I get a buck then?"

"I'll buy you a whole three-course meal. Who was the elf, sir?"

"A golden elf."

"Do you mean he had blond hair?"

"Spun gold, like the sun, he was."

"I'll take that as a yes," David sighed. He knew this guy would be useless as a witness in court, even if they found his blond elf. David didn't care. If this was a description of the killer, then at least it gave them a place to start. He'd worry about viable witnesses later. "Can you tell us what the elf was wearing?"

"Wearing?" he said, blinking at both David and Martinez. "Wearing?"

"Yes," David mustered all the patience he could. "What kind of clothes did he have on?"

"Isn't that odd?" The elf man screwed up his booze-bloated face. "He was wearing jeans. Now why on earth would an elf wear jeans?"

Later, after he had been dispatched with Schmidt to get a sandwich and another coffee, they retreated to their car in the next alley.

"We've got a possible blond killer who wears blue jeans," Martinez said.

David took a slug of lukewarm water from a bottle he had stashed there earlier. "And drives a golden chariot. Don't forget the chariot."

"Yellow car? Truck?" Martinez snorted. "Not too many of them around."

"Let's put out a bolo"—cop jargon for be on the lookout—"on all local elves in or out of chariots. That ought to get us some action."

"Think he really saw something?"

"Who knows?" David crushed the empty water bottle. A Be on the Lookout wouldn't be out of place if they had something more definite to look for. For now the elf man's words were useless. Out of habit he dumped the bottle in the backseat so as not to contaminate the crime scene.

"Our boy's too damned slick," Martinez said. "He's not leaving anything behind he doesn't mean to leave."

Wearily David climbed out of the unmarked car. "No I.D. this time. So why didn't he want us to know this vic's name?"

"Maybe no one cares about this one. Hustler?" Martinez followed him back through the alley toward the crime scene. The media had dispersed once the body was removed. "It's a notoriously easy target group."

Give any horny young guy a few drinks and his judgment went to hell. Which was why David made sure all his drinking took place in cop bars. He was never tempted to overindulge and get stupid when he was with other cops. Once they got on the brag and started boasting about all the pussy they got, he was usually in a mood to leave anyway.

So far he'd kept his private life separate from his professional life by time and distance. No one cared that he took his yearly holidays to Palm Springs—he always went out for the Palm Springs Classic Car Show and everyone knew of his passion for old cars. If he booked a room at the Hacienda it wasn't like he had to tell anyone he was cruising for a secret love. It was the single brush with another life that he allowed himself in his normally low-key existence.

One even his partner, Martinez, didn't know about.

CHAPTER 8

Monday, 8:00 A.M., DataTEK headquarters, Studio City, San Fernando Valley, Los Angeles

"MR. MCGILL?" DAVID held his shield in one hand while he extended the other to Peter McGill, the Brooks Brothers–suited CIO of DataTEK. "Detective David Laine. Thank you for seeing me on such short notice."

Martinez had been called into court for a morning arraignment and David had opted to interview McGill alone.

"Yes, well." He ran a hand through his thinning, rust-red hair. "I try to help the local authorities when I can."

McGill's office held a massive mahogany desk and four leather chairs. Prints of snowy forests occupied by deer and elk hung from beige walls. Behind the desk a large double window looked east, toward the San Gabriel Mountains; the snowless peak of Mount Wilson lay behind a brown haze.

"I'd like to ask a few questions, Mr. McGill. Background information on one of your employees. Just routine stuff." David opened his notebook. "You have a Christopher Bellamere in your employ?"

"Yes." McGill frowned. "Has Bellamere done something?"

"There was an incident involving his vehicle and I'm investigating. How long has Mr. Bellamere been employed by your company, Mr. McGill?"

"Chris started six years ago."

"Good employee?"

McGill's frown deepened. He played with a monitor-shaped

paperweight. "Christopher's performance has always been up to company expectations."

That sounded too carefully phrased to be good. "Does Mr. Bellamere have trouble fitting in?"

"He's not a rule follower. His . . . lifestyle leaves much to be desired."

Bingo.

"How would you characterize his behavior in the last few weeks?"

"I'm not sure what you mean."

"Has he been unusually anxious? Expectant? Did he seem preoccupied?"

"No, not at all . . . "

"Is Mr. Bellamere available to speak to us?"

McGill still seemed puzzled by the whole conversation; he frowned. "He won't be in until this afternoon—"

"I'd like to see Mr. Bellamere's work space, if that's not a problem."

"You mean his cubicle? I suppose that can be arranged." McGill picked up his phone and punched in three digits. "Tom? Could you come to my office for a moment?"

A few minutes later a blond, preppy-looking man strode into McGill's office. He stopped when he saw David.

"Detective," McGill said. "This is Tom Clarke, one of our senior I.T. people."

"Mr. Clarke." David extended his hand. Tom shook it vigorously. "I'm making some inquires into a fellow employee. Mr. McGill thought you might be able to help me."

Tom looked from David to McGill, one eyebrow arching.

"He wants to see Bellamere's desk." McGill waved them both out. "Show him around. Answer his questions."

"I have that meeting with the IBM people—"

"I assure you I won't keep you long," David said.

Tom used a card key in the elevator to access the ninth floor.

"How many people work here?" David asked.

Tom shrugged. "Fifty? Sixty? Besides our group, there's a mainframe team, several D.B.A.s—database administrators—and a handful of programmers and Web designers."

"What exactly does Mr. Bellamere do?"

"Chris and I do everything from handling data storage and backup to building secure networks from scratch. When our clients have problems, they call us." The elevator door whispered open and they stepped out onto a dove-gray carpet. Tom turned right. "Just this Saturday Chris and I were involved in getting a major pharmaceutical company back up and running. Took us hours."

"You've worked with Mr. Bellamere awhile? How would you characterize him on a personal level?"

"Personal? What's this about? Do you think the guy molested someone?"

"What would make you think he'd molest someone?"

"You've talked to Peter—I mean Mr. McGill, right? Did he tell you Chris was gay?"

"Who would he have molested?"

"Boys, what else." Tom smirked.

"You have reason to suspect Mr. Bellamere is a pedophile?" That one was off the radar. Could it be true? It didn't fit with the profile they'd generated on their killer.

David didn't want to believe it. He repeated his question, adding: "That's a pretty serious charge."

Tom looked sullen. "No. Let's just say I know he's a sick fuck."

"You need to be careful about charging people with crimes like that. We don't take that sort of accusation lightly—"

"Okay, I overreacted."

"To what?"

"Nothing, I was wrong. Forget it."

They entered an area of cubicles. The walls matched the carpet and each cubicle held a steel desk, a black flat-screen monitor, and a phone that looked like it had more buttons than a NASA console.

Each cubicle had an engraved nameplate. Bellamere had personalized his space by covering the walls with framed Dilbert and Maxine comics; a Dilbert desk calendar still showed Friday's date. A red message light blinked on his phone.

"How does Chris get along with people?" David changed the subject abruptly. He picked up the desk calendar and flipped forward, glancing at the cartoons, looking for notes or names. "He argue with people? Cause fights?"

"Chris do something that might cause a fight?" Tom looked amused. "You're joking, right?"

David set the calendar down. He glanced at a notepad beside the phone. 'Lunch with Des—B Cactus—Trev???' The name Trev was underlined two times in bold strokes. He flipped through a leather folder. It had more notes; most seemed to be work-related. "You don't like gays much, do you, Mr. Clarke?"

"Long as they leave me alone, who cares."

"How would you characterize Mr. Bellamere as an employee? Does he do his job competently?"

"Competently?" Tucked against his side, Tom's hands curled into fists and he avoided David's gaze. "I guess so. He's a good talker, got lots of people convinced he knows it all."

"But not you?"

"Listen, I have a lot of work to do—"

"Sure." David put his notebook away. "I've got all I need for today. Thanks for all your help, sir."

"That's it?"

"That's it. I believe I can find my way out."

Monday, 9:35 A.M., Cove Avenue, Silver Lake, Los Angeles

At first Chris ignored the pounding. One glance at his bedside clock told him it was barely nine-thirty. He wasn't expecting anyone this early and all his friends knew enough to call before dropping by. He hadn't returned home from a Glendale call-out to take care of some misbehaving servers until nearly three, and even Petey knew better than to expect him before noon after nights like that.

But the hammering on his door persisted. Growling under his breath, Chris threw on a robe and lurched down the stairs. He yanked the heavy door open.

"What the fuck—"

Detective Laine stood inside the gated courtyard, between the two short Italian cypresses that flanked the door, studying his notebook as though it would tell him why his knocking wasn't being answered. When Chris opened the door he snapped it shut and slid it into his jacket pocket.

"Mr. Bellamere—"

"Jesus, don't tell me, you just have a few more questions?"

"Yes, sir. If it's convenient."

"Why do I feel like I'm in a bad *Columbo* movie? So, you're saying if it's not convenient you'll leave me alone?"

Laine stepped closer. The dusty breeze blew through the open door. "I thought you might be interested in getting your vehicle back."

"What's this? Giving me a ride to grill me for more information?" Chris couldn't resist a smile at the thought of David coming all the way up here to give him a ride.

"No, no . . . I wanted to talk to you without Martinez."

"Why?"

"You don't seem to like Martinez."

"You mean there are people who do?"

David actually laughed. "Your body shop picked it up from impound yesterday morning just as you instructed. I just called and they said it's ready."

Chris went inside to get dressed, while Laine waited outside in his car, a wine-colored Crown Victoria that had a serious dent in the passenger door. Chris had to jerk at the door several times before he could get it open, and when he did it scattered flakes of rust all over the cobblestone driveway.

Heat swamped him immediately. He looked around, wondering why the air conditioner wasn't on. It was the middle of August, for God's sake. Belatedly he realized Laine's window was down.

"No air?" he croaked.

"'Fraid not. Your tax dollars at work."

The window proved more stubborn than the door.

"Here. There's a trick to it." Laine brought the Crown Vic to a stop under a massive crape myrtle tree whose electric-pink flowers trailed nearly to the hood of the car. Laine slid off his seat belt and leaned over Chris. His arm brushed Chris's chest, muscles bulging as he yanked down on the handle.

The window moved down a couple of inches. Hot air poured into the gap. From inside the car Chris could smell soap and Kenneth Cole. He was so close the pores of the older man's skin looked like miniature craters. A single bead of sweat poised on Laine's temple, catching on a strand of dark hair. Chris saw some silver mixed in with the sable. David had taken his jacket off, and Chris saw that his arms were thick with more dark hair. He was a real bear. David pushed again at the stubborn window. The glass protested, but this time it went all the way down.

He met Chris's eyes. "There," he said. "That should help."

Chris nodded, wishing they'd start driving again. Then he realized the other man was staring at his mouth. Without thinking about it, Chris licked his lips.

Instantly Laine jerked away. He swung the car out into the

street and eventually turned north on Silver Lake Boulevard. "Has anything else occurred to you since Saturday night?"

For some inexplicable reason Chris thought of his dream. He shook the memory away. "You mean do I remember seeing someone with a can of spray paint trotting down Hyperion? No."

"This Jay guy, you sure you never saw him with anyone else?"

"He didn't come in often." Chris rubbed the fleshy part of his thumb. "The one time we were, ah, together he said he was from Anaheim. I took it to mean he cruised somewhere else."

"He ever say where?"

"No."

The cop left it at that, though Chris had the distinct impression he wasn't done yet.

At the body shop the Lexus squatted regally between a rusted-out Saturn and a newer-model Volvo. The late-morning sun caught the metallic finish so that it gleamed like a newly minted gold coin.

Chris climbed out of the Crown Victoria. He did a walk around his Lexus, pleased to note that they had done a good job. There was no way to tell how badly marked up the vehicle had been.

He looked up to find that Laine had followed him.

"Thanks for bringing me," he said.

"Nice wheels. What color do you call this?"

Chris pursed his lips. "Prasecca metallic. Always thought it looked gold to me, but I guess the marketing department didn't agree."

"Yeah, they do like to fancy things up," Laine murmured, trailing a hand along the sleek curves of the SUV. He paused briefly at the back bumper, and Chris wondered if he'd spotted a scratch. Finally he circled around the other side and came back to the driver's side. "Nothing's ever what it seems anymore," he said. "Get pretty good mileage out of it, do you?"

"Not bad, considering." Chris got into the driver's seat, slid the key in, and cranked the engine. It purred. "Was there anything else, detective?"

"No, nothing—" the cop turned away, then swung back before Chris could shut the door. "One question, Mr. Bellamere. Just a quick one."

"God, you really are Columbo!"

"You don't strike me as the type, but, do you wear glasses?"

"Glasses—no. I don't. Why?"

"Have good vision do you? Or do you wear contacts?"

"Twenty-twenty," Chris said. "What's this about? You think I might have missed something the other day?"

"No, chances are whoever did this was long gone by the time you got there. Just idle curiosity."

Chris didn't think this cop had an idle bone in his body, but he kept the thought to himself. "Fact is, I have nearly perfect vision."

"You're very lucky, sir."

He stepped away from the truck and Chris backed out. He flipped his hand at Laine, who nodded, still fixated on the back of his truck.

He was still staring when Chris pulled out of the lot and headed west.

Monday, 11:35 A.M., DataTEK, Studio City, San Fernando Valley, Los Angeles

"Thomas, good to see you again. Glad to see you've settled in."

Executive row was a maze of small offices and conference rooms. The walls were cubicle-thin, without doors. Chris glanced up from the VP's computer he'd been working on for the last ten minutes. He recognized the voice of Saul Ruben, DataTEK's chief financial officer. Then he also recognized Tom Clarke's voice.

"Uncle Saul. I thought you were on your way to San Francisco."

"This evening." The distaste was heavy in Ruben's voice. "I prefer to spend as little time as possible in that Sodom and Gomorrah."

Tom made noises of agreement.

"How's your father these days?" Ruben asked. "I haven't seen him since the last stockholders' meeting."

"He's fine. Enjoying his retirement."

"That's right, he left his firm, didn't he?" A desk drawer slammed shut. "Still think he should have taken that House seat. We need more men with his fortitude in Washington. Too many of these pantywaists running things these days."

"Yes, sir."

"I'm glad you stopped by," Ruben said. "Your aunt wants you to come by this Sunday. We're having some people over. The Armstrongs' daughter is visiting from Boston and she needs an escort."

"Uncle— "

"Could do worse, boy."

"Yes, sir."

Chris grinned at the pain in Tom's voice. A pair of shadows crossed in front of the frosted glass fronting the VP's office.

Chris watched Ruben pass by in his Brooks Brothers suit. At least he knew where Petey got his fashion sense. Tom followed in his knockoff Calvin Kleins. He needed a little more of his uncle's money to afford the real thing.

Chris finished up with the VP's computer. He found Tom in the cafeteria picking at a mandarin chicken salad. Chris dragged a chair around and straddled it.

"Well that explains a lot," he said softly.

Tom's tentative smile froze, became a grimace. "What the hell's your problem, Bellamere?"

"Just wondering how a guy like you got here with nothing going for him but brass balls."

"At least I've got balls."

"So, Uncle bought you a job, did he? He trying to buy you a

society wife, too?"

Tom clenched his fists so hard Chris swore he heard the knuckles crack. "I earned this position, same as you. Why the hell can't you give me any credit?"

"Because I've seen your work. And if you think I don't know about you trying to get Petey to can me, think again." Chris thumped to his feet. "You want respect, don't ride in here on someone else's coattails. I could drag in a dozen guys who have forgotten more than you ever knew, who don't have cushy jobs because daddy sits on the board of directors. Even Petey knows it." Even if he'd never admit it.

"I'll bet you could drag in a dozen guys—bunch of faggots standing in line for a blow job."

"You say that like it's a bad thing." Chris smiled. Leaning forward he took his time selecting a mandarin slice from Tom's salad and popped it in his mouth.

Tom flushed, his mouth a thin white line. "There are going to be some serious changes around here, just you wait. I don't care how irreplaceable you think you are. We'll see who's laughing then."

Chris was thoughtful as he made his way back to his desk. He knew the CFO, Saul Ruben. At least he knew his reputation. But what didn't he know?

His cubicle neighbor, Becky Chapman, slapped their shared wall, then rolled her chair around into his cubicle. She glanced at his computer, where he had just opened Google. "Working on something?"

"You know who Clarke is?"

"Trick question?" She grabbed an apple out of his ever-present fruit basket. "Last time I checked his name tag, it said Tom Clarke. I miss something?"

"His father's a major stockholder. And our esteemed CFO's brother. How much you wanna bet Petey gets a fat bonus at year end for bringing the kid in?"

She grinned sourly and took a bite of apple. "You should try giving him a chance. Maybe he's not as bad as you make out."

"You think?"

"No. But we *are* stuck with him."

"Ever the pragmatist."

"That's me. Plays well with others, too."

When she rolled back to her desk Chris checked his phone messages while he did a scattershot search for information on Saul Ruben.

One message was from Des. "Let's do the Pit tonight. Kyle's got an audition. We can have dinner. Your choice. Call me."

Chris did. The phone was picked up on the third ring.

"Masturbation corporation—can I give you a hand?"

"Aren't we just the cutest." Chris rolled his eyes. "Is Des there, Kyle?"

"Haven't seen you in a while, Mary," Kyle said. "The interstate rest stop reopen for business?"

Chris ground his teeth. "Give it a rest, will you? This hostility is so yesterday. Is Des there?"

"No, he isn't. And if you'd stop horning in on us I wouldn't care what you did."

"Des and I are old friends, that's it. It never was anything else." Not entirely true. For a two-month period, during their sophomore year at UCLA, he and Des had tried to take their new friendship to another level. It had failed so miserably they had sworn never to try anything so foolish again.

"Yeah, right. I see the way he looks at you."

The dial tone filled his ear. Chris held the phone away from him and stared at it.

Becky popped her head around the corner. "You aren't going to do something stupid, are you?"

"Who, me? Never." Chris quickly hung up and swept his fingers through his spiked hair. "Stupid how?"

"I've heard some things about Ruben . . . "

"Oh?" Chris straightened, Kyle forgotten. "Juicy things? Tell."

"I heard he's a real hard-ass. Doesn't give slack to anybody."

"Boring. Is that all?"

"He's also a raving homophobe."

Chris shrugged. "Him and all the other Republicans. Anything else?"

"He apparently disowned his own sister when she came out. When she died last year he refused to go to her funeral." She lowered her voice. "Refused to let anyone else in the family go, either. Said anyone who went was out of his will. Disowned."

"So anybody go?"

"Never heard. Want to bet Tommy's daddy didn't? Maybe DataTEK is Tommy's reward."

"Well there's a cheery thought."

"Ain't it?"

CHAPTER 9

Monday, 11:20 A.M., Northeast Community Police Station, San Fernando Road, Los Angeles

WHAT DID I *see in Bellamere's vehicle?*

David grabbed coffee from the pot, which had the dubious distinction of always being full. He sipped and grimaced. Even copious amounts of cream couldn't cut the bitterness of squad-room coffee.

The words of the elf man who had found the last body returned. The man he had claimed to see had been blond, driving a golden vehicle. David and Martinez had been quick to assume he meant yellow. But what if he had truly meant golden?

As in Prasecca metallic?

And what had he seen behind the driver's seat in the back of Chris's SUV? Eyeglasses?

Jason Blake had worn glasses. That had been in the initial report.

His desk was its usual clutter of half-finished reports and must-read documents. A new one lay on top of the Jason Blake report. It was Blake's autopsy.

A sticky note was attached to it. Martinez had scribbled a hasty "Check the tox report" in his sloppy handwriting. While David's fevered mind worked over the possibilities, he skimmed the autopsy. "Substantial quantities of chlorophenyl dimethylamino cycolhexanone hydrochloride present in the victim's liver and stomach."

"Nice, eh?" Martinez slid his rump gingerly onto the edge of

David's desk, almost dislodging a stack of paperwork. David caught the papers and moved them out of danger. "Well, at least we know how he immobilizes them."

"Ketamine," David muttered. "Special K."

"Raver's drug," Martinez said. "Think our vics are being picked up in raves?"

"It's also big in the gay scene. I think it's time we paid a visit to this Nosh Pit."

"*Madre de dios*."

David looked at him sharply, but Martinez wasn't even looking at him. Instead he was eyeing one of the new female junior D's.

"Your wife catches you looking at that and you and your *cojones* have got some serious explaining to do."

Martinez grinned. "No harm looking, right? You telling me that's illegal?"

David glanced across the room at the tall, statuesque blond. Thank God she was ignoring them. He forced himself to smile, flipping back through the report as though that distracted him.

"Probably is in some states. Now about this." He tapped the paperwork in front of him. "We need to put some D's out in the more popular clubs."

"Talk about being popular—man, you're ratings are gonna go through the roof when you assign that one."

"They'll survive."

"Guys should get hazard pay. They touch you and your dick falls off. Talk about the heebie-jeebies."

David knew his partner didn't really believe that. No one was that ignorant in this day and age. But he knew it reflected a view shared by many in the department. The new tolerant attitude only went skin-deep with many of the older cops. They remembered all too well when nobody had to tolerate anyone who wasn't "normal."

Martinez was grinning, and David braced himself for his next dig. "Maybe this is one of those cases where you can't ask the rank and file to do what you wouldn't do yourself."

David picked up the report and read through it again. "You talked to Lopez about the others? I want to make sure they run tox screens on all of them."

"Sure," Martinez said. "Said she'd have them to us early next week. So, you gonna do it?"

David's jaw clenched and he stared down at the tox report. "Sure, why not?"

"You get hit on, I don't want to know, okay?" Martinez laughed all the way back to his own desk.

David pulled up Jason Blake's murder book. The older brother lived in Orange County. He had provided most of the background for the report. It was woefully thin, so it didn't take David long to find the entry.

Brother remarked that Blake wore glasses for astigmatism. Neither the glasses, nor any other item of clothing, had been recovered. The report described the glasses. The description matched the glasses in Chris's vehicle.

David knew he'd never get a search warrant. All he had were suspicious circumstances. No probable cause. No evidence even the most pro-cop judge would look at.

So it was time to find the evidence. Laine dialed the Orange County number.

A cool-sounding woman answered the phone with the words "Gilbert, Michelson and Gabronni," and acknowledged that Mr. Blake was a partner there. She rung his extension and a male voice said, "Hello?"

"Mr. Blake." David pulled up a new database entry form on his desktop PC and entered the day's date while he listened to Blake ask who was there. Before answering he entered Richard Blake's name and his relationship to the deceased. "This is Detective Laine. We spoke—"

"I remember," Richard Blake interrupted him. "Are you calling to tell me you have someone in custody for killing my brother?"

"I'd like to meet with you," David said, rubbing his temple with the tips of his fingers. "I can come out to your workplace if that's more convenient—"

"I hear there have been others. Is that true?"

"Mr. Blake—"

"Is it true?"

"I'm sorry, Mr. Blake. I can't comment on an ongoing investigation. As a lawyer, you must be aware of that."

"Lawyer," Blake spat. "I'm an entertainment lawyer. I handle spoiled, nihilistic musicians who think every word out of their empty minds is a pearl of unaccounted wisdom." Blake sucked in a breath and let it out in a long sigh. "Do you really think it's going to do any good talking to me again?"

Several seconds of silence floated down the phone line. David was sure the man was going to hang up, then he sighed again.

"Fine, come by my office at two. I'll keep my calendar clear for the rest of the day."

•

Richard Blake was a heavy-set, dark-haired man of at least thirty-five who wore his custom-made suits with ill grace. He looked more like a beefy truck driver than an entertainment lawyer with a wealthy, if uncultured, clientele.

He came around the melamine desk and held out his hand. David took it. Blake's handshake was firm. He waved David to a chair.

David flipped open his notepad. "First of all, would you have a recent photograph of Jay?"

"Sure, I can probably dig one up." Blake grimaced and pressed his fingers together. "Sorry. I just keep thinking of Jay . . . Jesus!

Who could do something like that to another human being? I guess you see this sort of thing all the time. You must be used to it."

"No, sir," David said. "You never get used to it. Never want to."

"Poor Jay. He wasn't the brightest bulb, but he really was a sweet kid. Guys used to tell him he was cute and sexy." He shook his dark head. "He always thought he was going to meet some swank angel who would take him in and rescue him. I told him the kind of guys he met out there weren't interested in saving anyone. He'd always say sure, he knew that, but then another opportunistic troll would whisper a few sweet words in his ear and he'd be off again."

"You know the names of any of these men?"

"No. Never wanted to." Blake leaned forward, his elbows on the gleaming desktop. "You have to understand, I never approved of Jay's lifestyle, but he was my brother. I wasn't going to abandon him, too."

Blake's fingers worried the silver pen, as though they would snap it in two.

"My—our parents could never reconcile themselves to what Jay was. They were old-fashioned. I think they blamed themselves for his 'condition,' like those old notions that homosexuality was caused by a weak father and a domineering mother, which if you ever met my family is a laugh. Mom couldn't dominate a strand of spaghetti and there was never anything weak about my father. He worked in the merchant marines during the war, then stayed on the ships until we were born, when he took a job down at the docks. Jay never could do anything to please the old man. You have children, detective?"

"No, I don't."

"I have two. Boys. And let me tell you, detective, I can't say either one of them is what I would have expected in any child of mine. But that doesn't stop me from loving them with everything I've got."

"Did they know your brother?"

"Sure, Jay loved those kids. I guess he knew he'd never have any of his own."

"Jay have problems with people?"

"He was a gay teenager," Blake said dryly. "What do you think?"

"He have trouble with anyone in particular? Get into fights, that sort of thing?"

"I wouldn't say he got into fights. He got beat up a lot in high school—all those civilized savages who thought it was cool to bash a kid because he was different."

"Anyone ever get into trouble for that?"

"You wondering if some homophobic asshole got revenge on Jay for getting him in trouble?"

"It happens."

"I'm sure it does. Just not to Jay. He never would point fingers. He'd just shrug and say he knew what he was, and he knew what they were and anyone who thought he was the loser missed the point altogether."

"You gave me the names of a couple of friends last time. Can you think of anyone else I might speak with?"

"You really think you have a hope in hell of finding this guy?"

"I intend to try, sir."

•

Leroy Gillie was a slight, taciturn youth wearing a clown-motif T-shirt and baggy jeans that rode so low they exposed several inches of red and black boxers. According to Richard Blake, he had been Jay's closest straight friend.

Leroy barely glanced at David. He fed coins into a Coke machine, popped the tab on his drink, and slid sideways into a molded plastic chair.

"You the cop?" Leroy took a deep drink of Coke, his Adam's apple bobbing up and down with each chug. He wiped his mouth with the back of his hand. "Richie said you're on Jay's case."

"How well did you know Jay?" David asked.

"We were best buds in school. At least until he started letting on that he was, you know, gay." Leroy made a face and glanced away. "After that, we didn't really hang out much."

"Why is that?"

"He was gay. If we were buds, everyone'd think I'm gay."

"And you're not. Gay, that is?"

"Shit no." Leroy looked around frantically as though someone might overhear the question. "I'm not a fag."

"Did it surprise you that Jay was?"

"I knew this guy for years, man. We were in first grade together. How could he be a faggot?"

"That bother you?"

Leroy chugged the rest of his Coke, crushing the can with one fist, and tossed it into a nearby garbage can. "Yeah, I hated not being buds anymore. But what could I do? Assholes were already calling me names cause they knew we was friends."

David scribbled. "These assholes got names? Any of them ever give Jay a hard time?"

"They're assholes. What do you think?"

"It ever go beyond name-calling? Any of them ever get physical?"

Leroy shrugged, his skinny shoulders rolling loosely. "Jay'd show up with a black eye or a split lip. But he'd never say who done it. He'd always say he might be a faggot but he weren't no pussy," Leroy said "He took a lot of shit."

"Think any of them might have got more serious? Maybe someone who thought Jay was hitting on him."

"You think one of them pussies kacked Jay? Not a chance."

"Ever see Jay with anyone?"

"Like a boyfriend?"

"Like that."

Leroy fidgeted in his chair, plucking at the short strands of hair on the side of his head. His face twisted into a grimace. "Me and Jay went into Hollywood once," he said. "We was going to a new Vin Diesel flick. Coupla guys stopped him on the street. Real friendly like. One of them wanted Jay to go with him. But me and Jay wanted to see this movie, so he said no. One guy, he weren't very happy 'bout it."

"What did they look like? Do you remember?"

Again Leroy's face screwed up. "One was a black guy, but it was the other one that got nasty when Jay said no."

"Was he black too?"

"Him? Nah, he was blond, looked like a West Hollywood pansy. All dressed up fancy, expensive shit. Jay told me later his jeans cost eight hundred bucks. Who the hell spends eight hundred bucks on a pair of fuckin' jeans?"

"Was he driving or did you see them on the street?"

"They was walking, like us."

"When did this happen, Leroy? How long ago?"

"Last summer, I think. It was after we graduated. I think maybe my girl was back in school—she's in grade eleven this year, only repeated one grade. Like Jay 'n' me."

"So she was back in school." David steered him back to the topic at hand. "So it had to be after September, that right?"

"September? Sure. Musta been. Before Halloween, though. That was the last time Jay 'n' me did anything together." Leroy fidgeted and grimaced. "He wanted us to go to West Hollywood for the Halloween parade, but why would I wanna see a bunch of flaming queens goin' down the street dressed as *girls*? Buncha sickos. I told him I ain't doin' that."

"Did Jay go anyway?"

"He stayed here, but I could tell he wasn't happy. After that we stopped hangin' out so much."

"This guy you saw in Hollywood. Would you recognize him again?"

"I dunno. It's been awhile. You think he might've had something to do with Jay?" Leroy straightened. "Think he's the one did Jay? No way, man, he was too fuckin' soft. A real queer boy."

"At this point I'm just trying to find anyone who might have known Jay. That's all. What about specific bars Jay hung out in. He ever give you any names?"

David watched as the younger man dug into his memory. His eyes squinted as he stared over David's left shoulder.

"There was one place . . . Nosh something. Dumb name. Pit, the Nosh Pit, that was it." Leroy plucked at the loose folds of his jeans. "You really think you gonna find out who killed Jay? You do, I want five minutes with him."

"Thank you, Mr. Gillie. I appreciate you giving me this time."

He seemed reluctant to let David go.

"Think you'll find him?"

David tucked his notebook back into his pocket. "We'll find him."

"What's gonna happen to him when you do?"

"He'll get due process."

"Sure," Leroy said. "You gotta say that, don't you? After what he done, he don't deserve—what'd you call it?—due process."

David handed over one of his cards, and watched as Leroy labored over the printed words. His lips moved over David's full name and rank.

"If you think of anything else," David said, "you'll let me know?"

"Sure."

"If I come by with some pictures, would you look them over and see if there's anyone you recognize?"

"Like a lineup? Could you get me into a real lineup? You tell me who to finger and I'll make sure the asshole don't walk."

"It doesn't quite work that way," David said gently.

"I won't tell." Leroy stared down at the painted cement floor. He sighed. "You're not gonna get him, are you?"

The kid seemed so downhearted, David had to reassure him. “Sure we will. We’ve already got some leads—”

“No!” Leroy sprang to his feet. David tensed. “Even if you do, my dad says the bleeding-heart liberals will make everyone feel sorry for the ass-wipe and let him off. He ought to die for what he done to Jay, but you watch, they won’t do nothing to him. You watch.” Leroy sniffed and wiped his face with the sleeve of his T-shirt. “They’ll let him off. Like they always do.”

CHAPTER 10

Monday, 6:35 P.M., The Nosh Pit, Hyperion Avenue, Silver Lake, Los Angeles

THE NOSH PIT was jammed. The air was thick with testosterone, poppers, and a dozen conflicting colognes. The bar was packed two deep, the mood still jovial, without the taint of desperation that crept in as last call approached. Ramsey was wiping down the spotless mahogany and leather bar with a rag. He waved at Chris and pointed off to his right.

Des had grabbed a table along the far wall and successfully defended a second seat, which Chris now slid into. Under a giant poster of a manic-looking Bette Davis, clichéd darling of the drag-queen set, tormenting Joan Crawford in *Whatever Happened to Baby Jane?*, he leaned down over and kissed Des. He eyed Des's sidecar sitting in a damp circle on the red and white chintz tablecloth.

"Been here long?" he shouted.

Des offered his familiar lopsided grin, the one that set off his white teeth perfectly against mocha-colored skin.

"Not that long," he shouted back. He waved languidly at Ramsey, who held up two fingers and barely waited for Des's nod before he grabbed bottles off the top shelf and began mixing Chris's Cîroc martini and another sidecar. Des bounced to his feet. "I'll get those."

"Thanks," Chris said when Des returned and handed him his drink. He leaned closer so he wouldn't have to talk so loud. "Where do you want to—oh, shit, what's he doing here?"

Kyle, the boyish, twenty-one-year-old dancer Des was hooked on like bad smack, appeared at the end of the bar.

"He asked to come." Des sucked on his drink, avoiding Chris's eyes. "His audition went sour. He didn't want to be alone tonight. You know his parents threw him out when he came out. He didn't have family like yours that left him expensive homes when they passed on."

"Well aren't you a fucking ray of sunshine. You know I never asked my grandmother for anything."

"But you got it anyway," Des said. "Just like my folks didn't disinherit me. You ever think how it might have turned out if they had?"

"I got to school under my own steam. You could have, too."

"And done what? I took philosophy and English lit., for Christ's sake."

"Then you'd have taken a different major if push came to shove."

Des shook his head. "I'm not smart like you. The only thing I'm good at is retail. That would have meant minimum-wage rag jockey down on Melrose. At least Kyle has talent. I want to see him make something of himself."

Like that was ever going to happen. Hollywood was full of talented wannabes and never-weres. "There are better guys out there. Guys who can appreciate you—who don't think you owe them."

"And I guess you'd know that better than anyone, wouldn't you, Miss Queen of the One-Night Stands."

"Hey, not fair. They're not all one-night stands."

"Oh?" Des said. "When was the last time you went to bed with the same guy two nights in a row?"

Chris stared into his martini, groping through his memory for a rebuttal. "It happens."

"You don't remember, do you?" Des made a point of looking around them. "If you really know where all the decent men are, why are we here?"

"Just because you like being alone," Des said, "you think everyone does."

Movement by the front door caught Chris's eye. As though on cue, Bobby the actor made his entrance. A peacock couldn't have strutted any prouder before a yard full of squawking hens.

"Is that one of those better guys?" Des jerked his chin toward Bobby. "Because I know what that one is, even if you don't. You are such a hypocrite, Bellamere."

Chris looked away from Bobby. He was startled by Des's anger and was tempted to deny knowing the guy. But one look at Des's face told him the lie would not fly.

"At least with Kyle I'm trying," Des said. "You can't see past a pair of tight jeans and a pretty face."

"Des—"

"Rick, I was hoping to see you." Bobby slid his hand down Chris's neck, kneading the tight skin above his collarbone. "Spare a seat?"

"This one's free—" Des stood up so fast his chair crashed into the table behind them. A heavily rouged and hennaed drag queen shot them an evil look before going back to her Manhattan, her three-inch fuchsia nails beating an irritated tattoo on her glass.

Chris scrambled for the door, but Des was faster. By the time he hit the sidewalk Des had already snared Kyle and was walking down the boulevard toward Sunset.

Chris got in front of them and forced Des to stop.

"What are you doing?"

"Leaving." Des walked around him, his hand firmly tucked into Kyle's. "I've had enough of your lectures. I'm going home with the man I love."

"Jesus, Des." Chris eyeballed Kyle with a jaundiced eye. The look was returned. "Let's at least have dinner—"

"I'll call you tomorrow," Des said.

Kyle squeezed Des's hip and nuzzled his throat. "That's if I let you out of bed, stud muffin."

Chris watched them disappear behind a wall of jostling men. A shiver crab-crawled up his spine. Suddenly it was as if he was back in the disturbing dream he'd had the day after his Lexus was vandalized. All at once he didn't want to leave the safety of the bar. But he didn't want Des to walk off like that.

Did he dare follow? Was he willing to risk his friendship with Des over a stupid argument they'd both forget the next day? Spinning around, he hurried back into the noisy, crowded Pit.

He squeezed past the press of bodies crowded around the bar. Bobby was sitting at their table, drinking what was left of Chris's martini. Clearly, he was already drunk.

"Shit, man." He tilted the glass back and drained the last mouthful. "Why don't you drink something decent like Bud?"

"Feel free to order what you want." Chris snatched his drink back. He grimaced, put the glass back on the chintz tablecloth, and stood up. "On second thought, I'm going anyway."

"Why don't you grab some shooters while you're at it?" He smirked. "Get me a blowjob."

Chris had no intention of indulging in a game of downing shooters with this guy. If he got drunk he'd probably do something stupid like take Bobby home. He came back with the beer, another martini, and the Kahlúa, Bailey's, and Amaretto concoction for Bobby, which he downed with smooth practice. Only then did Bobby seem to realize Chris had not indulged.

"Waiting for another emergency?"

Chris shrugged. "I'm on call."

"Life sucks." Bobby swallowed half his beer and burped. "And then you die. Well I'm not—on call that is, or dead." He lurched to his feet, waving his shot glass. "I'm gonna have some fun. Hey, bartender, another one of these."

Even half drunk, Bobby moved with a grace that was enviable. Chris sipped his martini and watched, remembering what Bobby looked like in bed. Naked and hungry. All a brilliant fake-out.

Chris suddenly didn't feel like playing the game.

"Most people come to these places to have fun," the voice in his ear made him jump.

He swung around to find Trevor smiling down at him.

"You do not look like a man having fun," Trevor said.

"You just don't recognize extreme ecstasy when you see it."

Trevor leaned down until his warm breath brushed Chris's face. "Hmm, you're right. I don't." He slid his fingers through Chris's short hair. Lowering his head, he covered Chris's mouth with his.

After some serious tonsil hockey Trevor finally backed off. He straddled a chair and grinned across at Chris.

Chris's mouth was numb and his heart beat a rough tattoo. "Jesus, what was that for?"

Trevor ran his thumb over Chris's lips. "I don't need a reason. Do you?"

Chris shivered. He thought of what Des had said and wondered if there was any truth to his words. And would going home with Trevor change anything? It would be fun, but would it end up being just another one-night stand he regretted the next day?

"Hey, lover, let's ditch this dump and go have some fun." Bobby slid back into the seat he had vacated only minutes before. "I got some nose candy. Or I know where we can score some X, if you're interested."

"He's not," Trevor said. He tugged at Chris's ear and slipped warm hands up under Chris's Izod shirt. "Let's go back to your place. We can crack open another bottle of wine and compare notes."

"Maybe," Chris said, refusing to commit, tempted all the same by Trevor's offer. He wished Bobby would take the hint and find someone else. Still, he couldn't resist saying, "Maybe I'll go home alone."

"That'd be a real waste," Trevor said.

The noise level in the bar cranked up. A band was warming up on the tiny stage, and the sound check throbbed over the speakers.

It was retro night at the Pit. The band struck up the opening chords of ABBA's "Dancing Queen." Chris leaned back, letting the noise and a warm haze of lust wash over him. Maybe this evening wouldn't be such a waste after all.

The yelling sounded like it was outside at first. It quickly moved inside. A surge of bodies near the door broke apart as someone came hurtling in from the street. In the garish light from the stage the blood covering him looked black on his dark skin.

"Oh, God," Des shouted. "They're going to kill him!"

Monday, 7:10 P.M., The Nosh Pit, Hyperion Avenue, Silver Lake, Los Angeles

David could still make out the words "cock" and "*joto*," the Spanish slang term for faggot, on the whitewashed walls of the Nosh Pit. He stared at the windowless building with growing apprehension. Did he really want to go in there? More obscenities covered the sidewalk and the business next door. It looked like someone had wielded a sloppy brush in an attempt to cover up the nastier obscenities.

Joto was a term he'd heard all too recently, when he'd called Martinez to tell him he was going to check out the Nosh Pit.

"Better you than me, *mi hermano*," Martinez had said. "Do me a favor, and don't tell me all about it tomorrow, especially if some cute little *joto* hits on you."

There was a knot of men crowding around the recessed entrance, and at first David thought it was a queue. Then he realized the tension in the crowd had nothing to do with waiting.

He heard the yelling and grabbed his radio, calling for backup.

A motley collection of four Latino teens had pinned a fifth man to the graffiti-covered wall. They had already given him a bloody nose and split lip. Ignoring David's shouted warning they pushed their victim to the sidewalk and one raised a booted foot.

"Police," David shouted, hand resting on the butt of his gun. "Stand down. Hands where I can see them. Now!"

One of the teens looked at David and sneered. "*Bastardo . . . joto . . . usted merece esto.*" When the black-and-white skidded to the curb, doors flying open before it came to a stop, the teens broke and ran. David grabbed one and slammed him against the wall, jerking his arm back and sliding out his cuffs all in one move. He snicked the cuffs in place and shoved the teenager to the ground. With a grunt he stepped sideways to avoid the man's boot. He shot his left foot out and clipped a second one on the kneecap. The teen yelled and stumbled backward.

David was on him before he could recover his balance. Under a barrage of curses in Spanish and English, David cuffed him, then knelt by the battered man slumped against the wall, making a quick assessment of the victim. Blood from his face dripped onto the sidewalk, collecting in a dark pool. His lip had been split and already one eye was puffing out. In a few more hours he'd have a nice shiner. David flipped out his cell.

"I'm calling an ambulance, sir—" he said as he started punching in numbers.

"What the hell is going on here?"

Fingers still poised over the keypad, David spun around to find Chris Bellamere standing less than three feet away, arms folded over his chest. "Jesus. What's going on here? You always bring this kind of trouble with you?"

CHAPTER 11

**Monday, 7:35 P.M., The Nosh Pit,
Hyperion Avenue, Silver Lake, Los Angeles**

"HEY." TREVOR SKIDDED to a halt beside Chris. "What the hell's going on—"

"I'm not sure." He turned away when Trevor slipped his arm around his waist. The guy was definitely into staking his claim tonight. "Des, are you okay?"

"Kyle! Oh, honey, are you all right—" A battered Des darted forward and fell to his knees at Kyle's side. His lover's normally pretty, perpetually sneering face was a mask of pain. He flinched when Des gently touched him.

"Excuse me, Mr. Bellamere," David said. "You know these people?"

"Yes." Chris shook off Trevor's possessive arm. "Des, hon, why don't you get Kyle to a hospital—"

"Ambulance is on its way," David said. He snapped his cell phone shut.

"Thank you, officer," Des said.

"While we wait, can I get a statement?"

"They just came out of nowhere," Des said. "They started shouting, then one of them hit me. The next thing I know Kyle was screaming—"

From the ground Kyle protested, "I was not screaming."

"Honey, it's okay. They're animals. We were both afraid."

Chris studied the two shackled bodies lying on their stomachs on the sidewalk and the other two who had already been deposited in the back of the black-and-white. The grungier of the two, his nose a smear of blood from his abrupt contact with the pavement, glared up at them.

"Did you see anything?" David asked Chris.

"What good would it do if I said I did?"

"We take these crimes very seriously—"

"Sure you do. What are you doing down here anyway?"

A siren howl warned of the approaching ambulance. Des helped Kyle to his feet.

"It's all over here." Trevor squeezed Chris's arm. "Why don't we go back to your place?"

Two EMTs emerged from the ambulance and began a low-voiced conversation with Kyle. One of them flashed a light in his eyes and probed his head for the extent of his injuries.

"You should accompany us to the hospital, sir," he said.

Kyle shook his head. "I'm fine."

"Come on, Kyle." Des tugged gently at his lover. "Go with them."

"I just want to go home."

David snapped his notebook shut. "I'll drop you at your place. You can finish giving me your statement there."

"Thank you, officer." Des all but dragged Kyle over to David's car. "We accept your offer."

"I'm going with you," Chris said.

Chris was sure David was going to protest. So when David jerked his shaggy head at his car he was surprised. Just then a second police car angled to a stop behind the ambulance.

After loading the two cuffed men into the back of the car, David spent another ten minutes giving a report while the uniformed cops eyed them all suspiciously. For a while Chris thought for sure they were all going to be arrested, then the cops took their prisoners and left.

Trevor tried one last time to dissuade Chris. He leaned in through the open car door and said, "Come on, man, these guys can look after themselves."

Part of him wanted to go. He'd been looking forward to some fun before all this started. But he knew he'd feel like shit if he left now. "Des is my friend. I want to be there for him."

"Chris—"

Chris spoke through clenched teeth. "Not tonight, Trev."

Trevor threw Des a look of pure frustration before he stalked off. Chris sighed and slid into the front passenger seat.

David cranked the engine. "Where to?"

"North Palm Drive."

"Sure you don't want to go to the hospital?" David asked.

"We're sure. They said there's no sign of concussion," Des said. "He's just bruised."

The house Des shared with Kyle in the flats of Beverly Hills was a well-tended two-story cottage that, according to Des, had once been owned by Imogene Coca. It was concealed behind a screen of trimmed boxwood and a towering jacaranda tree. While Des led Kyle into the living room, Chris ditched his jacket in the front foyer and went into the kitchen to prepare an ice pack.

Des eased the pack over Kyle's swelling eye. The younger man winced.

"Keep it on," Des said firmly when he tried to push it aside. "It'll take the swelling down."

David perched on the edge of the spindly-looking Louis XIV chair that matched the sofa Des and Kyle occupied. He had his notebook out. The cheap vinyl briefcase was on the floor beside the chair.

Chris made himself scarce in the kitchen. He fussed with the kettle and put a pot of coffee on, and readied a tray with mugs, cream, and sugar. He could hear the drone of voices from the living room.

David stood when Chris reentered the room. He left Des to comfort his lover. "Any idea what happened back there?"

Chris shrugged. “They left the bar together. Next thing Des is back, yelling that they’re killing him.” He studied David’s lean face, wondering what lay behind that enigmatic countenance. What was it with cops that they always seemed so cold? Were the unemotional ones drawn to the job or did they have to learn to be unemotional? “What brought you around so conveniently in the nick of time?” A thought just occurred to him. “You weren’t following me, were you?”

Monday, 8:10 P.M., North Palm Drive, Beverly Hills

DAVID THUMBED OPEN his briefcase and pulled out one of the photos Richard Blake had given him earlier. It was a picture Richard had taken on a family picnic at the Los Angeles Zoo. It was the last family outing Jay had attended.

He passed the photos over. “I’m looking for information on this guy, Jason Blake.”

Chris took the picture and stared down at the head shot of the twenty-year-old Jason Blake. It was obvious he recognized the young man.

David’s chest tightened. He didn’t realize until that moment that he hoped Chris would say that he didn’t know him. The knowledge disturbed him. Maybe that was why his next question came out sounding harsh: “Where did you meet him? The Nosh Pit? How long ago?”

“Months,” Chris murmured. “I don’t remember exactly.”

David drew out a second photo and studied it, trying not to think of the way Blake had looked when the killer got through with him. “Good-looking guy.” Jason Blake had matured from the scrawny, too-thin kid David had first seen in his high-school photo to a sleek-looking, dark-haired man who must have stirred a lot of libidos, male and female.

Chris stood up. “Let me check to see if the coffee’s ready.”

David almost let him go, then abruptly changed his mind. Maybe it was time to put some pressure on Mr. Christopher Bellamere. He followed him into the kitchen. It was all brushed steel and granite countertops, totally out of place with the rest of the house. It had all the warmth of a meat locker. Chris must have seen him staring because he grunted.

"Kyle's idea of ultrachic. I always feel like I'm in a giant tin can when I come in here. What do you take in your coffee?"

"Nothing." David quickly amended that. "I mean, no thanks. I don't need anything."

Chris shrugged and filled a large mug and threw in a splash of Hazelnut-flavored cream. He came to stand beside David, who shifted uncomfortably at his nearness.

"What do you really want from me?" Chris asked. There was a plaintiveness to his question that stirred a longing in David, which he quickly suppressed. Chris was a suspect, for heaven's sake. And even if he wasn't, Christopher Bellamere was way out of David's league, now or ever.

"What do I want?" he asked. "Try the truth."

"I've told you the truth. I barely knew the guy."

"Then tell me anything you can—"

Des reappeared. "Kyle wants to go to bed," he said. "Do you have any more questions, officer?"

Monday, 8:40 P.M., North Palm Drive, Beverly Hills

Chris sipped his cooling coffee while David slipped out of the room. He looked over to find Des grinning at him.

"What?"

"Did you see it?"

"See what? Chris scowled. "Okay, what's so funny?"

"You really didn't catch it?"

"Catch what?" Chris felt like shaking him. "Des."

"That guy had such a boner for you."

"Who—*what? The detective*?"

"Yeah." Des smirked. "Him. Come on, you know I have the best gaydar in the state. Have I ever been wrong?"

"Well, there was that UCLA football halfback—"

"Oh honey, just because *he* wouldn't admit it doesn't mean he wasn't."

"Honey," Chris said acidly. "The man broke your arm. He came damn close to breaking your neck. If it hadn't been for me you'd have spent the next term in traction."

"Oh pish." Des dismissed his words with a scented wave of his hand. "Maybe I misjudged him, but I'm right about this one. He's got a boner for you."

"Would you stop saying that."

Des sniffed. "Just you wait and see."

•

As long as Chris had known him, Des had collected Hollywood memorabilia. Nearly every inch of wall outside the kitchen was covered with movie posters. Horror flicks mingled uneasily with frantic comedies. Chris knew some of the posters were worth thousands. An ancient, carefully framed *Gone With the Wind* had been rumored to be valued at nearly a hundred grand.

David perched on the edge of the sofa beside Kyle, who was hunched over, holding the melting ice pack to his eye. The look of concern on David's rough face seemed genuine. He touched Kyle's shoulder and when the younger man looked sideways at him David smiled. Chris was amazed to see Kyle smile in return.

He was still smiling when he caught sight of Chris. The smile died and David looked up. He rose.

Kyle stumbled to his feet. "I'd like to go to bed."

David frowned. "Of course, Mr. Paige. I can see my own way

out—"

"Good." Kyle brushed past Chris and Des, barely acknowledging his lover's "Hey—"

"Listen," Des said to Chris. "I'll call you tomorrow. Right now I just want to make sure Kyle is okay."

"Sure." Chris barely nodded. He was still holding David's gaze. "Call me."

Chris studied David. Could Des be right? Did it mean anything if he was? The man wasn't his type. Even if he was intriguing as hell. It sure as hell didn't mean Chris wanted to sleep with him.

"Are you done, then?" Chris asked.

"Yes."

David eyed the wall full of posters. "Mr. Hayward is in the industry?"

"Des owns a clothing store. Mind you, it's a store in Beverly Hills. He lived with an assistant director once, if that counts."

"You've been friends a long time."

"Did Kyle tell you that?" Chris could just imagine that conversation. Kyle couldn't seem to forgive Des for having a past that didn't include him. He sighed. "You going to take me back?"

"If you're ready."

Chris stepped closer to the much taller man. He wasn't used to looking up to anyone; at six feet he was eye-to-eye with most men. David made him crane his neck. His mouth was at eye-level. Chris dropped his gaze to the plain gray cotton shirt covering David's broad chest. It was buttoned almost up to his throat and finished with a sedate blue and gray tie he had tugged open, providing a glimpse of a mat of black chest hair. Chris wasn't normally into bears, but he found himself wondering what David looked like under all that cotton.

He smelled damned good.

"Why are you always following me?" he said softly.

"You said that before." David folded his arms over his chest, making himself look even more massive. His mustache bristled. "What makes you think I'm following you?"

"Is that a cop thing?"

"What?"

"Answering a question with a question? Never giving a straight answer—pardon the pun."

David's eyes narrowed. The thick muscles of his forearms bulged. "I'm not following you."

"You won't even admit it to yourself, will you?"

Spinning around Chris stalked toward the front door. He wasn't really surprised when David followed.

"What does that mean?" David demanded.

"Buried in the closet like you are, it must get pretty damned stuffy when you never come up for air."

Chris was nearly at the front door when David wrapped one big hand around his elbow and pulled him to an abrupt stop. Chris eyed the wall of flesh in front of him and fought the urge to step back. Not that the grip on his arm would have allowed it.

He glared at David, ignoring the way the heat from David's fingers scalded his flesh.

"Why do you think I'm following you?" David asked. "Doesn't that strike you as a bit paranoid. I am conducting a homicide investigation."

Chris dismissed his words. "It's pretty obvious."

"Not to me."

"Nobody can be that thick."

When David would have moved away, Chris slammed his hand against the wall, blocking his retreat.

"You don't understand?" Chris cupped David's head in both hands. "Maybe you'll understand this."

He rammed his mouth over David's.

David went rigid with shock. Chris froze. David's mouth was closed, shut tight against Chris's invading tongue. Oh, Jesus, now he'd done it. David was going to bust him for assault. If he didn't break him in two. How the hell could he have listened to Des? Des and his stupid gaydar. How could he have thought David was queer—

Massive hands closed into fists around the material of Chris's T-shirt and David shoved him back against the wall, at the same time his lips opened and his tongue filled Chris's mouth. The coarse bristles of David's mustache and his incipient beard chafed Chris's face. Beside them a coat rack crashed to the floor, flinging umbrellas and jackets across the floor.

Chris barely noticed. His heart was pounding so hard he swore the wall behind him vibrated. He closed his eyes and hung on to David just to stay upright.

Pinned to the wall, Chris matched David's sudden fervor. Flashing between them was raw lust as uncontrollable as a river roaring downhill. David pressed against Chris with his hard body. Chris went after bare skin, shoving his hands up under David's shirt, clutching warm flesh.

"What the hell is going on down there? Dammit, I'm trying to get Kyle to sleep—shit, I—oh damn—I'm sorry—sorry . . . "

Chris dragged his mouth off David's in time to see a red-faced Des backpedal down the hall.

Des fled. His feet thumped as he tripped on the stair riser and he grabbed the banister to keep from falling. He took the short flight of stairs two at a time.

"Oh man," Chris muttered. He blinked and met David's glazed eyes. Then his gaze wandered back down to David's half-open mouth. His thick dark mustache looked delicious enough to chew on.

He wanted to kiss him again. Damn Des for interrupting.

David's breathing was ragged, and Chris could see a pulse beat in the five o'clock shadow under David's chin.

He leaned forward. "David—"

"Don't." David shuddered and backed away. He stooped down and grabbed the coat rack, fumbling to pick up the umbrella that had popped open in its tumble to the floor. "We're going to pretend that didn't happen."

"No—" Chris reached for David, his hands skittering across skin where he had pulled the shirt out of David's pants. "How can you say that wasn't real?"

David jerked away as though scalded. "Let me take you back to your vehicle, Chris. I'm calling it a night. I suggest you do the same."

"Come back to my place," Chris said. "We can talk—"

"I'm on duty." With that he pulled completely free of Chris's touch. He was breathing hard, which was some consolation. When Chris moved toward him, he stepped back. That wasn't good. Damn. The man had a hell of a lot more willpower than Chris had.

"David . . . " With a sigh Chris scooped his jacket off the floor and slipped it on. "Forget it. Fine, I'm ready."

David already had the car started when Chris climbed into the passenger's seat; he grabbed the seat belt when David shot out of the narrow driveway.

Chris glanced at the dashboard clock. After midnight. He felt a crushing exhaustion; he should have been home in bed by now. Which is exactly where he wanted to be.

Only not alone.

He peered sideways at David, taking in the grim set of his jaw and knew talking wasn't going to work. He tried anyway. David wasn't the only one with a stubborn streak.

"If you don't want to go back to my place, why don't we grab a coffee—the Flip Side is just down the street."

"Forget it, Chris."

"Can't." Chris tried to keep it light, hoping that would break through David's stiff-necked pride. "Anyone ever tell you, you make quite an impression? You—"

"Don't."

Chris was silent while David maneuvered along the nearly empty streets of Beverly Hills. He only spoke again once they passed through the more boisterous Boystown and turned onto Sunset.

"We need to talk, David."

"There's nothing to talk about. Whatever you think happened, didn't. End of story."

"End of nothing. God, you're so deep in denial it's scary. How the hell can you live like that? What do you think they're going to do if they find out?"

David didn't answer. But Chris could see the tension in his shoulders and the stranglehold grip he had on the wheel.

Finally he ventured, "Are you going to keep telling yourself you didn't kiss me back? Or that you aren't as hard as I am right now—"

"Don't you know when to leave something alone?" David swung the car into the curb and slammed on the brakes. Headlights washed the back of Chris's SUV. "Just let it go."

Chris opened his mouth to retort, then bit his lip. He threw the car door open and scrambled out, slamming the door.

He didn't watch as David peeled away from the curb. Down the sidewalk light flared when someone emerged from the Nosh Pit. Chris glanced at his SUV. He should go home, get some sleep . . .

The Nosh Pit was still hopping, but now there was a familiar tension to the place. The desperation of the still-single clung to everyone present.

Chris nearly stumbled over a groping couple in the dim front vestibule. Muttering that maybe it was time to take it home, he passed into the bar. Behind the counter Ramsey raised his eyebrows. Chris lifted his hand in greeting but didn't go over, knowing the bartender would only want to know why he had returned.

He spotted Bobby at the same time the younger man saw him.

Bobby bounced to his feet, ending the conversation he'd been having with an older queen, who looked pissed at the interruption.

"Hey, man." Bobby grabbed Chris around the waist. "Thought you were gone for the night."

"So did I."

"Come on, buy me a drink and cheer yourself up." He squeezed Chris's still semi-hard dick through his jeans. "I'll make it all better, I promise."

CHAPTER 12

Tuesday, 7:25 A.M., Northeast Community Police Station, San Fernando Road, Los Angeles

"YOU GET LUCKY last night, *perro Viejo*," Martinez said from his desk. He never looked up from the file he was studying.

David nearly tipped his second coffee of the day into his lap. He opened his mouth to snap a retort, then shut it again. Martinez wasn't even listening.

"Gotta hand it to you," Martinez finally said. "You got more balls than me, spending the night with a bunch of *jotos*—"

"Stop saying that!"

"What?"

"*Jotos. Jotos*! You act like they're not human."

"Hey, it's just an expression—"

"Yeah, the same one those punks used last night before they tried to kill one of them."

"What the hell—"

He told Martinez about the gay bashers.

"*Idiotas.* Don't they know they should stay down in the barrio?" He shook his head, then caught David's look. "*Dios,* you don't think I'm like that, do you? I told you, it's just an expression."

"An ugly one. Do me a favor and stop using it."

David liked Martinez, respected him as a cop, and for all his blatant displays of intolerance, Martinez *was* a good cop. He treated everyone, perp and civilian, with a mild contempt that was almost casual in its delivery.

Still, David could all too easily imagine what Martinez would say if he found out what had really happened last night.

David couldn't believe what he had done. Letting a suspect get through his guard like that. Letting himself be kissed—worse, losing it and kissing the guy back.

Tuesday, 9:40 A.M., Cove Avenue, Silver Lake, Los Angeles

Chris woke amid a tangle of sweat-soaked sheets. He blinked away sleep and groaned when the bedside phone rang. Who the hell would call this early—then he looked at his clock.

"You planning on coming in today, Bellamere?" Becky's voice was pitched low as though to keep someone from overhearing. "I'm holding Petey at bay with some story about you talking to clients off-site, but he's getting nasty. Wants to know when you're checking in. You sick?"

"Jesus, Chapman, why'd you wait so long to call."

"Last time I checked, Bellamere, you were old enough to wipe your own ass."

Chris groaned.

"Must have been some night," Becky said. "You fit to work?"

"Let me go stick my head in a bucket of water. I'll be right there."

Fifty-five minutes later he nearly ran down Tom Clarke as he stepped off the elevator.

"You expect everyone to get out of your way, Bellamere?" Tom glanced at his watch. "Running late?"

Becky wrinkled her nose when she saw him. "Wow. Who was he?"

"Nobody!" Chris snapped. A sudden image of David flashed through his head. Could he have been wrong about the way David responded last night? Had he misread things that badly? "Maybe I just overindulged."

"Ha, Bellamere." She popped a stick of Juicy Fruit in her mouth. "So, who was he?"

"Don't go there, Chapman."

Chris spent the morning fielding phone calls from various clients. At lunch he settled for take-out, *chiles rellenos* from a nearby Mexican place. His phone rang. He let it go to voice mail.

He got iced tea out of the vending machine and ate half the chiles, then played his messages. Damn, that last call had been from Des.

Chris had his speed-dial on the BlackBerry, so he grabbed that. Des picked up on the third ring.

"I was right?" Des giggled. "That cop's gay? Man, he looked like he was ready to do you right in my front hall. So, you guys go back to his place? I know you didn't go home, I called often enough."

Chris rubbed the back of his neck, sorry now he had called. He really didn't want to talk about last night. "Maybe I wasn't answering the phone."

"You took him to your place? I want gory details. Give me the dish, boyfriend."

"Nothing to dish," Chris sighed and popped the last batter-covered Anaheim chili into his mouth. "He dropped me at my car. I went home."

"Right. So, are you going to see him again?"

•

The phone rang as he let himself into his house later that afternoon.

"Chrissy, you're a hard man to find." Trevor's smoky voice smoothed Chris's nerves, even though he hated being called Chrissy. "I've been calling for hours."

"Gotta keep the tax man happy. What's up?"

"I was hoping we could get together, but I'm heading out of town on a job."

Trevor worked for one of the fringe production companies as a script supervisor, a tedious job he once explained meant watching out that if an actress wore pink slippers in one scene, she had on the same footwear when the next scene was shot two weeks later. Trevor had a hundred catty stories about the newest Hollywood talent. Especially the cute little gay hotties who tried so hard to play it straight.

"Too bad. I was thinking of heading down to the Pit for a drink later," Chris said. Trevor was the only man Chris had ever met who could actually purr when he spoke. So many men tried for the effect, but no one did it better than Trevor. A shiver of lust raced along Chris's nerve endings. Trevor was just what he needed to take the sting out of David's rejection. He tried for some purr of his own. "How about you leave in the morning? I'll serve breakfast in bed."

"No can do, babe. Got business to attend to," he said, sounding distracted. "But you and me, we got some unfinished business of our own to take care of, don't we?"

"When will you be back?"

"That's what I like to hear. Enthusiasm. I'll only be gone a few days. Keep next weekend open for me, okay?"

"Consider it yours."

Tuesday, 5:25 P.M., Piedmont Avenue, Glendale

David unlocked his car. His cell chirped.

"Davey," Martinez said. "Got something you might want to see. How soon can you get back here?"

It was nearly five-thirty. "Why don't you grab something from the deli?" David said. "I'll meet you in twenty."

Thirty minutes later David found a pastrami on rye on his cluttered desk. Martinez was nowhere to be seen.

Half a dozen folders lay beside the sandwich, plus one manila envelope with his name on a computer-addressed label. There was no postmark. He picked up the envelope after unwrapping his pastrami. Martinez had remembered to get extra mustard.

Martinez appeared at his elbow, nearly knocking the other half of the sandwich off the desk as he planted his butt.

David rescued his dinner and waved the envelope at him. "When did this come in?"

"Front desk called just after four."

David slit it open with a fingernail and peered uneasily inside. What he saw made him glance up at Martinez. "Got a pair of gloves handy?"

Martinez handed him a pair. David slipped them on, and Martinez leaned forward as David reached in and pulled out a California driver's license and a photograph.

Daniel Anstrom. Nineteen-year-old sophomore at the University of Southern California. North Hollywood address. Both of them stared at the young face. David felt despair tighten the muscles of his stomach as he studied the photo, which had been printed out on flimsy paper from a digital file. It showed a dumpster, this one with a backdrop of mountains. Somewhere north of Los Angeles proper. He flipped to the next image, recognizing it easily: Angeles Crest Highway.

"Think anyone filed on him?" Martinez asked, but even his voice sounded strained.

It took less than ten minutes to find the report, taken three weeks earlier. Anstrom's parents had called it in, waiting the requisite forty-eight hours after their son disappeared, though they insisted he wasn't the type to just vanish.

David called the California Highway Patrol and told them what to look for. Then he sent the envelope and all its contents down to the lab for analysis.

The rest of the day was spent trying to locate Anstrom's parents, who weren't answering their phone. David spent the next day catching up on paperwork, which was never in short supply.

Thursday night he ate a hastily prepared supper of frozen stir-fry tossed with soy sauce on some left-over rice while catching the tail end of a Dodger's home game. When the Dodger's lost seven to two he knew it was time to call it a night.

He almost made it to sleep before the bedside phone shrilled.

"Better get down here," Martinez said.

David sat up. "Highway Patrol found something?"

"No. Looks like our boy delivered a fresh one to our doorstep."

Thursday, 7:45 P.M., County Coroner's Office, North Mission Road, Los Angeles

The morgue assistant brought out the sealed body bag, and David signed off on it.

No confirmation yet it was their killer's work, but David's gut told him it was. The fact the body's temperature was still 95.2 degrees when discovered proved to be the only definite piece of evidence. A patrolling officer had spotted something suspicious on her rounds and left her car to investigate. Rigor hadn't even set in.

"Our boy's got brass balls." Martinez casually appraised the body on the table. "Getting bigger every day, too. Brazen, dumping a body like that."

David frowned. The latest John Doe had been dumped on the front steps of a house undergoing renovations less than five hundred yards from the Northeast station. So far no one inside or outside the station had reported seeing anything. Brazen wasn't even the word.

Lopez used sterile water and the first of many clean swabs to wipe the blood off the damaged face. The morgue assistant captured the results of her work on film. David knew he'd be heading back to the Nosh Pit with those pictures. His stomach rolled over at the idea.

"Interesting," Lopez muttered. "What do we have here?"

She used a pair of forceps to tease something out of the bloody folds of skin around the victim's throat. From where David stood it looked like dark strands of gore-covered linguine.

"What is that? Film?" David leaned in to get a closer look.

"VHS stock, if I'm not mistaken." She continued to work the material out one inch at a time, taking care not to break it.

"He wasn't strangled with it, was he?" Martinez asked.

"Not strong enough," Lopez said. "I suspect the ligature strangulation was performed by something else, and this was wound around before the actual strangulation occurred."

"What makes you say that?"

"The material's all but embedded in the skin. That could only occur if the force of the ligature material acted to drive the tape under the skin."

David leaned forward. "Can it be cleaned?"

"We'll isolate any latents, and test for DNA, but sure, I think it can be cleaned up."

"Haven't been to a good movie in ages," Martinez said. "Think this is a blockbuster?"

"I think it's a message."

"Original," Martinez muttered. "Why can't he be like everyone else and send badly composed poems?"

Lopez slid the bloodstained film into a steel bowl and handed it to the morgue assistant. "Check into cleaning this. Carefully, we don't want it damaged."

The morgue assistant nodded and carried the bowl toward the sink where racks of chemicals were stored.

Lopez patiently continued to clean the corpse, exposing a face that had probably been handsome, though it now bore the unmistakable marks of someone else's rage.

"Does this one seem more personal to you?" David moved around to study the body from another angle. He kept rubbing his temple, where a headache lurked. "Another question: Was he drugged?"

"Something eating you?" Martinez asked.

"He's decompensating fast." Psychiatric jargon for falling apart. Their killer was losing it. "Getting sloppy."

"Sloppy is good. We can use sloppy."

David thought of Chris. Psychopaths were cool, until they decompensated, but as cool as Chris was? If he was guilty, then he was a veritable iceberg and his lies were Oscar quality.

He stared down at the ruined body on the slab. Who was he to the killer? Had Chris known him?

As soon as possible David got them to roll the body's prints and run them through the Automated Fingerprint Identification System, but no hits came back.

Returning to the station, David and Martinez went over what they knew. Not much. It was back to legwork. David already had a pair of newly assigned D's canvassing the area where the body had been dumped. He couldn't find out any more here; it was time to hit the Nosh Pit again.

He told Martinez as much.

After several minutes Martinez picked up the nearly empty murder book that had been started for the latest victim and flipped through it. He met David's gaze.

"You want me along?"

Technically David knew they should go together. It was a solid lead he had developed on his own, but now it should be worked by both partners. Only, he didn't want his *partner* around for this one.

"It's a no-brainer, so if you got something you want to work on your own . . . " he murmured.

Martinez kept worrying the murder book as though he wished he could produce answers out of it.

"I'm thinking that film angle should be addressed," he said.

"Go for it, then," David said.

Martinez looked grateful. "You want me there, I'm beside you, man, but I gotta confess those place give my *cojones* the willies."

Which pretty well summed it up, David thought sadly.

"Just make sure you let me know if you find anything, eh, *compadre*?"

"How about we report back with our findings, say, around one?" He flipped his sleeve back to look at this watch. Nine-thirty. "That ought to give us both time to do our thing."

"I'll bring the pizza."

"Forget the anchovies this time, okay?"

"And you call yourself a cop." Martinez was still shaking his head as he strode away from his desk. He spun around and glared back at his partner. "Don't tell me you want me to forget the hot peppers, too?"

David grinned. "Nah, those I can handle." He kept a bottle of Rolaids in his upper drawer just for that situation.

David watched him go, then clipped his cell to his belt, slid his sunglasses into his jacket pocket—though he wouldn't be needing them where he was going—and with briefcase firmly in hand, headed out to sign a car out.

Only when he slid onto the sun-baked seat did he think of the other guy who had been with Chris that night. Des. Des what? He pulled his notebook out and skimmed until he found it. Desmond Hayward. He stared down at the phone number he had taken down, remembering all too clearly how Des had come down the stairs, catching him in the act of kissing Chris, knowing what Des must be thinking.

But first the Nosh Pit.

CHAPTER 13

Thursday, 10:45 P.M., The Nosh Pit, Hyperion Avenue, Silver Lake, Los Angeles

DAVID KNEW THE bartender made him the minute he entered the Nosh Pit. The man eyed him coldly while David made his way through the press of bodies. David flashed his shield and watched the crush melt away. He was left facing the angry bartender.

"Do something for you, officer?" The bartender lifted a beer mug out of the draining rack and rubbed it dry with a towel. Muscled arms bulged out of his sleeveless shirt. A tattoo on his left arm said SEMPER FI. A snake coiled around his other arm, the head peering out from under his armpit.

David passed over a business card. "Got a name?"

"William Ramsey. But everyone just calls me Ramsey."

"Well, Mr. Ramsey, we might want to find someplace private for this conversation."

Ramsey hesitated, but David knew he was all too aware of the bar patrons watching them. "This way."

David followed him into a backroom filled with cases of beer and alcohol. The room smelled faintly of smoke.

"This won't take long." David hoisted his briefcase onto a case of Smirnoff. He popped the latches and made a show of dragging out his pictures. He indicated Ramsey's tattoo. "Where were you stationed?"

Ramsey looked bemused. He folded his arms over his broad chest. "Pendleton."

"See any action?"

"Spent some time looking for weapons of mass destruction. Never did find anything but sand."

"Heard Iraq was nasty."

"It had its moments."

"Know this guy?" David watched Ramsey's stony face when he dumped the half dozen pictures of the dead John Doe in front of him.

Ramsey jerked away from the images. "What the fuck you doing?"

"Asking if you know this guy."

"Who the hell is he?"

"You tell me."

"I don't—"

"Look at it!" David slammed the nearest picture with his index finger. Sick of the games. Sick of the secrets that kept his stomach tied in knots. Somebody was going to talk and they were going to talk now. "I want to know when he came in here. Who he was with. Where he lives. His name."

"I don't know his name," Ramsey said.

"But you recognize him, right? Did he come in alone or with someone?"

Ramsey shrugged. "Alone."

"He leave the same way?"

"What happened to him? Who did that?"

"He leave here alone?"

Ramsey dragged his gaze away from the photos. "He came in a lot. He left with whoever he wanted."

"Anyone in particular?"

A shrewd look entered Ramsey's eyes. "Different guys," he said.

"Who?"

David sighed and pulled out his cell phone. He tapped in a series of numbers, then met the quizzical bartender's eyes. "You sure you don't want to talk to me?"

"What are you doing?"

"Putting a call in to the station—they can send a couple of uniforms down here to help me question everyone in the place," David said. "If we keep at it long enough someone's bound to remember something, especially if the guy was as good-looking as you say."

"No call for that. I told you I don't know anything."

"Doesn't mean no one else does." David depressed the send button. "This is a homicide investigation and I'm tired of being jerked around."

Ramsey held his hand up, almost touching David's. "Don't. We can talk."

David hit END and set the cell down on the counter. "When was the last time you saw him?"

"Few days ago . . . Monday night."

David was startled. That was the night he had broken up the gay bashers.

"What time Monday?"

"He was here till last call." Ramsey's intense green eyes wandered uneasily around the small room.

David leaned forward. "He alone?"

"He spent the night chatting guys up. Talked to a lot of people. Said he was an actor."

"Any reason to think he was?"

"He was full of the usual Hollywood bullshit, if that's what you mean." Again the wary look. "Never saw him in anything."

"Anybody in particular he talk to?"

"Few people."

"Give me some names."

Ramsey frowned, tugged on his bristling mustache. Ice glinted in his eyes. David thought he was going to play hardball and refuse to answer.

"I need names."

"Chris. Guy's name was Chris," Ramsey said. "But if you think he had anything to do with *that*, you're crazy. I know the guy. He'd never hurt a fly."

Usually when David scored a major hit, he felt a surge of adrenaline that made the catch all the sweeter. This time his stomach roiled and he swallowed past the sudden taste of bile.

"Bellamere? Christopher Bellamere? That the one you mean?"

"Could be. Don't get into last names much here."

"Good-looking guy, maybe six feet. Blond. Blue eyes. Expensive dresser? Works with computers."

Ramsey raised one eyebrow and looked him up and down as though he was seeing him for the first time. David was annoyed to feel himself flush, hoping the darkened room kept it from being obvious.

"Sounds like him," Ramsey said.

"That the first time you ever saw them together?"

Ramsey curled his hand into a fist. "No."

"When did they meet before?"

"You're wrong about Chris. He couldn't have done what you think."

"He's not a suspect at this point," David lied. "I just need to talk to him. Clear some things up."

"Sure."

"I want to thank you for your cooperation, Mr. Ramsey." David scooped his pictures up and slid them back into the briefcase, forcing it closed with a solid thump. "I'd like to think this conversation won't go beyond our ears. Got a problem with that?"

"No."

"I'll be on my way then. Try to have a good one."

"Like that's going to happen now."

David had barely cleared the door before he had his cell out, launching a D.M.V. check on both Christopher Bellamere and Desmond Hayward. He checked his notes from Monday and added

Kyle Paige to his search list. While he waited for his requests to be processed and displayed on his dashboard monitor, he ran over the notes he had taken that night.

Des and Chris had been friends since their college days. At least ten years. Just how well did Mr. Hayward know his long-time pal? David put the car in gear. Time to find out.

Kyle answered his knock, scowling when he saw who it was. The bruises on his face had congealed into a rainbow of mauves and sickly yellows and his already full lips remained puffed up.

"Mr. Hayward available?"

"Yeah, he's here." Kyle remained standing in the doorway, effectively blocking the way. "What do you want?"

David crowded in on the much smaller man. He filled the suddenly narrow doorway. "To talk to him."

"I'll see if he's up."

David glanced at his watch. It was past midnight. But the kid was fully dressed when he answered the door. Maybe he'd interrupted something. Which at least would explain the kid's hostility.

Des appeared less than five minutes later, dressed in faded jeans and a gold turtle neck sweater that showed off his dusky skin. His head was freshly shaved. Des was one of those men who looked sexy as hell with his head shaved.

Not that he came anywhere close to Chris in terms of physical beauty.

David shoved the dangerous thought aside. He had to stop thinking that way.

"I need to ask you a few questions, Mr. Hayward." He glanced at Kyle. "If you're not too busy."

"No, that's okay. We were just watching TV. Kyle, babe, you want to put the kettle on? Would you like coffee, Detective Laine?"

"Thanks, I'm fine. But you go ahead. This won't take long."

David thought he heard Kyle snort as he vanished toward the kitchen. Neither Des nor David watched him go.

"What's this about, detective?" Des signaled that David should precede him into the living room, where they had held their earlier interview. "Has something come up about those men who jumped us?"

"No, it's not that, Mr. Hayward. I'd like to ask you a few questions about your friend, Mr. Bellamere."

"Chris? What do you want to know?"

Kyle slipped onto the couch beside Des. On the wall behind them framed posters from a slew of old Hollywood sci-fi flicks lent an air of comic menace. Kyle leaned forward. "What's the asshole done now?"

David flipped out his notepad and a pen and scribbled down the date.

"Why, Kyle? Are you aware of anything that would warrant police involvement?"

"No, he's just a jerk. Full of himself." Kyle smirked. "But then you two were getting pretty cozy the other night. Maybe he got full of something else."

David ignored the crude insinuation, turning to Des.

"What about you? Have you seen Mr. Bellamere since I drove him back to his vehicle Monday night?"

Des shook his head. "I've been busy—"

"Have you spoken to him?"

"Sure," Des said. "Talked to him the next day—"

"Yeah, after you spent half the night calling," Kyle sounded bitter. "I kept trying to get him to bed, but he *had* to talk to Chris."

Was the kid jealous? According to Kyle, Des and Chris had a relationship that spanned years. How could anyone compete with that kind of history?

David leaned forward. "You couldn't reach Mr. Bellamere that night? How late are we talking here?"

Des shot Kyle a dirty look. "I thought he went home with you," he said. The look Des gave David was shrewd and full of questions.

"I saw you two kissing, you know. You can pretend I didn't, but I know what I saw."

"That may be, sir, but Mr. Bellamere and I went our separate ways once I dropped him off. How late did you try calling him?"

This time Des shrugged. "Two o'clock maybe. I talked to him early the next day." Des glanced at Kyle. "Babe, can you get me some of that coffee?"

David waited until the younger man left, since it was obvious Des didn't want to talk in front of Kyle. Once he was gone, David asked, "He call you or you call him?"

"I called—no, wait . . . He called me."

"What time was this?"

"Twelve, twelve-thirty."

"Do you have call display? Where was he calling from?"

Des shrugged. "Work, I guess. You should come down to the store sometime. I've got some Perry Ellis that would look sharp on you—"

"Can you verify that he was calling from work?"

"What's this about? So Chris called me on his cell."

"So you can't verify he was at work?"

"It was lunch time." Des smoothed his fingers over his bare scalp. "Where else would he be? Jesus, if you knew Chris, you wouldn't ask. The guy's a fucking workaholic. He's always at work early and stays late—works weekends, the whole nine yards."

Kyle returned with two mugs of coffee. He handed one to Des.

"Thanks, hon," Des said.

Kyle sat back down beside him, crowding close. Des patted his knee.

Not wanting to lose the conversation, David pressed on. "How often have you talked to him since then?"

"Not much. We don't live in each other's pockets, you know." He glanced at Kyle, then back at David. "What exactly is it you think Chris did?"

"Just gathering information. My job is like working a jigsaw puzzle. Before I can start doing anything, I need to assemble as many pieces as I can."

"And what piece does Chris represent?"

"Like I said. I'm just gathering information."

David stood. He held out his hand to Des, who took it gingerly.

He left Des standing in the middle of his living room, surrounded by memorabilia from ancient films and dead actors. It struck David that the place was like a tomb, housing the immortal remains of the bygone famous.

Outside, David took a deep breath, tasting car exhaust and ozone. It was time to bring Chris in for some formal questioning, maybe a lineup with Leroy, the guy who could link the suspect with Jason Blake. But first, he had some legal issues to take care of. He wasn't going to let Chris get off because he let himself get sloppy.

He headed back toward the station, where Martinez would be waiting with his pepper-laden pizza.

Which David would force himself to eat, though he no longer had any appetite.

CHAPTER 14

Friday, 7:45 A.M., Cove Avenue,
Silver Lake, Los Angeles

CHRIS STARED DOWN at the folded parchment the sheriff's deputy held out to him.

"Mr. Christopher Bellamere?" the deputy said.

"Y-yes? What is this—"

The sheriff pressed the folded paper into Chris's hand. "This subpoena requires you to present yourself at the Northeast Community Police Station—"

"What?" Chris snatched the document and unfolded it. He read through the legalese as best he could. A lineup. They wanted him to show up for a lineup. "What the hell is this?"

"That's not for me to say, sir."

Chris stepped back inside his cool foyer and shut the door, before he could be tempted to share his thoughts with the uniformed jerk. Dazed, he scooped up his phone.

Des answered on the third ring.

"I got trouble. I need a lawyer."

"What's wrong?"

Chris scrubbed his face with one hand, feeling the rasp of early morning beard. "I don't know." He told Des about the subpoena.

"A lineup?" Des sounded agitated. That didn't help. "He sure didn't let any grass grow under him, did he?"

"What? Who?"

"That cop, David, came by our place last night, asking all kinds of questions."

"David?" Chris's gears did a rapid shift. "What the hell did you tell him?"

"Nothing!"

"The fuck. You must have said something—"

"I swear I never said anything."

"Goddamn it, Des—" Chris pressed the fingers of his left hand against his eyelids, flashes of light exploded behind his eyes. "I need a lawyer. You gotta help me."

"S-sure. I'll find somebody, I got some connections."

"Good." Chris hung up before he said something he'd regret. He slumped down in the nearest chair, cradling his head in his hands.

Now what? Go to work like nothing was happening? What the hell was he supposed to do? Put his life on hold while he sorted this mess out?

What did David think he had done?

•

Simon Weiss didn't look like a Beverly Hills lawyer. He was a short, balding man with a pronounced gut and a fringe of white hair that stuck up on either side of his round head like a pair of soft horns.

But he dressed the part. A twenty-five-hundred-dollar Versace suit worn with Italian leather shoes and a tie that would have set Chris back a day's pay. He sat behind an acre-sized desk of granite and steel that held nothing but an off-white phone, an ornate letter opener that looked like it dated back to Washington's day, and an exquisitely framed, professional studio shot of an unsmiling woman and two unsmiling children, a boy and a girl. The rest of the office held only framed prints of a Stanford law degree and a couple of pictures of presidents, past and present, and of the current California governor.

Simon held out his hand. They shook and Simon pointed to an oxblood leather chair.

"Please, Mr. Bellamere. Have a seat."

Chris sank into the supple leather. He set his laptop case beside him on the Berber rug.

"I think I'm about to be screwed," Chris said, ignoring the startled look the man gave him. "I want you to stop them."

Friday, 4:40 P.M., Northeast Community Police Station, San Fernando Road, Los Angeles

DAVID LED LEROY Gillie into observation room 2. Martinez was already there, along with Simon Weiss, Bellamere's lawyer, and Barry Lords, the assistant D.A.

Leroy bobbed nervously in place, his Adam's apple convulsing when he caught sight of the polarized-glass window separating them from the room next door.

From his vantage point behind Leroy, David watched a uniformed cop lead six men into the room beyond the glass.

There were lines on the wall to mark off heights and more marks to tell members of the lineup where to stand. It still took a uniformed cop a few minutes to get them all in place and facing the mirror. David recognized a couple of beat cops picked to be in the lineup because they bore enough of a resemblance to Bellamere's overall coloring and body shape to satisfy the high-priced legal help Bellamere had shown up with less than an hour ago.

"No one inside the room can see us in here, Mr. Gillie," David said. "You're quite safe."

Leroy puffed out his skinny chest, a pouter pigeon determined to show how tough he was. "I know that. I watch *Law & Order*."

David suppressed a grin at the indignation in the young man's voice. "Okay, Mr. Gillie. Take your time. We'll have each man step forward in turn. Look them over and tell us if any one of them looks like the man you saw Jason Blake with. It's important that you be sure of your identification, so again, take your time."

"Please, Detective Laine," Bellamere's lawyer said. "No coaching of the witness."

David didn't bother protesting. Instead he reached forward and depressed the intercom button. "Put 'em through their paces, Officer Larch."

Then he stepped back, leaving Leroy at the window.

Each man's number was called and he stepped forward, into the light. Bellamere was third in line. He wore the blue jeans he'd been told to wear. Eight-hundred-dollar jeans? David wondered. Even in this crowd of look-alikes he stood out, like a diamond among pieces of colored glass.

He turned to find Bellamere's lawyer watching him with cool eyes. David felt as though his desires were written all over his face. A warm flush crept up his neck.

"Number three, step forward," Larch's voice could easily be heard over the intercom.

Bellamere stepped into the full light. David held his breath. Then, rather than risk betraying more than he already had, he focused all his attention on Leroy.

The young man leaned forward, looking for all the world like a little kid staring at a roomful of puppies. And Bellamere was clearly his favorite.

"Turn to the right, number three," Larch said. "Now step back. Number four, step forward."

Leroy suddenly bolted forward, his finger stabbing at the window. "That's him. That's the one I saw Jay with."

"Which one is that, Mr. Gillie?" Ice settled in David's gut. But he had to hear the words. "I need you to say the number, sir."

"Three. It's number three. That's the guy you want, isn't it?"

"Thank you, Mr. Gillie." David clamped down on his own disappointment. He glanced at Bellamere's lawyer. "As I see it, that's two for two. We can now place your client with two of our deceased victims."

Martinez's smile was wolfish. "We'll see you in court, counselor."

The lawyer glanced at Leroy, then at David. His face held only boredom. "I doubt it, detective."

Once Weiss was gone, Martinez's grin threatened to split his dark face in half.

"You did great, kid," he said to Leroy. Then to David: "Let's go get those warrants."

Monday, 10:15 A.M., Lincoln Boulevard, Venice, Los Angeles

CHRIS SPENT MONDAY morning trapped in the subbasement of the Venice Savings and Loan, where he had struggled for hours to fix a mysterious software glitch that had invaded the bank's main database, threatening their data integrity. Thank God for backups and redundant systems. They hadn't lost a single byte of customer information. Chris had tested it a half a dozen times against their latest backups and found no corruption anywhere. Finally he was able to have the bank manager sign off on the work and could crawl back to DataTEK to find out what new disasters awaited. He knew it was going to be that kind of week.

He climbed back into daylight and blinked at the midmorning sun burning through the sullen layer of smog hanging over the beach town. The man who had envisioned Venice a century ago had seen something that would rival the Italian city of the same name. A Venice West with canals filled with boats and pretty people riding upon the placid waterways.

His BlackBerry vibrated as he stepped off the elevator at DataTEK. "Chris here."

"Chris!" It was Des, panic-stricken and frantic. "What's going on? Two cops were just at the store looking for you. Kyle called and said there was someone at our place too."

"What—"

He lapsed into uneasy silence when two uniformed cops stepped out of his cubicle. Behind them stood a pale-faced Becky and someone he wouldn't have wanted to see under any circumstances, and especially not these: a smug-looking Tom Clarke.

"Christopher Bellamere?" the older of the two cops said.

He nodded slowly, wondering whether even that admission might be too much information.

"We need you to come with us, sir," the older cop said. "Right now."

The younger one, a huge, burly guy who looked like his hobby was lifting refrigerators, closed his hand over Chris's wrist, pulling the BlackBerry away from his ear. Chris could faintly hear Des screaming something about David, then the device was wrenched away from him and the voice stopped.

Weakly he tried to shake off the fridge lifter. "Hey, I was talking to someone."

"You can call anyone you want later, sir. Right now we need you to come with us."

"What is this about?"

"You'll find out everything you need to know at the station."

Chris was tempted to refuse. If he put up a fight would they drag him out? No one had said anything about arresting him and they seemed polite enough. What if he insisted on calling Simon?

"What station?" he asked, hating that his voice still sounded weak. God, they probably already had him pegged as some kind of pansy faggot.

"Northeast," the older one said, his voice still polite, despite the contempt that radiated off him.

They steered him back into the elevator. Chris stared at the silver-paneled door, embroiled in his own thoughts, only belatedly realizing the fridge lifter was talking to him.

"Do you have your car keys, sir?"

"Car keys? What for?"

The other cop handed over a folded legal-sized piece of paper. Chris stared at it like it might open up and bite him.

"We have a warrant to impound your vehicle. Please give me your keys, sir."

Chris could almost hear the unspoken "faggot" in his words. He resisted arguing, and held his silence all the way down to the Northeast Community Police Station. Simon would have been proud.

They put him in a room with a single, scarred table surrounded by four equally battered chairs. A large, fingerprint-smeared window took up one wall; Chris watched enough TV to know it was two-way glass. Who was on the other side? David? He stared at the metal bolts on the table. It added a grim overtone he didn't like one bit. What the hell did they do with those? Handcuff people to them?

He kept waiting for David to appear and tell him it was all a mistake. But when the door opened it was to reveal a stout, florid Latino man in a muddy green jacket and a lemon-yellow shirt over blue-and-green checkered pants.

David's partner.

Chris couldn't remember his name. He watched the fashion-challenged man set a briefcase on the table and pull out a chair, glancing only briefly at Chris before opening the case and shuffling through some papers in it.

Chris could stand it no more.

"Who are you?"

David's partner blinked at him. Surprised he'd speak up? He went back to shuffling paper, then slid his oversized rump into the chair. Before Chris could speak again he drew out a tape recorder and set it on the table between them.

"You mind if we record this session?"

"Why?"

"For your protection, as well as ours. This way no one puts words into anyone's mouth. Fair enough?"

"Tell me who you are, first."

"I'm Detective Martinez Diego of the Los Angeles Police Department. That answer your question?" Martinez indicated the recorder. "Shall we continue?"

Chris debated telling him to go to hell. But he was sick of not knowing what was going on. If this guy could tell him anything it would be worth the hassle. Hell, Chris hadn't done anything. He had nothing to hide.

He temporized. "I want to call my lawyer."

"Fair enough," Martinez said. "Call him."

But when Chris connected with Weiss's law offices a placid-voiced woman told him that Mr. Weiss was in court all day and would not be available until much later. Did he wish to leave a message?

What Chris wanted was to talk to his damned lawyer; instead all he said was, "Sure, tell him Christopher Bellamere called." He fixed Martinez with a jaundiced eye. "And the cops have dragged him back down here. I want him to find out why they're still hassling me."

He hung up and glared at the fat cop. "Go ahead."

Martinez flipped on the recorder and immediately repeated his name, rank, and the day's date and time.

"You want some coffee while we wait for your lawyer?"

"No. Why am I here?"

Martinez smiled politely.

"Would it be breaking confidence if you were to tell me your full name and current address?"

Chris hesitated then recited both.

"Where do you work, Mr. Bellamere?"

"You ought to know that, you had your men drag me out of there just now."

"It's for the record. Don't worry, your lawyer will get to hear the whole thing once he gets here."

Chris sighed. "I work for DataTEK Systems, in Studio City, on Moorpark."

"And how long have you worked there, sir?"

"Six years."

"And what exactly do you do at DataTEK Systems?"

Something niggled into Chris's mind. Martinez was being too nice. What was up? "What is it you people think I did? I'm telling you right now, you're wrong—"

"Don't worry about that right now." As well as recording the conversation, Martinez took notes. "Demanding job?"

"It can be . . . "

"What sort of hours you keep in a job like that?"

"I'm on call," Chris said. "Someone wants me, they call."

"Doesn't leave much time for a social life." Martinez's muddy brown eyes met Chris's, measuring, weighing. "Or girlfriends."

Chris cracked a smile. "Sorry, wrong sex. Didn't we do this already?"

"Excuse me?"

"I'm gay, remember? I have boyfriends."

Without changing expression Martinez scribbled something down. "Got one now?"

"No."

"Playing the field?"

"You could say that." Chris thought of David and wondered if this guy even had a clue about his partner. "You didn't bring me down here to ask about my work habits or my bedroom partners, so what is it, detective?"

Instead of answering, Martinez fished around in the briefcase and withdrew four eight-by-ten glossy photographs, which he dropped on the table between them.

"Know this man?"

"What the fuck?"

He shoved the pictures back but Martinez held them in place.

"Take another look. You recognize this man?"

"No—" Then Chris realized to his horror he did. It was Bobby. "Oh, my God."

Martinez leaned forward, his swarthy face flat, his eyes like a shark's, unmoving, watching, dissecting. "You do recognize him. Who is he? Give me a name."

Chris looked away. "His name was Bobby."

"Bobby who?"

"I don't know." Chris refused to look at the images. He stared at a stain on the green wall behind Martinez. "He never gave me his last name."

"What was your relationship to this Bobby?"

"We were . . . friends."

"Friends? But you don't know his last name? How long did you know him?"

"We'd only met a couple of times."

"Where did you meet?"

"Why all the questions?" Chris tried to glare at the fat cop. "What happened to him? Who did that?"

"Where did you meet Bobby?"

"A bar."

"What bar?"

"What difference does it make?"

"What bar?"

"The Nosh Pit." Chris was beginning to feel afraid. Goose bumps crowded the bare skin of his arms. The knot at the base of his head began to resolve into a pounding headache. "What is going on here?"

"Where is this Nosh Pit?"

"Hyperion. In Silver Lake."

"Gay bar?"

"What do you think?"

"I think you better answer my questions," Martinez snapped. "Before things go bad for you."

"What does that mean? Is that a threat?"

"When did you last see this Bobby?"

"I don't remember."

"Try."

"I don't—last week, I guess. Monday, I guess." Chris rubbed the skin of his knuckles. He found himself staring at his distorted image in the mirrored glass. Who was watching from the other side? "We had a couple of drinks at the Pit. I never saw him again."

"Did he get into your vehicle?"

"What?"

"Did he enter your vehicle that night?"

"Sure," Chris said. "He wanted me to take him home . . . to my place. I didn't want to. We argued. He got out and I never saw him again."

"What did you do while you were in the vehicle?"

"What do you mean?"

"Did you solicit him for sex?"

"No, it wasn't like that."

"What was it like then, *sir*?"

Chris rubbed the back of his neck, startled to find it was damp with sweat. Suddenly he'd had enough of this fat, overbearing cop.

"So we fooled around," he said. "This is the twenty-first century, right? Hell, according to Clinton it isn't even sex."

"Are you saying you and Bobby engaged in fellatio?"

God, what a stupid word. "Shit, we were just fooling around. End of story."

"Except it's not the end of the story, is it, Mr. Bellamere." Martinez pulled out a bulging handful of colored eight-by-tens. He threw the pictures down on the table in front of Chris. "Want to have another look at your handiwork, Mr. Bellamere?"

Chris glanced down at the images as they came to rest atop the cigarette burns and knife work that adorned the battered table. He was expecting more images of Bobby for him to I.D., but what he saw made his flesh flash ice cold and his stomach roll over.

"What'd he do, Bellamere?" Martinez was over the table, in his face, screaming. "Look at you wrong? Say the wrong thing to you?"

It was Bobby. No mistaking that. But these images showed a Bobby who had been hideously abused, his skin flayed and ripped off his once gorgeous body. A circlet of blood ringed his neck and in one image it looked like he was on his stomach, and the gaping wound between his legs made Chris lose it.

He threw himself away from the table. Away from the images. His hand went to his mouth, but it was like stemming a flood with straw. Vomit spattered all over his legs.

Distantly he thought he heard Martinez yell, "*Hijo de puto*. You asshole."

Then the door swung open and he looked up through a blur of tears to see David enter the room.

"Put those away. Shut that tape off."

Someone else entered the room and there was a whispered conversation that Chris couldn't make out. The next thing he knew someone was guiding him out of the room, away from his own stink. Almost immediately they turned into another room, a washroom. The door closed and he was guided to the sink.

"Do you want a drink of water? Coffee?"

It was David. He brushed by Chris and turned on the taps.

Chris blinked up at him. He took the damp paper towels that were handed to him.

"Here," David said. "Clean yourself up."

Chris forced himself to focus on David. He clutched the towels in one hand.

"How could you let him do that to me?"

"I'll take that to mean you don't want a drink. Okay, can you answer some more questions?"

"*More* questions? Are you fucking nuts?"

David perched on the sink and Chris nearly screamed when he pulled out his notepad.

"Tell me what happened after Bobby and you entered your vehicle."

"You want a blow by blow account?" Chris snarled. "I'm sitting here with fucking puke all over me and you want to know about my *sex life*? Rent a video like everybody else does."

"Like the kind Bobby made?"

"How the hell did you know about that—"

"If you had looked closely at those pictures Martinez threw at you, you would have seen a strip of film around the deceased's neck. It was a porno loop, starring one Bobby Starrz."

"Bobby Starrz?"

"His stage name. His real name was Robert Allen Dvorak."

"And what does any of this have to do with me?"

"You are so far the last person to have seen him alive."

"And you think I had something to do with *that*?"

"Where were you Tuesday morning?"

"Jesus, if I'd known I was going to need an alibi—"

"Yes?" David leaned forward. "What would you have done, Mr. Bellamere?"

"I'd have done something to be noticed. Maybe dance naked on my front lawn so the neighbors could tell you I was home. Would that have made you happy?"

"What time would you have felt compelled to create this alibi?"

Chris opened his mouth to retort, then closed it. His skin grew clammy. "You're trying to trick me, aren't you? Anything I say is going to incriminate me now, isn't it?"

"Do you feel you're incriminating yourself, Chris? Is there something you'd like to tell me?" David's voice was gentle, almost hypnotic. “You can talk to me, you know.”

Chris’s mouth hung open. Finally he pulled away from David, holding his arms wrapped around his chest.

“You really think I killed him, don’t you?” he whispered. “My God, what kind of monster do you think I am?”

“Talk to me, Chris. We can work this out.”

“Fuck you, David.” Chris was still whispering. He staggered backward. “I’m not saying another word to you without my lawyer.”

CHAPTER 15

Monday, 12:20 P.M., Northeast Community Police Station, San Fernando Road, Los Angeles

"WELL THAT WENT well," David said wearily as he rejoined Martinez in the detectives' squad room.

"Still think we shoulda held him. Let him spend a few hours in lockup. Pansy like him, he'd break like that." Martinez snapped his thick fingers. "Look how he fell apart when I showed him those pictures."

"He hardly acted like he was seeing his own handiwork."

"He's fucking psychotic, what do you expect? Should have let him have a look at those loonies down in lockup. He'd have been squealing to save his pretty ass."

David's hands closed into fists at the thought of Chris being abused by animals like that. But all he said was, "We don't have enough to make a convincing arrest. You know the D.A.'s demanding we bring her some solid forensics. She's scared of his lawyer. This Weiss is a cobra, I guess."

"You know those faggots got no guts." Martinez slammed his hand down on the desk. "Oh hell. He'd probably like it. Let those damned *vatos* plow his ass from one end to the other and he'd be begging for more. Sick fuck."

David suppressed a wince. "His vehicle been checked out yet?"

A phone call confirmed the SUV was still being processed. They grabbed a quick lunch at a nearby sub shop and met over the freshly delivered report back at David's desk.

"Fingerprints all over the passenger's side—some match this

Bobby character," Martinez said. "No surprise. Miss Swish admits to having the fudge packer in his car. Nothing to suggest him or anyone else was ever carried in the back."

"So we have nothing," David said. God, why did that make him feel relief? What was happening to him?

"We have them together. We have opportunity. Can he alibi the times?"

David shook his head.

"Why doesn't that surprise me? We already got the two at work telling us he came in late Tuesday and that was unusual enough to be noticed by both of them." Martinez consulted his notes. "They put him over two hours late for work, which would jibe if he was busy playing with his latest vic in his hidey hole."

They knew the killer had to have a secure place he could stash his victims. All the evidence so far suggested each had been held for hours before being killed. The killer's hiding place had to be a location where he felt safe. Probably isolated, too. David thought of Chris's Silver Lake house. With neighbors crowding in on either side it hardly qualified as isolated. And none of those houses had basements, either. Then again, Jeffrey Dahmer had kidnapped and dismembered over a dozen guys in an apartment building and gone unnoticed for years.

Still, maybe it was time to do a property search on the guy. Maybe he had access to a second location. Someplace he could come and go once his victim was secured.

David picked up the typed list of items found in Chris's SUV. It included one pair of black frame glasses and a T-shirt bearing unknown stains. The shirt was still in the lab being processed. But it hadn't tested positive for blood or semen. Traces of semen had been discovered in the vehicle's front seat, so they were going to have to type Chris and see whom it matched.

David tried to imagine the Chris who had responded so hotly to his kiss being a calculating killer, aroused by another person's pain. He couldn't reconcile it.

The glasses, though—that looked bad . . .

"Jason Blake wore glasses," David said. "But can we get a match on them?"

"I'm going back to Bellamere's workplace," Martinez said. "See if anyone noticed anything else unusual. This guy's job gave him lots of freedom and with the damned cell phones they all carry he could have called in from anywhere, claiming to be on the job."

"He'd have to record his time. Maybe even get employers to sign off." David tapped the top sheet of the report. "Let's find out what jobs he was supposed to be doing the last six months. Match it up with the job sites to see what he actually was doing."

"Right." Martinez grinned. "Nail him with the discrepancies. Still think we should have let him go?"

"He's got money. You saw his lawyer."

"Right. We push, the next thing you know we're all a bunch of antigay bigots persecuting this poor faggot," Martinez said. He wiped his mouth as though tasting something foul. "*Dios,* that stinks."

David pushed his own traitorous thoughts aside. This wasn't the time or the place. "So let's make sure our case is unsinkable. You check out the workplace. I'll chase down Blake. While I'm at it, I'm going to look at Daniel Anstrom. If I can talk to his parents, figure out Anstrom's activities before he went missing, maybe we can place Bellamere with him."

"Let him explain that away."

Monday, 12:25 P.M., Northeast Community Police Station, San Fernando Road, Los Angeles

Chris stumbled out of the station. Only when the sun started baking the vomit into his legs did he remember he had no ride home.

Hailing a cab proved challenging. Two whizzed by without slowing; when a third stopped, the driver took one look at the vomit and hit the accelerator. The fifth demanded a fifty-dollar surcharge up-front.

At home, he threw the ruined jeans into a garbage bag and tossed it outside. Then he crawled into the downstairs shower and turned it up as hot as his skin could handle, emerging in a cloud of steam, pink and tingling from his near scalding. But at least the smell of his own vomit no longer clogged his nose. He reconsidered tossing the jeans—at eight hundred a pop he could swallow the shame. He dashed outside and dragged the bag to the back step.

Retreating to the living room he flopped down on the sofa and dialed Des's number. Just his luck, Kyle answered.

"What the hell do you want?" Kyle snapped. "We don't need you bringing your cop troubles here. What did you do, anyway?"

What could Chris tell him? That the cops suspected him of picking up a guy in a bar and butchering him? That the cops thought he was the Carpet Killer?

"I just need to talk to Des. Put him on."

"He's not here," Kyle said. "Leave him alone, asshole."

When he slammed the phone down, Chris lay back staring at it for several minutes before it started beeping and he reached over to hang it up.

Monday, 2:24 P.M., Offices of Gilbert, Michelson & Gabronni, West La Palmas Avenue, Anaheim

"I'd like you to look at something, Mr. Blake, if you have a few minutes."

Richard Blake rose from behind his melamine-topped desk. His face paled as though he was expecting David to ask him to look at something gut-wrenching. David flashed back to Chris and how violently he had reacted to the stark, brutal images of the killer's latest victim.

He hadn't approved of Martinez's approach, but had seen it as a way to wring a reaction from the smart-ass younger man. It had gone far beyond that and David couldn't help but wonder how much damage they had done. Chris hadn't deserved it. Chris—

"Detective?"

"Your brother wore glasses, is that correct?" Focus on the facts. Bellamere had known the last victim. He had been the last one to see him alive.

"Yes—"

"And they were never recovered?"

"Yes. What—"

David pulled out the pictures he had secured of the glasses found in the back of Chris's SUV. He laid them on the desk in front of Richard.

"Can you identify these?"

Richard looked down at the images and frowned. He flipped through the pages, spreading them out to show all five pictures. Occasionally he would pick one up to study it more closely.

"You found his glasses? Where?"

"That's not the issue right now, sir. I need to know if you can identify them. Do they look like the pair Jay wore?"

Richard dropped the last picture back on the desk. He was still frowning and David felt something in him give way.

"Those look like Jay's. If you found them, you must have found my brother's killer?"

"We're still investigating." David retrieved the pictures and dropped them back in his briefcase. He felt a tightness in his chest that he refused to define. "What about these?"

The T-shirt bore no logo or brand label. The stains on it were inconclusive. But the shirt was a distinctive peach color that might be remembered by someone's big brother.

This time Richard was shaking his head.

"I couldn't swear to it," he said. "But Jay usually wore shirts, that designer crap."

David leaned forward. "How did Jay afford designer clothes?"

"Bought secondhand. Knockoffs." Richard dropped heavily into the leather chair and rubbed his neck. "Hell, maybe his lovers traded him clothes for sex."

David left, after promising to keep Richard in the loop. He paused in the outer reception room to put on his own sunglasses against the glare he could see beyond the tinted windows.

He called Martinez.

"Any luck with DataTEK?" David asked. "Anyone remembering anything?"

"That one guy, Clarke? He sure has a hard-on for our boy, and I don't mean that in any way Bellamere would fancy. He keeps reminding me how Bellamere is in and out all day, how he was late last Tuesday—something they all agree is really unusual. Guy doesn't have a clue what we're working on, but he's all set to testify in court that Bellamere's guilty."

"Any chance this Clarke is a closet case? Could Chris have hit on him? I'd hate for it to come out later he's got some kind of vendetta against Chris."

"Nothing stands out. If it's jealousy, I'd say it's professional."

That was the impression David had, too. He nodded as he rolled out of the parking lot.

"What now?" Martinez asked.

"Finally got hold of Daniel Anstrom's mother," David said. "They live in North Hollywood. I'm going to see her now. I'll be just down the road from you—we can grab some supper," he suggested.

The Anstroms' was a three-story Cape Cod–style "cottage" nestled among half a dozen large crepe myrtles. A circular flowerbed was planted with a tasteful arrangement of roses, geraniums, snapdragons, and tall gladiolas, all wilting in the lingering afternoon heat.

Daniel Anstrom's mother was a tall, slender woman who might have been anywhere from forty-five to sixty years of age. She had an elegant, unlined face capped by a carefully coifed bowl of gray hair. Sharp hazel eyes held his when he introduced himself. After a beat, where David wondered if she was going to forbid him entry, she stepped away from the door and signaled him to precede her into her tidy foyer.

It looked as though Mrs. Anstrom was alone in the house. David recalled that the report had been submitted by both of Daniel's parents. He figured the husband must out of the house for the afternoon.

She led him into a tidy yellow and blue kitchen.

"I presume you are here to tell me my son is dead. That is why you came, isn't it?"

"Ma'am?" David was taken back by her bluntness. "Your son is still listed as a missing person. Do you have some reason to assume he is dead?"

"Of course." She abruptly sat down on a high-backed wooden chair. Her gaze swept the room filled with light and hanging copper pots without seeing anything, including David. "My son would not remain a missing person this long unless something terrible had happened to him. My son is dead. I know this."

"I'm sorry, ma'am," he said. "But I don't know any such thing. But I do have a possible match. I was hoping you might be able to—"

"Identify? You want me to look at this corpse and tell you if it's my son?"

"I've brought some photos you might recognize." He stopped when she took a deep breath, the skin around her mouth whitening almost imperceptibly. "Ma'am?"

"Oh please, call me Edith. My husband would tell you I am abrupt. I prefer to think I have lived too long to dance around silly conventions. I have known for some weeks now that Daniel is dead. I used to think knowing how he died was the most important thing, but now I'm no longer so sure of that." Her eyes, when they met his, were clear and piercing. "Do I want to know how my son died, detective?"

"First I have to establish that your son is our victim." David didn't tell her that as the horror show escalated and the media sank their teeth into the story they might tell her more than she ever wanted to know. "Is your husband home, ma'am? Edith?"

"Yes, he is. But I'm afraid it would do you no good to talk to him. He had a stroke a little over three weeks ago and is confined to bed. His vocal cords are paralyzed."

"I'm sorry."

She nodded. "May I see these pictures, young man?"

He pulled out the pictures they had I.D.'d as Daniel Anstrom from the driver's license that had been dropped off at the station.

Edith closed her eyes. David felt her shaking, though their only contact was through the picture. Suddenly she dropped it with a cry and her hands flew to her face.

David knew they had their sixth victim.

Monday, 5:10 P.M., Cove Avenue,
Silver Lake, Los Angeles

Chris found himself moving through his house like a victim in some kind of gothic horror film. He tried flipping on the TV, but the only things he could find were news shows or game shows. He needed someone to help him forget. Somebody who could take his mind of this horrible mess. Somebody who could make forgetting fun.

Trevor answered on the third ring.

"Trev, how's it going?"

"Hey, Chrissy," Trevor's voice was liquid heat. "Sorry I missed you this weekend. Got tied up with work."

"Know how that goes." Chris laughed, relaxing for the first time that day. "What are you up to?"

"Right now?"

"Now. An hour from now. Tonight?" He dropped his voice. Nothing could get his mind off his problems better than some sexy company. "Tomorrow morning."

"I like that. Eagerness. You missed me?"

"Come over and I'll show you."

"Supper?"

"I'll cook."

"You're already cooking."

Monday, 5:50 P.M., Glendale Boulevard, Glendale

"Daniel Anstrom," David said. "Twenty years old, worked at Safeway as a box boy. If he was gay, his mother didn't know."

David and Martinez sat in the back of the overbright deli. David's pastrami and Swiss on rye tasted like cardboard.

"How many of them don't tell?" Martinez plowed through his Reuben with gusto. The sharp smell of sauerkraut filled the small booth. "They stay—where do they call it?—in the closet?"

David changed the subject fast. "Or it could mean he doesn't always target gays."

Some sauerkraut juice dribbled down Martinez's chin. He swiped it with a napkin, missed. "Poor guy if he wasn't gay."

David felt the skin of his face tighten and grow hot. "You think it's easier for the guys who were gay?" He forced his voice lower when he realized it was rising and heads were turning. "You think getting a knife shoved up your ass is easy if you've had a cock up there?"

"Jesus, man, no." Martinez scowled. "What's up your—" He abruptly fell silent. "Forget it. I didn't mean anything by it."

David rubbed one hand over his face, closing his eyes against the look on his partner's face. "I know you didn't. It's this case. It's hard to take, you know?"

"Oh, *hombre,* don't I though."

They finished their meal. Small talk dwindled into stilted silence.

"What now?" Martinez asked after they had both handed tens to the waitress and she had retreated to make change.

"See if we can link Chris to Anstrom. I got the name of a couple of places his mother said he frequented. An arcade and a nearby McDonald's."

"An arcade." Martinez nodded. "Good place to hustle young boys."

Monday, 6:15 P.M., Cove Avenue, Silver Lake, Los Angeles

Chris bounced to his feet after Trevor rang off. Company meant he had some domestic chores to do. Change the sheets, get some chicken in a marinade for barbecuing later, make sure he had wine ready. Distractions he welcomed. He put some coffee on and went to make his bed.

In the middle of ripping the old sheets off he flashed on the night he had spent with Bobby at the motel. His hands froze and his mind spun away into darkness. He sat down hard, still clutching the top sheet in numb fingers. How could Bobby be dead? Who could have done such a thing?

He shook his head, trying to clear it of the images. Bobby brutalized. By whom? Why? Had the killer known Bobby? Had he had the bad luck to stumble across this Carpet Killer after leaving Chris that night? The thought made Chris sick. If he had taken the younger man home with him like Bobby had wanted, would none of this have happened? How the hell could the cops have taken an innocent encounter as a sign of guilt? It was like they wanted him to be guilty.

He pounded the wall above the bed. Dammit, he wasn't going to let them railroad him. Screw the LAPD, he was through being a victim.

Downstairs he booted up his computer. By the time the coffee was ready and he poured himself a mug, he was logged in and online, ready to launch his queries. First he ran some simple searches on Bobby Starrz that brought back several links of film credits. Bobby had been a busy boy. The videos went back over three years, which meant Bobby had started when he was underage, since Chris doubted he'd been much over twenty-one. He printed off a couple of pages that listed the production company that had done most of the videos. StarFlight Productions. A quick Google search returned a hit for an office on Ventura Boulevard in North Hollywood. Even better, it gave him his first lead. A Web site. Bingo.

Opening StarFlight's Web site landed him on a smarmy page featuring suggestive images without substance and a lengthy list of available titles. They even had a secure site for making online purchases. MasterCard, Visa, or PayPal. Convenient. The videos could be ordered as VHS or DVD or downloaded as streaming video. Instant porno without leaving home.

StarFlight even sold a line of sex toys for the connoisseur. Dildos, specialty condoms, and the really fun stuff like butt plugs and bondage and S & M gear in every material from silk to leather.

All that merchandise meant a back-end-database to store customer information and inventory. Was there also an employee database for the talent? The only way to find out was to gain access to it.

Chris dove into his laptop case and pulled out an unmarked CD binder. Leafing through it he found one labeled simply TOOLS. He slipped it into his D-drive, and the CD demanded a password before it opened a Web page with a list of options.

He knew if StarFlight paid big bucks to the right people their site would be nearly impregnable. But if, like most businesses, they were lazy with their I.T. dollars, this was going to be a snap. It took Chris all of ten minutes to determine that StarFlight didn't invest in I.T. security. The site was wide open.

He needed only one more thing. He wasn't about to launch this attack from his own PC. If anyone at StarFlight realized they were being hacked he didn't want them—or the cops—tracing it back to him. He had to find a vulnerable PC he could hijack.

He launched his port-snooping tools from the same CD and left to refresh his coffee while his software went out on the Internet in search of a computer that hadn't been secured against hackers. He knew it wouldn't take long. Home users were notorious for not securing their machines. No matter how often the media warned them, their blissful ignorance making them ideal targets for what he needed.

Back with his second coffee he found his sniffers had discovered opened ports on several vulnerable machines and launched tiny, malformed packets that caused a buffer overflow. The vulnerable machines had no way to handle the overflow, so they allowed the packet in and allowed Chris in. He looked around his hijacked PC. All it had on it were a few cheesy games, chat software, and several dozen spyware gadgets installed by other unscrupulous netizens. The owner of this machine was a perfect dupe.

Chris launched his second set of tools. These would set up the hijacked machine to run the processes he needed in the background, so that even if the owner was working on his computer he'd never know what was happening.

The hidden processes ran flawlessly, and within minutes he had a perfect little zombie doing his bidding. That was when he set to work hacking StarFlight's back-end server.

The tools he used for that were a lot more sophisticated and he was sure the police would be very interested in knowing he had them. He had password-cracking tools and decrypters as well as a whole range of key-loggers.

While the crackers and the decrypters ran against the database he refreshed his coffee one more time. Then back to check the progress of his hacking job. He was pleased to see that StarFlight most likely had chosen their operating system and their security model on the basis of office politics and management schmoozing, instead of good I.T. judgment—their system was the easiest one in the world to hack.

In another ten minutes his zombie machine registered success. He was in.

Within minutes Chris had a list of every movie Bobby had participated in—Chris refused to think of it as acting—and something even better. Bobby Starrz's real name and his social security number.

Just like David had said: his name was Robert "Bobby" Allen Dvorak. Born in Topeka, Kansas, June 9, twenty-one years ago. Quit high school at sixteen, and like so many before him, took off for granola land to become a star. And like so many before him, he was eaten up by the big machine.

Best of all, a street address on Western Avenue in the still-ungentrified part of Hollywood. Maybe ten minutes from Chris's. He jotted down the full address anyway, just in case his memory failed him.

He knew he should call David. Dump what he had found in his lap. Only, how would he explain how he came by it? Admit to hacking StarFlight? That wouldn't help his credibility.

Could he just give them the information without saying how he got it? No, David would think he'd known it all along.

So, nix telling David.

Which left him playing sleuth.

That or let David and his homophobic partner hang him out to dry, which they were doing a damned good job of right now.

It was nearly six o'clock when a knock announced Trevor had arrived. Chris saved his information, released his captive PC, and shut his tools down.

Trevor handed Chris a plastic bag that clanked heavily. Chris opened it to find two bottles of wine, a Diamond Hill Cabernet and a Kistler Chardonnay.

Trevor shrugged. "Wasn't sure what you were cooking."

"Kistler's perfect. Only had it once. Let me get this put away—"

"Hey, no welcome kiss?"

Before Chris could respond, Trevor pulled him forward, his hand closing over the rapidly swelling bulge between Chris's legs.

Both of them were breathing hard by the time Trevor let them up for air.

"So, what are you feeding me?"

"Chicken."

"Good." Trevor didn't move away. He pressed his mouth against the hollow of Chris's throat. "I love chicken."

He slapped Chris's butt and shoved him toward the kitchen. "Go on, let's open this wine and get cooking."

A pair of pepper trees in a stone alcove flanked the barbecue. A chaise longue and a couple of Adirondack chairs with cushions crowded around a small, round table, filling the rest of the narrow space. Chris set the bowl of marinating chicken on the table and got the propane grill cranked up.

When he turned around, Trevor was sprawled on the lounger with a full glass of wine in one hand. He beckoned Chris over and held out the wine glass.

"Come here." Trevor hooked an arm around his waist and pulled him down on the chaise. "I want you here with me. This is one night you're not getting away from me."

Chris didn't bother telling him he wasn't trying to get away. Then he wasn't able to talk as Trevor pulled him into an embrace.

He had Chris's shirt off and was working on his jeans when his hands skidded off the BlackBerry still attached to Chris's belt.

"Get rid of that damn thing, will you?"

Chris set it under the chaise longue where it wouldn't get crushed by a misplaced foot. Things got very hot very fast.

From under the lounger came the soft but insistent chirp of his BlackBerry.

Chris groaned and groped for it. Trevor grabbed his hand.

"Fuck, no," he growled. "Don't—"

"I have to. It could be work. An emergency—"

He flipped the handheld on and plastered it to his ear, trying to ignore both Trevor's scowl and the sight of his aroused, half-naked body.

It was Des.

"Oh God, Chris, he's gone. I don't know where but I just know something bad has happened—"

"Who's gone?" Chris slithered out of Trevor's octopus arms and sat up on the edge of the lounger. "What's going on, Des?"

"It's Kyle. He's been so depressed lately. Ever since that horrible thing at the Pit. He says his looks are gone and he'll never work again."

Chris tried to ignore the way Trevor's hands wandered across the landscape of his bare chest, or how his erection pressed against Chris's back. Trevor bit his other ear and murmured some very enticing obscenities into it.

Des burst into sobs. "Oh God, I'll die if anything happens to him. It's all my fault. He's been so full of self-doubt lately. I should have been there for him—"

"Come on, Des. Kyle isn't going to do anything. He's just being a drama queen. You know how he is—"

"No! He's not like that. He's full of pain and I should have helped him. Now he's gone and I have to find him before he—I have to find him."

Chris nearly groaned aloud when Trevor slid the zipper of his jeans down. He forced himself to focus on Des's voice.

"Okay, I'll come by in the morning. We can look for him

together"—and maybe the damn fool would come home by then. "I'll call you—"

Trevor took the phone out of his hand and spoke into it, "Call him later," and hung up.

"Hey—"

Trevor stood up and dragged Chris to his feet. "You are coming with me." Back inside, Trevor extracted a DVD from his jacket pocket. "I brought something to inspire us—"

In the bedroom the phone rang. Chris ran for it, ignoring Trevor's furious look.

It was Kyle.

At least it sounded like Kyle, though Chris had never heard the younger man sound so panicked.

"I can't find Des. He's not at home. Where is he, Chris? Where's Des?"

"Looking for you. Where are you? What's wrong—"

"Someone's following me."

"What?" Chris sat down on the bed, shoving Trevor away when he tried to take the phone away. Trevor responded by stripping his jeans off. "Who's following you?"

"I don't know." Fresh panic tightened Kyle's voice, raising it in pitch. "I don't know, but they're right behind me in a truck."

Oh good. California good old boys out for a night of fun.

"Where are you now?" Shit, if anything happened to Kyle, Des would never forgive him. He might as well kiss their friendship good-bye forever. "Do you know where you are?"

"Santa Monica. I just passed Bundy."

Chris reached for his shirt, still protecting the phone from an amorous Trevor. "What are you driving, Kyle?"

"My Boxster, of course."

That had been a major sore point between Chris and Des. Chris had thought it a foolish indulgence to buy any car for his latest boy-toy, let alone a pricey little sports car like the Porsche Boxster.

But Des had insisted, and now Kyle drove everywhere in it. At least when he wasn't letting Des chauffeur him around in the Mercedes.

Right now Kyle was driving through territory ripe for car-jacking. He refrained from telling Kyle that—no sense having the fool freak out even more.

"Come to my place—"

"I can't. I'm almost out of gas. I didn't bring my bank cards—"

Idiot, Chris wanted to say. Instead he took a deep breath. "Okay, whatever you do, don't stop until you get to a well-lit place with lots of people. In fact," he thought hard. "Go to Freddie's. Then call me back on my cell."

"Are you going to call Des?"

"I'll call him, but in the meantime I'm coming out there. Go to Freddie's." Trevor reached for him; Chris twisted away.

"You can't be serious," Trevor muttered. "You're leaving?"

Chris hung up and scrambled to his feet, tucking himself back into his jeans.

"Kyle's gotten himself lost out in Santa Monica. He's begging me for help. Des is my best friend, Trev. I can't leave Kyle out there on his own. Des'd kill me if anything happened to him."

"You're killing *me*, is what you're doing."

Chris tried to smile as he admired Trevor's naked body. "Wait for me. I won't be long—"

"Fuck that." Trevor grabbed discarded clothes off the floor and threw them back on. "Trevor doesn't wait."

"Give me a lift—" Chris stared at the empty doorway. Downstairs the front door slammed. He sighed. "Or not."

Trevor was long gone by the time Chris left the house to wait for his cab.

CHAPTER 16

**Monday, 11:00 P.M., Cove Avenue,
Silver Lake, Los Angeles**

IT TOOK CHRIS forty minutes to reach Santa Monica. His BlackBerry remained stubbornly silent the whole way. Freddie's was packed. In the barely legal crowd it took Chris nearly half an hour to establish that Kyle wasn't there. Pushing through the solid press of bodies he forced his way back outside.

He scanned the street. No sign of Kyle or his Boxster.

Idiot. How the hell was he going to explain this to Des? Where was Kyle?

He pulled out his BlackBerry. "Hey, Des," he said when his friend answered. "Any word?"

"No," Des said.

"Call the cops, Des—"

"You know what they'd tell me?" Des's voice rose a notch. "They'd tell me I'm some hysterical queen who had a tiff with his boyfriend."

"You called them already, didn't you?"

"Twice. They won't even take a report for forty-eight hours—what's it to you anyway? Since when do you care about Kyle?"

"Des—" Chris stared into the half-filled parking lot attached to Freddie's. No Boxster. "Des, you gotta call them again. Kyle's in trouble."

"What are you talking about?"

"He was being followed. You tell the cops that. They have to do something if they know that."

Monday, 11:20 P.M., Northeast Community Police Station, San Fernando Road, Los Angeles

David wearily tossed his jacket aside and dropped into his chair, his elbows finding support on the desk. His phone rang. It was Martinez.

He sounded as exhausted as David. "I'm heading home."

"The arcade a bust?"

"Found a couple of guys claim to be good friends of Anstrom. They may have seen him around the time he disappeared. Any way you can round up some pictures of Bellamere?"

David looked around the squad room. "Don't we have a camera here somewhere?"

"Check the top drawer of my desk."

The camera David pulled out fit into the palm of his hand.

"Digital?"

"Beauty, ain't it? Plug it in tonight and it'll be ready in the morning."

"I'll catch him before he leaves for work."

"Sounds good. I have to get the kids ready for school, Inez's sister is in the hospital having a baby, so I may be a few minutes late. Get your pics, we'll head out to the valley later."

David managed to grab a few hours' sleep, and woke himself up with a shower while Sweeney prowled the bathroom, impatient for breakfast. By seven David was parked up the street from Chris's in his unmarked. Less than thirty minutes later a cab edged its way around him and pulled into Chris's driveway.

David couldn't see inside the courtyard, so he didn't see Chris come out, but he did see him slide into the backseat of the cab. Within minutes the cabby's lights flared and they headed down the hill.

David stayed on their tail in the light traffic that got heavier as they cut over to Santa Monica. He managed to keep the cab's dome light in view. The cab finally stopped at a Hertz. Parked across the street, David watched Chris rent a car and emerge thirty minutes later in a pale blue Lexus.

But instead of heading back over the mountain to work, Chris turned west toward Beverly Hills. Once he parked and David saw where he was going, he cursed low and grabbed his cell phone off the seat beside him.

"He's in with his lawyer," David said when Martinez answered. He could hear kids talking in the background and a TV blaring.

"Think he's on to us?" Martinez sounded harried. "Our boy must be shitting bricks—"

Abruptly Martinez cut off. David could hear a small voice in the background.

"No, honey, er, Daddy didn't mean to say that. So don't tell Mommy, okay? Now you go pick out a toy to take to school."

Martinez was trying to suppress his laughter when he got back on the phone. "*Dios*, how much you want to bet she asks Mom about that tonight?"

David laughed. "Your wife's gonna kill you."

"Let's see if we can take our boy down with me. Any luck getting pictures?"

"Not yet." David glanced around the busy street. "I think I can catch him coming out of the office, if I can get into position. Call you later."

He dropped the phone back on the seat and picked up the camera. A car pulled away from the curb three cars down from Chris's rental and David grabbed the spot away from an irate Jaguar driver. When the driver approached him with a scowl and a few choice words David settled the beef by flashing his tin.

While he waited he managed to capture a couple of other young, blond men as they left the building, knowing it would be useless to present a photo lineup unless they had a variety of similar types to show potential witnesses.

By the time Chris emerged from Weiss's building, David had half a dozen pictures saved in memory. He snapped four more in rapid succession as Chris made his way to his rental.

Martinez called a few minutes later.

"All done here," David said. "I'll stop at Keiko's and get prints made.

"We're gonna be early. Grab some breakfast?"

"Sure. As long as it doesn't involve sauerkraut."

"Even the Germans aren't that crazy."

They met in a greasy spoon two blocks from the arcade where Anstrom had hung out. Martinez looked over the shots and between them they picked out half a dozen, all similar in body type, dress, and hair color.

"Now that's an honest lineup," Martinez said, rearranging the pictures so Chris's was on top. He tapped the picture.

David had considered how he was going to put this, but in the end he just said, "Do we both need to run this lineup?"

"What have you got in mind?"

"Think you can get another warrant from Judge Harris?"

"What do you want it for?"

"Chris's work place. Let's find out what his schedule should have been and get a list of who to contact to confirm if he showed up when he claims he did on those off-site jobs. And let's have a look at his computer. Maybe we'll get lucky. Meanwhile, I'll hit the arcade, snoop around, see if anyone recognizes Chris from this lineup."

Tuesday, 8:30 A.M., Canon Drive, Beverly Hills

Simon frowned across at Chris, clearly not happy with his newest client. Chris didn't really care. He had spent half the night prowling the streets of Santa Monica, without any luck.

Finally he had called Des back and insisted they file another report with the Santa Monica Police, but Chris could tell they weren't going to be taken seriously.

"So, the police impounded your vehicle and have probably already searched it." Simon studied Chris shrewdly. "What might such a search yield?"

"What do you mean?" Chris felt renewed panic. He had thought once Simon heard his story he would dismiss the police allegations without hesitation. "They won't find anything! Jesus, I've never done anything to anyone in my life."

"Except you misunderstand the role of evidence in the police mind. They are looking for proof that this man you met, this Bobby, was in your vehicle. You admitted as much to them."

"I drove him around. Is that a crime?"

"Sexual misconduct will strengthen their case."

"What sexual misconduct?"

"Proof that sex of any kind occurred in your vehicle." Simon opened a drawer and pulled out a legal-sized pad of yellow paper and a gold pen. The pen scratched as he wrote. "We must immediately seek to have the warrant and subsequent search quashed. Then it won't matter what they find."

"Are you saying if they can prove this guy and I had sex it means I killed him? Is it because we're gay?"

"In their minds, your sexual orientation may strengthen their case."

"*What case*?" Chris couldn't believe this. "I didn't *do* anything. How often do I have to say that?"

"I agree their case is weak. They know it, too, otherwise they would have moved to arrest you by now." Simon tapped his thumbs together and held Chris's gaze, as though testing his fortitude. Abruptly he nodded. "We will move to strike the results of the search. Then they will have no case. That will force them to act quickly to secure one, which should play in our favor."

"What are you talking about? I don't want to force them to do anything—except leave me alone. Can't you do that?"

"In the long run—yes. But for the short term, the police are like bulldogs, very tenacious. They will not want to give you up since I'm sure they have convinced themselves you look better than you do."

"Maybe if I talked to them again—"

"No, that will definitely not do. At this point anything you say will only further their interest. You should not have talked to them at all." Simon looked hard at him. "If they come for you again, you will not only not speak to them, you will invoke my name and refuse any comment until I am beside you. And I mean any comment. That was an incredibly foolish thing you did."

Chris ignored the jibe. "If they come for me—you think they're going to arrest me?"

"Doubtful. But neither are they going to leave you alone."

Chris swore and ground his teeth together. "How long do I have to live with them watching me, trying to trip me up?"

"Until they find a better suspect."

Tuesday, 11:30 A.M., Vanowen Street, North Hollywood, Los Angeles

The Jungle Arcade was filled with a mix of teenage boys and girls. Even the proprietor barely looked old enough to be out of school. His prime job seemed to be dispensing quarters to feed the insatiable video machines.

The front lobby, littered with the usual gang tags, opened into a cavernous hall lined with video machines. The noise was a steady roar. Behind the counter, the proprietor's head bobbed to music from his headphones.

He noticed David the minute he walked in. The headphones came off and he watched David approach.

"Yeah?"

"I'm looking for Smitty."

"That's me. Who's looking?"

David flashed his shield. "I got some pictures I'd like you to look over."

"Pictures of who?"

"You just tell me if you recognize anyone." He laid the six-pack of images out on the scratched, glass-topped counter. "Any of these people ever come in here?"

A girl drifted over, thin as an apology, pink hair tied back in a careless bun, wearing enough metal piercings to keep an airport security checkpoint buzzing. Her kohl-blackened eyes fastened on the six pictures and she studied them avidly, picking the sheet up with fingers that sported inch-long bright-fuchsia nails.

"Who's that?" She was pointing a nail at Chris's picture.

"Ever see him around?" David asked casually.

She shook her pink head. "Nah. Too bad. He's cute."

Smitty scowled at her words.

"How 'bout you?" David asked him. "See any of them?"

Smitty glared at the girl, then shook his head at David. "Sorry."

"Mind if I ask around?"

"Go ahead. Marcia." Smitty laid the sarcasm on thick. "Take him back and find Ant and Digger."

She stuck her tongue—pierced in two places—out at him and sauntered back toward the dimly lit central arcade. David picked up the pictures and followed.

"Miss . . . Marcia," he called as she strode through the crowded machine-filled room. "Marcia."

She stopped so suddenly he nearly plowed into her. She twisted around to look at him.

"What did you call me?"

"Marcia . . . That's not your name?" David felt as though there was some big joke going on around him and everyone else was in on it. "That *is* what Smitty called you."

"He's always calling me something. Marcia's his 'get off your high horse, bitch' name for me."

David just looked at her, knowing he was missing something, without a clue as to what.

"You don't get it?" She rolled her eyes. "Marcia? *The Brady Bunch*?"

"Wasn't that a seventies show?"

Another roll of the eyes said it all. Suddenly she caught sight of someone and abandoned the jaded act, squealing like the sixteen-year-old he figured she probably was.

"Hey, Dig!" She flashed a huge grin his way. "He's the one you wanna talk to. Oh, man, he's so hot."

David suppressed a smile when the skinny blond "hunk" squeezed through the crowd in answer to her call. Digger was dressed like all the others in the pseudo-gang style they all affected; his baggy pants hung off his hips, showing a pair of red and black boxers underneath. His plaid flannel shirt flopped open at the neck to reveal a concave chest that hadn't filled out yet with any muscle. The kid couldn't have been over eighteen.

Not-Marcia had gone back to affecting a pose of bored sophistication.

"We still going to see that show tonight?" she asked, her nails raking through strands of hot-pink hair.

"Sure, whatever."

"You Digger?" David stepped between the two before their budding romance could take over. "Either of you know a Daniel Anstrom?"

"DJ? Sure, I know him." Digger's dark eyes moved from Not-Marcia to David. "What's up?"

"He's got some pictures he wants you to look at," Not-Marcia said.

"I'm looking for anyone with a connection to Daniel—DJ."

"Ain't seen D.J. in ages. What gives there, huh?"

Apparently word hadn't filtered down that their friend was dead. David didn't want to tell them here, like this.

"Listen, is there someplace we can talk?" he asked. "Bring along anyone else who might have known Daniel."

"Oh, you want to talk to Ant. Him and DJ were like this." Not-Marcia crossed her fingers.

Digger and the girl found Ant, who looked like a Digger clone, and they moved toward the rear of the arcade, where some kind of renovation was under way. The floor underfoot was littered with paint chips and old plaster board. David sidestepped a rusted tin can filled with old nails.

Light came from a pair of overhead bulbs. A drop cloth covered a counter like Smitty's. David set his six-pack of pictures down on it.

"I'm afraid I have bad news," he said, catching Not-Marcia's gaze, then moving on to Digger and Ant's. "Daniel Anstrom, DJ, is dead."

Not-Marcia looked dazed. "Dead?"

"DJ?" Digger shook his head. "No way, he can't be—"

"I'm afraid he is," David said gently. "He died several weeks ago. His mother has identified his body."

"But I saw him—" Digger froze. "Shit, maybe that was a while ago. I don't believe this. How—?"

David dug out his tin and held it out for them to see. "Daniel was murdered. That's why I'm here." He pinned Digger with his gaze. "When and where did you see him last?"

"Here," Digger said. "He was always here. 'Less he was working . . . Man, homicide?"

"Did you ever see any of these men here? Ever see Daniel talking to any of them?

All three youths bent over the pictures, as though they could fathom what had happened to their friend by studying them. Digger was first to shake his head.

"Never seen any of them."

"Ever see Daniel talking to anyone you didn't know? Probably an older guy."

"How old?" Ant wanted to know.

"At least late twenties. Probably thirties."

"Wow, old, then," the girl murmured. "Sometimes they come in. Usually trying to hit on us." She made a face. "It's so lame. They're like, ancient. I might as well date my father."

"But not these guys?" David indicated the pictures. Trying not to think how ancient he was at thirty-seven.

"Sorry, no," Digger said.

"Except for his uncle," Ant muttered. He rubbed one chewed up finger along his fuzz-covered face. "That time he got sick, remember?"

David felt a stir of excitement. "Who was sick? Daniel's uncle?"

"Nah," Ant said. "DJ was here playing as usual. This guy comes in, hell, none of us pay any attention, and DJ never said who he was, but then DJ got real sick. And that's when this guy said he was DJ's uncle and he was gonna take him home." Ant glared at Digger. "You don't remember that?"

"Don't remember no uncle," Digger said. "I thought DJ was stoned."

"He was sick."

"The uncle tell you that?" David kept the excitement out of his voice. "What did his uncle look like?"

Ant shrugged. "Old." He glanced at the pictures. "Like that, maybe older."

"White?"

The look Ant gave him said "Of course" as though David was stupid.

"What about hair color? You remember that?"

"I don't know. Light, I guess. Blond."

In frustration, though he knew if a defense attorney like Weiss ever heard of it, he'd be raked over the hottest legal coals, David tapped the sheet of pictures on the counter.

"You're sure it wasn't one of these guys?"

Ant studied the pictures again, even going so far as to pick up Chris's, but he was firmly shaking his head when he dropped it back down.

"No. None of them is DJ's uncle."

Then David did something he knew would get him nailed good. He reached into his jacket pocket and pulled out the rest of the pictures he had taken of Chris that morning.

"Here," he said. "Look these over."

Again Ant peered down at the three new pictures, his face screwed up in a scowl. He eventually tossed the three images on top of the old ones.

"Nope. Ain't him."

•

"Could we have the wrong guy?" David threw the photos down on the hood of Martinez's car.

Martinez stood blinking down at them. They had met up in the parking lot of the building across the street from DataTEK shortly after three o'clock.

"They're kids," Martinez said. "They make a wrong I.D. based on one picture."

David considered a second, then sighed and dropped the other three pictures on top of the first six. "Except I also showed them these. They were still adamant."

"Shit, even a first-year PD could get a lineup like that tossed, even if your wits had copped to knowing him." Martinez frowned. "This ain't like you, Davey."

David ignored that. "We have nothing else on this guy."

"He knew the last vic," Martinez said with some exasperation. "He admits to fucking him, cops to having him in his truck. We got the vic's glasses in his truck."

"Glasses I.D.'d from a photo. You know how many glasses of that type there are in this city? Your first-year P.D. would love us to walk into court with that one."

"Get the prescription—"

"I've requested that from the brother."

"So we'll still get him."

David ticked off the problems he was having with the whole "Bellamere as perp" scenario. "We got the bartender's testimony of the last guy the vic hustled. If it went down like Chris said and the vic stormed off in a huff, he could just as easily have been picked up by someone else." He scooped up the useless images. "We don't even know for sure he was picked up that night. For all we know it was the next night."

"Except we got no wits who saw this Bobby character again, right? After he was seen with Bellamere he vanished, until he turns up dead. We know he worked porno. Probably hustled, too."

"No record."

Martinez's irritation grew. "Do we have anyone else?"

"No," David conceded.

"Then let's do like we planned. If we can't find anything from his employment, we put him on the back burner. I still think he's good for it and something's going to show up."

"You got the warrant then?"

"Ever know me to fail?"

David dropped the photos into his briefcase, clicked it shut, and stepped away from Martinez's unmarked.

"Let's do it then."

CHAPTER 17

Tuesday, 1:15 P.M., Western Avenue, Hollywood, Los Angeles

FROM THE PERFUMED corridors of Beverly Hills to the piss-drenched streets of a low-rent apartment on Western took less than forty minutes. Chris felt like he'd traveled to another planet. Was this why Bobby hadn't wanted to bring him home the night they connected up?

He made his way along the dimly lit corridor on the first floor, easing by a pile of filthy blankets and trying to keep his Dockers from touching anything. When the blankets moved, he nearly jumped out of his nerve-mangled skin.

A gaunt, dirt-blackened face peered up at him hopefully.

"Dollar, mister?" A cracked, wheezing voice asked. "Spare a dollar?"

A life spent in L.A. had inured Chris to the multitude of panhandlers and street people who lived out shadow lives on the fringes of his world. He sometimes dropped careless coins into the battered guitar cases of street musicians, or the hands of old women who followed their steel shopping carts like faithful dogs as they wended their way along the cracked sidewalks of East Hollywood. They always seemed to him to be searching for memories that had fled them long ago.

Was this what Bobby would have come to? Once his looks had faded with age and abuse, would he have moved from this shabby apartment to the streets, just one more failed dreamer?

He felt sick as he fumbled in his back pocket for a handful of coins and dropped them into the outstretched hand, refusing to meet the man's rheumy eyes.

On the second floor the muffled screams of Eminem came from farther up. When a baby's screams joined Eminem, Chris winced.

Bobby's roommate turned out to be a skinny teenager with a vague midwestern accent and a head full of dreadlocks, which Chris figured had less to do with the Rastafarian cult than a refusal to brush her hair. Her lemon bright T-shirt bared one shoulder and most of her midriff, showing off a skull tattoo and belly-button ring.

Chris held out his hand.

"Chris Bellamere."

She stared at his hand for several heartbeats, then touched his fingertips. "Skull. You another cop?"

When she grinned she displayed tobacco stained teeth. Chris stared—she had filed her incisors down into pale spikes. She proudly fingered the skull tattoo on her hip, then stared pointedly at his crotch. He felt himself shrivel up inside his boxers. A horrible thought occurred to him. Bobby hadn't been bi, had he? Had he slept with this creature?

"The cops were here?" he asked.

She disappeared into the apartment, forcing him to follow. She patted a yellow and brown flowered sofa. When she sat, her sagging belly flowed out around her too-tight jeans. Her pierced navel looked inflamed. She grinned again and bounced on the sofa. "They were here, asking all kinds of questions. You a friend of Bobby's?"

She seemed pretty jazzed about being questioned by the police. Like it was all a game.

"If you ain't a cop who are you? One of his tricks?" She smiled slyly.

"Do you know the names of the cops who were here?"

"Nah. They left me a card; it's around here someplace. Who reads that shit, right?"

"What did they look like?"

"One of them was this fat Mex, the other guy was big, had stuff all over his face. Can't say either one of them turned my crank. Why can't I get a cop looks like Brad Pitt? This is Hollywood, ain't it? Oughtta be a law."

"What did they want to know?"

"Who Bobby was seeing." She giggled. "Like he dated the guys he was porking. I told them Bobby never brought his tricks home with him."

"I was hoping to find something that would tell me what Bobby had been up to the last weeks of his life."

"You and the cops both. Say, you one of his tricks?" She looked him up and down and licked her lips. "Bobby could get 'em, that's for sure."

"So he didn't keep an address book or anything?"

She scratched at a festering pimple on the side of her nose. "What's in it for me if he did?"

Before he could ask her what she meant, she vanished into a backroom. She returned several minutes later with the last thing Chris would have expected.

A Palm Pilot.

She held it out. "I didn't tell the cops about it. They would have just taken it from me. Now what good's that to me? I gotta survive too, y'know."

Chris took the device from her. He fumbled in his wallet and found two twenties and a ten. He offered them to her.

She looked up at him. "You wanna buy it?"

"If you got the power adapter to go with it."

She eyed the money, then hugged the PDA to her chest. "That's all? Maybe I should just give it to the cops."

He pulled another twenty out, showing her his wallet was now empty. She scurried out of the room and came back with the AC adapter. She snatched the bills from him.

He left before she could change her mind.

Tuesday, 2:40 P.M., DataTEK, Studio City

“What exactly was it you wanted, officers?”

The officious CIO of DataTEK, Peter McGill, had been joined by a fox-faced woman who glared at everyone in Peter’s outer office as if they were personally responsible for her extra workload.

David handed the warrant to McGill.

“Specifically we want to see any records that relate to Mr. Christopher Bellamere’s employment with you in the last ninety days. We need to see records of where he worked when he was off-site and who he worked for.”

McGill nodded brusquely at the fox-faced woman. “Mildred can provide that for you. She’s our director of human resources. Was there anything else?”

“We also have a list of items we are to secure from Mr. Bellamere’s work cubicle, including any computer equipment he may have worked on.”

McGill frowned. “That equipment is company property. Will it be returned?”

“The equipment in question will be held for the duration of our investigation; then it will be returned to you.”

McGill glared at Mildred. “I want him off our payroll,” he snapped. “Can you start the ball rolling on that?”

“You might want to reconsider, Mr. McGill.” The woman glanced at David, then murmured something in a low voice to her boss.

McGill’s glare was transferred to David. Then he reluctantly nodded at her. “I’ll consult with our legal department, then. Mildred, can I count on you to get the documents these gentlemen require?”

“Yes, sir.”

“I’ll leave that in your capable hands, then. Gentlemen.” McGill nodded at David and Martinez, then retreated to his office and closed the door.

David and Martinez followed the woman into the hallway.

"Not a happy camper," Martinez said. He eyed the HR director uneasily. She led them down the hallway to a second office, where she asked them to wait.

They did as she directed, and after they had cooled their heels for twenty minutes she returned, producing a sheaf of papers that she handed to David. He glanced at them and saw Chris's name on top.

"Mr. Bellamere's hours and work locations for the last three months. Will you need a list of contacts at those businesses?"

"Yes, we will," David said. "We'd like to start at Mr. Bellamere's desk. Can you have someone show us the way?"

She nodded. "I'll bring that contact list by there later."

"Thank you, ma'am."

He and Martinez retreated to the hall, where they waited for their escort. Eventually another woman showed up to lead them to Chris's cubicle. Like the last time, his phone was blinking and several handwritten notes littered the desk.

An outraged Becky Chapman planted herself in front of David. "What are you doing?"

"Police business," Martinez said, all but shoving the warrant under her nose. Becky backed up a step, but continued to glower.

"We only need this black box, right?" David muttered after crouching to determine how many computers Chris had at his desk. He found only one under the monitor.

Still kneeling, he opened his cell and dialed the station, and asked to be put through to a computer-forensics technician. Soon the whiny voice of someone who sounded as though he was barely out of grade school came on the line.

When the tech found out what they were doing he sighed and said, "Okay, is the computer still on?"

"Yes."

"Unhook the colored network cable at the back."

David found a blue cable that plugged into what looked like a telephone jack. He described it to the tech.

"That's it. Unplug it, then unplug the power. Once it's off, unhook everything else and bring it back here."

"This is related to a murder investigation," David said, trying to keep his voice low, aware of eavesdroppers. "How soon can you get to it."

"As soon as I can get to it," the bored-sounding tech said before hanging up.

David did as he was told. He hefted the black box onto the top of Chris's desk and found Becky still there, glaring at him.

"What are you doing?" Her contempt was open. "Where are you taking that?"

"Computer-forensics lab."

She turned away in disgust. The disgust deepened when Tom Clarke appeared beside her. "What are you doing here?"

"Peter is concerned about the corporate image," Tom said. "He wanted me to help these gentlemen get what they needed as quickly as possible."

Translation: get what they came for and get out. David took advantage of Tom's arrival. He pointed to Chris's workstation.

"Are there any other machines that Mr. Bellamere would use?"

"Nah, that's his only workstation," Tom said. "So, did you finally get around to arresting Bellamere?"

"Are you aware of something he should be arrested for?"

"His lifestyle, for one. The guy's clearly up to something. Late all the time. Out on so-called service calls. No one really knows what he's doing when he leaves here."

David thumbed through a couple of the files Martinez had pulled from Chris's file cabinet. They all bore company names and clear dates.

"He appears to keep meticulous records."

"He might have been telling DataTEK one thing, but I'll bet you find he wasn't doing half the work he claimed."

"You are so full of shit," Becky said. "If Chris didn't do his work, why was he always called back? When half of those companies put in requests for our services, they ask for Chris. They don't want anyone else touching their systems. Wonder why that is, eh, Tommy?"

Tom's lip curled at her. "He's snowed you all, hasn't he?"

"Yeah," she said. "He's snowed us all by doing the best work anyone in this company can produce." Her brown eyes turned toward David. "You believe who you want, but Chris isn't cheating anyone. And he hasn't done anything illegal, either."

She turned and stalked off. Tom lingered, then sauntered after her a couple of minutes later.

Once in the elevator David shifted the weight of the computer in his arms.

"You were right, that guy has it in for Chris," David said. "You get the impression he thinks he should have Chris's status in the company?"

"That girl doesn't think so," Martinez said. "If he wasn't a faggot I'd think something was going on between them."

"It doesn't always come down to sex, you know."

"Since when?"

David stared at the elevator door the rest of the trip.

Tuesday, 3:10 P.M., Western Avenue, Hollywood, Los Angeles

Chris's BlackBerry vibrated as he escaped Bobby's building.

"Yeah?" he murmured.

"What the hell kind of trouble you getting yourself into now?"

Chris recognized Becky's voice instantly. "Hi to you, too, Chapman. To tell the truth, I figured my life was getting way too tame, so I thought I'd liven it up a bit."

"Right." Her normally husky voice dropped several octaves and he could almost imagine her looking around, searching for eavesdroppers. "I'm in the bathroom."

"Gee, Chapman, thanks for sharing that."

"The cops just came in here with a big story about having a warrant to search your workspace. They've taken your PC."

Chris nearly slammed the car door on his fingers. He stared sightlessly out the tinted window at the traffic on Western. A black-and-white crawled by and he felt like shrinking down in his seat, away from the watchful eyes.

"What?" he finally managed.

"They're after you hard, man. I don't know what they think you did, but that little shit is right there in the middle of it, spinning all kinds of stories for them."

"Little shi—you mean Clarke, don't you."

"What are they doing, Chris? What do they want?"

"Damned if I know. I mean that, Becky. They got some crazy idea I'm involved in something I'm not and they aren't listening to anybody, least of all me."

"If I was you I'd find myself a good lawyer and give it to them. Jesus, you hear about them railroading innocent people, but you never expect . . . Get a lawyer, Chris. Now. Before this goes any further."

"Already done." Chris started the car. He glanced at the dashboard clock. Nearly three-thirty. "In fact I think I'll give him a call now, let him know what's going on."

"I'd say that's a good idea."

"Call me later, okay? Don't do anything that will get you in trouble, but if you happen to overhear something . . . "

"Gotcha. Talk to you later then."

He could hear the sound of a toilet flushing, then the line went dead. He dialed Simon Weiss's number.

"You were right about them acting quickly," Chris said. "They've shown up at my work with another one of their damned warrants. No way have I got a job after this. How the hell can they just walk in and fuck up my life this way?"

"Tell me what happened," Simon said.

Chris did. Then something else occurred to him. "Becky isn't going to get into trouble, is she? For calling me like that, I mean?"

"We do not yet live in a Gestapo state," Simon reassured him. "You are not a fugitive, so there is no legal reason to prohibit a person from calling you. Is she discreet?"

"As a Holmsby Hills madam. She's going to call me later and let me know what happened when she got back to her desk."

"I will begin making phone calls now. Do not worry, Christopher. The police are on a fishing expedition, nothing more. They will come up empty-handed, which will make subsequent attempts more difficult. Even the most hard-nosed of judges cannot justify harassment in the name of justice."

Chris stared down at the Palm Pilot full of information written by a dead man.

"I might have something for you—let me get back to you."

"What are you up to, Christopher?"

"Nothing, I swear."

"Hmmm . . . " Weiss didn't sound like he believed him. "See you keep doing that."

Tuesday 4:20 P.M., Northeast Community Police Station, San Fernando Road, Los Angeles

Chris's computer went down to the techies with their gadgets designed to decrypt and recover files people thought they could cleverly hide by deleting.

In the meantime he and Martinez got on the phone with DataTEK's clients and proceeded to query I.T. managers at DataTEK's client firms about their recollection of Chris's time on-site with them.

Just as David got off the phone with his sixth puzzled and harried I.T. manager, Martinez also slammed his phone down. He yanked his red tie with its dimpled-golf-ball motif away from his thick neck and swore. "What is this guy, some kind of fucking saint? He never overbills?"

"Doesn't look like it." David made a note in the margin of his notepad about the last call. "So far his hours billed match what he turned in to DataTEK, and in some cases I get the impression he may have put in some extra time he didn't bill."

"Fuck." Martinez threw his pen across the desk. "*Dios,* you see what this guy charges for his time? No wonder he doesn't have to overbill. I'm in the wrong field."

"You're only figuring that out now?" David drew out the billing sheet for a place called Pharmaden. Billed hours: seven. Hourly charge: one-fifty. "Of course that's the company charge. Our guy only gets part of it."

"Want to bet he still gets five times what we make? No wonder he can afford Weiss." Martinez scowled. "What now?"

"We got the court order for these things, we may as well check them all. Maybe by then the tech guys will have something to tell us about his files."

"What about his truck? Anything come up on that search?"

"I think it's still in processing." David flipped the phone up and pressed it to his ear. "Let me check." When he hung up ten minutes later he grimaced. "Nothing. Not one fingerprint besides Bobby's anywhere in the vehicle. Minuscule traces of semen in the front seat, not Bobby's, not any of the other vics, either."

"Probably the fudge packer's." Martinez scowled. "Getting off with guys in the front seat. Too bad patrol never caught him. A criminal record for indecent would have looked good for us right now." He slammed a hand down on the folders in front of him. "Woulda sullied his saintly reputation."

David felt like asking if he'd never fooled around with girls in his car. He knew the answer and he knew what Martinez would say, too. It wasn't the same thing. It was never the same thing.

David could visualize the look on Martinez's face if he faced him right now and said, "Guess what, I'm gay. I'm one of those fudge packers. A faggot."

But every time he imagined that conversation he shied away. He wasn't ready. He doubted he ever would be.

He envied Chris the ease with which he faced a hostile world and got on with his life. But it went beyond envy, didn't it? If he was honest with himself he wanted to do more than be like Chris.

But there wasn't room in his crowded closet for another man, no matter how attractive.

David picked up the phone and read off the number for Venice Savings and Loan.

"I'd like to speak with a Terrence Miller, please. Yes, I'll hold."

Martinez's phone rang. David heard his partner answer it, saw the thundercloud roll over his dark face, and finished up with Terrence as fast as he could. It was all the same story anyway. Chris had done his job efficiently and billed the hours he reported to DataTEK—no anomalies.

He half listened to Martinez's end of the conversation; it wasn't good. He leafed through another folder. This one was a different listing. He caught the name of a hotel chain at the same time Martinez slammed his phone down.

"God damn it, we can't cut a break." He stabbed a thick finger at the phone. "That was the lieut. Bellamere's lawyer is contesting the search warrants. He's got a judge looking at them right now. And those glasses you found in Bellamere's truck, the prints don't match Bellamere or Blake."

If the warrants got tossed, then anything they had secured from those searches would be thrown out. David knew it validated his belief that Chris was innocent. "Looks like we're barking up the wrong tree here, wouldn't you say?" David sighed at the look his partner gave him. "Have we even found anything? So far these searches have been a monumental waste of time."

"Not the point. How the hell can we do our job if these assholes can just have some stupid bleeding-heart judge toss it out on a whim."

David knew his frustrations were legitimate, but he also knew you had to learn to pick your fights.

"I'd hardly call someone else's prints nothing."

"I still think this guy's perfect for it. He's just cagier than most. Why the hell should we drop it?"

David glanced down at the folder he'd been half studying. A date caught his eye. He sat up. Then he reached for the murder book.

"When did Blake go missing? August?" David found the report. "July fifteenth. He was found Saturday morning, the nineteenth. No way his death occurred before Thursday."

"Okay, sure," Martinez said. "He was picked up Wednesday, the sixteenth. Killed the next day. What's your point?"

David slid the folder to the end of the desk. Reluctantly Martinez got up and they both looked down at the report. David tapped the relevant line.

"Christopher Bellamere booked a hotel room in Salt Lake City Sunday night for the entire week. He wasn't even in town when Blake was killed."

"Why are you so hot to clear this guy?"

"Why are you so hot to convict him?"

They glared at each other across David's desk.

"Call the Salt Lake City P.D.," David said. "Find out what you can about this conference. You find something that stinks, I'll stay on this with you. Otherwise—"

"You bailing on me, partner?"

"We got the wrong guy, Martinez."

"I don't believe it. Goddamn pansy freak did something, sure as shit."

"Jesus, you want to nail him because he's *gay*? Or because he's gay and doesn't try to hide it?"

"He's a freak, and he's been waving it in our faces that he's a freak. 'I'm gay. I have boyfriends.'" Martinez mimicked Chris's words in the interrogation room. "He's a sick fuck, is what he is. Hey, where you going?"

David couldn't listen anymore. He grabbed his jacket and cell phone off its charger.

"I'm going back to the Nosh Pit," he said, forcing himself to speak levelly. "I'm going to keep going back until I find someone who saw Blake leave with someone. I'm going to take a sketch artist out to the Jungle Arcade and get those kids to give me an eyewitness account of Anstrom's phony uncle. That's your killer. Not Chris. And I'm not wasting any more time hounding an innocent man. I don't care who he sleeps with."

CHAPTER 18

Tuesday, 10:00 P.M., Cove Avenue, Silver Lake, Los Angeles

CHRIS FLIPPED THROUGH the channels, restlessly looking for something to occupy his overstimulated mind. He'd spent half the day with Simon. The search warrant hadn't been quashed yet, but Simon seemed to think it was only a matter of time.

He was even going to get his SUV back tomorrow. Finally, at nearly five o'clock, he had called Petey and practically begged to keep his job. It had not been pretty. It probably hadn't even been necessary—Petey let slip toward the end of their conversation that he'd been advised by HR not to be too hasty in terminating an employee who hadn't been charged with anything.

Chris had nearly blown it then, but he'd bitten his tongue and kept the words inside, where they'd festered and given him a headache that persisted through the rest of the night.

Only now, three glasses of wine into the evening, had he managed to knock the headache back.

Finally he called Becky. She was on the way out the door with Clay, her live-in boyfriend.

"You coming in to work tomorrow?" she asked quietly.

"Petey and I have agreed that I should take the rest of the week off. It's about the only thing we ever have agreed on in the last six years—oh, that and the fact that I do still have a job."

"Oh, Chris, I'm glad." She let out a gust of air. "I was so sure he was gonna can you."

"You and me both. I still got the taste in my mouth."

"What taste?"

"Of Petey's ass. Jesus, and that was one butt I never wanted to touch in a million years."

"You are bad." She actually giggled. "Tommy's going to be one disappointed puppy. He was so sure you were history."

"So, what else did our cop friends do while they were there? Anything interesting?"

"They took your files."

"My files? What would they want those for? Check to see if I'm double billing?"

"Hey, you're a serial biller." The weak joke lay between them.

Chris loved her for it.

"They really must be desperate," she said. "I mean, what are they going to find on your PC? Links to support sites? Software patches. He's been doing his job too diligently, arrest him."

"Thanks, Beck."

Chris hung up and went on to spend the evening channel-surfing. Eventually he must have dozed off. When he jerked awake an ancient western was playing.

He wiped his mouth clean of sour drool and sat up on the love seat. He flicked the TV through a few more channels, but now it was either news or old movies and neither interested him tonight.

He finally gave up and climbed to his feet; his bare toes curled away from the cold tile in the kitchen. He rinsed his wine glass in the sink and set it on the draining board, then washed his mouth out with tepid water from the tap.

He was halfway up the earth-tone tiled stairs when someone started pounding on his front door.

Chris turned on the atrium light. He peered outside, dancing from foot to foot; the tile cold compared to the promised warmth of his carpeted bedroom.

It was David.

He was leaning against the inner courtyard wall, his tie

lying askew on his thick neck. His shirt looked like it had been unbuttoned, then done back up crooked. Dark hair peeked out from between buttons. He raised his hand to pound on the door again and nearly fell down the single stone step into the driveway.

David was drunk.

Opening the door carefully so as not to startle him, Chris waited for David to notice him. David tried to smile when he caught sight of him. It looked ghastly.

"Wasn't sure you'd be home," he said. "You're just like me, always working . . . workaholic. Kind of a two."

"You mean two of a kind?"

"Said that. You gonna let me in?"

David immediately wandered past him into the living room. Chris hoped he wasn't going to throw up or anything.

Chris went into the kitchen to put the kettle on. If ever someone needed coffee it was David. Whatever had possessed the guy to get drunk? More, whatever had possessed him to come *here*?

"The bathroom's through there—" Chris came out to find David nowhere in sight. He heard a banging sound upstairs. "Shit."

He took the stairs two at a time.

David was sitting on the edge of Chris's bed, his tie off completely, his shirt open to the waist. His chest was covered with a thick matt of black hair that thinned out over the soft mound of his stomach. He'd laid his gun belt over Chris's armoire. The belt to his cotton pants were open, revealing boxers underneath.

"What are you doing?" Chris asked.

"Well, aren't you gonna?"

"Going to what?" Chris watched the other man warily, unsure how he might react. Not sure what he was up to.

"Kiss me. I won't stop you this time."

Chris flushed. "No David, I'm not going to kiss you. I'm going to take you home."

"Don't wanna go home."

"You have to," Chris said, as if he were talking to a five- year-old. "You have to go to bed."

"Go to bed here." Awkwardly he patted the pillow beside him. "You can tuck me in." He tried to leer, but it came out as a grimace.

"David, what are you doing? Simon will kill me—I'm not supposed to talk to you—"

"Then don't talk—" David reached for him. "Don't you wanna take me to bed?"

"Jesus, David. What's got into you? Aren't you investigating me for this homicide?" What kind of trouble was David going to be in for this? Hell, what kind of trouble was *he* going to be in?

"Not anymore. Cleared you. Wrong person . . . "

Chris's jaw dropped. "What? Since when?"

"S'afternoon. You were in Salt-Salt-Utah. You were in Utah when Jay was sliced."

"Utah? That conference?" A wave of dizziness swept through him. "Jesus, I almost didn't go," he whispered. "I hate those things."

"Good thing for you. Perfect alibi. Got the wrong guy . . . Not even your fingerprints . . . Martinez still wants you, though. Had a fight over that. My own partner . . . God, if he knew . . . "

"Knew what, David?" Chris wanted to laugh aloud and jump up and down. He was off the hook. Then it clicked. "Martinez doesn't know you're gay, does he, David?"

David grimaced. "God, I hate that word." He twisted around to look up at Chris and tried to leer again. "But I like you. Want to fuck? I want to fuck you."

"Let's get you home, okay?" Chris tried to wrestle him up, but it was like lifting a two-hundred-pound sack of sand. He couldn't control the heavier man and David wouldn't do a thing to help. Every time Chris got near him David groped his crotch. It didn't help that Chris had a raging boner and David knew it.

Chris rocked back on his heels. "You have to go home, David. You're going to hate yourself in the morning if you don't."

“Wanted you to know. Not a suspect anymore.”

“Thank you, David. I appreciate that, you have no idea . . . but really, you have to go—”

“Sleep with me, Chris.”

“If you weren’t drunk, I’d be glad to, David.” Chris stroked his head, feeling the crisp hair curl under his fingers. “But you’d hate me in the morning. I’d hate me in the morning.”

“You probably think I’m some boring stick-in-the-mud rule follower.”

What could Chris say? David was a stickler for the rules. He wore his dress shirts buttoned up tight and never let his guard down. Chris wouldn’t necessarily say he was boring, but—

David cracked a yawn. He blinked at Chris. “I think I had too much.”

“Yeah, I think so,” Chris said gently. “You’re going to feel like shit tomorrow.”

“Sleep with me, Chris. I can’t stop thinking about you. Ever since you kissed me. Even when I was supposed to think of you as a suspect . . . ”

“Not tonight—get some sleep now, okay, big guy?”

Chris thought he was going to argue some more, but his body went limp. Chris wrestled him under the covers, pulling the duvet up to his shoulders. He gave the slumbering man a light kiss on the cheek. Already his soft snores filled the bedroom.

Chris padded back downstairs to his office, where he pulled out the small futon bed he kept for out-of-town guests. He grabbed a blanket and a set of sheets from the linen closet and crawled under the covers around two o’clock in the morning.

He wished he wasn’t so damned noble. David might be a stick in the mud, but he was turning out to be one of the most complex men Chris had ever known. He was also sexy in a way Chris couldn’t begin to explain. He just knew he wanted to go upstairs and crawl in beside him and find out what being fucked by David

Laine would be like.

A small sound awoke him. He looked up, blinking, to find David standing in the doorway staring down at him with flat, unreadable eyes. He was dressed again; even from the doorway Chris could smell the reek of alcohol coming off his clothes.

"How did I get here?"

"You don't remember?" Chris sat up, glad he had decided to wear pajamas last night. Normally he slept naked, but that hadn't seemed like a good idea with a drunk and overly amorous David in the house.

"If I remembered, would I ask?"

"You came banging on my door last night."

"What time was that?"

"Around one o'clock."

"My car's not in the driveway."

"I don't know how you got here." Chris shrugged. "You never said."

Suspicion darkened David's face. "Why didn't you just send me home? There's money in my wallet. You could have paid a cab."

Chris bristled. "I tried to get you out of here. You refused to go. I had no choice but to put you to bed." Chris untangled himself from the futon and stood. "Look, I'm going to make coffee. We can continue this discussion in the kitchen."

David put his hand on Chris's arm. "What happened last night, Chris?"

Chris snatched his arm away. "You mean did I take advantage of you? Fuck you, David."

Before he could respond, Chris shoved by him and stormed into the kitchen, where he banged around refilling the kettle and grinding coffee until his anger subsided.

David appeared in the kitchen doorway. He looked tired.

"I'm sorry, Chris," he said. "That was uncalled for."

"What's this about a fight with Martinez?"

"I told you that? Sorry, that was just stupid."

"You said I wasn't a suspect anymore, but Martinez didn't want to let it go. Is it because I'm gay?"

David winced. He rubbed his head. "Yeah, well Martinez has some problems with that."

"Martinez is a narrow-minded bigot." Big news there. David already knew that. He's the guy who had to live with it. Chris banged around in the cupboard, producing two mugs for his efforts. "Where did you go last night?"

"Some bar up in La Canada. Country and western place. I don't remember leaving. Next thing, I'm waking up in your bed, practically naked."

"If you'd had your way, you'd have been completely naked. And I'd have been there with you."

David blushed scarlet.

"Do me a big favor," Chris said. "Next time you come over, do it sober. Then I won't have to say no. I don't want to say no. I don't think you do either. Where does that leave us, David?"

"Maybe we need to talk."

"That sounds like a good start—"

"Is that coffee ready?" David rubbed his forehead again. "I could really use some."

Chris poured him a mug.

He sighed when he took his first sip. "Now I remember why I don't do that."

"Go on benders?"

"Right. Was I really bad?"

"Blotto. Totally and completely blotto. I've rarely seen anyone that stinking—"

"Okay, I get the picture." David set his mug down and looked around the kitchen. "Where's your phone? I have to call a cab."

"Let me give you a ride. I still got my rental. It's the least I can do after compromising you."

"Compromising—" His eyes narrowed. "According to you, we didn't do anything."

"I can fix that soon enough." Chris moved closer, grasped David's powerful arms, and drew him down until their mouths touched. "How about this?"

The passion that had burst between them the first time was still there, untamed. David tasted of coffee and mint; he had clearly taken advantage of Chris's mouthwash before he came downstairs. Chris groaned when David's hands moved down to his ass and pressed their growing erections together, proving the lust was not one-sided.

Chris murmured against his throat, "You sure you can't stay? I could make you breakfast. Wash your clothes for you. Take you to bed and ravish you."

David broke away, laughing shakily. "In that order?"

"Any order you like."

"This is getting too complicated."

"David—"

"I can't, Chris. Not now. Maybe not ever."

"Is it your partner?"

"It's everything. It's who I am."

"I don't think I like who you are very much."

"Sometimes neither do I."

Chris stared at him for several seconds. David looked away.

"Fine," Chris sighed. "Come on, let's go find your wheels. Jesus, I hope you can remember where this place is."

"A western bar in La Canada?" He shook his head. "This should be fun."

Wednesday, 11:30 A.M., Baptiste Way, La Canada, Los Angeles

It took them nearly two hours to track down the bar, a tiny, nondescript cinder-block building tucked behind a dirt parking lot near Foothill. It barely looked inhabited, but when they pulled into the lot at two minutes after ten, two Latino guys came out of the building. One of them carried two cases of empties out to a blue pickup.

"They here last night?" Chris asked as they watched the two dump the empties and head back, presumably for more.

"*I* barely remember being here last night," David said.

"This your car?"

Chris strolled around the '56 Chevy Two-Ten sport coupe David was struggling to restore. On his salary it was a project destined to take years. But Chris seemed to see beyond the damaged body and faded paint.

"Wow, haven't seen one of these in years. Where'd you find it? And what happened to that horrible Ford?"

"That's an LAPD car. I bought this from a guy in Palmdale two years ago."

"Beautiful. Hard to find parts?"

"There are places." David shrugged. "You into classics?"

"Go to all the shows. Unfortunately I'm mechanically challenged. I figure I'm doing pretty good to pump my own gas."

David laughed and unlocked the door. He reached in and popped the hood. They peered inside.

"I did a complete rebuild of the carburetor," David said, pointing out the piece. "The manifold's new, too."

Chris leaned in; their shoulders brushed and David could smell him. A pulse beat in his head. Maybe this wasn't such a good idea. But he didn't move away.

"I go to all the shows, too," David said. "When I can."

"Yeah? Which ones?"

Their eyes met. "Palm Springs. San Diego once. The L.A. shows, of course."

Chris swallowed. "Palm Springs is nice."

This was insane. Standing in the middle of a dusty parking lot in broad daylight and all David wanted to do was kiss this man. Where had all his discipline gone? All his hardwon resolve?

Chris's phone rang. David jerked back. He slammed the hood down and retreated to the open door and got in the car.

"Des, how's it going—"

Even from where he sat, David could hear Chris's friend. Chris tried to break in but Des wasn't letting up.

"I'll try—"

Des's voice dropped and Chris hunched over the phone, straining to hear. Beginning to look worried.

"Des—"

Chris stared at his cell. With a low curse he shut it off and met David's gaze.

"Trouble?" David asked.

Chris started to shake his head, then stopped. "Kyle's disappeared."

"Kyle—oh, right. Des's friend. What do you mean, disappeared?"

"He called me the other night from Santa Monica. He thought someone was following him." Chris shrugged, an uneasy gesture. "I told him I'd come get him but when I got there I couldn't find him."

"When was this?"

"Yesterday." Chris bent down, leaning his elbows on the window's lip. "Do me a favor?"

Warily David met his eyes. "What?"

"Can you do anything for him?" Chris held up his hand, palm out. "We already filed a report with the Santa Monica Police, but I could tell they were giving us the brush-off."

David opened his mouth to say something, but Chris didn't give him a chance.

"Kyle had no reason to run away. And he was being followed. Des is worried."

"Chris, I don't know—"

"Just run one of your checks, can you?"

"You mean check the morgues? The hospitals?"

Chris winced and looked away. When he looked back his face was pale but stoic. "Yes. If that's what it takes."

"I'll see what I can do."

"Thanks," Chris said quietly. He smiled. "Let's hope I'm wasting your time."

"Sure."

Chris patted the side of the Chevy. "You'll have to take me for a ride sometime."

"Ah, sure." David settled both hands on the worn steering wheel. "We can do that."

"Have dinner with me tonight, David."

"I don't know if that's a good idea." Hell, he knew it wasn't. Could he really spend the evening with this guy and keep it safe?

"Dinner, David. What's the harm in that?"

David looked at him like he was crazy. He should know just being in the same room raised thoughts that David had long ago forsworn. He squeezed the wheel in his big hands.

"Okay," he said, knowing it was a big mistake, but beginning to feel like a moth in front of a brilliant flame. "Dinner."

"Hermosa Beach," Chris said. His fingers caressed the ivory door panel. "You can drive. Pick me up at my place, six?"

"Six, sure."

David slammed the door shut with a solid *thunk*. He rolled the window down and propped his elbow on the lip.

"Tonight then."

He drove off the lot in a plume of dust.

"Brilliant," David muttered. "Absolutely brilliant."

His cell phone rang.

It was Martinez. "I got a positive I.D. on our first John Doe. Meet me at the station in thirty minutes."

Traffic was heavy leaving Verdugo; he saw the flashing lights of the California Works Department ahead of him. Heat shivered off the stalled traffic and blacktop. He wasn't getting anywhere in thirty minutes. The work crew stood around looking into a hole they had made in the ground, while their machinery stood by idle. Nobody was moving in the torpid heat.

David calculated how long it would take to get home and have a quick shower and change his clothes.

"Make it ninety minutes. I'm stuck in traffic."

"Ninety then." Martinez clicked off.

In his rearview he saw Chris two cars behind him in the left lane. All his windows were rolled up and even from here he looked cool and unruffled in his air-conditioned car. A guy who had it all.

Who was David kidding? He did have it all, and then some. Of what interest would a closeted cop at least ten years his senior be to a man like that?

David sighed and leaned over to crank the other window down. It didn't help much, but it was better than nothing. He turned on the radio and caught the tail end of Garth Brooks wailing on about walking in the fire. Then it was Patsy Cline's turn.

•

"This one disappeared out of Silver Lake in early July. No doubt there, according to his numerous friends." Martinez sucked on a mint, scowling. "And no doubt about which way he swung. Found his roommate and he was happy to give up these."

Martinez handed over a pair of three-by-fives. They showed another slender guy with dark hair cut short and streaked. He was dressed in leather. At least he was partly dressed, as Martinez was quick to point out.

"Get a look at that outfit. Can you believe they wear that shit?"

David hadn't seen too many men in full leather regalia. In his experience they were a private bunch who kept to their own clubs and rarely wore their gear in public. This one had on leather chaps over bare skin—only a leather pouch covered his genitals. A harness studded with metal rings, exposing a well-muscled chest, covered his upper body. Both nipples were pierced. Dark eyes peered out from under a stiff leather cap. In one picture a pair of black shades dangled from his fingers. In the second one he had donned the mirrored sunglasses to put the finishing touch on the ensemble. He looked like something out of a Kafka western.

David glanced down at the missing-person report Martinez had dug up. Jeff Charette. Apartment in Newport Beach at the time he went missing. Twenty-three. The oldest identified victim so far.

"His friends know where he hung out?"

Martinez flipped through his notes. "Couple of places. Joint called the Gauntlet. Silver Lake. Another one in West Hollywood."

"Guess we plan a visit." Again he studied the report. "Missing somewhere between the thirtieth of June and the first of July. Body found July third. Dead at least twenty-four hours at that point."

"If our perp went by his standard MO then he was held several hours." Martinez narrowed his dark eyes and chewed fiercely on his mint as he glared at David. "We? What do you mean 'we'?"

"Wouldn't want you to miss anything."

"Thanks, *partner*. Has anyone informed the sheriff's department about this? This guy seems to be operating in their backyard just as freely as he is in ours."

"Lieutenant says they're apprised and they're willing to share the investigation, but they figure it's our call. Body dumps are ours, no way to know where the perp's stashing them, but unless we can prove he's doing them in West Hollywood—"

"—they want no part of it."

David shrugged. "It's a political hot potato no one wants to catch."

"I know how they feel. 'We,' huh? *Madre de dios*, my mother would be turning over in her grave if she could see her eldest son now."

•

From the outside, the Gauntlet didn't look like much. Plain dark brick and a door curtained with a heavy black cloth. Martinez stood on the sidewalk and stared at it as if it was the entrance to a man-eating dragon's lair.

David pushed the curtain aside. Beside him Martinez hitched up his purple herringbone pants and followed.

The instant they were inside David could smell the old reek of hops, stale sex, and cigar smoke.

The interior of the club was deliberately dark and secretive. Light came from wall sconces and a pair of fluorescent lights above the bar. There were a lot of wood-paneled walls posted with images of men. The bartender was a tall, narrow-hipped guy in full leather, including a peaked hat on his hairless head. No pierced nipples on this one, but he did have a black and gold leather dog collar around his neck and several gold earrings in both earlobes.

He watched them approach with flat brown eyes.

"*Dios*." Martinez breathed shallowly through his mouth. His eyes didn't stop anywhere for long.

David took in the long mahogany bar on one side and the narrow row of small tables crammed along the opposite wall.

Acres of glass surrounded a tiled dance floor that wasn't much bigger than a kitchen table but was already packed with at least a dozen men writhing to the deep bass that thundered out of hidden speakers. Lights bounced off the mirrored walls and the watchful patrons, most of whom had gigged themselves up in leather.

David stared at a tall black guy leaning against the bar who wore nothing but chaps and a leather thong that did a poor job of concealing his equipment. David could even make out the cock ring the guy wore. His body was hairless and oiled, showing off his sculptured ebony chest and tight abs.

His eyes met David's and held them. He showed white teeth

in a smile that completely unnerved David. As if he knew David's secrets. Even the ones he barely acknowledged. He broke out in a hot sweat.

Everyone in the bar watched them. Especially Martinez, who along with the purple pants sported a loud yellow and green plaid blazer that had to be one of the ugliest things David had ever seen. Add to that a wide, purple tie and he definitely stood out in this field of cowhide.

"Help you?" the bartender asked.

David and Martinez both flipped out their gold shields. Then David pulled out the police-artist sketch he had had prepared from Digger and Ant's descriptions of Anstrom's phony uncle the day before and showed it to the bartender. "Have you ever seen this man?"

The bartender sucked on the ragged end of his Fu Manchu mustache. "Maybe," he drawled. "Not a regular."

"When did you see him?"

"Didn't say I did, now did I?" the bartender said. "Just . . . maybe."

"Ever see him with anyone?"

The bartender shrugged. "Maybe. Who pays attention?"

"How long you worked here?" Martinez leaned his bulk over the bar, crowding the bartender's space. "Most bartenders I know, they don't miss anything that goes on in their place."

The bartender looked Martinez up and down, unfazed by his nearness. "I don't think we travel in the same circles, friend. I run a place where guys come in, have a few drinks, maybe meet new people."

Martinez sneered. "Pollyanna's dating service." He looked around the crowded bar. "If I was to start carding guys, what do you think I might find?"

"That a threat?"

"Sure it's a threat," Martinez said. "How come no one ever

recognizes plain old police threats anymore?"

"We just came to ask some questions. Let's start with your name."

"Barry Lakowski. What's this about, anyway?"

"Can you recall when this man"—David tapped the police sketch—"was in here? Any regular customers interact with him? You see him leave with anyone? Nothing too difficult there, right?"

"Like I said, he's not a regular. He might have come in a while ago." He glared at Martinez. "If he left with someone, that's what they come here for."

"Did he ever appear to be helping anyone? Maybe somebody got sick all of a sudden?"

"Sick?"

"Sick, falling down drunk, that kind of thing."

"I cut people off all the time they have too much. Take their keys if I have to."

"But what if someone offered to take the guy home? Anyone going to object to that?"

Behind him, Martinez approached the nearest table along the wall. He dropped something among the litter of beer bottles and shooters and leaned in close.

"What's he doing?" Barry asked in alarm.

"Showing some people pictures." David tried not to show his dismay once he realized whose picture Martinez was flashing around. "See if anyone can I.D. them."

Martinez left the table and approached the bar again. He laid the six images of Chris and the others out and invited the bartender to study them.

"Ever see any of these guys in here before?"

Martinez didn't object when a couple of leather-clad men crowded close to the bar to peer at the pictures. David could smell their aftershave and sweat.

Barry looked confused. David tapped the sketch. "I need you to try to remember when you last saw him."

"What this guy do, anyway? Kill someone?" Barry laughed.

Neither David or Martinez joined him.

"Christ," Barry said.

David tried not to watch Martinez in his determination to prove Chris guilty. "Give him to me, Barry. When was he here?"

Sliding his leather cap off his head, revealing a recently shaved scalp, Barry stared at the sketch, then to David's dismay he glanced back at the image of Chris that lay on top of the six-pack of pictures.

"I know the face." He cocked his head. "But not recently. I'd have to say it's been at least a couple of months."

Martinez pulled out his notebook. "Really?" he murmured. "Two and a half months ago . . . That was Jeff Charette."

"Who?"

David reluctantly dug out the two pictures of the leather-clad Charette and dropped them on top of the sketch.

Barry paled.

"What are you doing with those?"

"You know him?" Martinez leaned over the bar. "He come in here?"

"Regularly." Barry frowned. "At least he used to. Haven't seen him in a while."

"How long's a while?"

"A month, maybe six weeks."

"Mid-June? July?"

"Could have been." Barry's gaze fell back on the police artist's sketch. He frowned.

"Anything unusual happen the last night you saw Jeff?"

"Like what?"

"I don't know, you tell me."

Barry tugged at his bottom earring. Then his face grew pinched. "Jeff must have been putting the screwdrivers away too fast. Usually he's not a heavy drinker, but he got totally wasted that night. I was gonna take his keys, but this guy he was drinking with said he'd take him home."

Bingo. "And you knew this guy hadn't been drinking so you were happy to see Jeff taken care of."

"Didn't see any harm in it? Why? What are you telling me?"

"Know where we can get in touch with this guy?" David tapped the sketch. He kept his voice casual. "Got a name on him? Anything?"

Barry shook his head violently. "He never gave me a name. Who is this guy? What the hell is this about?"

"How often was he here?"

"Once, twice maybe." Barry was starting to look worried. "Does this have something to do with the fact that Jeff's never come back? What happened?"

"Jeff Charette is dead. His body was found July third, but was only identified recently."

Barry grew even paler. His gaze fell on the sketch, then skated over to the picture of Chris. He frowned. "And you think one of these guys had something to do with it?"

"We don't know that, sir. We need to talk to them is all."

At the other end of the bar someone rapped the counter. "Hey, Barry, you stopped working for the night? We're dry down here."

Barry jumped, but then he seemed to welcome the interruption. David waved him off.

"Go on, if we have any other questions, we'll find you."

A grateful Barry moved off down the bar.

Martinez scooped up the sketch. "I'm going to call down a couple of D's, get them canvassing the area for any other wits." Martinez slapped the pictures. "Told you we'd get him, partner." Then he seemed to catch something on David's face. He narrowed his dark eyes. "Something wrong?"

David glanced at his watch, knowing he had to escape from

Martinez. It was nearly five. "I have some personal business to take care of. Catch up with you later?"

"Sure. Personal, heh? Got a hot date?"

David thought of Chris. He shook his head. "No, it's not like that." Even as the traitorous thought came: *I wish it were.*

"Sure." Martinez grinned. "I believe you. Thousands wouldn't."

"Glad to have a partner who trusts me."

"Hey, I trust you." Martinez clapped David on the back. "Do me a favor, amigo. At least *try* to get lucky, okay?"

Martinez gathered everything up and shoved it back into his briefcase.

"Come on," he said. "Call the station and get those D's assigned. Then you go take care of your personal business. If I don't see you till tomorrow morning, I'll understand, really."

David followed him out the door, trying to ignore his crude laughter. Wishing he hadn't said anything.

Already looking forward to seeing Chris again.

CHAPTER 19

Wednesday, 1:45 P.M., Police Impound Lot, East Commercial Street, Los Angeles

UNDER THE WATCHFUL glare of two uniformed cops, Chris was shown to his impounded SUV. He popped the door and instantly backed off as a wave of chemical fumes enveloped him. The younger of the two cops smirked.

"They use heated superglue to lift prints." The cop was still grinning at his discomfort.

"Superglue?" Chris sniffed again. He recognized the smell now. "Great, so I get stoned on the drive home."

"I suggest you keep your windows down until you hit the freeway, sir." The sneer was obvious now. The cop was baiting him. "Don't stop to pick up anybody."

Meaning what? Jesus, were they telling him they were going to follow him?

Chris suppressed the temptation to flip them the bird as he wheeled out of the lot. The drive home seemed interminable as he struggled to breathe shallowly to avoid the heavy fumes.

At home he showered and shaved, then took his time selecting his outfit. As he stood in front of his overstuffed closet, frowning over what he should wear, he wondered why he was going to such lengths for this guy. There was nothing special about David. Chris wasn't a cop groupie, attracted to the uniform and the gun, like some guys he knew.

Not that Chris wanted a relationship with anyone. He was happy playing the field. Safe, anonymous sex. No strings. That suited him just fine.

Sure it did.

He finally settled on a tight-fitting pair of black denim Diesels and a body-molding Izod shirt in soft yellow that he knew set off his skin tone. He moussed his hair and spiked it with stiff fingers, which emphasized his blond streaks, full mouth, and high cheekbones.

He looked good. Would David think so?

He was halfway out of the bedroom when the phone rang. He scooped it up. Silence greeted his hello. The caller I.D. window said only unknown number, unknown name.

A soft knock broke through his preoccupation.

David.

He took the stairs two at a time and flung the front door open just as David got ready to knock again.

He looked like he had just stepped out of the shower. His dark, curly hair was still damp. He had changed, too, out of his usual suit and tie to a pair of simple navy linen pants and a crisp pale-blue shirt. No tie. The shirt was open at the throat and the tight curls of his chest hair peaked through.

Chris wanted to lean over and bury his face in it.

David took in Chris's lean form and his eyes darkened. He licked his lips and looked away when he realized Chris was watching.

"Ready?" he asked.

In the driveway David's Chevy coupe ticked and pinged as it cooled.

"See you got your truck back," David said as they slid into the bench seat of the coupe.

"Oh yeah," Chris muttered. "Superglue and all."

"What?"

"Never mind." He'd left the windows of the SUV down an inch on either side, figuring eventually the chemical reek would fade. "You like curry?"

"Thai or Indian?"

Chris grinned. "I think you can do both at this place. It's pretty eclectic."

Hermosa Beach was south of Marina del Rey. A tiny beach community sandwiched between Manhattan Beach and Redondo, it was less well known than its kitschy cousin Venice or more upscale Santa Monica.

The restaurant was run by an Indian couple, but the chef was Thai. Chris ordered a bottle of Australian Chardonnay and they munched on crisp fried pappadums as they studied the handwritten menu board. The restaurant filled up rapidly and over the soft flow of piped-in flute music the noise level rose and the delicious smells of cumin, garlic, and curries scented the evening air.

David ordered lamb curry. Chris chose Kerala chicken.

Talk was light, never moving beyond the weather, the promise of another nasty fire season, and the last car show they had both been to. Only when their meal arrived and they fell to eating in earnest did Chris venture a question.

"You find anything?"

"About Des's friend?" David shook his head. "I did run some checks on local emergency rooms."

Chris played with the base of his wine glass. Finally he raised his head and met David's gaze. "What about the other places . . . "

"Morgues? No John Does that come close to matching Kyle."

"Good. That's good, right?" Chris sipped his wine. He suddenly didn't want to talk about Kyle. Changing the subject, he said, "You find out any more about Bobby?"

David fished a piece of lamb out of his rice and dipped it in yogurt. "We talked to his sister."

Chris avoided David's gaze. "She able to tell you anything?"

"His parents live in Topeka, Kansas. They're on their way in to claim the body."

Chris sipped his wine.

"You're not involved in this anymore, Chris, so stay away from it."

"Your partner ready to do the same?"

Chris knew he'd hit a sore spot when David winced. "We found a better lead today. He'll come around."

"You got a suspect?"

David scowled. "I can't say. You can answer one question for me," he said.

"Sure. What?"

"What were those glasses doing in the back of your SUV? They weren't yours. So whose are they?"

"Glasses?" Suddenly Chris burst out laughing. "Those things? They were a Halloween gag. I wore them to look like a geek. Why? Who did you think they belonged to?"

"Jason Blake."

"Jay?" Chris felt the blood draining from his face. "Is that why you suspected me?"

"If figured into the evidence. Forget it."

Chris managed to scoop the bill when it came and ignored David's frown when he fished out his American Express card and handed it over to the obsequious waiter.

Once they were back outside Chris turned away from where David's car was parked. If this had been West Hollywood, or even Silver Lake, he might have grabbed David's hand, but he settled for walking close by his side. They drew near a pink and mauve building with signs and crowds lined up outside. Half the crowd carried massive hand-dipped ice-cream cones. The signs said it all: "We make the best ice cream in the world!"

"Hey, you want to spend money on me, buy dessert. Something with pralines and fudge and lots of caramel."

David got in line and twenty minutes later returned carrying two cones. He handed one to Chris, who swirled his tongue agilely around the dripping mound of ice cream. David had already started on his chocolate cone.

Chris eyed his choice. "At least it's not vanilla."

"What?"

"Never mind. Let's walk down by the beach."

The sun was just slipping behind a haze of offshore pollution and the masts of a dozen sailboats heading back to the marina. They stayed back on the boardwalk, away from the sand until Chris finished his cone. He reached down and slipped off his Dockers and socks. He rolled his jeans up a couple of inches.

"Come on, let's go down to the water."

David hesitated only a minute, then followed suit. Shoes and socks in hand they stepped onto the cooling sand and within minutes were at the water's edge.

A gentle surf hissed and rolled over the golden sand, darkened at the surf line. Water splattered Chris's legs, sand flecked his ankles and encased his toes.

"Now you can't get back in my car," David said.

"Oh yeah?" Chris leaned down and threw a handful of water at David, who laughed and jumped back. A spray of sand coated his hairy legs. "Now we're even."

David stamped his feet, but it only scattered more sand around his ankles. Finally he shook his curly head and shoved Chris toward the open ocean.

"Go soak your head."

"Only if you come in with me."

David looked regretful. He turned away from the ocean. "Not tonight. I have to get back to work."

Chris had been expecting that. He sighed but followed David back up the beach. "What about this weekend? You can't work all the time."

"Depends on this case. It's not my weekend on call, but we're working some hot leads. This is no time to take it easy."

"Man, you gotta rest."

David rubbed his face with his free hand and didn't speak.

They walked along the boardwalk awhile, finally sitting down on a vacant bench to pull socks and shoes back on. Chris wiggled his toes to clear most of the sand off. He could still feel the grit even after his feet were encased in leather again.

Streetlights came on as they headed back to David's car. The crowds thinned, but Chris still walked close, his hip brushing David's occasionally.

Back in the car, David cut over to Aviation Boulevard and headed north, eventually joining the stream of taillights on the Santa Monica Freeway. Once they settled into traffic, Chris slipped his seat belt off and scooted over on the bench seat, settling his head on David's shoulder, his left hand on the other man's knee.

"I forgot how much fun these kind of seats are. Wonder why they stopped making them."

"Put your seat belt back on."

"I'd rather hold on to you."

"Chris—"

Chris compromised and used the middle set. His hand went back to David's knee.

"Better?"

David didn't answer. The tension in his big body was palpable.

Chris wasn't going to let him go back into his shell so easily. "You have fun tonight?"

No answer.

"David?"

"Yeah," he said. "I had fun. But I'm not going to make a habit of this. I like you, Chris, but this can't go anywhere—"

"We can see how it's going to play out. Give us that much at least."

They cut through Century City, then David turned onto Sunset. Forty minutes later they were on Silver Lake Boulevard. Ten minutes after that he pulled into Chris's driveway. The engine died with a choking grunt.

"Thanks for dinner—"

David's lips were open when Chris pressed his mouth down on them. He groaned when David's tongue joined his. Instantly his hand was between David's legs, stroking his growing hardness.

He broke free long enough to ask, "Come in for coffee."

"I can't." David's breath was warm and still tasted of ice cream with just a hint of curry.

"Just for a little bit." Without giving him any chance to object, Chris had David's fly open and was holding him. Then he was tasting him and he didn't taste at all like ice cream.

The steering wheel bumped his head more than once but Chris didn't care. David moaned Chris's name and held his head with hands that shook. Then just as abruptly it was over. David sagged back against the vinyl seat, breathing hard.

"You shouldn't have done that," David said.

"I want to do a lot more than that. Come in with me. I'll make coffee—"

"I can't."

"Oh God, David. Don't brush me off."

"I'm not. I won't."

"Let me call you then. This weekend. Tell me when."

At first he thought David wasn't going to say anything, then he twined shaky fingers through Chris's.

"Saturday night. I'm getting tickets to an Angels game. Martinez sometimes goes with me, but he's got family in town this weekend. You like baseball?"

Chris hated sports. But he wasn't about to tell David that. For a chance to spend a few hours together he'd tolerate just about anything.

"Sure. What time?"

"Game starts at six. I'll pick you up at five."

"I'll be ready." He started to get out of the car, then he suddenly turned and jammed his mouth down on David's. Then: "Will you come in for coffee after?"

"I don't know. I'll see."

Chris had to be content with that. He waited in the driveway until David's taillights vanished down the street. Then he let himself into his empty house. The message light was blinking on his phone, but when he went to listen, all he heard was the soft swish of traffic in the background. Nobody spoke. Not even heavy breathing.

"Can't even get a decent obscene phone call."

He stared at the phone as though something more interesting would come on it if he waited. Finally he gave up and erased the non-message. Then he had another shower and went to bed.

•

After a restless night of achingly erotic dreams Chris dragged himself out of bed just after nine o'clock. He had barely plugged the kettle in for coffee when his BlackBerry vibrated. It was Petey.

"We've got a problem, Bellamere."

"We do? Pray tell."

"Becky was supposed to go to Colorado next week. Now she's got some kind of family emergency and can't make it."

Chris knew what was coming, but his first rule of business with Petey was "Never make things easy for the man."

"I need a representative there."

"Okay," he dragged the word out. "And just how does this become my problem?"

"I want you to go in her place."

"To Colorado?"

"Denver."

"I hate the mountains. All that thin air."

"Your flight leaves at nine, Sunday night. Becky's already emailed you the itinerary. The main item is meeting Tamura Yamamoto, the CEO of Tand-Howser. They're opening an office in L.A. and we're in talks about setting up their infrastructure. But I want the maintenance contract, too. It's your job to convince him we can do the best job."

Chris rolled his eyes. "Is that all?"

"Becky had some conferences booked, too. They'll be in her notes. I think she said the full itinerary was online. If there are other conferences you want, maybe you can switch to them. But take that meeting with Yamamoto."

Chris turned off the phone. He poured boiling water through the Melitta and went in to check his email. Sure enough, there were a couple from Becky. One was her itinerary, the other gave the link to the conference Web site. Chris spent half an hour perusing the site, booking a couple of seminars that were more interesting than what Becky had chosen. Finally he printed off the entire itinerary and stuffed it into his laptop case.

After his second coffee, he called Simon and told him about his conversation with David. At least the parts that related to the case. Simon seemed pleased, but still insisted on pushing through the motion to quash the search warrants. "In case there is any change of heart later on," he said.

"David and I talked last night," Chris said. "He says I'm not a suspect anymore."

"It is not a good idea, Christopher, talking to the police. Do us both a favor. Let *me* decide when to speak to them."

"I don't know if I can do that anymore."

"Is something going on I should know about, Christopher?"

"David's gay," Chris blurted out. "We're . . . seeing each other."

"This could change things. You realize that, don't you?"

"For who?"

Simon didn't answer. He didn't need to; Chris knew. If it hurt anyone, it was going to be David.

Damn, why did everything have to be so complicated?

•

The message light on his phone was blinking when he returned from picking up some papers Simon wanted him to read and sign before Monday. Call display said the last call had come from Des.

Immediately he called back, but only got the answering machine. At seven the same machine tried to take another message from him.

"Shit." Chris slammed the phone down. Had Des heard from Kyle? Had this all been one of Kyle's prima donna stunts? The least Des could do was leave a message.

At seven-thirty the phone rang and Chris snatched it up before it could ring a second time. Call display again said it was Des.

"Damn it, man, I've been calling—"

Heavy breathing and the background hiss of a bad connection.

"Des?"

Silence. Then the breathing started again. Thick and labored, like someone had been running a long distance.

"Okay, Kyle. What's the game? Put Des on—"

The phone went dead. He hit recall and Des's number popped up on the display. It rang and rang, but no one answered.

A chill marched up Chris's bare arms. Without another thought he grabbed his BlackBerry and car keys, and ran out of the house, barely pausing to lock up behind himself.

The SUV still smelled faintly of superglue. It took him over forty minutes to reach Des's place. The house was wrapped in shadows when he wheeled into an empty spot in front.

Des's Mercedes sat in the narrow driveway, nose up to the gate that led to the backyard. Chris stared at Kyle's Boxster parked behind it. He dragged his gaze away and looked toward the house.

The inner door was open. The screen door unlocked. No one answered his knock.

Chris speed-dialed the number and listened to the phone ring in the living room. He glanced again at both cars in the driveway. He was in Beverly Hills. No one walked anywhere in Beverly Hills.

Inside, the machine picked up and Des's voice invited him to leave a message. He hung up.

The screen door opened silently and he stepped into the cool foyer. Past the brass mirror dominating the foyer, around the tight corner into the crowded living room.

Which was even more crowded than usual.

Kyle sat in the spindly Louis XIV chair, his open eyes staring at the poster-covered wall. Only, Kyle was past seeing anything. A strip of silver duct tape had been wrapped around his face, gagging him. His death had been a silent one. As Chris watched, a fly landed on Kyle's unblinking eye and wandered around pausing now and then to sample.

One of Kyle's hands had fallen off the arm of the chair, the open fingers brushing the Kashmir rug. A line of blood dribbled down his index finger, soaking into the knotted wool fiber. A second fly alighted on Kyle's bare chest. More blood marred the once smooth, hairless skin. Some of it had pooled in his crotch.

Chris smelled blood and something nastier underlying it. In death Kyle had voided his bowels.

Chris choked back a cry. His hand went to his mouth, as his stomach slammed into his throat. He backpedaled out of the room and managed not to throw up until he was outside in the blessedly hot industrial-stink beyond Des's door.

On his knees he vomited into the nearest boxwood. A car crawled down the street. He ignored it as he fumbled with his cell.

"Laine here." David's voice had never sounded sweeter.

"Oh God, David. It's Kyle . . . He's . . . It's—You have to come. Now."

Thursday, 7:50 P.M., North Palm Drive, Beverly Hills

David skidded his unmarked to an angled stop in front of Chris's SUV. The usually quiet residential street was crowded with Beverly Hills cop cars and the coroner's wagon. There were also a pair of EMTs on the sidelines in case any injured parties showed up.

According to Chris, Des was missing. He spotted Chris sitting in the back seat of a black-and-white, talking to a uniformed officer. Further talk with him would have to wait.

Inside the crowded house David found the on-site criminalist and the crime-scene investigation team who did contract work for the county processing the living room. Chris had already I.D.'d the body—a single glance confirmed it.

So where was Des?

A man approached him in the foyer. David held up his gold shield and the other man nodded. They shook hands.

"Ernie Copland, Detective second grade, Beverly Hills."

"Detective David Laine, LAPD What's it look like?" David asked.

"Bad domestic. We're getting a statement from the guy who called it in. No weapon found on him, but my guess is we'll find it nearby. We're bringing in dogs."

"Have you been able to contact the owner?" David thought of Des's car in the driveway. "The Mercedes belongs to him, the other car belongs to the vic."

Copland frowned. "You're familiar with these people?"

David glanced at Kyle's bloodstained body. "Yes." He decided not to elaborate.

Copland jerked his head toward the front door. "Our caller admits being close to the missing home owner. Says he followed the vic into Santa Monica the other day. He's not saying, but I'll hazard we'll find it was your typical gay triangle. He offed the vic to eliminate the competition."

"Have you talked to him yet?"

"One of my men spoke with him. Claims he got a phone call that spooked him and he came over to see for himself what was going on, walked in on this."

David kept his voice flat. "You don't believe him?"

"You don't think it was a domestic?"

"Can I talk to them?" David indicated the C.S.I. people bent over Kyle's body.

"What are you looking for?"

"I'll tell you if I find it."

The criminalist, a young Asian David recognized from other crime scenes, looked up at his approach. David nodded down at the body.

"What can you tell me?" he asked.

"What's your interest?"

David studied the wound pattern on Kyle's exposed skin. He frowned. "I'm working the Carpet Killer—you familiar?"

The criminalist nodded.

"So what have you got here?"

The criminalist stripped off his bloody gloves and pulled on a second pair. The first pair went into a disposal bag beside their equipment case.

"Extensive piquerism is evidenced in the cuts on the upper torso. He was raped, but it looks like a condom, or condoms, were used. Severe anal tearing is also consistent, I believe—"

David nodded. "It is. We've seen the duct tape before, too. Sometimes he needs to keep them quiet. Anything strike you as unusual?"

The criminalist waved toward a pair of C.S.I. techs collecting something off the carpet near the sofa. "Blood. On the arm of the sofa and floor. Not spatter, it dripped from someone sitting on the sofa."

"A second victim?"

"We'll have to type it to be sure."

The C.S.I. techs waved a light wand slowly over the back of the sofa, then the seat. Looking for more blood.

Des's blood? Or the killer's?

"Our perp's never taken out two before," David said. "This is a radical change in his M.O."

"Don't know about that," the criminalist said. "All I know is, I'm thinking there were three people here. One of them was wearing latex—and he used the phone after he worked on this guy." He indicated Kyle's body. "Handset tests positive for his blood."

"Guy who found the body got a nonresponsive phone call from this residence. Came over to check, that's how he found the vic."

"This guy wanted him to find his friend."

"Looks that way."

"Nice guy."

"You have no idea." David sighed. "No sign of what happened to our second bleeder?"

"He's not here. We searched the house top to bottom and they're taking a dog through the backyard. Nothing."

"Could he have walked away?"

"Not with this kind of blood loss."

David walked back to where Copland was talking to one of the C.S.I. techs. They both looked up at this approach.

"Find what you were looking for?"

David nodded brusquely. "I think we're looking at the Carpet Killer."

"I thought he usually dumped his bodies. You've never found the kill site before."

"That's what's got me worried. I think our guy's decompensating fast."

A uniformed officer entered the house and approached Copland. The two spoke briefly. Copland waited for him to leave before he turned back to David.

"It looks like the vic's car was towed recently. Gibes with what the witness claims about the car going missing in Santa Monica." Copland rubbed his chin. "You think Desmond Hayward's been taken hostage by this Carpet Killer?"

"Maybe. More likely he means Des to be his next plaything. He usually likes to hold them several hours. Take his time."

"We're canvassing the neighborhood," Copland said. "Hopefully someone saw something. It's quiet, though. Not many people answering their doors."

The Asian criminalist entered the room. He was stripping off yet another pair of gloves. He held on to them.

"There are three blood types present," he said. "Someone fought back and the perp was injured. Left his blood on the floor by the body."

David perked up. "We can get a DNA match then?"

"We can."

David headed for the front door. Copland followed.

"My men will keep asking around."

"Good." From the door, David could see Chris still sitting in the black-and-white. "Mind if I talk to the wit?"

Copland waved him forward. "Go ahead. Gallagher's probably almost done, anyway."

Gallagher was done. Chris caught sight of David and flew out of the backseat. His handsome face was marred with tears and his skin was chalky white. He touched David's arm and it was all David could do not to grab him and wrap him in a safe embrace.

"I'm sorry, Chris. Let's go someplace and talk."

They slid into the front seat of David's unmarked.

"Can you tell me about it?" David said gently.

"Oh, God, David. Where's Des? That guy was trying to tell me he thought Des did that. Are they nuts? Des would never hurt anyone. He loved Kyle."

"It wasn't Des."

Chris froze and stared at David. "Then what—Jesus, do they think I did it?

"No!" David touched his face, trying to give him strength for what he had to tell him. "I think Des was taken."

"Who is it, David? Who did this?"

David grabbed Chris's cold hands in both of his. He no longer cared who might be watching. He forced Chris to meet his gaze.

"I think it's the Carpet Killer."

Chris stared at him blankly. In an instant David saw how he would look in twenty years.

"Des . . . Is he?"

David shook his head. "I don't know. Do you want to go home now?"

When Chris nodded, David left him and went in search of Copland. He found him back in the house, talking on a cell. He hung up when David appeared.

David handed him one of his cards. "I'm taking Mr. Bellamere home. I was planning on staying with him awhile, so if you have any other questions, call this number. If anything else comes to him, I'll let you know."

Copland's cool, measuring look made David wonder what the man suspected. What he was proposing wasn't exactly S.O.P. He was surprised at how little he cared.

"I'm going to call my partner, too," David said. "Apprise him of the latest activity. Between us maybe we can come up with something."

Copland nodded and turned away. "We'll be in touch."

David left.

Chris hadn't moved. David slid in beside him and started the motor of the unmarked. "You want someone to bring your truck around later?"

"What? Oh, sure. I guess." Chris stared out the window toward Des's house.

David touched his knee. "Give me the keys. I'll have it brought up to your place."

"Sure . . . " Chris fumbled in his pocket and dropped the SUV's keys in David's hand.

"You have house keys?"

"Yeah, I'm fine."

It took David five minutes to find an officer who promised to drive the truck to Silver Lake later that evening. He'd leave the keys in the mailbox.

At Chris's place David took the house keys from Chris's limp hand and led him through the gated courtyard. He unlocked the door, then aimed Chris at the alarm system so that he could punch in the code, commenting, "I don't think you want Securicor coming up here for a false alarm."

David led Chris into the living room and set him down on the sofa. But when he moved away to take another seat, Chris grabbed him.

"Don't," he said. "Don't leave."

"I'm not going anywhere," David said, lowering himself beside Chris. "Tell you what. How 'bout I just sit here for now."

"Good."

Chris melted back into the stiff cushions. His eyes stared blindly ahead, through the massive picture window to the lights spreading out beyond the lake that gave the area its name. David wondered what kind of waking nightmare he saw through those eyes.

"He's dead," Chris whispered. "Isn't he?"

"We don't know that."

Chris didn't even seem to hear him. "Like Kyle," he said. "Like Bobby."

"Chris."

"He's dead. I know it."

David slid his arm around Chris's stiff shoulders. "Try to relax. I'll wait with you."

"Who's doing this? Who is this guy?"

"I don't know."

Chris twisted away from him, his face a mask of hate.

"Why is he doing this to me? Why—"

David's cell phone rang. He snatched it up and in the frozen silence that fell between them, then barked his name.

It was Copland.

"We found a man matching the description of your missing kidnapped vic. Witnesses have him falling or jumping out of a truck on Pacific Coast Highway, north of Santa Monica."

"Where is he now?" David leaned forward, shielding the phone with his free hand, all too aware of Chris watching him with unblinking eyes. Praying Copland wasn't going to say "the morgue."

"Santa Monica Hospital. Far as I know he's being prepped for surgery as we speak."

David straightened. "Was he processed first?"

"You'll be happy to know we collected more than enough skin tissue from under his nails to get a solid DNA match. This guy was a fighter, I'll give him that."

"He had a lot to fight for," David said softly. "Good work, detective." David met Chris's gaze. "We're on our way."

He slapped the phone shut and jumped to his feet, dragging Chris with him.

"It's Des. He's hurt, but he's alive."

Chris's beautiful face lit up. "Where?"

"I'll take you."

Slapping the bubble light on the unmarked car's dash helped them speed through the traffic to Santa Monica. They made it to the hospital in under forty minutes. David parked in the emergency lot, dropped an LAPD OFFICER ON DUTY board on the dash, and led Chris inside.

Fifteen minutes later a white-coated doctor floated through the doors of the emergency room and beckoned them into an empty alcove.

"Detective Laine?" she asked, glancing from David to Chris. "I'm Dr. Melanie Anderson."

"David Laine. This is Christopher Bellamere. He's a good friend of Mr. Hayward's. How is he?"

"Mr. Hayward is still in surgery. His condition has been guardedly listed as critical."

"Can I see him?" Chris asked. David wasn't sure he'd even heard her words.

Dr. Anderson shook her short mop of red hair. "He's in surgery. Even when he's moved to the intensive-care unit it's unlikely he'll be allowed visitors for some time."

"I want to see that he's okay."

She looked to David for help. "At this point all we can do is wait and see. Your friend's condition is critical and the next twenty-four hours he'll be under constant watch."

David led Chris over to an orange vinyl chair along the waiting-room wall. "Wait here. I want to talk to the doctor a minute."

"What? I want to see Des—"

David pointed at the chair. "I'll see what I can do. Stay."

Chris subsided. David turned back to Dr. Anderson. He took her arm and guided her away from Chris.

"There's an officer waiting outside the I.C.U.," she said. "I told her the same thing I'm telling you. This man is not going to be talking to anyone for some time."

Unspoken between them lay the words "if ever." A critically ill man in surgery might not make it out of surgery.

"What are his injuries?"

"Head trauma," she said. "More than likely from the fall from the vehicle. Skin abrasions to the spinal column. Shoulders, ditto. Other wounds consistent with a weapon—probably a knife. And he was raped."

He pulled out his notepad and wrote, thinking all the while: How am I to tell Chris?

"Was a rape kit run?"

She nodded. "No fluids were recovered. Indications are a condom was used.

"Who brought him in?"

"An ambulance was dispatched. The EMTs probably saved his life. Jumping out of a moving vehicle on the Pacific Coast Highway. He's damned lucky he wasn't turned into road smear."

"He'd have been dead if he'd stayed in the vehicle."

She nodded her head. "I thought it might be like that."

"Can you let us know when he's out of surgery?" David tucked his notepad back in his jacket pocket. "In the meantime, I'd like to speak to the other officer."

"Sure. I'm just making my rounds. I'll show you the way."

Officer Barbara Morelli was a first-year rookie who had been on patrol in Santa Monica when the call came in that an injured man had been found on the Pacific Coast Highway. She and her senior partner, Foster Dean, arrived on-site shortly after the EMTs.

They had worked on the injured man while Morelli and Dean had done a quick canvas for witnesses. They found four. At this point Morelli consulted her own notes.

"Vehicle was described as a bright or dark yellow sport-utility vehicle. Possibly a Ford Explorer. Year unknown, but probably new."

"Anybody get a look at the driver?"

"Not enough to matter. Male. Likely Caucasian."

David briefly thought of giving her a copy of the police sketch, then remembered Martinez had it.

"You get names? Contacts?"

"Of course—"

"If I get you a sketch, can you run it by your wits? See if it rings any bells."

"No prob. Who is this guy?"

"Don't know yet."

"Nasty piece of work, whoever he is."

David found Chris still sitting in the tacky orange chair in emergency. He jumped to his feet the instant he saw David.

"Is he okay? When can I see him? What's happening—"

"He's still in surgery." David guided him over to a more comfortable sofa where they could sit together.

"But he's alive? He's going to make it, isn't he?"

"They're doing the best they can."

Chris leaned into him. David stroked the short, spiked hair where it rested against his shoulder. Chris's eyes closed.

David held still so as not to disturb whatever measure of rest Chris was able to get. An hour passed. Then two. People passed through. He grew stiff and the back of his head throbbed.

Finally the door opened and Dr. Anderson stepped out. She looked nearly as wasted as David felt. Their eyes met. She took in the sight of Chris in his arms and one eyebrow went up, then she nodded as though something now made sense to her.

"Doctor?"

"Mr. Hayward is out of surgery. He's still critical, but stable." She offered him a tired smile. "The prognosis is guardedly optimistic."

"Any idea when he might be available for a statement?"

"Twenty-four to thirty-six hours, if you're lucky."

David frowned.

"If I was you, I'd take your friend home. You're not going to be in any shape to ask anyone questions if you hang around here another day."

"Can I leave a number to call if his status changes?"

"Of course."

Once she was gone, taking his cell phone number and Chris's home phone with her, David gently tapped Chris awake.

"Des is out of surgery. But he can't have visitors for another day at least. Let's go back to your place. We can wait there."

"He's okay?" Chris blinked up at him owlishly.

David nodded. "I'm sure he'll be all right. He's through the worst of it."

Chris blinked some more. "God, I can't keep my eyes open."

"Come on then. I'll get you home."

"Stay with me?"

"Of course."

Chris slept in the car and barely woke up enough to get them past the alarm system at his place. The SUV was nose up to the gated courtyard. David unlocked the mailbox with Chris's key to find the SUV keys.

David guided him upstairs and left him to undress while he went to check the house and make sure everything was locked up tight. The message light on the phone wasn't blinking.

When he returned to the master bedroom, Chris was sitting up groggily in the bed, wearing only his boxers. He froze when he saw David.

"I thought you'd left."

"No, I'm staying. I'll be downstairs—"

"No. Stay here. Please."

David stood by the edge of the bed. Chris smiled up at him.

"Hey, I promise I won't take advantage of you," he said.

"Don't," David said, not sure if he meant don't promise, or don't start. He returned Chris's smile and slipped off his jacket and holster and hung them on a hook on the bedroom door before sliding into the bed beside the younger man. "Now go to sleep."

Within minutes Chris was breathing softly and lay completely relaxed in David's arms. David tried to follow suit, but it was a long time before sleep came. Just before he drifted off he realized he hadn't called Martinez to tell him about the evening's events.

He wondered if his partner would find out from some other source. And what he was going to think when he did.

CHAPTER 20

Friday, 4:10 A.M., Cove Avenue,
Silver Lake, Los Angeles

CHRIS ROLLED OVER and bumped up against a solid wall of muscle. He blinked both eyes open and met David's bemused stare.

"You always sleep this restless?"

"David? I thought I was dreaming . . . "

"No dream." David's arms enfolded him; his heart beat a staccato tempo.

Chris's hand splayed over David's thickly furred, naked chest. "Your shirt," he muttered.

"I didn't want it to get wrinkled," David said.

Chris nodded as though that made perfect sense. His fingers fanned through the dark hair, stopping to play with a fat brown nipple.

David's eyes were half closed.

"Any word on Des?"

"He's been moved off the critical list," David murmured. "We'll probably be able to go see him tomorrow, or early the next day."

Chris closed his eyes. "Thank God." Then he opened them again. "What did the doctor tell you?"

David shifted on the king-sized bed. One of his hands moved down Chris's hip. "He's going to be fine. Now I've got a question for you."

"Yes?"

"You interested in proving once and for all that you're innocent?"

"I am innocent."

David's warm gaze slid over Chris's bare chest. "Somehow I doubt that. But I'm talking about this case."

"Very funny. What do I need to do?"

"Give us a DNA sample."

"Jesus, I don't know . . . "

"Listen," David said with urgency. "I know you didn't kill anyone. But I'm not the only detective on the case. I need something to convince Martinez once and for all that we need to look elsewhere for our Carpet Killer. Please, Chris . . . talk it over with your lawyer." David smoothed his hand up Chris's hip, rubbing the bare skin above his boxers. Chris shivered. "I'm not trying to pressure you here, Chris."

"No?" Chris whispered, all too aware of David's erection pressed between his thighs. It matched his own. "What *are* you trying to do?"

"You okay?"

"Yeah, what—"

"You're sure? You haven't been drinking, have you?"

"No." Chris frowned at the odd question. "What—?"

"Good. Neither have I," David said. "One more question."

He pulled Chris tightly against him, pressing his mouth against the hollow of Chris's throat. David's unshaven face and mustache stroked Chris's skin. Desire pooled in his gut.

"David!"

"You got protection?"

"Top drawer, lube and skins. Oh, God, David. Are you sure?"

"Oh yeah, I'm sure." He lowered his mouth to Chris's.

•

Chris struggled to get his breath back. He thought he'd never had anyone make love to him with such single-minded intensity.

"Wow." Chris touched the side of David's face. His swarthy, pockmarked skin felt rough under his fingertips. "You haven't done this for a while, have you?"

"Is it that obvious?"

"Oh, yeah. So." Chris sobered. "What happens now?"

"We wait," David said. "Wait for Des to tell us what happened."

"Are you going to get into trouble?"

David sighed and pressed his lips together. "It's a little late to worry about that, don't you think?"

Chris drifted off to sleep with the feel of David's arms around him.

He dozed, very aware of David above him. His weight felt good. Chris wanted to reach for him, but couldn't find the energy.

Then sleep claimed him.

Friday, 5:40 A.M., Cove Avenue, Silver Lake, Los Angeles

THE PHONE RANG. When Chris didn't answer it, David reached for it over his body. Maybe it was the hospital again with more information about Des.

"You shouldn't have done that." The soft, whispery voice spoke so low David had to strain to hear the words. "He doesn't belong to you. He's mine."

"What? Who is this—"

The phone went dead.

David swung upright on the king-sized bed, his gaze shooting around the room as though he expected the owner of the voice to materialize in front of him. The darkened window, overlooking an even darker backyard that was pitched down into wooded blackness, drew his wandering eye. They were two stories up, perched on the edge of a hill overlooking the Silver Lake Reservoir; there were no curtains on the broad windows.

Strips of light leaked into the bedroom from a room down the hall. David lunged off the bed into a half crouch and slammed the bedroom door shut, plunging them into total darkness.

His fingers closed over the leather case of the police-issue Beretta he had hung on the door hook earlier. The familiar weight of the weapon felt good in his hands. He quickly put on his linen pants.

The phone shattered the silence again. Chris rolled over into the space David had just vacated, one hand groping sleepily for something that wasn't there. He sat up, the thin sheet falling into his lap.

"David?"

"Get down, Chris!"

"What the hell—" Chris leaned sideways and snapped on the bedside lamp.

David swung the nine-millimeter semiautomatic up at the ceiling at the same time he dove across the room and shoved Chris off the bed, sending the phone and the bedside light crashing to the hardwood floor.

"Get down and stay down."

"What the hell are you doing?" Chris tried to crab-crawl out of the tangled sheets wrapped around his legs. "What's wrong with you—"

"He's out there."

Chris froze and David took advantage of his stillness to swing over the bed and creep up the wall beside the window.

"Shut that light off!"

The room was plunged back into darkness.

David peered out through the thin pane of glass, all too aware of his vulnerability. He couldn't see anything in the tangled, tree-filled yard beyond the sweep of spidery branches. Somewhere close by a dog barked. A coyote answered it.

He couldn't see any lights from any of the nearby houses. He could barely make out a distant brightening on the horizon. Day would be coming soon, relieving the night of its secrets.

The dog's barking became frenzied. On the other side of the bed he heard the phone's dial tone change to the *blatt-blatt* sound.

"Hang it up," David said. "If it rings, don't answer it. Does that phone have call display?"

"Yes." The phone clanked against the wooden floor as Chris fumbled to find it, then there was an abrupt click and the annoying sound died, as he put the receiver down. Almost immediately the phone rang again.

"Don't answer it! What does the call display say?"

"Unknown number. What the hell is going on, David—"

"Probably a cell." It occurred to David that Chris might recognize the voice. He left the window and eased around to the foot of the bed. "Answer it."

"*What?*"

"Answer it. Tell me if you know who it is."

He picked up the receiver, cutting off the ring in midtone. "H-hello?"

The oppressive silence that filled the small room thickened. After a century of failing nerves, Chris set the phone back down.

"He hung up." Chris's voice grew stronger. "Who was it, David? Will you please tell me what is going on?" His voice changed again, grew scared. "That was him, wasn't it? Kyle's killer?"

"That was him." David eased around to Chris's side of the bed. He crouched down on the floor and almost immediately Chris was in his arms. He hugged him with one arm, keeping his gun arm free. "He seems to have developed a bit of a fixation on you."

"You think?"

Outside the dog went ballistic. The sun's early light was beginning to fill the room.

David stood up. "Get dressed."

Chris grabbed the clothes he had hastily discarded last night and struggled into them. He rubbed the sleeve of his shirt over the blond stubble on his face. His red-rimmed, bloodshot eyes met David's over the curve of his arm.

"You think he's out there *now*?" Chris asked.

"He was close enough to know we spent the night together." David set the Beretta down on the rumpled bed long enough to slide his shirt on over his linen pants and do up the first three buttons. He scooped the gun up again. "He wasn't very happy about it."

"He's watching us?"

"'Fraid so."

"And you think I know this guy?"

Friday, 5:55 A.M., Cove Avenue, Silver Lake, Los Angeles

David's face changed, seemed to grow colder, flatter. His cop face. Chris hated the change.

"He's targeting you. That much is clear."

Up the hill, the Templetons' terminally stupid yellow Lab was giving itself a voice hernia. Chris's eyes tracked to the window, now streaked with shadows from the leafy branches beyond.

The dog abruptly went silent. Someone next door had finally woken up and dragged him inside.

"You don't think he's still out there, do you?"

"I don't know." David pulled his shoes on, lacing them up quickly. "I want you to let me out, then come back up here. Stay away from the windows."

Chris didn't bother with shoes. In bare feet he followed David down the cool tile steps into the atrium. Light spilled over the transom, and the walls of the atrium glowed pink in the morning light. With hands that shook, Chris keyed in the security code.

David unlocked the door and eased it open, the black gun in his hand held flat alongside his right leg.

Chris crowded in behind when he stepped out into the stone courtyard. From the nearest crepe myrtle a pair of mockingbirds complained of the intrusion.

Shadows still gripped most of the hillside. Chris stared at the grille of his SUV. He blinked. There was something wrong with it.

"Get back inside," David said.

Against the gold wraparound grill of the SUV something red was just visible in the growing light. Chris ignored David as he stepped out of the courtyard. A sharp, familiar smell invaded his nostrils.

"Chris—"

David tried to grab him, but he slipped past the outstretched hand. He knew that smell all too well.

The SUV was spray-painted bumper to bumper with blood-red foot-high letters, words that screamed FAGGOT and COP FUCKER and DAVID FUCKS BOYS. Too late, David's fingers closed over his arm and jerked him back into the enclosed courtyard.

•

Twenty minutes later, Chris could see the other cops' thoughts tracking fast and furiously over what they knew and what they guessed. He could see a lot of them reaching conclusions that now seemed so obvious.

"It would explain a lot," he heard one cop mutter to another, who nodded sagely.

"It explains everything."

"Jesus, you think you know a guy . . . "

"Always thought he was kind of funny."

And so on and so on, round and round the fucking mulberry bush. The air crackled with the mechanical voices of radio calls being broadcast over the morning airwaves. Car doors opened and closed and Chris caught the flash of a camera lens as it captured David's ruin.

Three black-and-whites already crowded the narrow, dusty street when an unmarked car approached. Light from the newly risen sun streamed from behind the ghostly trunks of the native Sycamores and the Italian cypress trees and reflected off the untinted windshield as the car halted behind David's unmarked.

David's partner stepped out, shading his unreadable eyes behind a pair of cheap Ray-Bans.

David's face closed up. He approached Martinez stiffly, nodding coolly at him as both men took in the defaced truck.

"I heard the radio squeal, caught the address." Martinez's dark eyes swept once over Chris, then dismissed him. "No one said you were involved," he said carefully.

David said something Chris couldn't catch. But he had no problem seeing the way Martinez's gaze lingered over the nasty words or the way he kept glancing at David, taking in his partner's unshaven face and half-buttoned shirt.

At one point he threw a narrow-eyed, speculative look at Chris, staring so hard at his bare feet that Chris felt like tucking them up behind his ankles. He glared back, daring Martinez to say something.

David ignored all the inquisitive looks he got from his colleagues. Only when Martinez pointed to the edge of the house did David react. With a terse nod he drifted over to stand under the larger of the two crape myrtles, which Chris's grandmother had planted forty years before.

Ignored by everyone, Chris drifted with him. He stopped near a spray of lavender blooms, his toes sinking into the prickly Manzanita groundcover underfoot, wondering what the hell he was doing. Did he want to hear what this nasty piece of work was going to say?

Martinez's voice carried far in the still morning air.

"You want to tell me what's going on, partner?" he said. "I get this squeal, and I'm thinking we got a line on this perp, then I show up and . . . what?"

"What do you want me to tell you, Martinez?"

"Tell me to fuck off. Bop me in the nose for thinking what I'm thinking. Anything. Just don't tell me this looks like what I think it looks like."

"And what's that?"

"*Dios*, Davey, don't make me say it. We'll find who did this; I'll personally rearrange his face for him. Just tell me it ain't true."

Friday, 7:35 A.M., Cove Avenue,
Silver Lake, Los Angeles

David stared at his partner of six years and thought about lying. Martinez was giving him an easy out. Pretend like it hadn't happened, that he was a victim of a sick prank pulled off by deviant freaks.

He could lie and Martinez would pretend to believe him. Safety in fiction. Then he glanced over at Chris, hovering on the edge of his own house, trying so hard to be invisible. The worry on his beautiful face twisted David's gut. Chris was already blaming himself for this mess. For ruining David's life.

A lie would only seal the grave of any relationship he might have forged with the younger man. Some things couldn't survive that level of betrayal.

He faced Martinez, folding his arms over the thick barrel of his chest. The weight of his service weapon pressed into his ribs.

"I'm gay, Martinez. And I think it's time I stopped pretending otherwise."

"Come on, man. That's crazy—"

David froze him with a look. Martinez pressed his lips into a thin line and muttered something in Spanish. David only caught the word "*loco.*" Crazy, again.

David glanced at Chris.

"Crazy or not, it's what I am."

And he turned and walked back to Chris.

Without a word he took Chris's arm and led him up the step to the front door. Only when he closed the door behind them did he drop Chris's arm and march through the atrium into the living room. Chris hurried after him.

"Why did you do that?"

Silently David yanked shut the vertical blinds on the picture window. The room was plunged into shadow.

"David—"

He took the stairs two at a time. Chris followed.

David stepped into Chris's walk-in closet, dragging out a matching leather luggage set and carelessly tossing them onto the unmade bed.

"Pack," David said. He pointed at the suitcases. "Enough for at least a week. You can stay at my place tonight, but after that things are likely to get too hairy, so you'll have to book a hotel somewhere. If you want, get one out by the hospital, then you can visit Des once he comes around—"

"Why am I not just coming back here?"

"Alone?"

"Why not with you?" Chris planted himself in front of David. "What was that all about out there with Martinez if you're just going to brush me off?"

"I'll be lucky to be employed next week, let alone in a position to be of any use to you or anyone."

When Chris made no move to pack, David started pulling things out of the closet, with no regard to what he was grabbing. Wool pants fell on the floor amid silk blazers and something that looked like a zoot suit straight out of the fifties.

"They can't fire you!"

David frowned at him, holding two crumpled dress shirts in his big hands. His mind was working furiously, trying to see how things were going to unfold. Knowing it wasn't going to be pretty. He wondered if he'd even be able to shield Chris from the worst of it.

"It's going into the weekend. I'm damned lucky the captain's on vacation, or he might just put me on desk duty right now. As it is, the machinery won't get rolling until Monday, but if the damned tin collectors get involved, there's no telling what level they could take this to."

"Who or what are the tin collectors?"

"Internal Affairs. They collect badges. Sometimes they even take them off cops who deserve to lose them."

"I'm not even a suspect anymore. You said so yourself." Chris looked scared. David wished he had more time to explain things. "What can they charge you with?"

"Bad judgment. You may not be a suspect, but you've never formally been discharged, either. And fraternizing with victims or witnesses is not exactly a business practice the LAPD approves of."

"I was never charged with anything in the first place."

Chris sat down on the bed, surrounded by the clothes from his closet. David finally came over and sat down beside him. He picked up one of Chris's cold hands.

"If I can't stay here," Chris said, "then why can't I stay at your place? Oh, shit—"

"What is it?"

"I have to call Petey." Chris scrambled to pick up the bedside phone. "He thinks I'm going to Denver on Sunday—"

"Whoa, wait a minute." David grabbed Chris's hand again before he could lift the phone. "What do you mean, Denver?"

"He booked me for a conference there—I'm replacing Becky. It was a last-minute thing. I forgot all about it . . . "

David's eyes narrowed. His mind whirled with new thoughts. "Does anyone else know you're going on this junket?"

"No. I told you. It was last-minute. I only learned yesterday—"

David swung off the bed and drew Chris against him. He was smiling.

"That's perfect."

"What is?"

"You, my friend, are going to Colorado. No one will ever find you there."

The house echoed with the sound of someone's fist on the wooden door.

Chris jumped. David stepped back, his gaze gravitating toward the front of the house.

"Martinez." David tossed the last pair of shirts he'd been holding to Chris, who caught them limply. "I have to go talk to him. Be ready when I get back."

"David—"

"I'll drop you at my place, but then I'll have to go in to work for a while."

Suddenly David pulled Chris back into his arms. He kissed him soundly on the mouth. "You a half-decent cook?"

"Sure, I—"

"Good. There's a market down the street from my place. We can grab some stuff there. You stay for two days, and Sunday I'll take you to the airport."

"And when I get back?"

"With any luck the worst of this will be history." David cupped Chris's chin in his big hands. He forced a smile. "I can't promise anything beyond that, Chris. Maybe it won't be so bad. But if things do get bad, hell, I always wanted a sugar daddy."

Chris didn't know whether to laugh or scream. David kissed him again, leaving him a little breathless.

"I have to go talk to Martinez," David said when the pounding resumed. "Be down in twenty minutes, packed. I'll have the car ready."

Friday, 8:20 A.M., Cove Avenue, Silver Lake, Los Angeles

David was true to his word. He had the car unlocked and was standing beside it when Chris descended the front step. He passed the gauntlet of cold-eyed cops who stopped what they were doing to watch him dump his suitcases into the backseat of David's unmarked.

Martinez was standing beside David. It was obvious the two had been arguing. Martinez seemed loath to let the argument go.

"This is crazy, man. You want to throw your life away? For what? Some cheap *joto loco*?"

Chris curled his lip at the man. "Listen, you fat—"

David put his hand on Chris's shoulder, silencing him. He swung around to face Martinez. "That's the way it is, Martinez. This is one genie you can't put back in the bottle. I'm sorry it came out this way, but I'm not sorry for what I am."

Chris slipped into the passenger's seat and pulled the door shut; it made a solid clunk. He rolled the window down in time to hear Martinez say, "What you are is a cop."

David waved his arm impatiently. "I'm still a cop," he said. He slid in beside Chris and leaned out the open door. "And until someone says otherwise and makes it official, I'm going to keep doing my job, too."

Martinez stalked back to his car, which was parked behind David's. Chris tensed when he grabbed something off the front seat and walked stiffly back. David slammed his door shut.

Chris eyed Martinez as he approached his side of the car. He pulled his arm inside the open window.

Martinez leaned down to meet David's gaze. "You wanted these—well, here are your copies."

Ignoring Chris, he tossed a bundle of loose papers into the car. Most of them landed on Chris's lap, and several sheets skidded to the floor at his feet.

He bent to retrieve them.

The topmost image caught his eye. He frowned down at it.

"What are you doing with my picture?" He held up a five-by-eight photo taken of him on a street somewhere. In the reproduction the grainy background looked vaguely familiar, but he couldn't quite place it.

He glared up at Martinez, who smirked at David.

Martinez showed his teeth and his muddy brown eyes were full of malice when they met Chris's. "We were showing it around to see who might remember you. He forget to mention that?"

"He knows," David said. "He also knows he's no longer a suspect."

"Not sure everyone agrees with you on that. His friends have a nasty habit of ending up dead. You might want to remember that."

"Which in most people's books makes me a victim," Chris said. He was pissed at David for not telling the asshole to fuck off. The least he could do was tell him to shut up.

When David did neither, Chris jammed the pictures into a haphazard pile on his lap. He grabbed the other sheets to put them all together. That was when he saw the other image.

This one was a pencil sketch. Done in surprising detail.

"What are you doing with a picture of Trevor?"

CHAPTER 21

**Friday, 9:20 A.M., Cove Avenue,
Silver Lake, Los Angeles**

BOTH DAVID AND Martinez swung around to look at him.

"Who is Trevor?" David asked.

Chris shrugged uneasily, his gaze moving between both men. "A . . . guy I know," he said. "Just a guy . . . "

"Trevor who? What's his last name?" David reached in and snatched the picture out of Chris's fingers. "You got an address on him?"

He tried to sound casual, knowing he was unnerving Chris, but unable to keep the tension out of his voice. He could hear it in Martinez's, too, when he leaned down and braced his elbows on the open window and asked, "What's he to you, this *guy?*"

Chris pulled away from the window, spilling the other pictures onto the floor at his feet. "Nothing. I know him, that's all—"

"How well? You sleep with him?"

"Martinez."

But Martinez refused to let it go. David knew he was baiting Chris deliberately. "You and him like to play bedroom games?" Martinez's eyes blazed. "That how you found your buddy's friend so fast? You knew he was over there doing them and you wanted in on it—"

"No!" Chris was white and shaking. "No!"

"Martinez! That's enough." David walked quickly around the car and got in. He rammed the key into the ignition, jerked the gear into reverse, and glared at Martinez. "Back off."

David reversed out of the driveway, barely missing Martinez's bumper, then peeling out onto the cruiser-filled street.

David took in several deep breaths, trying to calm the roaring in his head. He'd really lost it that time. Stupid. Stupid not to try to deal with this calmly, rationally. They were both cops, for God's sake. Supposedly after the same thing. Instead they'd been going after each other like a couple of bulls.

He awkwardly patted Chris's knee. "Sorry, you shouldn't have had to hear that. Martinez is just—"

"Pig-headed? A walking advertisement for Rodney King's defenders? An asshole? Tell me, what exactly is he, David?"

David winced. He withdrew his hand and wrapped his fists around the steering wheel, wondering absently why it didn't buckle under his grip.

"Okay, forget Martinez. I need you to tell me everything you can about this Trevor."

Chris rubbed a shaking hand over his face. "Can we go to your place first? I don't want to talk in the car. Okay?"

It wasn't, but David knew he'd pushed him as far as he could. If Chris was going to cooperate, he needed to be handled gently right now.

He patted Chris's knee again, squeezing the bony cap. "Sure."

He doubted Chris was fooled.

Friday, 10:30 A.M., Piedmont Avenue, Glendale

David had bought his house several years before, after a drug dealer had nearly burned it down. It had taken a lot of sweat equity to restore the building to its present condition. It still needed a lot of work, but a cop's salary only stretched so far in the tight L.A. housing market, so he figured he had been lucky to get it.

His needs were simple. Up until now he had never considered what it might look like to others.

Now he saw the brown, stiff grass on the table-sized lawn for what it indicated—neglect. Paint was peeling off the wooden door jamb and the scarred siding had barely survived the fire. Even the bricks looked tired, as though the poisoned air of L.A. had leached out of them whatever vitality they might once have had. Under the gently pitched broad gables a pair of windows overlooked the street. A second gable sloped over the doorway.

David looked at Chris before he mounted the wooden steps to the front door. He dug out his key.

"Sorry if it's cluttered," he said, grabbing the largest suitcase. "I haven't been home much lately."

Chris passed him silently, carrying the other suitcase and his laptop case. He still clutched the picture of Trevor in one hand.

"Where's your car?"

"At the station," David said. "You can put that stuff in the backroom." It was more of a junk room than an extra bedroom, but it did have an old sofa bed that pulled out into a double. Right now David wasn't about to suggest any other sleeping arrangements.

The front room was shadowed, all the curtains closed. A musty smell rose from the old furniture he had picked up at garage sales and auctions over the years. Throwing open windows as he moved around, he felt a tepid breeze move through the room behind him.

Chris reappeared, empty-handed. David motioned him into the ancient kitchen. He pulled out a painted wooden chair and indicated Chris should sit. Sweeney appeared in the doorway, eyeing the stranger haughtily.

"Ready to talk?"

Chris nodded, returning the cat's unblinking stare. "What's your name?"

"That's Sweeney."

"Sweeney? As in Todd?"

"Yeah."

"I saw it at the Next Stage last year."

David's face brightened. "Me too. It was a pretty decent production."

Chris picked the cat up and stroked it. "You got coffee?"

"Nothing but instant," David said.

"Sure."

Chris toyed with the salt cellar on the vinyl tablecloth–covered table while David filled the kettle with water and pulled down two mugs. Milk and sugar followed and David sat down to wait for the water to boil. He pulled out his notepad and pencil.

"What can you tell me about this guy?"

"I—not much. I met him a few weeks ago. Des—" His slender fingers white-knuckled the saltcellar. "Jesus, Des introduced us. Des was always doing charity shows, usually AIDS stuff, since we've both had a lot of friends who—oh, never mind. It hardly matters. Des set us up."

"What's his last name?"

"Watson. Trevor Watson."

"Got an address on him?"

Chris refused to meet his eyes. He stared down at his knotted hands and shook his head.

"He never told you where he lived? Never took you there?"

"No."

"He give you a phone number?"

This time Chris nodded. "Yeah, he did. Wait . . . I have it in my BlackBerry—"

He vanished down the hall and reappeared moments later carrying a small, plastic rectangle that looked like a wide cell phone, which he poked at with something that looked like a pencil.

"Here it is." He rattled off a West Hollywood exchange. "But I think it's a cell."

David wrote it down. "We'll check it out. If it's a landline we can do a reverse lookup. If it's a cell, maybe we can get a warrant for the company records."

"But that takes time, right?"

"'Fraid so. Anything else you can think of that might help now?"

"He worked for a film company. He was some kind of film assistant. Something to do with continuity. Made sure the actors looked the same in all the shots."

"Remember the name of the company?"

"Strong . . . Strong-something Films. It was kind of a funny name, I remember that. But what do I know? I'm a Hollywood brat who hates movies." He offered David a small smile.

David took his hand in his. "You're doing great. I'm sorry any of this happened. I wish it could have been otherwise. Just . . . try to remember the name."

"I know. It's important." Chris sighed. "What happens now?"

David snapped his notepad shut when he realized Chris was finished. "I try to find this Trevor."

"Does he know you're looking for him?"

"I hope not."

Friday, 10:55 A.M., Northeast Community Police Station, San Fernando Road, Los Angeles

Striding through the door to the police station locker room, David paused. This time of day most of the staff were already out on patrol or buried behind mounds of paperwork at their desks.

At his entrance, a pair of new detectives looked up, and from the looks that crossed their faces he could see that they already knew. Gossip was like an L.A. firestorm. It came on fast and hot, and until it was spent no one knew how much damage it would do.

David nodded and headed for his locker. Their low-voiced whispers reached him, but he ignored them.

His locker had been pried open. Cautiously he approached.

Some enterprising spirit had used pink nail polish and painted something on the metal door. It looked like a six-year-old's idea of what a flower looked like. Using his notepad to tip the door open, David knew even before the door opened that it wasn't flowers they had gifted him with.

The stench wafted through the narrow room. The two cops who had been whispering looked up and grimaced. One of them muttered something, but before anyone else could speak, the outer door flew open and Martinez strode in.

He saw David and the open locker and froze. He wrinkled his nose at the smell.

"*Dios,* this some kind of sick joke?"

"You tell me."

Martinez peered in at the mound of shit carefully positioned on the top shelf. He furrowed his thick nose.

"I met some smart-ass who said I might find it amusing if I came in here. I think me and him are going to have a talk about defining funny. You sure as hell better not think I had anything to do with that."

"No," David said, jerking the door open. It bounced off the next locker and tried to shut again. "This came from someone with a finely tuned sense of humor."

Both David and Martinez glared at the junior D's.

"Either of you two see anything?" Martinez growled.

"No, sir. No one was here when we came in. Only Detective Laine came in after." The taller of the two eyed David as if they thought maybe he'd done it himself. They didn't hide their smirks very well. "Didn't see a thing."

"Now, why doesn't that surprise me?" Martinez muttered. "Get out, and if I hear stories about this circulating anytime soon, I'll personally nail your scrotes to the wall. Got that?"

"Yes, sir."

Both D's scrambled to leave.

"Like that's going to stop them," David said.

"Hey, it might slow them down for an hour or two." Martinez eyed the ruined locker. "Oh, Davey. How did it come to this?"

David opened his mouth to say something, then shut it again. When he did speak, it was going to be to tell the truth. Why bother lying anymore?

"You never fall in love?"

"Jesus, Davey. Don't say that. Not about this—"

"Why not? I didn't ask for it to happen. It wasn't in my life plan, but it did happen."

"How the hell can you—love! Jesus, he's a guy."

"I noticed."

"I don't believe this. You're a good cop. One of the best."

"I can't be a good cop and a faggot at the same time?"

Martinez winced.

The door opened again. They both looked up as Martinez muttered, "It's like Grand Fucking Central in here."

Bryan Williams, a D-2 who worked out of bunko, entered. David had been wondering when he'd show up. Bryan was the Northeast's gay and lesbian liaison officer for the department. David had never said more than a dozen words to the man.

They nodded at each other warily.

"I hear right, Laine?"

"You heard nothing, Williams," Martinez said. "Why don't you go find another fight?"

Bryan ignored him. He kept coming into the room, focused on David.

"You okay, man?" Then he caught sight of what lay in David's locker. "That your sick idea of a joke, Martinez?"

"Fuck you, asshole."

"Knock it off, both of you." David stomped over to the nearest paper-towel dispenser and yanked out a wad. Grabbing a garbage container, he disposed of the ugly mess, including the T-shirt underneath it.

"What are you doing?" Bryan stepped forward. "That needs to be documented—"

"I've got an investigation to run." David glared at Martinez. "You can either help or get out of my way. Same goes for you." This time he scowled at Bryan. "I'd rather not give idiots of that caliber the acknowledgment they even exist."

"They'll make your life a living hell if you don't fight back."

"Let them try," Martinez said.

Both David and Bryan turned toward the bristling Latino.

"Hey, you don't think I can stick up for my partner? What the hell kind of cop you think I am?"

"The wrong kind—"

"Later, Bryan." David pinned Martinez with his appraising gaze. "I've got a work site for our perp, and a possible phone. You in?"

"I'm in."

"David—"

"I'm not dropping this, okay? We'll talk . . . later."

He thought of the fight that was probably coming over his involvement with Chris and it occurred to him that having some political clout in his corner might not be a bad idea.

"In fact," he said, "I'll call you Monday."

Bryan looked like he wanted to object, but in the end he nodded. "Monday." He glared at Martinez. "I'd better not hear of any more problems or I'll have my guys all over it like flies on shit." He pointedly looked at the garbage container at David's feet.

"I'm counting on it," David said.

Friday, 11:10 A.M., Piedmont Avenue, Glendale

"Don't leave the house." Those had been David's last words before he went off to work. Of course *he* could go traipsing off, with no thought to what Chris was supposed to do all day. That David felt protective of him made Chris feel special. That he thought that meant Chris should be locked up like a princess in a tower left him cold.

He had called the hospital and using David's name was able to learn that Des was out of danger, but still too heavily sedated to be able to talk to anyone. Perhaps tomorrow. Perhaps next week. No one would commit.

David had given him no idea when he might return. What would happen if David found Trevor? That sent a shiver up Chris's spine. Was it possible Trevor had been involved in Kyle's death? In Bobby's? Had he tried to kill Des?

It was preposterous. He'd known Trevor how long? Five, six weeks? They'd almost been lovers. How could he be a killer? Chris's mind shied away from the images of Bobby. Of Kyle.

Trevor couldn't have done that.

Chris prowled the small, one-story bungalow. The kitchen was spotless; not a dish was in sight on the worn linoleum counter top. The sink looked freshly scrubbed. The stove was an old gas job that probably was new around the time the house was built.

He inhaled. The place smelled like David. He instantly liked it. The chintz curtains over the sink would let in the early-morning light and the small, plastic-covered table and its painted wooden chairs had enough room for the two of them to have breakfast and linger over coffee. Cozy. That was it, the place was cozy. On a shelf above the table a vintage fifties radio had its dial set to KZLA, a local country station.

The living room wasn't much bigger than the kitchen. A battered recliner with a TV tray beside it held the remote for the twenty-one-inch Sony occupying center place in the room. A potted Draconia filled one corner of the room, and a second, non-reclining chair was positioned on the other side of the TV tray. Both chairs looked well used.

The rest of the room was filled with old-fashioned radios and gramophones. A Philco console floor model that looked like it might have been new before television came along stood against the far wall. Chris ran his hand along the huge wooden Art Deco facade. The off-white walls held several neatly mounted posters and framed stock shots of classic cars. Buicks and old Chevies with monster fins and grinning grills looked down on him. He paused to study a photo of a '58 Caddy that could probably accommodate his SUV in its enormous trunk.

He strolled through the back of the house. There were two bedrooms and a narrow hallway leading to a back door.

The backroom where he had put his bags was cluttered with more old radios and ancient record players in various stages of repair. He found a stack of 78's and picked up the top one: Tommy Dorsey with Frank Sinatra. The next one in the stack was Bill Haley and the Comets.

He put the record back and slipped out of the room. The second bedroom was clearly David's. Like everything else in the tiny house, it was immaculate and filled with old furniture. The double bed was neatly made.

The cat he had seen earlier lay curled up atop the covers.

Chris smoothed one hand over what looked like a handmade quilt. It was old, too, but well tended.

"Hey, Sweeney," Chris said. "Don't make yourself too comfortable. Tonight this bed is mine."

The cat seemed to consider his words, then stretched one hind leg out and began licking itself. Chris grinned and left the room.

The backdoor was locked with a deadbolt, the key suspended from a wall hook. Chris palmed it, unlocked the door, and stepped out into a backyard that had seen better days.

Laundry hung from a limp clothesline in the yard next door. Down the street a car backfired and Chris heard the high-pitched squeal of children playing.

David kept his house the way he kept himself, neat and

controlled on the inside, inattentive to what the world saw on the outside.

Back inside he retrieved his laptop case from the spare room and took it into the kitchen. When he opened it up he found Bobby's Palm Pilot. After plugging in the laptop and booting it up, he powered on the Palm. It was dead. He found the power adapter in the laptop case. Leaving the thing to recharge, he made some configuration changes to his laptop and logged into his ISP, where he started by checking his email. Becky had sent him another note about some things she and Yamamoto had already discussed. Chris downloaded the email to his hard drive so he could refer to it later in Denver.

Then he hunkered down to some serious surfing.

What was the name of Trevor's film company? Strong Arm. Strong Box. Strong *something.* He played around with Google and Alta Vista, running Boolean searches on random-name choices. He loosed his search spiders on the Web and left them darting through channels cluttered with the zeros and ones of raw binary data. Eventually they all came back with whatever tidbits they had discovered and spread them out before him like a dog delivering a retrieved ball.

Strong Arm Playing Company. That was it. Had Trevor used it as a cover for his murderous activity?

Strong Arm Playing Company was no StarFlight Productions. If they had a database it was beyond the reach of Chris's skills to break into it. All he was able to find out beyond the basic particulars was some contact information and a list of independent producers who pedaled their wares to Strong Arm on a regular basis.

He started with the phone number and a cover story. A junior receptionist listened to his first attempt.

"Hi, I have to reach Mr. Trevor Watson. It's important."

He was put on hold and passed to another junior receptionist. She sounded bored when she took his request.

"What's this about?"

"Finding Trevor Watson. I know he works there—"

"And why is it important?"

"His mother's gravely ill."

He went back on hold. Chris cursed Alexander Graham Bell while Muzak played in the background.

"Strong Arm Playing Company, may I help you?"

"I hope so—"

The Muzak was back before he could finish. He tapped his fingers, belatedly realizing he was listening to an easy-listening rendition of an old Guns 'n' Roses song. God, what was next? Ice-T rendered into tuneful elevator music?

"Strong Arm Playing Company."

"I have to locate a Mr. Trevor Watson. His mother is dying."

"Oh, my, that's terrible," the woman sounded genuinely upset. "Who is it you're looking for?"

"Trevor, Trevor Watson. He works for your company and this was the only contact number he left us . . . "

"Let me check, sir."

This time something ancient by the Beatles. Or was it Elton John? The concerned woman returned.

"I'm sorry, Mr. Watson no longer works for this company."

"Do you have another number he can be reached at?"

"That information is confidential—"

"His mother keeps asking where he is," Chris murmured. "We tell her, Ma, we're trying to find him. Just hang on, but she's so frail . . . "

"The poor woman . . . Well, it looks like your brother last worked here August twenty-first. There's no mention of other employment."

"What about an address?"

"I'm sorry, sir."

"The doctor only gives her a week. Two at the most. We just

don't know what else to do. She hasn't seen Trev in six years . . . "

"I can't give you an address, but I'm sure it's okay if I give you his phone number." And she did, rattling off the same West Hollywood exchange Chris had given David.

He hid his disappointment. "Thank you, ma'am. My mother will be so relieved to know her baby is okay. Your records don't show why he left, do they? I always thought Trev loved making movies . . . "

"No, sir. I'm sorry. Just that he was terminated . . . " Her voice trailed off. "I'm sorry. I probably shouldn't have even told you that."

"Nobody else will know, ma'am." Chris hastily hung up.

Trevor hadn't worked for Strong Arm for nearly two weeks. But he had called last weekend and said he was out of town on a job. Chris knew some people might be embarrassed to admit they'd been canned, but . . . his mouth went dry.

That was the weekend Bobby had died. Nausea roiled in Chris's gut. Was that why Trevor had faked working? To give himself time to—Chris abruptly grabbed the phone again and dialed a number. He had to tell David.

"We're on our way out to his workplace now," David said when Chris told him what he'd found out. "Maybe we can get an address. But that's definitely interesting that he lied about being employed over that time frame. Let me get back to you." His voice dropped. "You're not going out, are you? I'll bring something back for supper. I want you to stay put—"

"I'll stay," Chris said. "But only if you promise not to be long. Otherwise . . . "

"I'll get back as soon as I can."

Chris decided he would spend the day digging through cyberspace. Maybe somebody else knew something about Trevor, or the Carpet Killer, or even his victims.

It was a long shot, but it beat sitting around waiting for a stubborn cop to show up.

Friday, 3:10 P.M., Café 50's, Santa Monica Boulevard, West Los Angeles

David shut the cell and stared over the roof of the car and through the café window at Martinez, who was flirting with the waitress bringing their coffee.

The ride so far had been a silent one. David was thankful Martinez wasn't demanding answers, but he missed their old camaraderie, even with Martinez's often crude mouth.

Was he supposed to be thankful they were still talking at all?

The passenger door closed with a soft *clunk* and David leaned down to stare into the open window. Martinez was already chewing noisily on a bear-claw pastry.

"Chris called," David said. "Seems Watson wasn't working where he claimed when Dvorak was taken. And Chris said he made a big deal of calling him that weekend, saying he was out of town."

Martinez chewed and swallowed the last bit of his bear-claw and washed it back with coffee. "Setting up an alibi? He'd have to know it wouldn't hold up under even the loosest investigation."

"When do psychopaths think things through? Could be he was figuring to avoid an investigation by taking himself out of suspicion early on."

"Any idea where he is now?"

"None. We got an address on his last employer." David glanced at the notes he had taken. "Out in Santa Monica. Feel like a trip to the beach?"

Santa Monica had gone upscale over the last decade. When Spielberg, Geffen, and Katzenberg moved their production offices out to the beach-side city, the money and glitter had followed. Now the small community was a thriving mini-Hollywood.

Strong Arm Playing Company was located in a cul-de-sac off Santa Monica Boulevard, housed in a refurbished stucco Art Deco building with tinted-glass windows. The lobby was furnished with muted pastel-on-gray love seats and a thick wall-to-wall carpet that ate their footsteps as they strode past a phalanx of lurid posters from the company's more successful films.

The girl who looked up from her computer couldn't have been more than eighteen. She had the uniform tan of the true Californian. She probably spent hours at the beach making sure her body was that perfect golden color all over. By thirty she'd be doing the same in the plastic surgeon's office trying to reclaim the skin she had ruined in her youth.

Martinez stepped forward to eyeball her. She looked from one man to the other, and sure of her power over both, smiled.

"Help you, gentlemen?"

"You got an HR department here, darling?" Martinez said.

"HR? What branch of film do they handle?"

"Human resources. Staffing." Martinez flipped his gold shield under her nose. "Who takes care of the employees?"

"Oh, that's all handled by an agency." She brightened. "That's how I got this gig."

"Maybe you can help us. We're looking for a guy used to work here. We need to talk to him, so we're looking for an address."

"What guy?"

"Trevor Watson."

"Never heard of him."

"Know anyone who might?"

She cocked her head. Teeth nibbled on her lower lip. "You want to talk to Kemp."

"Who?"

"Billy Kemp. He's the guy who deals with this agency. Tells them who we need, so they can send over the right people."

"Can we talk to this Billy Kemp?"

"Oh he's not in today. No one is but me and some of the editors." She giggled as though this should have been common knowledge. "He'll be back on Monday."

"We need to talk to him now."

David walked around the desk and crowded closer to her. Martinez leaned toward her. The combined effect worked.

"But he's at home."

David handed her the phone. "Call him. Tell him what we want. Better yet, let one of us talk to him."

Twenty minutes later they left with Trevor's last known address.

"She was hot for me, I could tell," Martinez said as he waited for David to dig out the keys and unlock the car. "You really telling me that little *Chiquita* didn't do anything for you?"

"Sorry, not a thing."

Martinez shook his head. "Un-fucking-believable."

David didn't bother contradicting him.

CHAPTER 22

Friday 4:15 P.M., Silver Lake Boulevard,
Silver Lake, Los Angeles

TREVOR WATSON'S APARTMENT was in a pale pink stucco walk-up containing a dozen apartments. Tired palms lined the center-court pool, where a stoop-shouldered Latina woman watched three kids splash in the shallow end.

David eyed the cracked parking lot, noting a half dozen cars lining the grassy verge.

"Our perp have a car?"

"He did." Martinez snatched up the car radio. "Let's get some details."

From where they sat, they had a front-on view of apartment 3A, where Trevor Watson had been in residence up to two weeks ago. At least Billy Kemp claimed that Watson's final check had been cut and sent to that address. The check had been cashed, too.

"Think our guy's home?"

"Be nice if it happened."

"See an eighty-nine Honda Civic?" Martinez rattled off a plate number.

David spotted the car, a gray two-door hatchback rusted out along the underside.

They approached the vehicle. The backseat held a box full of paperbacks, a roll of duct tape, and a blanket. There was also a plastic bag from a local video store.

"We should check out that video place," Martinez muttered. "See if they ever stocked any of Bobby's porno."

"Let's get working on a warrant for this thing." David pulled his cell out. He'd get one of the D's back at the station to start drafting the paperwork. "I especially want that duct tape examined. Maybe we can match it to the vics."

"Good," Martinez said. "Now let's go see if our guy's at home."

Almost simultaneously they checked their Berettas as they strode up the flagstone walkway.

The fat black man who answered their knock was not Trevor. Nor was he amused to have his afternoon disrupted by two cops.

"We're looking for Trevor Watson."

"Don't know him."

He stepped back and tried to shut the door. Martinez blocked it.

"Answer a couple of questions?"

"What kind of questions?"

Martinez showed him the sketch of Trevor. "Ever seen this guy before?"

"No."

"You sure?"

"Yeah, I'm sure. He might be whitebread but I'd still know if I'd seen him. What's this about, anyway?"

"Can I get your name, sir?" David asked.

"Clarence," the fat man said. "Clarence Dupont."

"How long you lived here?"

"Moved in Monday." Light dawned on Clarence's sweat-dappled face. "You looking for the guy lived here before me?"

"Maybe. Know when he moved out?"

"I see the 'for rent' sign go up Sunday. You wanna know more, talk to the landlord."

They banged on his door. "Call me Jackie," he told the two cops when he opened up. Behind him the TV blared with Pat Sajak cajoling the wheel to be good to someone. Jackson Stepanowski was the antithesis of Clarence: skinny, angular, and white.

David and Martinez introduced themselves. Martinez showed

Jackie the police artist's sketch of Trevor.

Jackie studied it closely, as though he was looking over each pencil stroke. Finally he handed it back to Martinez.

"Yeah, sure. Looks like one of our tenants. Guy's gone now, though. Split last weekend."

"He say where he was going?"

"Didn't even say he was going. Left me a note." Jackie frowned. "He was due to pay his rent, next thing I know I'm on his front door and there's no answer. Nothing but a goddamned note saying he's leaving, sorry about the rent. Yeah, sure. Ain't seen him since. At least I got first and last off him when he moved in. He do something?"

"How long ago precisely was that?"

"Guy left in a flippin' hurry's all I can say. Maybe a week ago Thursday, I guess."

"You guess?"

"I didn't know he was gone right away. Left food everywhere. I try to tell the damned tenants we all gotta fight to keep the roaches out, it ain't enough for me to come by every other month and spray. They gotta keep up their end, too. This guy, he was usually so tidy, you know. Any other time I went to his place it was spotless."

"Any sign this guy didn't just walk away? Anyone complain before you noticed him gone?"

"Nah, he was always quiet. Hardly knew he was there. If he ever had visitors I never saw 'em."

"How long he live there?"

"Three years. Hard to believe, huh? That long and he just vanishes."

"You aware Mr. Watson's car is still in the parking lot? Know why he wouldn't take his car with him?"

Jackie frowned. Behind him the studio audience was going crazy. Somebody had obviously just scored big.

"What's going on here, officer?" Jackie asked.

"What did you do with his property?" By law the landlord wouldn't be able to dispose of Trevor's things for at least six months. David wasn't surprised when Jackie grimaced.

"Put it in storage, what else? Means I gotta foot the bill unless he comes back and actually wants his stuff. Know what chance there is of that?"

"What storage company do you use?" David asked. He wrote down the name Jackie gave him. "We'll be getting a warrant for that soon. His vehicle, too. Do me a favor, don't touch it until we tell you it's okay."

"What do you want me to do if he comes back?"

"Call us immediately."

•

"He had another vehicle," Martinez said. They were sitting in the front seat of their car with both windows down trying to catch a cross breeze. The sun was setting behind the pool, now empty. "Remember our homeless wit who said the perp was driving a 'golden chariot.' I'm thinking truck or van. Yellow. Better for transporting his vics—dead or alive."

"Anything show up in D.M.V. under Watson?"

"Nada, nothing but the Honda. Doesn't mean he didn't have an unregistered vehicle. Hell, how many cars get jacked every day?"

"Let's check with Jackie, see if he remembers our guy driving anything else."

A laugh track and canned laughter coming from Jackie's apartment let them know he had moved on to sitcoms. The humor hadn't improved his temper.

"What now?"

"You remember Mr. Watson driving any vehicle other than the Honda Civic?"

"Never saw him drive anything else."

They thanked him again and retreated to their own car.

"What now?"

"I want to talk to Anstrom's parents again. See if they ever saw Watson. If we're right and he stalked his vics before making his move, someone besides those kids in the arcade might have seen something."

"Sure." Martinez glanced at his watch. It was nearly eight-thirty. "Let's call a code seven and grab supper, then we'll swing by their place. This time of night, surely they'll be in."

But they weren't, and none of their neighbors knew when they might return. At ten-thirty David called it a night. He already knew he'd pissed Chris off royally by not making it back earlier. Now he was too tired to think about anything but his pillow.

He caught Martinez in the middle of a massive yawn that made a lie of his partner's attempt to say he was all ready to keep going. They agreed to meet back at the station first thing in the morning, even though it was Saturday. There were still threads to be pursued. Someone had to know where Trevor Watson was.

•

David let himself into his house; a light burned in the kitchen, no doubt left on by Chris. The rest of the house was dark and silent. The door to the spare bedroom was closed.

David slid his shoes off in the front hall and tip-toed in stocking feet to his own room. He turned on the overhead light and gave a startled "oof" when Chris sat up in his bed. Sweeney opened one blue eye from where he had taken up residence on David's pillow.

"David?"

"Chris, what are you doing here?"

"Waiting for you. You're late."

"Yeah, well, sorry. Things came up. That's what happens in my work."

"Find him?"

"No, not yet. Found where he lived, though. Turns out he left last weekend."

"But I saw him Monday," Chris said. "He left before I went looking for Kyle . . . "

They traded glances. Had Trevor beaten Chris out to Santa Monica? Had he found Kyle first?

Chris didn't ask. David figured he didn't want to think about Bobby or Kyle and how they had died. Fair enough. David didn't want to think about Chris knowing this guy Trevor.

"I missed you at supper," Chris finally said.

David saw he had donned pajama bottoms, red silk. He hadn't bothered to put on the top and his well-defined chest looked like sculptured marble in the overhead light.

David swallowed against the sudden obstruction in his throat. "Er, why aren't you sleeping down the hall?"

"Didn't you miss me?" Chris looped his arms around his knees and smiled. "Did you think about me at all?"

It occurred to David that Chris was flirting with him. That was an entirely new experience.

"I don't like sleeping alone. Do you?" Chris asked.

David wouldn't have thought a desire for anything but sleep was possible, but now a different kind of desire pooled in his gut. He fought it. He scooped the cat up and cradled it in his arms. When he spoke his voice was hoarse.

"I don't know if this is a good idea, Chris."

"You aren't going to pretend it was a mistake, are you?" Chris moved around so he was sitting on the edge of the bed. He could have reached out and touched David. He didn't. "Because we both know what it was, and it wasn't wrong."

"How can you know that?"

"Because I remember how good it was." This time he did touch David, laying his fingers over the hand holding the cat. "I know how you made me feel. Please, David. Make love to me."

Sweat popped out on David's forehead. He abruptly turned toward the door, where he gently set Sweeney down in the hallway and shut the door. When he turned back Chris was staring at him.

"I hope you brought protection with you," David said. "Because I know I don't have anything."

"Hey, I was a Boy Scout. I'm always prepared."

Saturday, 1:35 A.M., Piedmont Avenue, Glendale

"You weren't really a Boy Scout, were you?"

Chris felt way too enervated to do anything but drift in and out of sleep. He barely felt the towel David used to wipe his damp skin. David's words were soft puffs of sound in his ears.

"For about five minutes," he murmured. "I'm not a bug person. Camping just makes me itch. But I did learn how to be prepared." Chris played with the thick hair on David's chest. "So, you have any luck tonight? You and Mr. Sensitivity."

"Besides finding out your friend split, no. We recovered his car. We may find something to link some of the victims to it. That would be a break."

"I still can't believe Trevor did any of those things . . . How can someone be that way and it doesn't *show*?"

"The experts will tell you psychopaths don't empathize with anyone. But a lot of them are smart enough to fake it. No one around them catches on, at least not right away."

"But not all people like that are killers, right?" Chris shook his head tiredly. "God, Trevor just didn't seem that . . . monstrous. He knew Des. They were friends . . . "

"Guys like that don't have friends, though on the surface they might seem to. They're empty."

It was too depressing a topic to continue, so Chris didn't. He snuggled under David's quilt, content to have David's arms around him. Soon the older man's soft snores provided another sort of comfort and Chris drifted off.

When he awoke the space beside him was empty. He groped across the still warm sheets, then sat up when he heard banging noises coming from the kitchen.

He grabbed his pajama bottoms from where he had discarded them the night before, then found the top, and did half the buttons up before venturing out of the room.

He found David, fully clothed, crouched in front of an open cupboard, dragging things out and piling them around him on the floor. A large cast-iron frying pan waited on the stovetop already filled with six slices of bacon. A bowl holding four eggs and a loaf of white bread sat on the counter top beside a battered toaster oven.

A kettle steamed gently on the front burner.

Suddenly David sat back on his haunches, triumphantly clutching a drip coffee pot. He handed it to Chris.

"I knew I had this somewhere. Coffee's in the freezer, so it should still be good. Filters are above the stove. Get that started while I put this stuff back."

Chris blinked at the clock over the sink. "You do realize it's six o'clock, right?"

"Sure, I've been up since five-thirty."

David finished putting his pots and pans back in the cupboard and stood up. He quickly found the filters and the frozen ground coffee and poured the boiling water through.

He sat opposite Chris. "Why don't you go back to bed then?"

"What are you doing up?"

Chris was afraid he knew the answer, but he still felt disappointed when David said, "I have to go in to work." He reached out and took Chris's hand. "But I swear I will get off early. We'll make an early night of it. Tomorrow I'll drive you to the airport."

"What do you have to do today?"

"Talk to some of the victims' families. We're still trying to link

Trevor with them."

"And if you can't?"

"Nobody, no matter how careful they are, can interact with a crime scene and not leave something behind. Just like they always take something with them. If Trevor was part of this, we'll find proof. And once we find it, he's ours. We were thwarted before because we didn't have any viable suspects. We'll get him, Chris, don't worry."

"I hope so," Chris said. He squeezed David's hand. "I'll have some of that coffee, if it's ready."

"Pack," David said. "Get ready for your trip. I'll be back by four."

An hour later Chris was crouching over Bobby's Palm Pilot. He called up a list of recently accessed data and found that Bobby kept a journal of sorts. Opening it he paged through the entries, most of which had to do with either jobs or the assorted men in his life. By the time Chris came across his own name his eyes had grown bleary with trying to read the small print.

Bobby didn't pull any punches. He liked florid description. Lots of it. Chris would never think of his dick in quite the same way again. Hearing a noise from the front hall, Chris quickly closed the program and deactivated the Palm. He looked up to find Sweeney watching him from the kitchen doorway.

"Busted."

Sweeney crossed the floor and rubbed against his ankles. He resisted the urge to pick the animal up. Instead he turned to his laptop and went online. Again he called up various search engines, and started with a quick look at the *L.A. Times* files on the killings. If Bobby had been an "actor," had any of the others?

Jason Blake and Bobby Starrz. He plugged in both names. Multiple links filled the screen.

He stared at the first link. Both names were in boldface, along with two other names Chris recognized—Jeff Charette and Frank Barker. He remembered Jeff from that leather bar. The guy had been into the gear big-time. Chris didn't gig himself out, but he liked the look on certain guys, and Jeff was a prime cut of meat. Frank was another Nosh Pit regular, a party animal with a penchant for fucking in public places. Chris's fingers caressed the ice-cold keyboard. What would he find on the other side of those innocuous looking links?

A fifth name puzzled him. Daniel Anstrom? Who was Daniel Anstrom?

His BlackBerry buzzed.

He'd had all his calls from his landline forwarded to his handheld, so it could be anybody. Somebody taking a survey. Charities asking for more money. Even his mother checking up on him.

But he knew who it was.

He reached out and scooped up the small handheld. It barely had enough weight to register in his hand. The display lit up.

Unknown name. Unknown number.

Not really, he thought. He knew exactly who it was.

He flipped it on. Took a deep breath.

"Bellamere here."

"Chrissy," Trevor's voice sounded tense. "Hey, man. Miss me?"

"Sure," Chris struggled to keep his voice level. "Where are you?"

"Around. Got things to work out. You know how it goes. But you and me, we're gonna get together soon."

"I don't think I can do that—"

"Sure you can." Was it his imagination or did Trevor sound pissed? "You owe me one, Chrissy."

Chris tried to sound casual. "You in town, Trev?"

"Oh, I'm around. I'll tell you all about it when I see you."

"Trev—why don't you tell me where you are. I could come around today—"

"Today's not good, man. Not good at all. But I'll let you know when it's time. You just keep thinking of Trev. We'll be together soon."

Trevor hung up.

A shaking Chris immediately dialed David.

"The party you are attempting to reach is not available—"

The officious prick who answered his call at the Northeast station wouldn't tell him anything. Just that David wasn't available. An attempt to his cell met with failure.

It was the tension of waiting. Of wondering what Trevor was planning, of what he might already have done . . . Chris tapped the enter key on his laptop and the Web page opened.

The linked images were thumbnails, with just enough detail to tease the visitor into wanting more. There was no way to see enough detail to know who lay behind each thumbnail. But the site's creator had helpfully named each link. He stared at the one labeled Bobby Starrz.

He called the station back, hoping to get someone more helpful. The same prick answered. No, Detective Laine was not able to take a phone call. If it was important police business he should leave a message. Someone would get back to him. He stared blankly at the laptop's fifteen-inch LED screen while the officious voice droned on . . . "If this is an emergency call dial nine one one . . . "

Did he really want to see this? Was he a coward if he didn't look? David saw this kind of stuff every day. He could look at it and still come to Chris with a gentleness Chris had only ever dreamed of in a lover.

Chris left a message with the prick, then hung up and clicked on the image of Bobby. Instantly another page opened.

The Carpet Killer clearly knew something about computers. He had used a Web cam to capture his atrocities, then made skillful use of some kind of Flash technology to both mask and enhance the images. Chris thought of Trevor, involved in professional filmmaking, picking up tips from the old pros with no idea how he was using their suggestions.

Though he forced himself to examine each streaming video

several times, tried to ignore the look of tortured pain and the terror of Bobby and the others as they were sliced and raped, first by a penis, then by a knife blade. Chris barely kept his lunch down. He never saw the Carpet Killer's face.

The phone rang fifteen minutes later. Chris jumped a foot off the chair. Hastily he wiped tears from his eyes and fumbled to grab the receiver.

Thank god, it was David.

"He called," Chris's voice broke. Then he froze. He couldn't talk about what he had seen over the phone. Not when the images of Bobby's last few minutes still burned in his mind with cold neon brightness. What could he even tell David? He needed to find the source of the Web site if he was going to be any help at all. Surely he could do that much at least.

"Trevor, he called."

"We'll be right there."

Twenty minutes later David and a reluctant Martinez filled the kitchen. Chris's BlackBerry lay on the table. It had remained stubbornly silent since Trevor's call.

"Any idea why he called you?" Martinez's gaze skittered from Chris to the BlackBerry, with the occasional side-trip toward David, who seemed oblivious to his partner's probing looks.

"Who's your service provider?" David asked.

Chris told him.

"We'll start monitoring incoming calls, maybe catch him if he calls again." David slammed his fist into his open palm. "Damn it, I should have anticipated this. I knew he had a fixation on you."

Under Martinez's watchful eyes Chris didn't feel at ease comforting his lover. He stared down at his own hands, rubbing the flesh of his thumb uneasily.

"We can't anticipate them all, Davey," Martinez said. "This guy's a loose cannon."

David's cell phone rang. He spoke briefly.

"Our warrant for the car and the storage locker came through. Let's check that out before we go any further. You"—he looked steadfastly at Chris—"call your service provider and see if you can talk to anyone who can take your authorization to monitor your cell. We'll call them, too, but it helps if the owner cooperates. They may still demand a court order, but we'll try to work around that for today."

Chris nodded and looked at the kitchen clock. Eleven-thirty. His flight left at nine the next night. Soon he'd be in Denver and for five days he wouldn't have to watch his back.

"If he calls, assume we're monitoring and *keep him on the line*."

Another nod and Chris followed them to the door, debating whether to pull David aside and tell him about the Web sites. Martinez left first. David half shut the door behind him and turned. He wrapped one hand around Chris's arm.

"I know, I know," Chris said. "Don't leave the house. Don't show my face in the street. Keep him on the phone—"

David silenced him with a finger to his lips. Then he pulled him into his arms.

"I'll get a patrol car to swing by as often as possible, but they won't let us assign someone full-time." He tilted Chris's head up. "I love you, Chris."

Before Chris could do more than stare in stunned silence, David was gone, closing the door firmly behind him.

Saturday, 11:50 A.M., Laurel Canyon Boulevard, Los Angeles

As they drove toward Judge Harris's to secure the signature on the warrants, David stared out the car's window. Warm air flowed over his flushed face, doing little to cool him.

What had possessed him to say he loved Chris?

He'd just complicated things tenfold. Chris had been fooling around, having fun seducing the cop-in-the-closet, making him admit how much David wanted him. Nothing more. Chris was a well-heeled, stunningly beautiful man; someone who had it all. Why would he be interested in having a dull, stick-in-the-mud detective in his life?

David mentally kicked himself. Well, no getting around it, he'd done it now. Maybe it would just speed up the process. Chris was bound to start distancing himself now. He'd have no choice; unless he was cruel enough to play with David's heart, and David didn't think that was Chris's style.

Too bad he'd promised to be home early, had told Chris to wait for him. He could have pleaded workload and hung around the station all evening, until he was sure Chris was safely asleep. Tomorrow he was leaving. In a week there would have been no reason for Chris to look him up when he came back. They all could have saved face.

But David always kept his promises.

They called a tow truck on the way out to Trevor's apartment. They would examine the car in situ, in the hopes that it might offer up some evidence they could use immediately; then it would be towed to the police impound lot, where the true forensic work would be done.

Martinez parked three spots over from the abandoned vehicle. David popped the trunk and hauled out their camera, checking to make sure it had a full charge, then dragged out their evidence kit. Martinez grabbed a pair of gloves and drew them over his thick fingers. David would take his pictures first.

The city-run tow truck bounced into the lot and the driver greeted them with a laconic nod. He immediately produced a shimmy and while David circled the car, shooting a round of film, he popped both doors open.

"She's all yours, man," the driver said, wiping a layer of sweat off his brown forehead with a greasy rag he pulled from his overalls.

"We'll let you know when we're done," David said.

The driver retreated to the cab of his truck where he promptly dug out a *Gents* magazine and fell to reading sideways.

Both David and Martinez peered into the hot, musty car.

David tried to imagine Trevor helping some guy he had just slipped Ketamine to into the passenger's seat. Strapping them both in. Already anticipating the evening to come. Driving where? Back to here? David glanced up at the three-story walk-up. Not here. Not if he held them for hours, as the medical examiner claimed. He had to have a stash site. Someplace more private, where he could take his time—have his fun.

Maybe a clue to the location of that place could be found in this nondescript-looking vehicle. A map or an address. A name.

They had already done a title search on Trevor's name and come up empty. If Trevor Watson owned property anywhere in Southern California, it wasn't registered in his name.

Did he have access to someone else's property? They'd had no luck tracking down any of Trevor's relatives. He hadn't provided any contact information to his employer and the landlord didn't have any names.

"Finished here?" David asked.

Martinez nodded, and David went over to let the tow-truck driver know they were ready. David shot more images once the car was removed—of the oil-covered pavement underneath the vehicle. Then they did a quick walk around, making sure nothing was overlooked.

Within twenty minutes they were back on the road, heading for Mascot Self-Storage, on North Hollywood Way, where the landlord had stored Trevor's belongings.

They met with the manager of Mascot's and showed him the warrant. Overhead a Boeing 767 with the American Airlines logo on its tail flew low, bound for the Bob Hope Airport. The manager eyed the warrant grudgingly and tottered out of his air-conditioned office and headed for the rows of low sheds that housed the eight-by-ten storage units that he leased by the month.

In unit 25 they turned on the single overhead light, which cast a yellow glow over the stacked boxes that lined two walls. A few rag-tag pieces of thrift-shop furniture filled the rest of the space.

"Got a couple of folding chairs we can borrow?" Martinez asked the manager.

Reluctantly the manager left, returning moments later with a pair of folding metal chairs with plastic lattice covering, one orange, the other blue.

Martinez took them, unfolded them, and plunked them in the middle of the cement floor. After dragging down several boxes they sat down and methodically began to go through each one. The job was tedious—sorting through mounds of dirty dishes, curios, and books that had been haphazardly packed. Whenever they came across paperwork they set it aside. Bills and receipts might be used to plot Trevor's movements over the last few months.

Once they had culled several boxes of paperwork, the search began in earnest.

There was too much to sort through in one afternoon. In the end they did a quick sort, arranged everything by year, and tossed everything back into boxes, each box holding at most two years' worth of paper. Then they lugged the whole lot down to the station.

By the time they got four D's working on resorting everything by month it was going on three-thirty.

David stretched, wincing when his back creaked and popped in protest. He had already told Martinez earlier he had to be home by four. Now he caught the other detective's gaze.

"If you catch anything interesting, call me. See if you can contact Anstrom's parents while you're at it. Maybe we can run up there later."

•

At four o'clock sharp David locked his front door behind him. From the living room he heard one of his radios playing. It had been changed from KZLA to something louder.

Chris emerged from the bedroom, and David stared at the vision in front of him.

Chris had changed from his red silks into a pair of skintight jeans that hugged his muscular thighs and clearly outlined the shape of his half-erect penis. The jade green shirt he was wearing stretched tight across his chest, showing off his sculptured body. Again David marveled at how utterly perfect he was. And how completely out of place he looked in David's shabby surroundings.

"Hi," Chris said.

David swallowed, but his throat had gone dry.

Chris looked at one of David's treasures, a Dutch cuckoo clock he had found in a North Hollywood flea market years ago and had painstakingly restored. It even kept reasonably accurate time.

"Right on time," he said.

"I promised."

"I'll have to get you to promise things more often then."

David wasn't sure what to make of it when Chris moved closer. His breath was warm on David's face. His body radiated heat and the erotic smell of aftershave and soap. David remembered how he tasted, the sounds he made when he came. He closed his eyes, fighting the memories.

"What are you doing?" David asked.

"I've been thinking about you all day. I've never had anyone prey on my mind like you do, Detective David Laine. Why do you think that is?"

David opened his mouth to speak but nothing came out. Chris didn't wait; he kissed him. David's resistance vanished in a wave of lust.

Sunday, 7:55 A.M., Piedmont Avenue, Glendale

Chris shut the bedroom door behind him, taking care not to wake David, who was still sleeping soundly, despite the hour. After last night Chris wasn't surprised.

Chris hadn't wanted to say anything about his find the night before. Between making love and cooking an intimate dinner for three—Sweeney insisted that pork tenderloin was vastly superior to dry cat food and wouldn't take no for an answer—the right moment hadn't arrived to show David the grisly playground Trevor had put online. So far, Chris's attempts to trace the site's origins had met with failure. Even at ARIN, the American Registry for Internet Numbers, the vast on-line repository of domain names, he had drawn a blank. Which meant the killer was spoofing his IP address. Every computer connected to the Internet had a unique IP, or Internet protocol, address, usually supplied by their Internet service provider. The killer was obviously skilled enough to fake his own IP so he couldn't be traced. He was using a labyrinthine technique to conceal his location behind legitimate addresses. He may even have jacked other machines and was using them as relays to host his site—if he activated enough of those and he could rotate the site's actual location often enough to avoid detection by nearly anyone.

But Chris wasn't just anyone. He dug into his bank of software tools and with some programming tweaks, set his own snoopers spidering along the Internet conduits. Sooner or later he would narrow the search down to something useful.

Two cups of coffee later, nothing had come back. With a sigh he rinsed his mug out and logged off. Maybe something would turn up before his plane took off.

Either way he was going to have to tell David.

David emerged half an hour later, wearing a bathrobe and blinking owlishly in the morning light. He smiled when he saw

Chris. Then the smile slipped.

"What is it?"

Chris explained his discovery of the trophy Web site and his technical search for the domain.

David exploded when Chris finished telling him about the Web site. "Dammit, why didn't you say something earlier—"

"I was trying to find out where it originated from. It could literally be anywhere in the world. I didn't think that was very useful to you."

"We have our own people who can do that—Never mind, tell me how to get to this site."

Chris wrote the URL down on the back of a piece of paper. David slid it into his pocket.

"Stop this, Chris. This is police business, we can get warrants—"

"How do you get warrants for something in cyberspace when you don't even know where it's located? I wanted to find out where it was coming from—that would have been a big help, right?"

"Well, yeah . . . But we can use the images, too. We can pick up location cues of the backgrounds. Maybe even sound cues—"

"I want this guy stopped. I hate what he did to Bobby, what he's done to Des, and the others—all six of them. I hate him. I want him dead—"

"Don't say that. I can't operate that way. I'm mandated to uphold the law—" David froze. "What do you mean 'six'?"

"Kyle, plus there were five on that horrible Web site . . . " Chris looked away. "I knew them all, except that one guy. Daniel? I never heard of him."

"Five? Do you remember their names?"

"I—"

"It's important, Chris. Who were they?"

Chris squeezed his eyes shut. Names. "Jason Blake," he whispered. "Bobby. Jeff. Frank—"

"Frank?" David was scanning his notes, frowning. "I don't have any Frank listed anywhere." He snapped the notebook shut. "It must be our last John Doe. We never did get an I.D. on him. What was the last name? Do you remember?"

"Frank," Chris said. "Frank . . . Barker."

David scribbled the name down on the same paper Chris had written the Web site URL.

"All I want to do is help," Chris said.

"Yes, well, you can help me by staying out of this. I've got enough things to worry about."

Chris bristled at the censure. For his part, David barely finished his coffee before he left the kitchen. Chris heard him in the living room making a phone call. No doubt to his partner. A couple of minutes later Chris heard the downstairs shower go on.

He was tempted to follow; he didn't want his trip to start with bad words lingering between them. Then his BlackBerry buzzed.

He flipped it open.

It was Phil DePalma, from Pharmaden.

"Hey, Chris," DePalma said. "I was hoping I'd catch you at home."

"What's up?" Chris couldn't imagine what DePalma wanted—all their dealings had been through DataTEK Systems and Petey.

"I've got six more servers coming in next week and I'm going to need help setting them up . . . "

"And you want my help? Sure, just call Petey—"

"I don't want DataTEK involved," DePalma insisted. "I want you."

"Well I don't know, Phil . . . "

"Just think about it, will you? I can guarantee you lots of work, either here or at one of our sister companies out in the Valley."

Chris's mind spun. Get out of DataTEK? He'd thought about it often, but never all that seriously.

"Listen, can I call you next week? I'm heading out of town for a couple of days."

“Sure, sure. If you can get back to me by Thursday that would be great. We need to make a decision by Friday.”

“It’s in my calendar.” Feeling a bit bemused, Chris closed the BlackBerry.

Then he jogged upstairs to finish his packing.

CHAPTER 23

Sunday, 5:20 P.M., Santa Monica Boulevard, West Hollywood

DAVID COULD SEE that the I-405 was jammed—even traffic on the ramps wasn't moving. He decided to cut over to Sepulveda and headed south. Chris leaned back in the passenger seat and closed his eyes, feeling their passage down the wide street. The sun's rays left warm tracks on his skin where it poured through the window. David wove handily in and out of the early-evening traffic. At some point he turned the radio on. Pearls of wisdom fell from Shania's unblemished lips.

It was pleasant to relax and remember the last two days. Sex with David was beyond incredible. He had a way of making Chris feel like nothing existed but his pleasure. His needs. It got better and better, hotter and hotter, and that had never happened before, not with anyone.

Even now he could feel David's touch, arousing him. He sighed, "David."

"Wake up, sleepy-head." David's voice held a rich undertone of amusement.

"I wasn't sleeping."

"You have a very romantic snore."

"And I don't snore." He looked around in consternation. They were in the Marina del Rey parking lot in front of the Waterfront Bar & Grill. "Do I?"

The hand on his knee moved to cup his chin. "Would such a perfect mouth ever do anything so vulgar?"

Chris straightened his spine, stretching his back muscles. They creaked alarmingly. "I was not sleeping."

"Come on, Rip, let's go snag ourselves a table before they're all gone and I end up eating at McDonald's. I get enough of that with Martinez."

David pulled the car up to the curb, got out, and tossed the keys to the parking valet who caught them and waited patiently for Chris to climb out.

The evening was wonderful. From their window seat they had an incredible view of a forest of masts backdropped by a sky spun with webs of red and gold.

They watched, enchanted, as a sixty-foot sailing yacht glided past. The deck blazed with more lights than the annual Christmas tree display on Rodeo Drive. A flag waved limply off the stern, a red maple leaf on a white field. The gilt lettering on the stern said EXECUTIVE DECISION. Lithe young women prowled the deck clutching untouched glasses. Men who weren't much more substantial moved among them. Chris swore he could hear the Salon de Mesnil bubbles popping.

"Looks like fun," he murmured.

"You think so? Why'd you never buy yourself a boat, then?"

Chris shrugged. "It looks like fun to go out like that when someone else is driving. I'm not the nautical type."

"I didn't think you 'drive' a boat."

"My point exactly. If I go to sea, it'll be on a luxury ship where I'll sail to exotic ports and let someone else do all the work."

"You're a spoiled brat."

"Is that a bad thing?"

David sighed. "On my salary, yes."

Chris stared out over the blood red ocean at the departing sailboat. "I'm not looking for a daddy," he said quietly. "I don't care how much money someone has."

"What are you looking for?"

A lean-hipped black-and-white clad waiter came around with menus and a wine list. Chris took the wine list, studying it while he considered his answer. He knew the future of their relationship—if they were to have one—rested on his response. And for the first time in his life he found he didn't want to blow this man off. He wanted a chance to make it work.

To become what, he didn't know. But he wanted the chance.

After he selected a Napa Valley Cabernet Sauvignon that gave excellent quality without breaking the bank, he raised his eyes to meet David's.

"I'm looking for the same thing you are, I think. Someone who's there for me, even if one or both of us is working a twelve-hour shift and I'm cranky and bitchy when I get home. Someone who forgives me when I do something stupid, like forget his birthday or burn dinner the day the in-laws come to town." He picked up the pepper mill and twisted it in his hands, sprinkling black flakes of fresh cracked pepper on the white tablecloth. Instantly the sharp smell of pepper tugged at his nose. "Does your whole family know you're gay?"

David nodded. "They've learned to live with it. My sister seems to have less trouble than anyone else."

"What would they do if you wanted to bring a friend for, say Christmas dinner?"

"I've never asked."

"My sister's okay with it. My parents . . . " Chris shrugged. "Well, that's another story."

Their waiter returned and they ordered. David got the daily special, Angus New York steak with grilled portobello mushrooms. Chris opted for Cuban black bean soup and blackened swordfish.

The sommelier brought the wine. After pouring them both glasses, Chris raised his to David. "To the future," he said. "May you catch all the bad guys and still have time left for all the good things in life. Like us."

David was being cagey. He smiled and dutifully sipped his wine. "The future."

The food was exquisite. The wine was everything the reviewers had promised. Outside, the last strands of sunlight drenched the sky in blood-orange red, finally fading to purple and midnight blue. A few feeble stars tried to show past the overwhelming light show cast by ten million Southern Californians.

They finished the bottle of wine. David refused a second one. Instead they settled on coffee, Chris his espresso, David a freshly roasted Colombian.

"You drink that," David said. "You won't be sleeping tonight."

Chris grinned. "Trust me, after last night, I'll sleep just fine." He reached across the table and touched David's fingertips. "I wish you were coming with me. Maybe next time?"

"You do these often?"

"Couple of times a year. Becky and I trade off. The next one is July, in Vegas. Think you could handle that?"

When the bill came Chris didn't protest when David reached for it. He knew a bit about pride and if David could keep his by paying for dinner, then Chris wasn't going to make a big deal out of it. He hoped there'd be plenty of future opportunities where David wasn't so touchy about money.

Back out in the car, Chris sighed and leaned his head against the seat.

"That was nice."

David tipped the parking attendant and expertly wheeled his vintage Chevy back onto Sepulveda. A steady stream of lights led the way south. They cruised at moderate speed, rarely topping fifty. Traffic lightened as they neared the airport. From behind them someone's high beams suddenly splashed into the car's interior, momentarily bringing a shot of daylight.

David muttered under his breath and looked away from the rearview mirror, blinking.

"Idiot," he said. He tapped his brakes as an SUV shot past, its horn dopplering as it pulled ahead before melting back into traffic.

Chris eased out of his seat belt and slid over to the middle of the bench seat. When David threw him a warning look he quickly buckled up the center seat belt before leaning his head against David's shoulder. His hand found a comfortable, familiar spot between David's legs.

"No funny stuff, now."

Chris smiled in the dark. He could feel David's erection pressing against his palm. "Wouldn't dream of it."

Lights flared along the stream of cars as brake lights came on. David swung onto Century Boulevard just as his cell rang.

"Grab it, will you?" Chris reached into David's pocket and drew out the phone. David took the phone from Chris and flashed him a smile before concentrating on whoever was calling. Judging from the one-sided conversation, Chris figured it was Martinez.

"Yeah? What time? I can be there. You can give me the details then."

He handed the phone back to Chris, who shut it and held it in his lap while he returned to stroking David.

"You have to go?" He had been hoping David could park the car and join him inside while he waited for his plane. He was running out of time.

"We got an anonymous tip—someone called in a location for Trevor Watson."

Chris could tell by his tone of voice that Trevor was still a sore point between them. He decided not to pursue it.

David pulled into a no-parking zone, flashing the overzealous airport cop his tin before getting out to help Chris drag his laptop case and the smaller Andiamo bag out of the trunk.

Then they stood awkwardly together on the brightly lit concourse while other travelers streamed around them. They didn't touch; Chris tried to think of something to say.

David finally broke the silence. "Call me when you get back. Chances are I'll be out in the Valley with Martinez."

"Well, good luck. Hope you catch him." Chris knew how lame that sounded. But it felt awkward not being able to do what seemed natural—kiss this man good-bye. Instead he had to settle for touching his hand and issuing a crooked smile.

"I'll call."

"I'll pick you up."

"Promise?"

"Yeah." David grinned. "Promise. And Chris?"

"Yes?"

"Stay away from those Web sites."

"No problem."

Chris walked through the terminal's open doors, and checked that his flight was still on schedule. He was early. More than enough time for a last-minute drink. When he saw the sign for a bar called the Encounter, he realized it was just what he needed: some light-hearted fun to take his mind off Trevor and Bobby and Kyle.

The Theme Building was one of the most recognized landmarks in L.A. after the HOLLYWOOD sign. The seventy-foot structure looked like something that had dropped in from outer space.

They carried the space-ship theme over into the interior. The Jetsons would have felt right at home amid the lava lamps and moon-cratered walls. The elevator played Esquival's *Harlem Nocturne*.

Chris selected a rear booth. A waiter sauntered over. Chris knew without asking that the guy was an actor. Tall, saturnine good looks were a staple in L.A. Still, he couldn't help it; he stared at the guy's well-packed groin. When he looked up it was to find him staring back in turn. A knowing look flashed between them.

"Hey," the waiter said.

"Draft," Chris said.

"Sure." But instead of heading for the bar he waited.

A month ago Chris would have had the guy's number in his

wallet by now. Two weeks ago he would have flaunted his own package and sauntered straight to the bathroom, knowing he would be followed. Now he just stared into a pair of sharp brown eyes and smiled, thinking of another pair of brown eyes flecked with green. Wishing he wasn't on his way to Denver.

"Dos Equis, if you have it."

"Sorry. Bud, Miller Lite, Rolling Rock."

Chris grimaced. "Bud." He thought of Bobby then. "No, make that a Rolling Rock instead."

While he waited, he pulled Bobby's Palm Pilot out and pulled up the boy's journal again. He began skimming, doing his best to ignore the entries Bobby had made on their encounter.

His beer arrived with a frothy head, a cocked hip, and knowing grin, which he ignored. Only after the waiter left did he suck off the head before savoring a mouthful of beer. It was cold. It had that much going for it.

His BlackBerry vibrated. He looked at the number. My god, it was Petey. The man was like the Black Death; he didn't know when to quit.

"I want you in my office the morning you get back from your trip."

Something solidified within Chris. "No," he said. He sat back and waited.

He didn't have to wait long. "What?"

"You heard me. But if it wasn't clear, then hear this: I quit. The only thing you'll find on your desk when I get back is my official resignation."

Silence. Then, "You're making a big mistake, Bellamere."

"I prefer to think I'm correcting one. I'll get this contract for you, then I'm finished with your bullshit. And don't think you can give me a bad reference, either, Petey. I know the kinds of sites you visit when you're sitting in your office all by yourself."

"Bellamere—"

Chris broke the connection. Then he punched in Phil DePalma's number and gave him the good news. Finally he shut the BlackBerry off. Now he just wanted to finish his drink in silence. He went back to reading the world according to Bobby—

"Figures I'd find you here."

Chris swung around in his booth and gazed up at Tom Clarke.

"What are you doing here?"

"Delivering this." He tossed a DataTEK inter-office mail envelope onto the acrylic tabletop.

Chris eyed the envelope, but made no move to open it. He didn't waste his time telling Tom he'd quit. He'd find out soon enough. Why make the guy's weekend?

"Hey." Tom grabbed Chris's beer and upended it, draining the glass. "Peter said you needed it."

"Hey!"

"Oh, was that yours? Here, I'll get you another one."

Chris watched in exasperation as Tom swaggered across the wildly lit bar and spent several minutes talking up the woman behind the bar. Chris looked away in disgust when he put his hand on her arm and leaned down to whisper in her ear.

Jesus, what a clown. He reached for the envelope, then caught sight of an entry in the Palm Pilot. He pulled it closer to study the small print. Tom plunked a full beer down in front of him, it's pale golden head wilted by the rough treatment.

Tom slid into the chair opposite Chris. He sipped his own drink, something dark on ice. The raw odor of top-shelf scotch wafted over the table.

Chris did his best to ignore the man.

Tom stared across the room at the bartender.

"Like to shove my ten-inch pole up that twat, eh? Have her screaming for more."

Chris buried his nose in the beer and gulped a large mouthful. The man was a pig.

"But I guess that's not your style, is it, queenie? You'd rather have that ten inches up your own chute."

Chris looked up from reading the Palm. "You volunteer for this or did Petey order you to be an ignorant asshole?"

Tom grinned.

Chris took another sip of beer. Bobby was writing about some incredible guy he had met who was going to get him into real films. Some guy who told the poor sap it didn't matter that he'd done porn, he was going to be the next Johnny Depp. Chris squinted at the blurred writing. Jesus, it couldn't be. He leaned closer, studying the output on the tiny screen. He recognized that name and how the hell was that possible?

"What's that?" Tom reached for the Palm Pilot.

Chris pulled it out of his reach. "Personal," he muttered, still squinting, trying to make sense of what he saw on the Palm Pilot's tiny screen, blinking away a sudden blurriness in his eyes. "That's not possible."

"What's not possible?"

Shaking his head and wishing Tom would shut up and go away, Chris stared in befuddled wonder at the fuzzy screen. "On top of everything this guy Tom's cute as hell. So far he hasn't made any moves and I don't want to blow it by spooking the guy with a pass if he's not ready, but man, he's hot. He's going to talk to this big producer he knows and maybe I can go for a reading next week. We'll form our own production company to take it to them. He wants to call it Clarke Pictures. I can hardly wait."

"What the hell . . . " The Palm Pilot slipped out of fingers that felt suddenly like wooden clubs. He reached for it, only to watch it spin out of control and skid across the table.

Tom caught it and held it up. "My, what's this, then?"

Their eyes met; Tom was grinning.

"Who knew the little faggot kept a diary, eh?" he said and his smile deepened. His eyes remained empty, Chris noticed. Like ice chips.

"Well don't think it hasn't been a slice," Chris said thickly. "But I gotta make like a tree and shove off—"

He made it halfway to his feet before his knees gave out on him. Dizzily he collapsed, rattling the table as he banged it with his hip.

He blinked at Tom, who swam in his vision and momentarily became two Toms, then a blur of pale flesh.

"Is something wrong, sir?"

Chris looked up to find the waiter bending over the table, bland curiosity on his wavering face. Chris shook his head in growing alarm and stared at Tom, who was suddenly standing beside him.

"He's the—"

"My friend's just had a bit too much to drink. I'll help him get on his flight." Tom was shaking his blond head. "His wife's going to be so disappointed. You swore you stopped drinking, buddy. Even did the AA thing. Now look at you."

The waiter receded, losing interest once he heard wife. Tom grabbed Chris's elbow in an iron grip.

"No . . . " Chris tried to pull away. His words came out as barely a whisper.

"Oh, I'm afraid yes. I'm going to take good care of you, aren't I, Chris?"

Chris fumbled with his BlackBerry, trying to hit keys with wooden fingers. Before he could do more than activate it, Tom wrenched it away and tossed it onto the chair beside Chris.

"You really won't be needing that anymore." Tom leaned over and his sour breath brushed Chris's face. "I don't think you'll be disappointed, Chris. It'll be a real scream."

Sunday, 9:50 P.M., Tyburn Street, Glendale

David pulled off the Hollywood Freeway. The clock on the dash said ten. He was running late. A two-car collision on the Santa Monica Freeway had slowed him down. He grabbed the cell off the seat where Chris had dropped it and speed-dialed Martinez.

"I'm about ten minutes away. Where are you?"

"Just pulling into Tyburn Street. How 'bout I wait for you and we go up together."

"Suits me."

David tossed the phone back on the seat. He caught the red and white running lights of a plane overhead and watched it briefly. Chris would be in the air by now. He wasn't sure what the future was going to bring them, but after the last couple of days he was no longer going to reject their relationship out of hand. Give it a chance, Chris had asked. He couldn't do less than that. He loved the man. He couldn't just turn his back, however big a fool that made him.

He pulled onto Tyburn Street, near the Los Angeles River, and drew up behind Martinez's brown Crown Victoria in front of a vacant lot. Martinez hopped out and strolled back. He stopped at the front fender.

They both stared at the vacant lot. The only sign of life was a wasted mongrel rooting around in a pile of garbage at the end of the block.

David kicked at the curb, loosening a fast-food wrapper that skittered off down the street. "Someone's jerking our chain. Tell me this wasn't a wild goose chase."

Martinez swore under his breath.

David laid his hand on his partner's arm. Martinez flinched away; David pretended not to notice. "It's a bust. Isn't the first time. But listen, we're not far from the Anstroms' place. Why don't we see if they're home? Maybe she remembers seeing Daniel with Trevor."

Before they could go anywhere David's cell rang. When he hung up he shook his head.

"That was the switchboard. The Highway Patrol pulled a body out of a dumpster in the Charlton Flat—in an area the Forest Service just closed off recently."

"So if our helpful perp hadn't sent that picture it would have stayed there for months."

"Years," David corrected. "They close portions of Charlton Flat for ten years. To improve erosion control."

"Who's got the d.b.?"

"They're going to bring the body down to the coroner's. We'll get the initial autopsy results early next week." David brushed his leg. "Ready to go talk to Daniel's mother?"

Martinez didn't have a better suggestion, so they wound their way through dark streets until they pulled onto the Anstroms' driveway.

Several spotlights lighted up the familiar three-story Cape Cod. Through the front window David could see the flickering blue glow of a television.

The woman David had met earlier, when he came with news of her son's death, opened the door. Edith Anstrom appeared older now, more careworn.

"Mrs. Anstrom?" David said. "We met earlier . . . ?"

"Yes, I remember you." She looked from David to Martinez.

"This is my partner, Detective Martinez Diego."

"What is this about?"

"We have a picture we'd like you to look at, see if you recognize someone."

"I was in the living room watching the news," Edith said. She lowered her voice. "Is this about Daniel?"

Preferring not to prejudice her into making an I.D. just to get closure on her son's death, David said, "We're looking for anyone who might have information regarding your son's disappearance."

Edith indicated a beveled wooden door with multiple panes of glass engraved with images were of old sailing ships. "We can do this in the living room."

If Edith wasn't a sailor, her husband must be one. The theme of ships and the East Coast permeated the cozy living room.

Above a fieldstone fireplace the wooden mantelpiece was packed with sailing treasures: a sextant, a pair of finely wrought reproductions of old sailing vessels complete with cotton sails that looked ready to catch a stiff southwest breeze.

A gray-muzzled basset hound raised its massive head when they entered the room. It looked at them with rheumy eyes, then seemed to decide they were no threat it could handle and promptly went back to sleep.

Edith watched them through piercing hazel eyes that had David mentally examining his state of dress. Had he left his fly open? Was his tie crooked?

"Whose picture is it?" she asked in a whiskey voice that spoke of years of smoking.

"We don't know, ma'am," David lied. "That's why we'd like you to look at it. Tell us if you recognize him."

"At least you admit it's a man's picture. You probably know a lot more than you're letting on, but you won't tell me anything. Don't want to influence me, do you?"

"Ma'am?"

"Oh, don't play dumb, young man," she said. "I hate it when men play dumb just because some woman lets them know she understands their game. Now, show me this picture."

Trying to hide his smile, David handed her the police artist's sketch of Trevor Watson. She laid it in her lap.

Immediately Edith's hands began to shake. She stared down at the picture in her lap.

"What on earth are you doing with a picture of our nephew?"

"Your *nephew*?" David leaned forward. "This man is related to you?"

"Well, not really." Edith fluttered her hands. "It's more a relationship by marriage. Trevor was my son-in-law's brother. Half-brother, actually. He used to work for some company that made atrocious movies."

"Do you see him often?" David asked.

"Once a month, perhaps. Holidays he would come for dinner. He had no other family. His own parents were dead, had been for years, as I understand it."

"When was the last time you saw him?"

"He was here last weekend. His landlord was hassling him about paying more rent for that dump he lived in so Trevor asked if he could stay here a few days."

"Did Trevor know Daniel?"

"Of course. They weren't exactly friends, Trevor being so much older than Daniel, but they got along well enough. At Christmas they used to horse around and if we had one of our big picnics on July Fourth they'd usually end up playing football or some other rough-and-tumble boy's game."

"Did you see him just before Daniel disappeared?" David was making less and less sense of this. Why would Trevor need to drug Anstrom to get him away from his friends? He could have taken him anytime, and not from in front of people who might know him.

Edith didn't answer right away. She stared across the room at the mantelpiece full of memories, her hand resting atop the Basset hound's head. The dog's snores filled the silence.

"Yes," she said. "Yes, I did see him. He brought Daniel home that night he got so dreadfully sick. Later we figured he must have eaten a bad hot dog earlier that afternoon. He was down for two days with that. Then, two days later, Daniel was on his way back to that place he hung out at and he vanished. Trevor was so upset over that, I think he half blamed himself."

David and Martinez traded glances. This was not looking good.

"Do you know where your nephew is right now, Mrs. Anstrom?"

"Why yes," she said. "He's in New York. He told me he had a job lined up there. He lost his job here, you know. Somebody he knew in New York thought he might have something for him. So he flew out on Tuesday."

"New York," David said woodenly.

"He'll be gone at least another week, then if he gets the job, he may have to move out there for a while at least. Is something wrong, officer?"

"No ma'am," Martinez said. "Do you have a number where your nephew can be reached?"

"Of course." Edith Anstrom leafed through some papers and stacked magazines neatly on a pristine antique end table, until she came up with her address book. Then she read off a New York exchange and a number.

David wrote it down. "We'd like to thank you for your time, Mrs. Anstrom."

Even before he reached the door David had his cell out and was dialing the number. It rang several times and he was about to hang up when a sleepy voice mumbled something unintelligible into the phone.

"Trevor Watson?"

The voice mumbled something else that might have been a question, or it might have been a curse.

"Is this Trevor Watson I'm speaking to?"

"Who wants to know?"

The voice still sounded blurry from sleep, but David was beginning to get a horrible feeling about this whole thing.

"It's Los Angeles calling. Is this Watson?"

"Didn't know a city could make a phone call. Who is this, really?"

"It's the LAPD I'm calling from your aunt's house. Is this Trevor Watson?"

"You're at Aunt Edith's place?" The voice sounded more alert now. And getting pissed. "What are you doing there?"

"Trying to find you. One more time, sir," David said. "Are you Trevor Watson?"

"Yeah, I'm Trevor. So what's the big deal? Why are you looking for me?"

Sunday, 11:15 P.M., Blackridge Road, Santa Monica Mountains

Chris woke once to find himself on the floor of a vehicle bouncing and jolting down what could only be unpaved road. Which meant they were outside the city. His cheek was pressing into a rough mat, the stench of hot oil, gas and human sweat filled his nostrils. He could hear the clatter and crunch of dirt and gravel on the undercarriage. How much time had passed? Chris groggily tried to roll over, but his movements were slow and uncoordinated. Barely conscious, he tried to brace himself against the vehicle's wall.

They hit a muffler-eating bump and Chris's head slammed back into the steel wall, ending all thought of sitting up. He passed out again.

Sunday, 11:20 P.M., Margate Street, North Hollywood, Los Angeles

David hung up on the irate Trevor. Trevor's voice wasn't the same as the voice on the phone whose owner had said that Chris belonged to him.

David stared helplessly at Martinez.

"We've been chasing the wrong guy." He glanced at his watch. "Listen, I want to make a couple of phone calls. Why don't you start with the airlines, see if you can nail down when Watson really took his New York flight."

Martinez immediately pulled out his phone and started dialing. David took advantage of his inattention to slip back to his car. He quickly dialed Chris's cell. Chris would be happy to know that it looked like his friend was no longer implicated in any of this.

Besides, David wanted to hear his lover's voice again.

"Uh, h-hello?" The tentative, soft female voice was definitely not Chris.

David took a shallow breath and let it out. "Who is this?"

"Ah, Loretta. Who's this?"

"Where's Chris?"

"You mean the guy who left this thing behind? He's gone. Some buddy of his helped him out an hour ago. I didn't even notice this was here until it started ringing. Who are you?"

A cold, gut-wrenching weight settled into David's stomach. He almost dropped the phone, then grabbed it and managed to say, "Where are you?"

"The Encounter. It's a bar at the airport—"

"I know what it is. This is Detective David Laine, LAPD" David's mind raced. God, no, it couldn't be. Don't let it be. Not Chris. No. "Where was the guy with the phone sitting? The bar? A table?"

"A table—"

"I need you to stay at that table until we get there. Don't let anyone near it. Can you do that for me, Loretta?"

"Who are you again?"

David told her.

"Yeah, sure, I guess . . . "

David bolted across the lawn to where Martinez was trying to browbeat someone on the other end of the phone into giving him information. David grabbed his arm.

Martinez jerked away, his eyes narrowing when he saw David's face.

"He's got Chris."

They leapt into the car and took off with a spray of gravel. The siren screaming, they raced south to the Hollywood Freeway, then followed I-405 south at breakneck speed.

CHAPTER 24

Sunday, 11:25 P.M., Blackridge Road, Santa Monica Mountains

CHRIS WOKE AGAIN. He was no longer moving and he felt plush carpet under his bare knees. He was kneeling, his arms held behind his back. Something dug into his throat. He opened his eyes. He had no idea where he was.

At some point Tom had tied him with a single piece of strong, thin rope. It held his hands together behind his back and passed around his neck. Any movement on his part only served to tighten the bindings, choking him. His shoulders burned with an icy fire that spread slowly down his upper torso.

He was naked.

He tried to look around. He was in a large finished basement. Dark wood paneling lined the walls. He could just make out the thick, carved leg of what looked like a pool table out of the corner of his eye. High above his head was the black rectangle of a window. It was still night. How much time had passed?

Diffuse golden light filled the otherwise shadowed room.

An Italian side-table held a Tiffany lamp that wasn't turned on and a Web cam with its unblinking red eye trained on him. Then he saw what lay beside the Web cam and fear pulsed through him.

It was a long, wicked-looking blade.

He licked his lips. His tongue felt dry and his lips stung. He swayed dizzily, trying hard not to move, knowing that any movement would only start him choking again. The muscles of his legs vibrated dully and cramps built up in his feet and calves.

He saw movement out of the corner of his eye, and before he could think he reacted. He jerked around, but his arms weren't there to balance him. He slammed sideways into the floor, tasting blood and carpet fiber as his mouth scraped the rug.

Two perfectly creased pant legs appeared in his field of vision. Rough hands grabbed the rope that held his wrists bound and hauled him upright. His shoulders felt as though they were being wrenched from their sockets. He couldn't help it, he screamed.

Tom's face was inches from his and Chris could see the dark desire dancing in the cold depths of his glacier blue eyes. Through the fog of pain Chris struggled to bite his tongue. Pain only excited this guy. Screaming roused no sympathy in him, only a gleeful need to cause more. Chris glared at him through tear-filled eyes.

"Hey, Bellamere." Chris saw the blade in Tom's hand and his terror returned. "I've been waiting for this day."

Chris spat out a bright red globule of blood and tried to still the erratic beating of his heart. His mouth tasted of copper. "Can't say I have."

"Cool little bitch, aren't you?" Tom lifted Chris's chin. "You really think you'll stay cool once I start? Don't you think the others tried to show me how butch they were, too?"

Chris was forced to pull his arms up to avoid choking. He grimaced and tried to squirm away.

Tom laid the narrow blade alongside Chris's face.

"If I cut you up and let you go, do you really think that pig would look at you twice afterward? Really, I thought you had better taste." The blade burned a solitary path down Chris's right cheek. Hot blood welled out. "Fucking a pig. When you could have had anyone."

The knife traced a second path beside the first down his cheek. "So pretty. But it's all so shallow. There's nothing underneath. Just blood. Blood and pain. That's all any of you are good for."

Tom grabbed his hair and pulled his head back. With his finger, he traced a bloody path through the free-flowing blood on Chris's face and smeared it over Chris's lips, jerking his head toward the camera. "Add a touch of color. Smile, Chris. Smile for David."

The pain was assaultive, overwhelming his senses and drowning out everything else. Chris ground his teeth to keep from crying out, but even so a soft whimper emerged.

"You killed them all, didn't you?"

Tom smiled. He circled Chris, who had to twist his head around to follow him. Tom hovered behind him, and Chris tensed, half expecting to feel the sting of the knife again. Not knowing where or when the cut would come was worse than the actual physical violence.

"Why?" Chris whispered.

Tom touched him again and Chris jumped, belatedly realizing it was just a finger. He cursed himself for giving Tom the reaction he wanted. But then, if he didn't maybe Tom would just go ahead and use the knife until Chris showed his fear. Chris was under no illusions that he could hold out for long. If Tom wanted him to scream, he'd scream. The knowledge was demoralizing.

Tom laughed softly. His hand touched him again, gliding over Chris's shrinking skin.

"Very dumb. Pretty, but dumb." He ruffled Chris's hair. "I guess dumb blonds come in both flavors." He grabbed his hair and tilted Chris's head back. "I killed them because they fucked you. They had no right to do that. You belong to me."

Chris's terrified mind grabbed a memory. "But who was Daniel Anstrom? I never even met anyone by that name."

"Hey, everybody can screw up. I meant to get that asshole uncle of his."

"Trevor?"

"Guess your friend got luckier than you did, eh?"

Chris's bound hands were slick with sweat and blood. He could feel the rope's knot when he twisted his fingers around. When Tom moved around in front of him again he jiggled his fingers against it, testing the bindings. Something moved under his fingers. Could he keep Tom distracted while he tried to wriggle free?

"Coward," he said. "Does your uncle know what a piece of shit you are? Do you think he would have bought you that job if he knew?"

Tom slid the flat of the knife alongside Chris's jaw, forcing his head up.

"My uncle doesn't care what I am, as long as I'm not a pansy." He suddenly looked quizzical. "Are you trying to make me mad? Now why would you do that? To make me slip up? I won't, you know. Failure isn't part of my plans for you. That's another thing my uncle could never abide. It doesn't matter anymore. Nothing does."

"You fucked up big time with Des. He got away from you. I saw him just yesterday and he's getting better every day. Soon he'll be able to tell the police everything they need to know about you. He'll tell your uncle, too." Chris didn't know if any of that was true. Even when Des did wake up, with his head injuries as serious as they were, what were the odds he would remember anything?

"Perhaps," Tom said softly, but Chris saw the rage flare in his blue eyes. "But it won't be soon enough to save you."

"You can't even admit you fucked up, can you? Useless queer faggot—"

Tom backhanded him. Chris never saw it coming and couldn't have braced for it anyway. He sprawled backwards, managing to roll sideways to take the worst of the damage on his side when he slammed into the floor. His arms jerked up and Chris was sure he had dislocated his shoulders. His scream was cut off as the rope around his throat tightened, his arms pinned beneath him. Gagging and coughing, he managed to roll onto his side and relieved some of the pressure on his neck. At least he could breathe again.

With his hands pressed into the carpeted floor he gained some leverage. Frantically he worked his nearly paralyzed fingers over the knot. Was it getting looser? Yes, it was. But not enough.

He needed more time.

Tom stood less than a foot away. Under the neatly pressed pants Chris was all too aware of Tom's erection. How long before he was raped?

He thought of David then, and how, despite his size, he was a gentle, considerate lover. Even at the height of passion, pain was anathema to David. Chris should have seen what was there all the time. The love David offered him, even when he was telling him it wouldn't work. So obvious now.

Chris squeezed his eyes shut at the tears. He had never told David he loved him. Never hinted that he even cared. Now he might never have the chance. Instead, the last thing David would see was a video image of his body being brutalized.

Tom nudged him with the toe of his dress shoe. Abruptly he grabbed Chris's left arm under the armpit and hauled him back to his knees. Chris ground his teeth to stop from crying out at the new wave of pain.

He spit out blood mixed with thick globs of saliva. His throat was raw and swollen; he could barely swallow. More blood came up. Tom shoved him back onto his knees. This time he caressed Chris's bare chest with the blade.

The knife blade turned in and circled his right nipple, drawing a line of fire across his pecs. Chris swallowed past the ground glass in his throat and groaned.

"Is that the best you can do? The camera is waiting." Tom leaned closer, his eyes gleaming with feral delight. "David is waiting. He'll be watching so avidly. Agonizing over every little scratch. Every little bloody stroke."

He grazed Chris with the knife again. More blood flowed down his straining chest muscles. With his free hand Tom slid the zipper of his dress pants open; Chris closed his eyes.

"I used to tell them that if they were really good I'd let them go."

Tom giggled, an obscenely incongruous sound. "Stupid faggots always believed me. Come on now, open up, Chrissy. Eat me."

The knife slid across his throat. He did as he was ordered.

"Your boyfriend Bobby was especially slow-witted. He actually told me we could sell the video, make money. Stupid faggot."

Chris gagged. Tears mingled with his blood as he struggled to keep his balance and not choke. Behind his back the bonds loosened, slipped away from his bloody wrists. One hand came free.

"Bite me and I'll cut you twenty ways from Sunday. Your faggot boyfriend will need dental records to I.D. you."

He knew he'd only get one shot at this. If he screwed up he was dead.

Chris whimpered, knowing the sound would excite Tom even more. The knife blade slipped away from his neck, Tom's hands moved toward the top of Chris's head, urging him on, burying himself deep in Chris's throat.

"Oh, yeah, cocksucker—"

Chris reared back. At the same time he swung his freed hand up to smash his fist into Tom's balls, hard enough to hear the solid *thunk* of soft flesh giving way under the hard bones of his hand. The impetus of the blow sent him rolling backwards.

Tom screamed and fell. Chris continued the roll, frantically scrambling with numb fingers at the remains of the bindings. The tension in his throat slackened for a second, then the other arm swung loose.

His muscles were so weak that both arms flopped around as though they were attached to lifeless rag dolls. When the feeling started coming back it was even worse. Pain flared along overstimulated nerve endings. He hunched forward on the carpet, burning his knees on the stiff fiber as he dragged himself further away from where Tom still lay writhing on the floor, clutching himself.

Chris looked for the knife but didn't see it anywhere. He spat out the foul taste of Tom and stumbled to his feet. The bloody rope pooled at his feet. The muscles in his legs quivered and threatened to dump him back on the ground. He grabbed the pool table, leaning over it. Heavy green felt grazed his bare skin. He left a trail of gore along the clean surface.

On the wall hung a rack of pool cues. He shambled toward it, pins and needles now playing along the nerves of his feet. His muscles twitched, cramps stabbed. He locked his arms on the pool table and forced his legs straight. Pain flared anew.

He managed to pull a wooden cue out of the rack. It took both hands to hold it steady.

He looked back. Tom struggled to his feet, one hand still cupping his bruised cock and balls. On his face a look of pure murder. In his hand the knife. Chris backed away from the wavering blade.

"You'll pay for that, faggot," Tom whispered.

"Not this time," Chris said.

He swung the pool cue and Tom skipped away. Chris hated the weakness that made chasing the other man foolhardy. But if he couldn't fight he could run. He snatched up the Tiffany lamp and stabbed at Tom with the cue again, keeping him at bay.

He raised the lamp and flung it at Tom as hard as he could, and followed it with the Web cam. Tom ducked both. Chris spun around and ran, plunging headlong up the stairs into the darkness beyond the circle of light.

CHAPTER 25

Sunday, 11:55 P.M., I-405, Los Angeles

DAVID GRIPPED THE steering wheel tightly enough to leave marks. His foot pressed down like a bar of lead, urging the already straining vehicle to move faster. The bubble light he had attached to the car's dash shot beams of red light down the windshield and car hood. The siren wailed its warning to traffic ahead of him in his unmarked and Martinez, behind him in the Crown Victoria.

"Airport security's been alerted," Martinez said over the two-way. "A couple of radio cars have been dispatched, too. They ought to be rolling in about now."

David nodded, knowing it was too late. Whoever had taken Chris was already gone.

"We'll find him, Davey."

Neither of them commented on the obvious. They'd find him, yes. But would he be alive?

The lights of the airport appeared off to the right. David swung onto the off ramp and let the siren and lights get him through the traffic.

David braked to a stop in front of the entrance where he had dropped Chris not four hours before. Martinez pulled in behind him. Both sirens wound down. The lights were still flashing, bathing startled pedestrians with a crimson glow.

They met on the concourse.

An airport security officer approached them.

"Sir?" The security officer flashed a nervous smile and David thought he was going to salute. Instead he fidgeted with his belt.

"We've canvassed the area and no one reports seeing anyone matching the description of either person you're seeking. Do you want us to continue?"

"Did Chris Bellamere take his flight to Denver?"

"No sir, he did not."

"Then keep looking, but I suspect the two have already fled the area."

"We do have a videotape of the main concourse, the area both of them would have had to cross to reach the Encounter."

David and Martinez traded glances. "Video? Show us."

The senior security officer, Norm Drover, was a dour, pot-bellied man in his late fifties with a thatch of graying hair combed over his bald dome and suspicious eyes that glinted at the world from behind a pair of glasses. He nodded curtly at David and Martinez.

"We've isolated the video loops for the time and area in question." Norm pulled out a chair on castors and indicated to the two detectives to take chairs nearby. Only Martinez accepted his offer.

David crowded close to the screen, studying each passing figure with intensity. He had no trouble recognizing Chris when he entered the concourse and moved down the corridor. He was alone.

"There," Norm said. "He enters the elevator that would take him up to the restaurant. One of my men recovered a BlackBerry, a laptop case, and an envelope from his table."

"Envelope?"

"Yes, from a DataTEK Systems. It was empty. Everything was secured into evidence by an officer from the LAPD"

David frowned. "Who would have brought an envelope from his work? It would have to be someone he worked with."

"Manager of the Encounter says he was in there less than half an hour before his friend helped him out of the place," Norm said.

"Did he appear drunk when he arrived?"

"No, the waitress claimed he seemed sober."

"Yet thirty minutes later he's supposed to be roaring drunk?" David felt his temper rising. He barely felt Martinez's hand on his arm.

Norm shrugged. "Drunks are a funny thing. Look sober one minute, falling down stupid the next. She figured he'd come in just under his limit. Said if he'd been female she might have wondered—but who expects a man to be drugged?"

David knew what he said was true, but he hated that after everything that had happened, it had been that easy to take Chris. Someone should have been watching. Someone like him.

"Hold on," Norm said. "We think this is him."

Another figure entered the same elevator Chris had gone up in moments before. All David could see was his back.

"No one else goes into the elevator. If we fast-forward this . . . " Norm did just that. "Is that Bellamere?"

Two figures emerged from the elevator this time. It was obvious one was supporting the other. Again, David had no trouble recognizing Chris, though his head was hanging down. He stumbled as he walked. Norm froze the image just before they walked off screen.

David also has no trouble recognizing the second man, carrying Chris's luggage.

"Tom Clarke."

Monday, 12:10 A.M., Blackridge Road, Santa Monica Mountains

Chris ran. The stairs were covered with thin carpeting that gave his bare feet purchase. He hit the door at the top with his shoulder and it flew open, nearly dumping him onto the tiled kitchen floor. He skidded past a massive refrigerator and barely avoided colliding with the counter beyond it.

His side ached and hot blood welled out of myriad small

cuts. He blinked away stinging blood as it dripped down his face, mingling with his tears.

He ran, heedless of where, aware of only one thing. Death followed him.

His bare feet gave him one advantage. He ran silently. Behind him, he could hear Tom blundering up the stairs, the solid soles of his dress shoes pounding noisily on the risers. His breathing was labored, and pain-filled.

Chris felt a hot satisfaction at the damage he had done. He only wished he could have done more.

Right now he had a more pressing issue. He had to get outside.

He eased through the doorway, trying not to knock anything over or crash into things. A thin light bled in through the open windows. The light had an odd color; at first he thought it was some kind of streetlight, but then he realized it was the moon. He caught a glimpse of it though the nearest window. It was nearly full. He could even make out some stars casting their own light.

He had no idea where he was. They were beyond the veil of light Los Angeles normally spilled into the night sky, drowning out all but the most persistent stars. How far from the city had they driven? What chance would anyone have of finding him?

The living room was filled with shadow and light. Dark shapes loomed—a floor lamp, a high-backed sofa, a big-screen TV. Deeper in the shadow, a matching high-backed chair faced the TV. Beside it was an end table. Light glinted off something plastic. A phone.

He grabbed the phone, knocked the end table with his hand, and lunged to catch it before everything fell. He plastered the receiver to his ear, feeling for buttons to dial 911. It was dead.

He tapped the button in the cradle to get a dial tone. Nothing. *Damn.*

Footsteps in the kitchen. Softer now. More focused. Tom was trying to sneak up on him.

He swung around the high-backed chair, crying out in surprise when he tripped over something. He fell sideways, and his hands were engulfed in cold stickiness. The smell of blood overwhelmed his senses.

He raised his head and stared into the sightless eyes of Saul Ruben, DataTEK's CFO. Cold moonlight shone on pale flesh, starkly illuminating the dark, fingernail-sized hole in the center of his forehead.

Tom really had taken care of his problem.

Monday, 12:20 A.M., Los Angeles International Airport

David reached up to touch the frozen video image. His fingers tracked across the cool screen, sliding over the grainy image of his lover. Icy fear slipped through his reserve.

Martinez was already on his cell. Vaguely, David heard him snapping at someone on the other end. Then he broke the connection and punched in another number, and a new argument started

" . . . employee records, Mr. McGill. I want this Clarke's address. No, not tomorrow. Now. Then find someone who can get them. Who lives closest? Rebecca? Who the hell is Rebecca—"

David touched his arm. "I've got her." He entered her number on his cell while Martinez continued to argue with Petey.

David held his breath when the line started ringing at the other end. He barely let it out when a sleepy female voice answered.

"Yeah? Who's this?"

"Rebecca Chapman?"

"Who wants to know?"

"Detective David Laine. We met a few days ago—"

"I remember." Becky's voice grew stronger and more pissed off. "What the hell is this about? Why are you calling me at . . . nearly one o'clock in the morning?"

"We're on the other line with your boss, Peter McGill. He tells me you're the closest to the DataTEK offices. We need you to go in and look up an address for us."

"An address? Now you're confusing me. Whose address could you possibly need at this time of night? Who are you hassling now—"

"This is important, Ms. Chapman. I can't go into details, but it involves Chris."

"Chris? How—"

"We need Tom Clarke's address. Don't argue, Ms. Chapman. Not now."

"Tom's address?"

"I need you to go into DataTEK. This is Chris's life, Ms. Chapman. I'm serious."

From the other end of the line he heard a male voice and Becky's muffled response. Then Becky came back on. "I don't have to go in. I can log on from here. Hold on, let me get to my laptop."

"Calling D.M.V.," Martinez said. "I'll find what they have on this Tom Clarke."

Becky came back on. "Okay, I'm dressed. You want to tell me what I'm looking for? Just what the hell has this got to do with Chris?"

"He's in . . . trouble," David said. "I can't really tell you any more than that. Not now. But we need to locate this Clarke guy."

Becky still sounded more confused than alarmed, which suited David just fine. Panic wouldn't help Chris right now.

"Okay, I'm logged on. It'll take me a couple of minutes to find the right HR records—damn, that means another password . . . Wait. Jesus, am I dumb or what? Chris left all that information."

"What do you mean? What did Chris leave?" Had he suspected Tom Clarke? But no, if he had, he would have said something to deflect suspicion from Trevor. "What is it, Ms. Chapman?"

"Oh for God's sake, call me Becky. Chris knew there was something flaky about Tom getting hired. He didn't have the experience or the knowledge. Chris found out the guy's uncle is DataTEK's CFO and Clarke's father is a major stockholder. So he ran down some information on both of them. Not that it would do any good, no matter what he found out. No way Petey's going to fire someone with that kind of clout."

"Would Tom have known about this?"

"He might have. Chris made no bones about not liking the guy. We all knew he was a phony."

"Who's the uncle?"

Silence. "Geez, you'd think I'd remember . . . Ruben. Paul, no, Saul Ruben."

"Check D.M.V. on a Saul Ruben, too," David said to Martinez. "See what they got on him." To Becky, "Find me an address on this guy. Please."

"He lives in Brentwood," she said and rattled off an address in the upscale side of town. "Pretty snazzy for someone just out of school."

David thought of Tom Clarke, who had to be on the other side of thirty. "He's a little old to be just graduating, isn't he?"

"Maybe he needed uncle's help getting into school. Hmm, this is interesting."

"What?"

"Chris really did some digging for just idle curiosity. The man's good. Looks like Ruben's got two places, one in Beverly Hills and another one up in Topanga Canyon. I always wanted a place out there. So rustic, you can hear the grass grow."

David and Martinez had always figured the perp had a hiding hole he took his vics to. Someplace isolated. In L.A. it didn't get much more isolated than Topanga Canyon. The entire area northwest of Los Angeles—a rugged, series of winding canyons that had resisted development for years—was riddled with barely traveled roads that at certain times of the year you needed an SUV to traverse. Was Saul Ruben's place on one of those?

"What can you tell me about the place in Topanga? Any information at all?"

"Just an address—Blackridge Road."

David took it, thanked her and hung up, glad he hadn't had to reveal just how much danger Chris was in. He clutched the notebook with the two addresses and caught Martinez's eye.

"Let's move."

"I'll check out his home address," Martinez said as they hurried through the concourse. "And call in some backup to meet me there."

"Think you can rustle up some warrants?"

"*No es problema*, we got more than enough juice." Martinez's eyes narrowed. "You got something in mind?"

"I want to check out the uncle's place. Get anything on him through D.M.V.?"

"Address, phone, he's got two vehicles registered to him. A BMW 330Ci coupe and a Ford Explorer—"

"Let's roll," David said. Martinez eyed him circumspectly. "Go nail this bastard, partner."

"Let's roll together," Martinez said. "This is no time for heroics, partner."

"Nothing heroic about talking to a man's uncle. We're not talking crime family here. I just need to know if Tommy's been keeping time with uncle lately. See if he's noticed anything hinky. I'll alert the sheriff's people I'm coming. They can meet me there."

"Keep me in the loop. Tight. You're in enough trouble without doing something really stupid."

"Wouldn't dream of it." David slapped the hood of his Chevy and unlocked the driver's side door. "Let's go."

He peeled out, the bubble light and siren on again to clear the way. Behind him he watched Martinez scramble to get into his own car and play catch-up. Flipping open his cell phone he dialed the Blackridge Road number first. No answer. Then he dialed the

Rubens' Beverly Hills number.

A woman answered his call. Her voice was sharp and abrupt. "Yes?"

"Is this the Ruben residence? Saul Ruben?"

"Yes, it is. Who is this?"

"This is Detective David Eric Laine, with the Los Angeles Police—"

"Oh dear God, did you find him?" The voice no longer sounded sharp. Now it sounded scared.

"Find who, ma'am?"

"My husband, Saul Ruben. We had a dinner appointment with friends but he never showed up. That's not like Saul—"

"Ma'am, did he say where he was going?"

"Yes." She drew in a deep breath and let it out. "To our place up in the canyon. One of our neighbors up there told him he'd seen someone on the property recently. He wanted to check and see if anyone had broken in . . . We've had break-ins before, you know. That place is so isolated."

"What time was this, ma'am?"

"He left here about one-thirty this afternoon." Her voice rose in fear again. "That's nearly twelve hours. I've called but all I get is voice mail. He would have called by now, I know he would have. Saul never just goes off—"

"Ma'am, I'm heading up that way. Would you like me to check out your place? I could look and see if anyone has been by the premises lately, maybe check with that neighbor."

She gave him the neighbor's address and phone number, someone named Chickie.

David thanked her and hung up. He tried Chickie's number. No one home. He drove north as fast as he could, his mind racing along with the car. Could Ruben have met up with Tom earlier today? Tom was clearly decompensating—no longer covering his tracks, no longer showing the care he took before to hide his actions. Did he know that he was at the end of his reign of terror and was setting it up to go out with one final, hated victim? Chris didn't fit the profile of his normal vics—the others were all dark-haired and butch—so David knew this one was personal.

Personal and up close.

His last call was to the sheriff's substation—only to be told a gas tanker had gone off the road in Malibu. The road was impassable and all units were tied up. Someone would be sent out to Blackridge as soon as a unit was available.

David snapped, "They better. This is urgent."

"So is a major fire in Malibu, sir," the dispatcher said coolly before disconnecting.

David jammed his foot down on the gas pedal. The car lurched forward as the engine roared.

Well, he could make it personal too.

Monday, 1:20 A.M., Fernwood Pacific Drive, Santa Monica Mountain

Topanga Canyon Road was a civilized stretch of paved roadway that cut a path from Pacific Coast Highway to the San Fernando Valley. Fernwood Pacific Drive, on the other hand was largely a series of switchbacks. Mud and rock slides frequently shut the road down even to SUVs.

Fortunately there hadn't been any rain for nearly seven months, and the road was dry and clear.

Except for the odd house light still burning at the end of half-hidden driveways everything lay shrouded in darkness. House numbers were often obscured by bracken fern and scrub oak. He was glad for the thick vegetation around—it muffled his approach. He crawled along, taking the switchbacks with caution, since an approaching car might easily catch them both unaware. He turned on the high beams, trying to see a few feet farther down the winding road. Then he saw his turnoff ahead and turned into Blackridge Road.

The engine labored as he ascended the unpaved road. A flash of color marked another roadside house number. He slammed on the brakes and skidded sideways, canting his high beams into a thicket of heavy brush.

The driveway was nearly as hidden as the wooden sign painted with something reflective. Ruben Saul must like his privacy. David turned on his overhead light long enough to double-check the number Ruben's wife had given him, then he backed up.

Flipping off his high beams he swung the nose of the Chevy down what was little more than a goat path, hemmed in by more bracken and thick, dust-choked brush. Farther in, the trunks of sycamores and live oaks danced furtively in his headlights.

The track switched back and forth past dense undergrowth thick with tree trunks. David wished he could turn his lights off but knew he'd be off the road in two seconds if he tried. He just had to hope no one in the house was watching.

If anyone was in the house.

If he was wrong about Tom bringing Chris here, then Chris was dead. He had no other means of guessing where Tom might have stashed his victims. He thought of calling the sheriff again, but didn't feel like dealing with the officious prick.

He edged past a border of untrimmed boxwood. Something glinted in his headlights and he made out the bumper of a car. A dark BMW was parked behind a light-colored Explorer. In the wan light it was hard to tell, but David knew without looking closer that the SUV was yellow.

Killing his lights David edged a few feet closer to the barely visible BMW. Gravel and dirt crunched under his tired Chevy as he glided to a stop.

He eased the window down and listened. The soft tick of his cooling engine was barely audible above the sighing of tree branches overhead. Close by an owl called; farther away another one answered.

The door clicked softly when he pushed it open. He fumbled for his cell phone, wondering if he'd get a connection, glad he was near the top of the canyon rather than down below.

The phone rang at the other end.

She answered on the second ring; David knew then she'd been waiting by the phone.

"Y-yes," she said.

"Mrs. Ruben?"

"Yes. Is this Detective Laine? Did you find my husband?"

"Ma'am, I just arrived," David said. "Could you tell me what kind of vehicle your husband was driving?"

"He drove the BMW. I told him he should use the four-wheel truck—what's happened to him, detective?" Her voice rose. "Where is my husband?"

"What four-wheel truck is that, ma'am?"

"The Explorer." She took a deep breath. "After Tom started driving it, my husband was only too happy to have his BMW. He just about gave the boy that thing."

"Do you mean Tom Clarke?"

"Yes." Disapproval thickened her voice, driving out the fear. "He spoiled that boy something fierce."

"Do you know where Tom is now, ma'am?"

"Tom? No. Why on earth would you be interested in Tom, detective? Is he in some kind of trouble again?"

Monday, 1:30 A.M., Blackridge Road, Santa Monica Mountains

Chris skidded backward, tangling in Saul Ruben's outstretched legs. He fell, rolled, and scrambled to his knees.

Praying the darkness would cover him, Chris half ran, half

crawled toward a dark rectangle he hoped was a door. He had a brief glimpse of Tom framed against the kitchen door, moonlight dappling his hunched figure, then he dove through the doorway.

The darkness lay like thick velvet, cloaking sounds as well as vision. Behind him Tom muttered in a pain-soaked voice. "Get you, motherfucker."

Chris's eyes had adjusted to the wavering darkness. Even when the moon moved behind a frieze of clouds there was still enough light to give shape to forms and keep him from a fatal, noisy blunder.

This time he was in a bedroom. A tall armoire filled one narrow wall; a single bed was positioned under a small curtained window.

He crouched and sidled from the armoire to the foot of the bed. He'd have to stand on it to reach the window. He would be a target when he tried to climb out the window if Tom entered the room.

Chris clenched his jaws to keep them from chattering. In shock from fear and pain, his entire body was covered with goose bumps.

Shuffling feet. The wheeze of harsh breathing, or was it only the far-off creak of an old building settling into its foundation? Every sound made him jump, magnified by the smothering silence all around. Adrenaline helped keep him preternaturally alert and even made him feel warmer, but how much could his body produce before it crashed in shock? His muscles were already growing stiff from oxygen depletion.

He slid toward the door, the pool cue raised. He poised on the balls of his feet, the wooden floor cold underneath his toes.

He didn't have a clue how long he'd been unconscious in Tom's car. Thirty minutes, an hour? Two? They could be anywhere between Antelope Valley and Santa Barbara, or beyond.

At the door, he held his breath, listened. Silence. Was Tom on the other side of the half-closed door, waiting? Or had he missed Chris entering the room and moved on to other parts of the house?

Chris waited for the telltale creak of the floor or Tom's stuttering, injured breathing.

Monday, 1:40 A.M., Blackridge Road, Santa Monica Mountains

David slid out of his car and approached the BMW. A hand on the hood told him the car had been there a while. It was cold. "Do I still have permission to enter the house, Mrs. Ruben? I'd like to check it out, make sure everything is okay."

"Of course, detective. The key is under a loose stone by the backdoor."

"Thank you."

"Will you call me back, detective? Will you let me know what has happened to my husband?"

"I'll do that, ma'am."

David immediately dialed Martinez.

"*Hola, amigo,* what's up?"

"How fast can you get to Topanga Canyon?"

"Topanga—how fast do you need me there?"

"Yesterday. The damn sheriff's caught in some highway accident."

"You found him?"

"I found him."

"Give me an address."

David did, then Martinez said, "I'll contact the sheriff's department again."

"Just tell them to make their approach low-key. I don't want some blue flamer spooking this guy."

"Gotcha," Martinez said and hung up.

David turned the cell off, not wanting its ring to give him away. He eased his Beretta out of its holster and made his way around the parked vehicles, keeping them between him and the house.

The house was dark. Not even an outside light. The side of the house was covered in beds of trimmed ficus, evening primrose, and other bedding plants. The air was heavy with their perfume.

Suddenly a light appeared to his right. It flickered in and out of the bush as he moved, and David realized it was a neighboring property. Had Chickie Lawson, the hippie wannabe, returned?

Should he check in and see what the man might have heard? Or should he try to enter the house with the key?

He was breaking regs by not waiting for backup but every nerve in his body screamed at him to do something. Chris was in that house.

He compromised by deciding he would walk around the perimeter. Cop instincts told him to wait for backup. Safety lay in numbers. Fear drove him on. Chris might not have time to wait.

Gun in hand, the blunt muzzle pointed toward the ground, he walked stiff-legged toward the deeper shadows in the rear of the house. Frosted moonlight glinted off a window, shadows pooled in a doorway. His eyes darted from side to side, seeking out anything that didn't belong.

The flowerbed was buried in shadow, but he easily spotted the large stone near the back step. Keeping one eye on the door, he crept along the grass bordering the bed of raised earth and knelt to pry the stone up. The key felt small in the palm of his hand. He slid it into his pant's pocket and brushed clammy dirt off on his thighs.

He slipped past the door, toward the back of the house.

Monday, 1:45 A.M., Blackridge Road, Santa Monica Mountains

Chris knew he couldn't wait any longer. Tom must be looking for him. He eased away from the door, crossed to the bed, and gingerly stepped onto it. It bowed under his weight, but thankfully didn't squeak.

The window made a grating sound as he opened it, and Chris held his breath, waiting for a shape to charge out of the darkness.

Pushing the screen off, he eased one leg over the sill, then the other. He jumped. There was nothing but air under his feet and he fell, stumbling into the damp earth. He squirmed at the prickly feel of ground cover and the sharp dig of pruned bushes on his bare skin.

Overhead, the moon slid behind a bank of silvering clouds. The darkness was more solid than any Chris had experienced. He prayed it would hide him.

Monday, 1:50 A.M., Blackridge Road, Santa Monica Mountains

A sound halted him. David tensed, both hands locked on the Beretta, muzzle still pointing at the ground.

The sound came again.

The slight scrape of wood on wood. A window sliding open.

David crouched behind a twisted mass of musk-scented sage as a pale figure slipped out of the newly opened window. In the wan light he could barely make out that the figure was unclothed.

David drew in a sharp breath. It was Chris. Glancing at the walls of the house, wondering if Tom was close behind, David eased forward.

Chris stepped away from the house, brushing past the ficus. David knew he dare not speak, nor allow Chris to make any noise that might alert Tom. In a half crouch David slid the Beretta into his shoulder holster and wrapped one arm around Chris, blocking his mouth with the other hand at the same time he dragged him into the protective shadows behind the sage. He felt Chris's startled intake of breath against the skin of his hand before his palm pressed down on the other man's mouth, sealing it.

Chris fought savagely. David scrabbled for purchase on the uneven ground as he dragged Chris backward, away from the open area. Chris even tried butting his head against David's, but he was totally off balance. He bit the fingers that covered his mouth and David grunted in pain. Thrashing, Chris bit harder.David hauled him upright and hissed in his ear, "Chris! It's me."

Chris went limp, and only David's grip kept him from tumbling to the ground. He spun Chris around and gathered him into his arms. "Oh God," he whispered, holding Chris's frozen body against his. "I didn't think I'd find you in time."

"D-David." Chris shook so hard he could barely speak for the chattering of his teeth. Shock.

Without another word David stripped off his jacket and wrapped it around Chris's shaking shoulders.

"Come on," he said. "We have to go. Martinez will be here soon, but I want you out of here."

Chris clung to David; goose bumps marbled his flesh. David rubbed his arms through the sleeves of his thin jacket.

"H-h-how—"

"Becky told me about this place. I talked to Ruben's wife. He's missing—"

David's hands were busy bringing life back to Chris's frozen limbs. Finally he was able to speak.

"H-he's dead. Tom shot him."

David frowned. He hadn't expected Tom to have a gun. That made their situation more precarious.

"Come on, let's get you to the car."

Chris stumbled wearily on the rough ground and stifled a cry as he nearly went down. David hauled him upright, ignoring his hiss of pain.

"Hang on, we're almost there—"

Gunshot cracked. David saw the flash of light at the same time Chris grunted. His arms were no longer around David. David had the barest glimpse of his face; eyes round in shock, mouth open as he fell away.

"Chris!"

Tom stepped away from the shadow of the house. David stared down the barrel of the blunt-nosed Walther nine-millimeter Tom held unwavering in both hands.

"Ironic, don't you think?" Tom's voice seemed to come from a long way off. David's answer, when it came, was a faint whisper, unintelligible.

"It was Uncle Saul's," Tom said. "For protection."

Chris hunched forward, wondering why his shoulder felt so numb. Why was he lying on the ground? It was cold and damp against his bare skin. Something lay atop him and it was a moment before he realized it was David's jacket, still draped over him.

Memories returned. He tried to roll over; the numbness in his shoulder gave way to a spreading ache that encompassed his left side. He could see Tom with his arms out in front of him, holding a heavy-barreled handgun in both hands. Pointed at David. Despite Chris's efforts to suppress it, a groan emerged.

Looking up he met David's eyes. Pain and relief co-mingled on his lover's face. Chris opened his mouth to speak, but no sound emerged.

"Ah, sleeping beauty's back with us," Tom said. The gun swung around, and Chris found himself staring down the bore of what looked like a cannon. "Good. That makes this a whole lot simpler. Drop your gun, detective."

Chris stared at the weapon in Tom's hands, at the stiff finger hovering over the trigger, finally at the man behind it. Out of the corner of his eye he saw David take a step forward.

Without blinking, Tom squeezed the trigger.

Chris twisted away. Dirt sprayed his twitching flesh. He felt the breeze of the bullet's passage on his shrinking skin.

"Move again and I punch a hole in his pretty face."

Chris pulled air into his lungs, fighting the terror. His heart hammered in his chest.

"What do you want?" David's hoarse voice was nearly unrecognizable.

"I want out of here."

"Then leave."

"Drop your gun." Tom motioned toward David. "I have to admit I didn't think you'd find the place so fast. How long before your buddies get here?"

"I don't know—"

The gun spat again. Searing pain erupted above Chris's hip; he screamed.

David went white. His weapon tumbled from his hand and hit the grass at his feet. Splattered dew glistened on the dark frame. He spread his arms.

"How long?"

"Sheriffs could be here anytime."

Tom's smile faltered, then returned. He stepped closer to Chris, who struggled to move away, sure he was going to die this time.

"Jesus, don't—" Chris said. "Tom—"

Tom's dress shoe nudged Chris's thigh. He spared a brief glance at the prone man.

"Get up, Chrissy."

"What—?"

"You're coming with me. That way I know your boyfriend will keep the pigs off my ass."

Chris struggled to rise, pain stroked his side, a flaming branding iron rippled along his nerve endings. He collapsed with a gasp.

"I can't—"

"No," David said.

David took a step forward. He froze when Tom's gun hand twitched. Grimly he folded his arms over his barrel chest.

"He's not going with you."

"Then he's a dead man—" Tom raised the gun's barrel and Chris steeled himself for the shot.

"No."

Tom froze, his smile finally fading altogether.

"You want a hostage," David said. "You take me. I'm not letting you take him anywhere."

"I'll kill him, I swear—"

"You'll kill him anyway. A bullet here's a lot quicker than what you have planned for him."

Chris stared at David. Mesmerized by his words. David's face was flat, devoid of expression. The hated cop face.

Tom seemed equally mesmerized. Then he grinned and waved the muzzle of the handgun toward the front of the house.

Obediently David stepped over his fallen gun. He spared Chris a glance, but his expression never changed.

"David . . . " Chris whispered.

But instead of David, Tom turned. He raised the gun, bringing it around in a shallow arc. "Right," he said. "Almost forgot—"

David swung around and caught Tom in the solar plexus. The smaller man stumbled back, his gun discharging in a shattering roar. David grunted and a dark stain blossomed above the pocket of his white shirt. He looked at Chris in surprise, then crumpled to the ground.

Chris screamed David's name. Pain forgotten in a surge of rage, he threw himself at Tom and the two of them went down in a tangle of arms and legs. The gun discharged a second time and Chris felt the *zing* of its passage through the short hairs on his temple. He attacked with frenzy, knowing only rage fed his fight.

"You killed him. You bastard. You bastard—" He pummeled Tom, madness lending him new strength. "Bastard. You killed him."

He wept in fury and pain as he slammed into David's killer. He didn't care if Tom turned and shot him, didn't care if he wound up dead too.

Wanting Tom dead more.

They rolled across the ground, struggling for possession of the gun still in Tom's hand. Chris bit and punched and screamed in fury.

Tom shoved Chris off and stumbled to his knees. He tried to raise the gun, and Chris kicked him. The gun flew from his hand, vanishing into the shadows that clung to the edges of the house.

Chris snarled more curses and tried to scramble upright. Tom swung his fist into Chris's chin, and everything exploded. Chris screamed and tumbled backward. Light flared in his head when Tom's fist connected with his temple, glancing off his skull.

Chris pummeled back, but he was too weak. His strength ebbed; half his body no longer responded to his commands. Tom's next blow slammed into his jaw.

He cried out and went down. Tom advanced. Chris rolled so that Tom's foot smashed uselessly into the flesh of his ass. Chris kicked his shins as he rolled again. Tom's next attempt was even farther off the mark, barely brushing his thigh.

But it was only a matter of time. If he couldn't get to his feet, Tom was going to kill him right here. His next kick put the toe of his shoe into Chris's already injured hip and pain ripped through him. Tom grunted and kicked again, catching him in the same place.

Chris roared at the pain. A third time the shoe descended, catching him in the kidneys this time. His vision grayed and Chris knew that with any more blows he'd succumb to the black peace that unconsciousness offered.

Blood patterned the ground around him. He caught sight of David's body in the encroaching light and an enervating sorrow filled him. Why was he fighting so hard? David was dead.

Except that would be giving in. Something David hadn't done, right to the end. Could he do less? He—

David moved.

Tom's foot slammed into Chris again, laying a trail of fire across his naked belly and ribs. Less than a yard away David lay on his back, a flowering crimson stain covering his upper shoulder. Chris blinked and strained to see through the spreading light. Had he really seen David's hand twitch?

His hand moved again.

With new hope came renewed energy. Chris lurched to his knees. Tom's eyes blazed with gleeful fury. He was fully aroused now, reveling in the destruction he caused.

With a yell, Chris made the final push to his feet, and ducked to avoid the next swing of Tom's fist. It glanced off his back.

He caught Tom around the hips and once more they ended up on the ground. Tom punched his head, hitting him on his cheek, another on his throat. Chris tried to strike back, but his arms could do little more than fold him in an empty embrace.

Too late he tried to deflect Tom's arm. It slid around Chris's throat.

Chris tasted blood and bile. Light exploded behind his eyes. His lungs screamed for air that wasn't there. Shadows lurched through the dazzling lights and he thought he heard David shouting something. Then Chris's scrabbling fingers encountered cold metal. A gun. His hand closed convulsively on it and he jerked it up between them. There was another explosion and almost instantly the tightness around Chris's throat vanished.

Tom staggered backward. His hand tried to stem the gush of blood from his chest. He collapsed.

Chris fell to his knees, gasping hungrily for air that now poured freely down his throat. His eyes were closed tight while he fought to grab all the sweet revitalizing air he could suck in.

David groaned and Chris scrambled to close the distance between them.

"David!"

His lover's mouth was a bloody rictus that might have been a smile. His swarthy face was pale.

"David." It emerged as a strangled whisper. Chris rubbed his throat and winced at the sensation of ground glass in his chest. "You look like shit."

"Hey. At least I don't look half as bad as you."

"Oh, right, flatter me." Chris tried to hold his arms out but he couldn't move. "David."

He lifted Chris up gently, his arms feeling wonderfully strong around his bruised shoulders. He stroked Chris's cheek.

"Don't ever scare me like that again, okay?" Chris murmured. "I thought you were dead."

"Just a flesh wound."

"Liar—"

They both heard the crunch and clatter of gravel as a car raced down the narrow drive.

They didn't have much time.

"I love you, David."

David stared down at him for several heartbeats. Then his face lit up in the most beautiful smile. How the hell had Chris ever thought he was plain?

"God, I love you too—"

"Drop the weapon."

Both David and Chris stared at the brown-shirted sheriff who crouched as he leveled his own weapon at them.

Belatedly Chris realized he still held Tom's gun in one shaking hand.

"Drop it. Now."

Chris let the weapon tumble from his hand. The sheriff held his weapon trained on them. The yard was suddenly filled with uniformed men. Red light strobed from a black-and-white parked on the grassy verge between the house and the driveway.

A voice said, "Put that away, *maricón*." For the first time since he had met the man, Chris was glad to see Martinez. "First you can't even get here on time, and now this? He's a God-damned cop, you idiot."

The sheriff's gun wavered and the uniformed man straightened, eyeing Chris uncertainly. Martinez waved him toward the house.

"Go secure the place. Take your stormtroopers with you."

Only when the others had gone did Martinez turn his attention to his partner.

"Call an ambulance," Chris managed to croak.

"On its way." Martinez knelt by David's side. "Hey, buddy. I thought you knew how to duck."

"Messed up this time."

Martinez's gaze moved from David to Chris. His eyes held a speculative warmth that surprised Chris. He studied Tom's unmoving body, then he stared down at the innocuous-looking gun lying on the trampled grass.

"Did you shoot him, Davey?"

Chris and David looked at each other. Martinez shook his head. He stared at Chris.

"You shot him?"

Chris nodded.

"You realize you both brought a shit storm down on you."

"Hey," David said. "Keeps things interesting."

In the distance an ambulance siren shattered the night.

"You guys got about five minutes before all hell breaks loose." Martinez straightened. "I'd say whatever you gotta say, because it may be a while before you can say anything to each other."

"But—"

"I'll be in the house anyone needs me." This time his eyes locked on Chris's. "You did good, man. I underestimated you. It won't happen again." He pointedly looked from Chris to David. "You better call Bryan Williams. I got a feeling you're gonna need his clout."

"Who's Bryan Williams?" Chris asked.

"Someone with enough political savvy to keep your boyfriend

from getting fragged by I.A. Internal Affairs just eats this kind of shit for breakfast."

"I.A.?"

"Just make him call, Chris."

"I'll call," David said.

Martinez abruptly turned away.

Chris took advantage of the lack of watchers to lower his mouth to David's. Just before they kissed he said, "I love you, David."

The kiss didn't last anywhere near long enough. Chris sighed when they broke apart.

"Get dressed," David said.

Chris found the jacket David had covered him with earlier and slipped it over his shivering shoulders. Fortunately it hung far enough below Chris's ass to let him keep a small shred of dignity. The ambulance crew came around the back of the house with stretchers five minutes later.

They checked over Tom, but Chris wasn't surprised when they couldn't revive him. They loaded both Chris and David into the ambulance and with siren's blazing, descended to the coast highway.

"Hey, this is yours." David ignored the protests of the EMTs and handed Chris his BlackBerry.

Chris stared down at the handheld. "Not anymore, it's not."

"What—"

"I talked to Petey." He let the device slide from his fingers and lay back down wearily. "I quit."

"Well."

When David didn't say anything else, Chris struggled back up. He found David staring at him, his face unreadable.

Suddenly David smiled.

"Well," he repeated. "There goes my dream of being a kept man."

CHAPTER 26

Wednesday 11:30 A.M., Santa Monica Hospital, Santa Monica

FAMILIAR SMELLS. HOSPITAL smells. Chris groaned and opened his eyes. Instantly David was at his side. The poor guy looked positively haggard. Chris reached for him, but his arm came up against the restraints of an IV and a nest of monitoring cables holding him down.

"Don't try to move," David said. The sleeve of his jacket hung loose; his arm was bound against his chest. "They've got you pretty well lashed to that bed."

"What gives?" Chris's throat felt like caustic sand had been poured down it. He swallowed and tried again. "David—"

"You're okay. You're in the Santa Monica Hospital."

"When—"

"It's Wednesday. You were in surgery Monday, but the doctor says you're okay now—"

Chris flexed his shoulders and groaned at the pain that sliced through him. Was David kidding? His insides felt like they'd been run through an industrial meat grinder. He said as much.

"The fact that you can complain so succinctly means you must be getting better," was David's laconic response. He seemed oddly reluctant when he added, "How much do you remember? About Tom, I mean?"

"Do you mean did he rape me?" Chris started to shake his head, then froze. Would it make a difference to David? Chris searched his face, but all he saw was pain and a naked love that made Chris wonder how he had ever doubted him. He reached his hand up and David grasped it in his good one. "No, he didn't. I think he just lost it at the end. He still thought he could get away with it. What happened . . . after?"

"They got a warrant and did a full search of all the houses, his and his uncle's. Found it all, his trophies, a stack of newspaper clippings on all the previous vics, he even kept a journal of each, ah, hunt. We also found Bobby's Palm Pilot, which went a long way to corroborating things."

Chris didn't bother telling him he'd had it in his possession briefly. Maybe later.

"Once we started looking," David said, "we found missing men up in the Berkeley area that coincide with the time Clarke was in school there. The Berkeley police will be taking another look at those in light of what we've told them. Apparently he was in trouble years ago for cutting up neighborhood cats." David glanced toward the TV set hanging above the end of the bed. His next words were casual, too casual. "You been watching the news? They've been covering it pretty extensively."

Something in David's voice alerted him. "What?"

Martinez strode into the room and answered the question. "They can't decide whether they want to crucify David or make him the next marshal in the Santa Claus parade."

His obvious good humor only served to emphasize how weak and sick Chris felt. Even David looked wan beside his robust partner. He also looked pissed.

"You're early," David snapped.

"No I'm not," Martinez said, pulling up a chair and straddling it, facing the bed. "I'm right on time. How you doing, Chris?"

"Fine. What's this about crucifying him?"

Martinez looked at David; Chris could tell he didn't want his partner talking.

"There's a segment of our fine citizenry that thinks Tom Clarke only died because of vigilantism, and that," he said solemnly, "has no place among the ranks of the new and enlightened LAPD"

"Vigilantism? Are they forgetting this guy was trying to kill both of us? That he butchered Bobby and Kyle—"

"As a matter of fact, I don't think that enters their equation. His rights were violated by the, ah, precipitous actions taken against him."

"So they don't care what that asshole did—" Chris's voice broke as ugly memories stirred and roiled in his brain. "How the hell can they vilify anyone for killing that monster?"

"Probably better you don't tell that to the press," Martinez said. He clearly approved of Chris's sentiments. Then he grew serious. "You up to answering a few questions, Chris?"

"Martinez—"

"He has to do this, David. Better me than one of the other guys." Martinez's gaze met Chris's. "I need to get your formal statement. It will probably be used in the inquest."

"Inquest?"

"They want to clear up the shooting. It's routine."

"Bull," Chris snapped. "It's not routine if they decide they want to hang David out to dry."

Martinez looked apologetically at David. "Give me half an hour."

In the end it took forty-five minutes and left Chris totally drained. By the time David slipped back into the room he was already dozing fitfully.

"Everything's going to be okay, Chris." David picked up Chris's hand where it lay atop the thin hospital blanket. "Don't let Martinez get you down. Even he thinks it will be a cakewalk."

Christmas Day, 6:10 A.M., Cove Avenue, Silver Lake, Los Angeles

The phone rang. Christopher Bellamere rolled away from the warm body he'd been cuddling in his sleep and fumbled for the bedside phone.

He squinted at the caller I.D. window, recognized the number, and grinned.

"It's Christmas," he grunted. "This had better be good."

"Hey," Des said. "Can't a buddy call and wish two of his best friends Merry Christmas?"

Chris glanced over at the shape concealed by the rumpled bedclothes. David was still sound asleep. Not surprising, after last night's performance. Who knew domestic champagne could be so inspiring?

"We still on for dinner tonight?" Des interrupted his heated thoughts.

"Sure." Chris checked the bedside clock. He winced. "In twelve hours. God, you're as bad as David, getting up at the crack of dawn."

Des laughed.

The sound still made Chris smile. It had been a long way back for Des. He had spent nearly four months in therapy, dealing with the trauma of his loss and the aftermath of the vicious rape. Chris had been luckier. His physical wounds had been relatively superficial and he had been released to David's tender care after three days of observation.

Chris felt a fierce joy at Des's ongoing recovery, both from his injuries and from the loss of Kyle. Chris knew he still missed the younger man, but he was coming along, talking about the future now. Chris had even caught him looking at a couple of good-looking guys on the street with more than casual interest.

The bed shifted. David's muscular arms came around him and

his thickly furred chest pressed against his back.

"Hey, I gotta go, Des," Chris said as David's unshaved cheek came down against the back of his neck. "Er, something's come up."

"Six, then?"

"Six." Chris nearly groaned when David's hand closed over his erection. "Yeah, six, ah, don't forget the wine."

"Like I'd ever."

Chris hung up and rolled over. He reached up and brought David's face down to his.

"Merry Christmas, sleepy-head. About time you woke up."

•

Bing Crosby and Rosemary Clooney crooned about dreaming of a white Christmas as snow fell on a sleepy Vermont village and an ex-general's inn was saved. Chris curled against David's side, sipping a glass of zinfandel, while he nibbled from a plate of mixed nuts.

The doorbell rang. Chris glanced at the digital display above the plasma TV. Four-thirty.

"Expecting anyone?"

David shook his head and stood up. He reached the front door two steps before Chris.

It was Martinez and a short Latino woman with dark, gentle eyes and oil-black hair piled atop her head. Even with her hairdo, she barely reached Martinez's shoulders.

Chris pulled the silk tie of his robe tighter as he shrank from the cool dampness flowing through the open door. Low threatening clouds looked ready to discharge another cold rainfall. Christmas in Southern California was never like a Vermont postcard.

David rarely talked about either his job or Martinez, but Chris knew a reticence had grown between the two partners. A reticence he knew bothered David.

The woman smiled anxiously before tugging on Martinez's arm.

"I hope we didn't interrupt—"

The woman poked him again. Martinez grimaced.

"My wife, Inez Yolanda Diego." He drew out a bottle of wine and handed it to David. "She wanted—we wanted—to wish you a Merry Christmas."

"Thanks," David said. He held out his hand to Inez, who shook it. "Would you like to come in?"

Chris extended his hand and swallowed hers. She smiled shyly at him.

"Hello! You must be Christopher. I have heard so much about you both." Inez spoke with a soft Spanish accent. She held his hand and smiled at David and Chris. "*Feliz Navidad.*"

Chris laid his other hand atop Inez's as he guided her into the living room. David and Martinez followed.

"*Gracias, señora. Feliz Navidad.*" Chris spoke passable Spanish. A lifetime in L.A. had seen to that. He wished her and Martinez a great holiday and hoped her family was well.

She brightened. Beside her Martinez murmured, "We can't stay long. The kids are at my mother's—"

"Martinez Diego," Inez said.

Her husband stared down at his feet. "But before we go, we'd like to invite you both to our place for New Year's." He raised his eyes and looked from Chris to David. "There are a few other guys and their wives dropping by. Nothing formal, and I know this is last minute . . . but we would really like it if you both could come . . . "

Where they would spend the evening being stared at by a bunch of off-duty cops and their spouses, like specimens at a freak show? What was Martinez up to? Chris's first reaction was to say forget it. Neither of them needed that hassle.

A quick glance at David and he knew the older man was startled by the invitation, but wanted to accept.

Could Chris deepen the wedge between the partners? Was he prepared to isolate David even more because of his insecurities?

Could he do that to this man he loved more than life?

He produced his most beguiling smile. "We accept. *Me alegro que nos invitán.*" He reached out to take the bottle of wine from David. "Now, let me break this open. You can stay for a glass, right?"

"We'd be happy to," Inez said.

David hung back when Martinez and Inez stepped into the living room. He slipped his hand into Chris's, who smiled up at him.

"Merry Christmas," David said, stooping to catch a quick kiss under the mistletoe Chris had hung in the alcove. "Love you."

"Hey, love you too. Now let's go and take care of your guests."

"Our guests, you mean."

Chris squeezed his hand. Then they followed their visitors into the living room.

ACKNOWLEDGMENTS

UNTIL IT'S FINISHED, a novel is a work in progress. Thanks to all the members of NovelDoc and NovelPros for their endless patience with my requests for help and for letting me know when it was time to let go. The critiques I got were immeasurably helpful in molding this work into the novel you hold in your hands. A special thanks to Jamie Lankford, Dave Shields, Jo Ann Hernandez, Sue Asher, Gloria Piper, Derek Armstrong, James McKinnon, Art Tirrel, Vicky Hunt, Rashmi Shankar, Alan Jackson, and Kate Johnston.

I would also like to express my endless gratitude to the Stratford Writing Group, especially Norah-Jean Perkins, Patti Miller, Meg Westley, and Beth Pratt, for always having an encouraging word even when they offered criticism.

And to Nick Archer, Mark Jesko, John Windham, and Lavenderquill, who have been there from the first iteration of Chris and David and always encouraged me to go further.

To Lyn Hamilton, creator of the Lara McClintoch mysteries, who believed in this book, and to Leona Trainer, agent extraordinaire, who was patient with all my newbie mistakes. To Nelson Clark, who assisted me with all my questions on Los Angeles, a special thanks.

A very special thanks also to Officer Manuel Portillo of the Los Angeles Airport Police and vice president of the Los Angeles Airport Peace Officers Association, who helped me get the police facts right. Any errors or omissions are my own negligence or artistic license.

Another special thanks to all the great people at Alyson who actually paid me to write! You rock.

And finally, thanks to the wonderful city of Los Angeles and the freaky, crazy, marvelous people who live there. Without you there would be no story.

$3 – Gen 9/1 K